RANDOM HOUSE
LARGE
PRINT

ALL THE
COLORS
OF THE
DARK

ALL THE
COLORS
OF THE
DARK

A NOVEL

CHRIS
WHITAKER

RANDOM HOUSE
LARGE PRINT

Copyright © 2024 by CW Storytelling Ltd.

Cover design by Anna Kochman
Cover photographs: Eerik/Getty Images (trees); Jonathan Knowles/Getty Images (paint)

The Library of Congress has established a Cataloging-in-Publication record for this title.

ISBN: 978-0-593-94900-9

www.penguinrandomhouse.com/large-print-format-books

FIRST LARGE PRINT EDITION

Printed in the United States of America

5th Printing

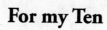

For my Ten

ALL THE
COLORS
OF THE
DARK

THE PIRATE AND THE BEEKEEPER

1975

1

From the flat roof of the kitchen Patch looked out through serried pin oaks and white pine to the loom of St. Francois Mountains that pressed the small town of Monta Clare into its shade no matter the season. At thirteen he believed entirely that there was gold beyond the Ozark Plateau. That there was a brighter world just waiting for him.

Though later that morning, when he lay dying in the woodland, he'd take that morning still and purse it till the colors ran because he knew it could not have been so beautiful. That nothing was ever so beautiful in his life.

He climbed back into his bedroom and wore a tricorne and waistcoat and tucked navy slacks into his socks and fanned the knees until they resembled breeches. Into his belt he slid a small dagger, metal alloy but the bladesmith was skilled enough.

Later that day the cops would crawl over the intricacies of his life and discover he was into pirates because he had been born with only one eye, and his mother peddled the romance of a cutlass and eye patch because often for kids like him the flair of fiction dulled a reality too severe.

In his bedroom they would note the black flag pinned to hide a hole in the drywall, the closet with no doors, the fan that did not work, and the Steepletone that did. The antique treasure chest his mother had found at a flea market in St. Louis, doubloon movie props, a replica one-shot flintlock pistol. They would bag a roll of firecrackers and the June 1965 **Playboy,** like they were evidence of something.

And then they would see the eye patches.

He looked them over carefully, then selected the purple with the silver star. His mother made them and some of them itched, but the purple was satin smooth. Eighteen in total, only one carried the skull and crossbones. He decided he might wear that one on his wedding day should he ever work up the courage to speak to Misty Meyer.

He removed the hat. His hair touched white in summer months and sand come winter, and he combed it but a tuft by the crown stood to attention like an antenna.

In the kitchen his mother sat. The night shift mortified her skin.

"You picking up signals with that thing?" she

said, and tried to fix his hair with her palm. "Pass me the Crisco."

He ducked away as she laughed. Patch liked his mother's laugh.

The weekend before she'd taken him to Branson to see about a job. Ivy Macauley chased near misses like acceptance of place was the greatest sin. He'd fill up the Fairlane with just enough gas and she'd fill up the cab with excitement, fixing her hair into a Fonda shag and squeezing his hand and telling him **this was it.** He'd wait the interview hour alone in towns he did not know.

She'd fixed eggs, and he wondered just how tough it was to be a parent, and if at times all poor kids were some kind of well-intentioned regret.

"Today will be the best day of my life," he said.

He said that often.

Because he could not know what would come.

2

He heard the mailman and ran for the door in case there was another letter from the school, but she took the envelope from him and closed her eyes and kissed it. "It's got a St. Louis postmark."

A month before, she'd interviewed at the botanical garden while Patch smiled at symmetrical families in the shade of Tower Grove House.

He held his breath till the sag of her shoulders.

Their Monta Clare rental was the kind of temporary already growing roots, the foundations knotting around his mother's ankles no matter how hard she hacked at them with declarations of women's lib, or how loud she played Dylan to remind herself that times were changing.

"We take something from every knock," he said, and screwed up the letter. He scanned the empty shelves in the refrigerator. "Black Bart Roberts took near five hundred ships in his time. But he started out when he was captured himself. A legendary navigator, his captors spotted his potential and let him live. Before long they voted him captain."

Sometimes she looked at him like he was the sum of her failings. Each night he lifted rusted dumbbells until his skinny arms burned, grinding his childhood away.

She noticed the bruise by his cheekbone as she removed his waistcoat and fixed his pants and licked her palm to smooth his hair down.

"Fighting, Joseph. Try to remember you're all I've got." She went to move the eye patch but he gripped her wrist and she softened.

"Then it sucks to be you." He added a smile.

Sometimes he took the album from beneath her bed and mapped the rise and fall of her.

"You need to eat breakfast," she said, as he pushed the plate down toward her.

"They give us something at school if we forget," he lied too easy.

"You nervous? My little pirate. No more trouble from here on. No stealing and no fighting. New school, new start, right?"

"Show me a pirate that never got in some kind of trouble."

"I'm serious, Joseph. I don't need the school on me. That woman who stopped by, she looked at me like I can't even care for you." Ivy cupped his face. "Promise me."

He could've told her he didn't ever start it. "No more trouble."

"You walking in with Saint?"

He nodded.

Ivy would go through this with the first responder, and then Chief Nix. She'd tell them she didn't notice anyone hanging around. Or see a dark van. Or anything much beyond the slow wake of Rosewood Avenue.

And later, when it got worse, she'd wonder how much of her son's life she had missed.

3

Across the street Mr. Roberts pushed his new Lawn Boy. The Robertses' house was painted each spring, white clapboard, navy gable. That night in place of **Hawaii Five-O** the Robertses would sit on their porch and watch the cops crawl over the Macauley house. Mrs. Roberts would pour them a couple of fingers of bourbon to steady the nerves as Mr. Roberts said it was **only a matter of time before something bad happened to that kid.**

Green grass. Buffed sedans. Flags hung limp and still. Their house was tall and maybe once was grand, but a generation of neglect dragged at its shine. The only rental on the street, Patch tore weeds from the yard, cleared leaves from the gutters, and hammered slates to the roof after each storm like he did not know he was furnishing someone else's future. He'd whistle as he worked, nodding hello to passing neighbors. Smiling. Always.

The next morning the cops would walk that same

road, knocking on doors and asking questions, trying to piece together events that would mar their town for years to come.

News vans would set up outside the small police station and ramp up the pressure on Chief Nix, who would stand before the flashing bulbs and stammer his way through an ill-prepared statement. For that one day, Patch would wrestle Lynette Fromme and her assassination attempt on Gerald Ford from the front page of the **St. Louis Post-Dispatch.**

He found a long stick and slashed at the air, then turned it into a gun and fired warning shots at the approaching armada.

"Man the cannon, sea hag," he said to the Anderson widow as she strolled past. She did not man the cannon.

At the foot of Main Street he looked for Saint, for the blue dungarees torn at each knee, the single braid she wore each day because she claimed it kept the hair from her eyes when she climbed the Morrisons' apple tree and tossed down the choice picks.

He gave her five minutes then kicked a can along Main Street. He affected his best Curt Gowdy cowboy and commentated, **"Patch Macauley, the first one-eyed boy to kick a seventy yarder."**

Outside Lacey's Diner sat a cherry-red Thunderbird. Chuck Bradley and his older brothers leaned against it.

"Vikings," Patch whispered beneath his breath.

He tried to turn when Chuck noticed him and nudged the other two.

It would take the cops two days to get to Chuck and his brothers, but only a half hour to confirm their alibis.

Patch ducked down the alleyway behind the stores.

He heard footsteps, turned and saw the three, so backed himself into a corner.

"Nowhere to run," Chuck said. He was tall and older and handsome enough. His brothers, wholesome copies. Chuck dated Misty Meyer, the feted beauty Patch had remained deeply in love with since kindergarten.

They moved a little closer. Patch backed up further until he felt the cool brick against him, and that was when he felt it, digging into his back.

He slipped the dagger from his belt and throttled the grip.

"No way you're using that," Chuck said, though Patch heard the doubt in his voice.

Patch stared at the blade as his knees shook. "November 1718, Robert Maynard finally captured the legend, Edward Teach. You'll know him as Blackbeard."

Chuck glanced at his brothers. One of them laughed.

"Maynard cut him twenty times with a knife just like this. Then grabbed a handful of his hair and hacked his head clean off."

"You're not a pirate. You're a one-eyed freak."

"Maynard hung Blackbeard's head from the bowsprit of his ship to let others know not to mess with him."

He held the dagger out.

And then he walked toward them, heart pounding as they backed off just enough. A yard past and he ran.

Threats were called.

He did not stop till he made it clear.

4

Pines rose through golds and blue shadow, the light leaves swept aside as he followed trails that skirted the town limits. A long way above he'd see Loess Hills buffeting the Missouri River, the low climb of industrial air over cities and farmland pinned by silver silos.

A Dodge with no fender was sunk in the earth, no wheels, just left for the wild, for kids to bullseye the windshield.

A leaflet caught in the spindles of Eastern redbud. The pinks wrapped a smiling Jimmy Carter, shirtsleeves rolled up like he was close to the kind of people he was calling on to vote for him.

The lake came into view. A faded sign warned of an undercurrent. In the summer, kids jumped from slick rocks the color of emerald. A boy named Colson had gone swimming and never come back, and rumor had it he lived at the bottom, watching the girls' legs as they kicked, choosing the right moment to reach out and take one.

Patch picked up a flat rock and counted six skims as the water coined toward blades of common reed.

He balanced along the rusted rails of the old Monta Clare railroad, arms out, the steels red and warped.

He watched a scissor-tailed flycatcher dart from its perch.

The scream stopped him.

A hard scream.

Down into a high-sided valley he saw splinters of a navy van, the brush so thick he moved nearer still. Maybe it was a rat rod or a Ford.

He knelt in the dirt as he saw her.

Misty Meyer.

For a moment he figured she was out with a boy and he'd misread it. She was in his math class, his age but passed too easy for older.

Then he saw the back of a man, his hood up despite the heat.

Patch desperately looked around for anyone at all. Anyone who could handle this, who could ease the responsibility, the acute burden of seeing a girl in trouble.

Another scream.

He whispered a curse, reached a hand up and touched the eye patch as his mind ran to Silver-Tongue Martin, and Wild Ned Lowe. The band of fearless.

He moved.

Misty screamed as Patch slid down the bank.

He bent low and wished he had his slingshot as he picked up a rock.

At ten feet away the man heard him and turned.

A balaclava hid all but the dead of his eyes.

Patch held his breath, hurled the rock and dropped low as he took the man down at the knees.

"Run," Patch yelled.

Misty stood frozen, fear claiming her muscles. Shirt torn, her bag in the dirt. Dazed like she'd been dragged into a nightmare.

The man rolled over him.

"Run," Patch managed to whisper, his lungs empty. He felt a hand on his throat, and he begged Misty with his eye.

Snap from it.

Finally, she saw him.

She was tall, a track star. Their eyes met, and then she turned and pumped her arms and lit out through the woodland.

The man was up and moving to follow her, but Patch was right up with him.

He pulled the dagger for the second time that morning.

The man grabbed his wrist and twisted.

Sun hit the blade till it met Patch's stomach.

He fell back to the ground and clutched at the wound and the forest around turned to night but he saw no moon and no stars.

The next day an army of walkers would beat the woodland to find a purple eye patch with a silver star.

Chief Nix would run over every bad man within a hundred miles.

His mother would fall apart entirely.

His best friend Saint would stalk the streets when hope had long since burned, getting herself into another world of trouble.

None would yet know of the evolving tragedy that would be their lives.

5

That same day Saint woke at dawn, crept down the stairs and out onto the rear porch.

Seven streets away Patch watched that same sunrise.

She rubbed her eyes as mist smoked from the grass like fire burned beneath.

Her morning routine, same each day since they arrived.

She was about to head in when she heard it.

Or didn't.

She crossed the yard, bare feet in the damp, stopping a few feet from the hive.

Saint crouched and peered inside at the stragglers.

She looked around, back at the tall house, the neighbors, the treetops.

Her eyes wide as she tried to make sense of it.

The bees had gone.

Inside she barreled up the old staircase and crashed into her grandmother's bedroom.

"Someone's stolen the bees," she said, breathless.

Norma turned from her spot by the window. "You're not wearing your glasses. Maybe the bees are there but you can't—"

Saint ran from the room.

"And brush your teeth," Norma called.

Up spiraling steps to her bedroom in the attic. She took the round glasses from her nightstand and watched the world come to focus through lenses so thick her eyes magnified as if in perpetual amazement.

She pulled on denim dungarees, both knees newly patched.

Saint cleaned her teeth with paste on her forefinger because she'd used her brush to dust mud from a fossil Patch delivered that later turned out to be dried dog shit.

Outside she found her grandmother standing before the empty hive, squinting toward the sky.

Norma cleared her throat, her silver hair cut short, wiry muscles in her forearms hinting at steel beneath. "But why would they—"

"Could be ants. But I laid the traps," Saint said, low panic in her voice.

"Can't be then."

"Like, if you keep interfering then they go. But I . . ."

Norma sighed. "You sit out here with them each day, sometimes for hours."

"They know me by now. It's been four years."

"Could be a skunk," Norma offered.

Saint straightened at that. "A rotten old skunk. I'll go fetch my slingshot."

"I read about a keeper over in Wayne County. . . . He got arrested for stealing hives."

Saint stopped dead, her small nose turning up into a snarl. "Someone stole my bees?" She paced up and down, oblivious to the burgeoning regret on her grandmother's face.

"I'll bet it was Mr. Lewis." Saint spat the name.

"The old deacon? He's—"

"He's a greedy old diabetic—"

"Language," Norma warned.

"He took three samples last time I laid out my stall. Licking it from his fat old fingers, didn't even buy a jar neither. I told Patch to limit the tasters. I'll go there and I'll—"

"You will not go there."

"I'll take it to Chief Nix then. He can cuff the fat old—"

"Enough."

Saint turned and ran from the side gate.

Norma sighed and shook her head in despair.

6

Saint spent more than an hour tramping woodland that fanned like a seashell around the back of the tall house and toward the Tooms farmland beyond, stopping now and then and hoping to God to hear the low hum of her bees, that they'd simply clustered on a tall elm while her scouts looked for a new home.

By the time she made it to Main Street her braid had pulled a little loose and sweat was beginning to dot her upper lip. In the small police station she was about ready to call for the arrest and swift beheading of Mr. Lewis when she saw Misty Meyer standing before a cop.

Young and scared and breathless.

The skin scraped from her knees.

Saint saw a stack of papers fluttering as the girl fell like she'd been robbed of the bones in her body. The cop caught her and helped her into a chair.

"Take a breath," he said, kneeling in front of her.

"He's there," Misty said, glancing back into the

bright of the street, her body shaking as she stared straight through Saint.

Saint noticed the red print on her arm. A hand. A big hand. A slight swelling by her eye, her shirt torn at the neck.

"You're safe now," the cop said. "There's no one out there."

"You don't get it," she said, still breathless. "He saved me."

"Who saved you?"

Misty took a drink of water, her lips full and pink against hair so light it touched platinum. A halo for a girl who already carried too much that shone.

Saint might have turned, left her bees for another day, but then she heard it, and her blood cooled and her skin pricked, and it was like she knew that things would be different from then on.

"The pirate kid," Misty said.

Saint moved toward them, instinct guided her. Instinct and that cold kind of dread.

"He hit him. But the guy was so big," Misty said, tears falling now.

Saint felt her pulse quicken. "Joseph Macauley?"

Both turned and noticed her. Saint stood there tiny, her frames balancing on a small nose with a smattering of freckles. Her collar bones stood proud, her braid thick over one shoulder. She wore a simple gold cross on a thin necklace. Her grandmother had given Patch a matching one.

"Where is he now?" Saint said.

The cop crouched, his muscles tight against a shirt bright and unblemished.

Saint knew about shock, the way it purged rational thought. She'd learned that the day she came home from school and found her grandfather lying in the kitchen as her grandmother pumped his chest, face straight like she was beating a mixture.

"Misty." Saint tried a smile. Her grandfather had said it was a good smile, the kind that lit January mornings, that recalled spring in the belly of Missouri winter.

"Where did this happen, Misty?" the cop tried.

Misty made no sound as the cop took a jacket and wrapped her in it to stay the shivering.

"Goddamn, where the hell is Patch?" Saint said, as the cop reared up.

"The clearing. By the old railroad," Misty said.

Saint heard the cop reach for the radio, and then she sprinted down Main Street, drawing looks as she seared toward the woodland.

7

Trees swayed as Saint parted the cover of a willow to roots rising like hands reaching up, preaching caution at each step.

She moved past the quake of aspens, white trunks thin and strong and pocked dark. An old metal sign rusted through, the letters too faint. The grove thickened. She smelled dust and Christmas. Sometimes when it rained she and Patch walked to the confluence three miles up to sail paper boats into the waters' fold.

Trees took the light as a low hill leveled out, her mind on her friend, on how he smiled too much for a kid with such a draw, on how his mother once told him of pirates because that made his difference more than affliction.

Her breath crowned in her ears.

She moved quick past fallen trees that bookended the clearing. Head up, she scouted, but it wasn't till she met the foot of the valley that she saw the spot.

The T-shirt.

The blood.

8

Word ate through the town. The easy wheels of local business ground to the kind of stop that left Main Street dying as they gathered at the edge of the woodland. Kids rode hard, red cheeked as they dumped bicycles, spoke beads still spinning as they joined the procession, watching and waiting for a dead kid to shade the color of their childhoods.

Saint stood apart from them and watched as Chief Nix rolled his cruiser past a line of local press, already backed up and herded by a barrier made from traffic cones and some tape.

He climbed out and blocked the sun with his hat. Most days his moustache framed a smile. He watched Saint as she watched a man photograph the tire tracks, like they weren't baked hard into the mud, the kind of fossilized nightmare Saint would pay homage to over the coming weeks.

Saint looked up at his handsome face, then back down at the mud again. A low pain spread in her stomach. A tightness across her bony shoulders that would mature and stop her sleeping each night until she no longer knew herself. Each part of that woodland was claimed with soft memories, and she battled tears. Her and Patch holding out stick guns and chasing phantom goons. Her hanging upside down from the twisting limbs of sweet gum, warning him not to try it because his missing eye fucked up his balance. Him trying to stand on one leg to prove her wrong. Her helping him back to his feet.

Nix crossed before her, hollering to the other cops, "All points. Got the whole damn county locked up tight. Highway 42 to 86, you can't get in or out without a flashlight in your face."

"Interstate 35," she spoke in a whisper that carried toward the big chief, who stepped toward her.

"You're the bus driver's granddaughter?"

She nodded.

"You're friends with this kid?"

She nodded again.

"He did a brave thing."

She might've screamed that he was not tough enough. She might've told them he once sat on the low roof by her bedroom window the whole winter night when she got sick with bad flu. That Norma found him blue in the early hours and brought him in to thaw. That he spent six hours rounding up silverfish, longhorn beetles, and even a luna moth when she fretted over her vacant bug motel. That he stole only what he needed, and not ever what he wanted.

Dogs jumped from the back of a white Taurus.

The scream hit them.

A cop stood his ground, one arm wrapped around the waist of Ivy Macauley as he struggled to keep hold of her.

Chief Nix waved a hand toward the cop who gratefully let her free. Ivy walked toward them slow, didn't lose it again till she saw the bloodied shirt in the bag. She was put together, always, even when she cleaned at night. When she scrubbed piss from the floor of bathrooms and swept tobacco from mahogany desks.

Ivy folded, arched her back and screamed the kind of wrenching sound that stained them all. The echo Saint would hear when she sat in the yard that night, shivering though it was warm. Trying hard not to cry out when news spread through the town.

A local, Pattie Rayburn, had seen the van.

It made a right turn onto Highway 35.

Patch was gone.

9

That first night was like none Saint had known.

She sat cross-legged on the front porch, the soles of her feet dark with dirt. Her grandmother standing when the low lights of a police cruiser passed by. Norma did not offer comfort or platitudes. Saint did not know a tougher woman to fear or emulate.

She could not smell the barbecue smoke or see church lanterns or the verdancy of Monta Clare, so beautiful it clung to memory when you left. Patch hung over the small town like city smog so turgid mothers ushered their children inside and made sure the news was deadbolted at the door. Saint had felt the pervade of those passing minutes as cops came from the towns of Pecaut and Lenard Creek. Chief Nix sent them out armed with a photograph that showed her friend smiling widely, eye patch in place.

At nine her grandmother climbed the stairs and told Saint that she should not stay up late because the boy would likely return soon enough, and she would need her energy to receive him.

At ten Saint climbed onto her rusted Spyder and pedaled hard in the direction of Main Street, breaking her grandmother's strict curfew.

Main Street was lit with locals gathered outside Lacey's Diner. She propped her bike outside the Aldon Funeral Parlor and listened as they talked of calls coming in from Jefferson City and Cedar Rapids and even one of the Amana Colonies. Later that night she would fix pins to the map that hung above her bookshelf.

I hear they got a guy over by Pike Creek.

I heard that.

Alibi has him working a double shift at the Roan Arnold Energy Center.

Could be. Midwest derecho wrecked a cooling tower.

And so it went.

She ducked through a cluster of onlookers and made it to the window of the station, and inside saw the kind of bustle that calmed her a little. The phone rang out as cops gathered around maps and pored over files. At the far end she saw Chief Nix pinch the bridge of his nose like the unfurling was too much.

In the state of Missouri two high school girls and a college kid had gone missing in the past eight months. Cops had shown up at Monta Clare High School and told the students the importance of vigilance, said it while they hooked their thumbs into their waistbands, fingers meeting the steel of their

Model 39s. For a while the town hung in the kind of rampant fear that meant Saint was no longer allowed out of her yard when the sun dropped.

They'll catch this devil, her grandmother had said as she sucked on a Marlboro and rocked on her chair.

"Go home, kid. Ain't you heard, there's a bad man out there," a Pecaut cop said as he passed by.

10

At eleven she rode down Main Street. Carved into a valley, the town of Monta Clare rose out and crept the low rise of the mountain, the roads neatly forged into acres of tilted green.

She coasted, then pedaled hard to meet the foot of the climb onto winding streets minted with Virginia bluebells and butterfly weed and bear's breeches. So much fucking color. Sheaves of warmth ached from grand homes. When the trail grew too steep she dumped her bicycle in a flourish of bushes and hiked the last couple of hundred yards.

Where the hell are you, Patch?

Up the wind of a steep driveway toward the spread of stucco and leaded glass; turreted rooflines of blue slate above a porch of natural stone topped with reclaimed wood gnarled just deep enough to tell it had traveled to adorn something so beautiful. Saint turned and saw the town spark a long way beneath.

She had not seen the Meyer house up close before. But she knew it. Everyone in town knew it.

The door opened before she could knock. A man filled it, and she noticed his tired eyes and the pavilion trusses behind him, his bare feet on parquet floor.

She swallowed back nerves of different kinds. "Mr. Meyer."

He fixed her with apathy like what had gone before had scooped out everything he thought he knew about their town and his daughter's place in it.

"You're Misty's friend," he said, like he knew nothing of his daughter's life.

A lamp burned behind, her shadow spearing the glow.

"Is she—"

"She's sleeping. You shouldn't be out this late."

Saint tried not to see everything the Meyer family had, instead how much they might have lost.

She glanced back and could just make out the tops of eastern white pine. Beneath them Patch Macauley had saved the life of his daughter. Saint blinked back her tears. "I have to talk with her."

"She'll speak with Chief Nix after she's slept. Her mother . . ." He swallowed. "You go on home now."

Saint knew that some people mistook money for class, anger for strength.

When he closed the door all she felt was his fear.

11

That night she did not sleep at all, instead stared at her map and marked with a yellow highlighter the route the van had taken. Her shelves bulged with books; the walls held no posters or photographs. She did not own makeup or perfume or a wardrobe that extended beyond school and church.

At dawn she found her grandmother sitting at the oak table, and the old lady's eyes told that she had not slept even though she would drive the bus that morning from Monta Clare through six towns and the forge of Palmer Valley.

"The bees?" Saint asked, and her grandmother shook her head.

Upstairs she wet a washcloth and wiped her face and beneath her arms and already noticed the red in her eyes and the unruly strands that fled from her braid. Her front tooth was crooked because she had lost her retainer while chasing Patch through the corn on the old Hinton farm. And after, when she caught him, the two had sat together, their bare arms touching. She recalled his face as well as her own, his mess of hair, how he too was skinny and pretty and when he aimed his smile just right . . .

God, let him come home today.

Her grandmother fixed eggs that neither of them ate.

"School is closed today," Norma said. Deep lines channeled from the corners of her eyes like rivulets forged from the hot tears spilled the day Saint's mother passed.

"I wasn't going to go," Saint said, looking up through her lenses like she was waiting on a rebuke. She had not ever missed a day of school. Some might've thought it was because Norma was hard on her, but sometimes Saint thought the truth was less palatable. She liked to learn.

"They'll find him," Norma said. "They will."

After breakfast Saint went to the woodland.

Chief Nix had put the call out late, that they'd need men to go trudge the woodland on the kind of grim journey where success and failure were one and the same.

Monta Clare answered, and near a hundred stood in weighted silence and listened to Chief Nix tell them what they mostly already knew. Walk in line and keep your mouth shut and your eyes open.

Chief Nix whittled them to only the most able, Saint swallowing dry when he shook his head at her.

Behind her fifty or so farmworkers and laborers and stone-faced teens with acned cheeks tried to dull their excitement. Midges steamed from the dirt and they batted at them idly, focused on the thrill of finding the kid's bloodied clothes.

12

Past white hawthorn blossoms she walked up Rosewood Avenue. The houses were old and large, and it was easy to spot the Macauley place because Patch had carved a skull and crossbones into the face of the red oak that guarded the yard.

Saint wore faded Nikes and did not hear the buzz of mowers. Mr. Hawes had left his fence half painted. The Atkinson twins' jump rope lay in the front yard.

Ivy Macauley wore a smart dress cut low on her chest like she wanted to show the world they were decent but did not own the right clothes for the occasion.

Saint followed her inside past wood panels and brickwork paper and sand-colored drapes against brutally florid walls. The kind of mismatch that screamed furnished rental, the cheapest end.

Saint watched the sway in Ivy's hips and sometimes tried to copy the walk.

"Goddam it, Saint," she said, and the girl stepped

into a hug that smelled faintly of smoke and vodka and perfume.

There was a steady drip from a leaking faucet, like a metronome that scaled up the tension.

"I heard Nix say there'll be a team come to search the house again," Saint said.

"Search it for what? You think he stole again?"

Saint shook her head, though knew it had been only a week since Patch stole the gold cufflinks from Dr. Tooms's bag when he visited the house. She'd ridden with him to the pawn shop two towns over to collect nine dollars.

"Look at you, Saint. How old are you now?"

Saint straightened a little. "Thirteen."

Ivy broke a smile that was hard and beautiful. Her hand shook as she lit a cigarette. Saint noticed the bulge of Ivy's hips, the way her skin plumped above each elbow. Sometimes she wondered if she herself would one day turn into a woman, if it would happen more suddenly for her because most of the girls in her class had tits arriving like they'd preordered and Saint had missed the window. Most times she reasoned they could do nothing but slow her down when she ran and climbed, and likely would make snaking beneath the Fullertons' front porch and searching for quarters near impossible.

"They'll find him today," Ivy said, holding the smoke deep. "It's not . . . I mean we all know what these men do with the girls. Those girls from Lewis County, and the college kid," Ivy said evenly, because even Saint knew. "Most men play at appearing decent; the rest aren't as good at the game." She blew smoke toward the window. "There's a lot of them today, down by the woodland?"

Saint nodded.

"It should be that girl missing. The Meyers, they have so damn much." She caught herself, raised a hand of apology to an audience Saint could not see. "Misty . . . is she okay?"

"I think so."

"I want to be there today, but Nix said no. In case there's a call. What fucking call?"

A little heat crept into Saint's cheeks when Ivy cursed.

Ivy reached out and settled Saint into the wooden kitchen chair and retied her braid with an expertise Saint could not ever match. Like it was a skill to be handed down solely from mother to daughter.

"He's alive," Ivy said. "I'd feel it if he wasn't."

13

At ten o'clock Saint leaned against a truck and watched the search party.

"He's dead."

She turned to see Chuck Bradley and two of his friends.

She heard a little laughter, but it didn't carry far, like it was rote, like even they knew it wasn't the place.

"Shit, those reporters in town, making the kid sound like a hero."

"He's a little thief. I remember when he broke into the Johnsons' garage. Stole a mower."

"We're at twenty-four hours, right?" Chuck said. "Everyone knows once that passes . . . kid's dead."

Saint swallowed when Chuck turned to her.

"Missing your boyfriend? Go cry to your dyke grandmother."

"Enough."

Saint stared up at Dr. Tooms, who sent the boys on their way. He wore a sport jacket and the kindest smile.

"Dr. T," she said.

He turned.

"All that blood . . ."

"Bleeding . . . it often looks worse than it is."

Chief Nix came over, touched the doctor's arm gently and sent him back to the walkers.

Chief Nix knelt to her level. She smelled his cologne and beneath it the sweat. "I asked around. I know you and him . . . you're close. More like family, right?"

"You have to bring him back now," she said.

"He wanted the girl. And he got your friend instead. Now we're taking that as a good sign. You've got to keep faith."

She saw Sammy, the drunkard owner of Monta Clare Fine Art, smart in his starched white shirt, five-button vest, and laced low tops. His eyes told that he had not slept either, like the entire town felt it. "How's the Meyer girl doing?" Sammy asked.

Nix was about to speak when they heard the call.

They stopped dead as one woman raised her hand.

Nix tried to keep Saint back, but she slipped from his grasp and ran toward, stopping cold when she saw it.

Nix pulled on a glove and held the small cloth up to the light.

Saint looked at the purple and the silver star and almost cried out.

They would search that land for three days. Through pleats of dogwood, breathing honeysuckle and witch hazel and elderberry. The group would thin, but Saint would stay with them, begging local kids to help out.

She would not sleep more than a few hours each night.

She would be there to watch each second of their summer die.

14

Saint had found the Langstroth hive the day they moved into the tall house on Pinehill Cemetery Road, buried beneath dwarf shrubs and succulents and bulbs. She picked a rusting hatchet from the woodshed and hacked a path, her grandmother busy with the movers, a couple of distant cousins with a U-Haul that leaned when they turned because the suspension was shot.

She stared at the boxes, the faded grain of the ten-frame, the three-quarter-inch lumber, each cut so neat she ran her fingers across the sawn edge. The summer unruly, they'd driven through a Burlington storm before the heat of Jefferson City, the windows open to a flat wall of air and the promise of something new. She'd been lured with talk of a backyard, room for her toys, a neighborhood where you didn't have to leave the street as the sun dropped.

She had dragged her grandmother into the yard while her bare-chested cousins heaved her bed frame up to the attic room.

"It's a hive," Norma said, then turned and left her.

"Can I—"

"No."

It took Saint the best part of that first year in Monta Clare to convince her grandmother that keeping bees was a good idea. She borrowed a book from the library, spoke of honey each morning and smacked her lips, chased bees around the yard to convince Norma she was entirely unafraid, and even managed to stem her tears when a worker reared on her and planted its tail in the lobe of her ear.

"Are you happy now?" Norma said, balancing Saint on her knee as she tweezed the stinger out.

"Very," Saint sniffed.

She saved her allowance and ordered in copies of **The Hive and the Honey Bee,** but fell short of the five dollars a year needed to subscribe to the **American Bee Journal.**

Saint was methodical in the breakdown of her grandmother, each Saturday morning riding Norma's bus route and perching herself on the seat just behind, her mouth level with Norma's ear so she might bend it with dazzling bee facts. Saint told her one out of three mouthfuls of food she consumed depended on pollinators. That the buff-tailed bumblebee had a brain the size of a poppy seed. That she had already planted primrose and buddleia and marigold to encourage nectaration, which she wasn't entirely sure was a real word, but Norma didn't question it.

And then she brought her A game. The waggle

dance. Maybe it was a communication technique, maybe it was a celebration of bee life—scientists weren't entirely sure—but Saint took to the center aisle as Norma crested Parade Hill, crouched a little and shook her ass while buzzing at the mouth.

"Jesus," Norma said, and she was not one to blaspheme.

The following weekend, under promise that it would be Saint's Christmas and birthday gift for the following two hundred years, Norma called a supplier over in Boonville and the order was placed.

They spent their summer in the yard. Saint watched intently as Norma wired the frame, handed her cigar box nails before she could ask, fetched iced tea when she began to sweat. Saint read from the limited instructions as she went about the repair, strengthening the comb, replacing the gunnysack, cursing at the goddamn pollen trap.

"How come you can do so much?" Saint said, as her grandmother fetched a block plane to smooth a wavelet.

"You ever ask that question to your grandfather when he was alive?"

Saint shook her head.

Norma went on.

Saint stood on their driveway waiting for three hours then screeched when she saw the white of the van on its approach.

"They're here," she screamed as she ran into the house and dragged her grandmother by the hand.

Norma did not sleep the night after the bees arrived, walking through the night garden to check on them, waking Saint because of the hum.

"Why aren't they sleeping?" Norma said.

Saint stood in the dark in her shorts and vest and rubbed at her eyes. "They're cooling the hive. They flap their wings at the same time and it sounds like an electric fan."

"I thought they were dying."

Saint clutched her hand as they walked back toward the house. "I'm glad you care about the bees, Grandma."

"Twenty bucks. I want my honey."

Norma looped a small cloth canopy over the tree beside the hive, and Saint did her schoolwork beneath it, watching the workers, and sometimes singing, "Be Thou My Vision" and "Abide with Me."

Saint did not make friends, though she aimed her smiles, did not raise her hand too much even though she knew the answers, and invited each girl in her class to come see the hive, spending an hour fashioning each invitation, dotting hand-drawn bees with glitter glue and crepe paper.

She finessed the drone escape and was stung two dozen times, appearing at the breakfast table with swellings and a smile.

The season was good. August rains kept the dry from total, and in September of 1973, as her grandmother mourned Jim Croce, she caught the final nectar flow. The honey capped, two supers primed. She could not afford a bee brush, so with Norma watching from the safety of the kitchen window she shook the bees free, remembering to release the stragglers the next morning from the old store, which her grandmother had repaired and turned into her honey house.

In early fall, after a procession of trial and error, of extraction dismay and filtration concerns, she jarred her first batch. They kept a little for themselves. She gave a few out to girls who had shown passing interest in her produce and potential friendship, and the rest she placed on a gingham tablecloth upon a folding table in the center of Main Street.

Sammy the drunk emerged from Monta Clare Fine Art and demanded to see her vendor permit, till Norma threatened to go fetch her Colt Python from their garage.

Saint grinned at locals and offered samples on graham crackers, stopped short of the waggle dance, and sold five jars.

"I'll reinvest the profit. Perhaps pick up a tank, a new brood box, maybe even a third super. Think of the yield. Honey money."

Norma frowned. "Technically you've realized a considerable loss."

It was on the last day of summer break, as Saint lay on her stomach in the soft grass, her feet kicked up behind her, that she noticed the boy standing by the side gate and staring at her.

She knew him from school, hard to miss with the patch covering his eye.

He wore jeans and a T-shirt, and when he yawned and stretched she noticed a hole beneath each arm.

Saint stood and glared and was about to see him off when she saw the small card in his hand. One of hers, handmade with a dashed glitter bee trail and dotted with cotton wool. Though as she neared she noticed he had crudely crossed out the name of the girl it was intended for and replaced it with his own.

"I'm here about the honey," he said, and stared past her as if he were seeking out a jar for himself.

"Oh."

"I received this invitation, which I believe is good for a sample, and perhaps a tour of the facility."

He was clearly an imbecile.

He noticed the hive and let out a long whistle. "Manuka, right?"

"Manuka honey is produced in Australia and New Zealand."

He closed his solitary eye and nodded, as if he were testing her.

His arms were more bone than flesh, and his hair long. He smelled faintly of mud and candy and carried grazes across his knuckles like he'd been pulled from a fight, and he wore a leather belt looped twice at his waist, and in it was tucked a wooden cutlass.

She might have told him to leave, but then he smiled. And it was the first time another kid had smiled her way since she had arrived in Monta Clare. And it was a good smile. Dimples. Neat teeth.

"I've heard it's the finest honey this side of . . ."

"I worked a whole six months on the hive," she said. Though clearly afflicted, he was the first kid to show real interest, and so she grabbed his hand and tugged him toward the Langstroth, took her moment and shone, dazzling him with bee facts he quickly claimed to already be aware of. Sometimes he chimed in with absolute nonsense.

"And these are pure bees?" he said.

She pretended not to hear.

When they came to the honey house his eye widened at the shelves. Two dozen jars, some glowed golden.

She handed him one, told him to wait as she headed into the kitchen to fetch a spoon, some crackers, a stack of napkins, and her honey apron.

Saint returned to find him sitting beneath a butterfly bush, the jar half-empty and his hand caked in honey.

She marched toward him, placed her hands on her small hips and glowered.

He looked up at her as honey ran from his chin. "Tell you what, I'd say this is the sweetest thing I ever saw . . . and then I saw you, Becky."

"Who the hell is Becky?"

He scratched his head, leaving a deposit of honey at his hairline. Then he reached for the invitation.

"Becky Thomas is the girl that invite was meant for," she said.

"Well . . . then who put my name on it? Maybe fate intervened. Cupid aimed his bow." Patch made an O with the forefinger and thumb of his left hand, before penetrating it with the index finger of his right.

"What was that?" Saint said.

"I see the older kids doing it. I believe it's cupid's arrow sticking right into my heart."

She rolled her eyes.

"You could smear this on chicken. Or maybe pork ribs. We should go into business together. Honey hustlers. Regional, then national. Maybe Latin America. It's highly addictive." He licked his entire hand, like a grooming cat.

Both looked up when they were cast into the forbidding shadow of Norma.

"The bus driver," Patch said, and offered her a sticky hand.

Norma turned to glare at Saint for an explanation.

Saint shrugged. "Apparently Cupid sent him."

Once again Patch made an O with the forefinger and thumb of his left hand, before penetrating it with the index finger of his right.

"Get off my property," Norma said.

15

Four days and she was remnants of before.

She had slept and eaten little, walked the woodland dawn till dusk, showed at the police station and took to sitting on the wooden chair like they needed the reminder. The cops had long since tired of telling her to leave.

The week had closed out in perceived progress, in the fever of missing youth patterns, tip cards, and school incident files.

"This kid," Officer Cortez had said as he flipped through minor indiscretions like they were gateways to something grander. His shirt opened to a swathe of tan chest, his sideburns thick like drops of tar.

"The pirate thing," Officer Harkness replied.

"That why he steals?"

"Nah, he steals 'cause they ain't got shit. You've seen the house."

"Kid carried a dagger and pulled it when he was outnumbered. Moxie."

"Served him well."

Cortez laughed.

Saint wondered how they could laugh, how they could sip black coffee and eat pastries and talk football.

She heard mention of a person pattern analysis and heard the name John Stokes and a little of his record. She knew those men existed, every kid did when they hit a certain age.

"The mother couldn't even find his birth certificate. Makes you wonder. Still, the ass on her though," Cortez said.

Friday Saint had been to see Daisy Creason from **The Tribune,** and to her credit Daisy had not laughed her out of the cluttered office above Monta Clare Insurance, instead took a little time to listen, to learn more about the pirate boy who saved the richest girl in town. Saint had sat there two hours and spilled all she had.

"So the boy likes honey," Daisy said, as things wrapped up.

Saint left with a promise that Daisy would not let the story drop.

"How about a reward?" Saint said.

A further promise was made. If Saint could squeeze dollars from townsfolk, Daisy would run it on the front page, print the posters, and put out calls to neighboring towns.

None of it eased it, that low pain that filtered through her blood and told her it was too long now.

Four days was too long.

16

She dressed in navy overalls with a white blouse beneath and downstairs found her grandmother at the table reading **The Tribune.**

"You look too skinny," Norma said.

Saint looked down at the jut of her hip bones. "I'm fine."

"You have dirt beneath your nails."

"I always do."

"Wear your wedge sandals. Church."

Beneath the fallow stone Saint stood in the colored flood of the sainted windows and did not sing with the others or listen to the old priest. He preached theirs was not a vengeful god, and Saint fought the urge to ask why the fuck not.

As they chorused about the fail of helpers and the flee of comforts a cruel hush fell for Ivy Macauley, who slipped in at the back and sat alone. She wore a corduroy A-line dress, buttoned high, her dark hair pulled back, her eyes' betrayal hidden only by a refusal to meet their gaze.

A kid from her class, Jimmy Walters, carried a single-chain thurible, but Saint did not see smoke, only the smile he aimed at her.

She ignored him, and her grandmother tutted at the slight.

"He smiled at you," Norma said.

"His brain is likely damaged from inhaling too much incense. He doesn't even realize he's smiling."

Norma sighed. "It's okay to have more than one friend."

"I don't need more than one friend."

The priest led them in prayer for the missing child. And at that Saint knelt on the cold and clasped her hands so tightly together her bones ground in plea. She had not had call to ask much of God in her short life, but she offered herself fully, made promises she did not yet understand, if only he would have her friend return safely.

At the close she picked her way through a straggling crowd of one-time mourners.

Misty Meyer wore a neat navy dress and flats and no makeup at all. Her lips were plump and her hair thick.

Together they sat on dry-laid stones.

"You're friends with the pirate," Misty said.

Saint nodded and felt a flutter of pride that Misty knew that.

"Every winter people say Monta Clare is too beautiful. It's like a bigger crime, right? Because it happened here. It's like none of us were prepared for the outside creeping in," Misty said.

Saint wondered how Misty could be so poised, so complete at that age when she should be ill-fitting parts and contradiction.

"Cops can't find him." Misty's eyes were warm blue and told her every thought before it reached her mouth. "My parents won't talk about him . . . the pirate kid. Or the man. They won't talk about what he might have done to me."

"You want to talk about that?"

"If I'd gone straight to school . . . instead of cutting in the woods. You think he would've tried it in the street? I keep looking at people and wondering about them. I can't see his face. When I sit with Chief Nix, he's so patient and I want to tell him, but . . . the guy, he wore a mask. And, I mean, I'm kind of used to ignoring boys."

Saint had been there when the Meyers came to the station, and through the window she'd watched them flip the pages, waiting for the nod, the call to go to some place likely upstate, maybe by the turnpike where the dozen or so hunters cabins sat. Most knew there were likely a hundred more not on any kind of map, just dug into land fed by the backwater. The low hum of a generator buried beneath the baldachin of nature. They'd find him dead. Of course. And they'd catch the guy, but there would not be reason for it.

"My grandmother says some people are born to make others work harder," Saint said.

"The dyke that drives the bus?"

"She's not a dyke."

"She has the short hair and she smokes cigars."

Saint shrugged. "She doesn't really smoke them much. She just smells them."

"She should beware, you know. Cancer of the snout."

"Excuse me?"

"My grandfather smoked thirty Pall Malls each day and his dog developed cancer of the snout from smelling the fumes."

Saint did not know what to do with that.

"Your grandmother isn't a hound," Misty offered.

Saint did not know what to do with that either.

"Why did you cut that morning, Misty?"

Misty looked over at her, studying her so finely Saint knew she could do nothing but disappoint.

"I didn't prepare for the math test."

"You ace every test, Misty. People think you're dumb because you act dumb for the boys. But you're—"

"It's a meaningless lie," Misty said.

They watched suited men, their hair long on their collars, trousers a little flared, and boots that carried a heel. Stomachs leaned over belts.

Saint plucked a cardinal from the long grass and shelled petals and waited. When it came her breathing quickened.

"I saw someone. I wanted to help him."

"Who did you see, Misty?"

Misty finally tore her eyes from the stone and looked at Saint. "I saw Dr. Tooms."

17

"You've got to stop this, kid," Nix said from across the desk.

The tired dragged her mind to the dark place that told her the wheels were slowing, the grind easing, and a low acceptance was beginning to pervade.

There were no photos on his desk, no wife or kids or handshakes with monied guys and golf buddies. His focus was total. He could not find her friend.

She picked the mud from beneath her nails, fussed with her braid, and pushed her frames up a nose too small to carry such weight. She knew when he looked at her, when most looked at her, they saw a poor girl. Not poor like Patch, because her grandmother drove the bus and they owned a decent home because her grandfather had insurance, but poor in an altogether more complex way. A poor girl who had no sense of style, or femininity, no chance of finding a boy and then a man. A girl who looked to books for answers to questions that would never be asked of her. Weighed questions that had nothing to do with fashion or baking or making a goddamn motherfucking home.

"Dr. T was just there that morning, in the woods right by where it happened?" she asked.

Nix glanced behind her at the glass-paneled door like he was trying to catch the eye of someone who would come save him. "He was just there, Saint."

She was too small, her feet stuffed into wedges that had fit her a year before, her arms scratched and cut at each elbow. She knew girls like Misty already powdered their cheeks and painted their lips and tweezed at their eyebrows.

At the door she stopped and turned. "Why was he there, though?"

"He was looking for his dog. The thing ran away. Your friend Misty was helping him search."

She tucked her hands into her pockets, rolled remnants of tissue and lint across her fingertips and stared at the big policeman. "He doesn't have a dog."

"Excuse me?"

"My grandmother's house backs onto the Tooms farm. In the winter when the trees are bare I can see the miles to his house. Me and Patch used to run through onto the farm. I didn't ever see a dog, Chief Nix. Not ever."

Nix was about to reply when the phone rang.

Saint watched the color drain from him.

That afternoon the news would spread through Monta Clare.

Another girl had gone missing.

18

Her name was Callie Montrose.

She lived in a town near seventy miles from Monta Clare and had not returned from school.

When Norma heard, she took the Colt from its place in the garage, checked it was loaded, and slept with it in the drawer of her nightstand.

That night Saint took her small rucksack and filled it with a pocket flashlight, a slingshot, a book of matches, and a jackknife so rusted the pivot caught.

She walked down sleeping streets, and at the Macauley house slipped in through the kitchen door and found Ivy passed out on the sofa. Saint covered her up, noting the empty bottle, and crept up the stairs. In the haunt of Patch's bedroom she retrieved the pistol from its dented biscuit tin and took a moment to stare at the empty bed.

"I'll bring you home," she said, quiet. "I swear it."

The pistol lay heavy in her hands, its origin heavy on her chest.

. . .

"What did you get for your birthday?" he said.

"Spyder," she said, and pointed toward the enamel-framed bicycle with the drum brake and the quilted banana seat. "It has a basket for my things."

So far her things were books, a chain of daisies, and a small rock she would later take to the library in Panora, where she would scan the geology section and discover it was not an emerald.

He let out a customary whistle. He wore a navy hussar waistcoat crossed with fine gold detail and pearl buttons, his eye aching for her to return the question.

She waited a full minute before he caved.

"The waistcoat. I got the waistcoat, Saint."

"It's not your birthday yet."

"I found it hidden in my mother's closet. Who can wait for such a thing?"

She saw it had been made from an old dress shirt, his mother a skilled enough seamstress.

"It's a thing of beauty, Patch. Really, it is."

Sometimes she was giddy about having a friend to call her own. At first she was mindful of the fact he was only after her honey, but then he suggested they run the corn maze together, and the roots of first friendship took hold. She was careful not to load him with too much of anything other kids deemed nerdy. She bit her tongue when he talked pirates, because she'd read three books on the subject to better understand his kind, and his facts were riddled with inaccuracies. She did not correct his English, his grammar, did not flinch when he cursed, which was often, and was something she would try to emulate, which thrilled her grandmother no end. She fought the urge to invite him for dinner when she found out his mother worked shifts that did not leave enough time for her to care for him. To her he was an exotic creature she would do well not to grasp too tightly for fear of scaring him off.

"I reckon it's the same kind Henry Every wore when he slaughtered the Mughal vessels," Patch said, then pulled a rusted spyglass telescope from his pocket and aimed it toward the frosted woodland.

Saint pulled back a thin branch and gamely joined in. "I read his crew also raped the slave girls."

He frowned, looked down at his waistcoat, and then frowned again. "So I look like a rapist?"

Jesus. "Not at all, if anything you look the opposite . . . like rape is the last thing on your mind."

He frowned once more.

Friendship was a difficult art to master.

Theirs had blossomed after he showed up at her house with a stolen spoon and a single cracker, bloomed when he sat next to her at lunch each day, eyeing her sack lunch to see if it contained honey. And now she knew several cogent facts about him.

His mother worked nights, and drank wine, and sometimes passed out cold from the combination.

He believed his one eye was more powerful than her two, and that he could read print from a hundred yards. A theory they had tested with his copy of Playboy in her backyard.

"Ursula Andress. Born March 10, 1936. Honey Ryder," he called, squinting at the page.

"Always with the honey," Saint said, though marveled at his skills.

He was both brave and stupid in a way she could not understand, like he knew nothing of risk or consequence. On their second outing she had confided in him her desire for a second hive to expand her empire. That same evening he had attempted to steal a colony from the Meltons' farmstead. The resulting massacre had seen him absent from school for three days.

"I guess I could give you your gift early too then," she said, and sprinted back into the house while he stayed in the yard.

She made him close his eye as she placed the one-shot flintlock replica gun into his small hands.

And when he saw it his mouth fell open. He looked at her, then the gun, then at her again. "How did you—"

"Lucky find." She would not tell him the luck was born of trawling the flea market, Goodwill stores, and pawn shops on her grandmother's bus route and beyond. Of emptying her piggy bank and still coming up short, and so striking a loan agreement with Norma whose terms involved Saint mowing the lawn and pulling weeds for the next seventy years.

He hugged her then.

Unexpected.

"You just wait till you see what I got for you," he said.

She did wait, and a week later was thrilled with the butterfly brooch he gave her, until she saw an impassioned plea from Miss Worth for its safe return on the church bulletin board.

19

Back in her yard Saint watched the empty hive, and through deep wades of moonlight walked along the foot of their land, the trees like guardians that wavered only in a single spot she had found with Patch that same evening two years before.

She stayed close behind as he forged them a path with a wooden cutlass.

"I carved our initials in the oak tree by the graveyard," he said.

"Defacing nature for me, be still my beating heart," she said, biting her lip to keep back her smile.

"I like that when we're gone, it'll be there. It'll last."

"Do you want to come to my birthday dinner tonight?" she said, and did not dare breathe for a long time.

He stopped dead, dropped to one knee, and tilled the leaves with a pale hand. "Wolf scat."

She wrinkled her nose and made a mental note to spray him with Lysol on their return.

"Ready the pistol," he announced.

Saint pulled the replica one-shot flintlock pistol from her satchel and cocked it, thrilled that she had been entrusted with such a prize.

"Does it fire?" she said.

"Doesn't need to. You stare down the barrel of that and you spill your pockets and your secrets. Or you take off running. If you see one it's best to aim for the eye," he said.

"Savage. Especially coming from you."

They moved on.

She cleared her throat. "Are you coming to this birthday dinner or not? Because I have lots of boys who might like—"

"Will there be cake?" he said, not looking back over his shoulder. She followed the shape of him, his bony shoulders and the narrow V of his waist. His trousers stopped an inch shy of ankle. He smelled strongly of cologne, a kind she did not know, a kind he had found in a box of his father's things that perhaps might have been better buried with the man, if only to ward off scavengers.

"What kind of party doesn't have cake?"

"Yes, but what kind of cake?"

"I mean . . . it carries a skull and crossbones . . . that's all they had left in the store." Her cheeks flamed a little at the lie. She had spent near a week working from the Wilton Yearbook of Cake

Decorating, had her grandmother pick up mint wafers, shoestring licorice, and two packs of chocolate fudge frosting so she could fashion the ship.

He turned slowly, his smile so wide she fought hard not to match it. "You have a pirate cake?"

"Indeed."

"I'll be there. And I'll bring a little offering. A gentleman corsair does not show with an empty hand."

Later that evening he would turn up with half a bottle of apricot schnapps, which he would make a show of pouring like wine for her grandmother, who could do little but shake her head at the whole sorry affair.

They met with nettle so dense their arms were streaked when they finally made it through onto Tooms's land, which pitched and fell in unruly pits.

In the distance lay a lone house, and above crowned a darkening sky that soon broke and hammered rain onto the land. Saint made to head for the trees, but Patch sat down on mats of grassland and then lay back.

"When the sky opens you got a better chance of seeing heaven," he said.

She lay beside him.

Their heads side by side, their feet the north and south of a compass.

"Will things be different now that I'm a year older?" she said.

"Your tits might finally arrive."

She nodded at that.

"Not that you need them or nothing."

"Excuse me?"

"You're smart, right? Already you know that you're smart. But also, in the right light, you look a little like Evelyn Cromer. She was the most beautiful pirate that ever sailed. Of course, she wore her hair in a braid, and slaughtered—"

"You think I'm beautiful?"

He nodded. "Entirely and absolutely."

The rain eased to gentle fall, and she turned from him and smiled, ran her tongue over her crooked front tooth and wondered if one day it would straighten by itself.

"Why is your name Saint?"

Her breath caught a little. "My grandparents named me."

"Because your mother died before she could."

She nodded.

"But the name . . ."

"They said I was every good thing, Patch. Can you believe that?"

He turned his head to look at her. "Sure, I can. Entirely and absolutely."

20

Saint snapped herself from the memory as she turned and looked back at the tall house one last time. Only the low purple from her attic lava lamp kept the smother from total.

She found the clearing and moved across arid fields, a path trodden over iced winters as they made it their gateway.

A black border marked the beginnings of Thurley State Park.

The house was grand and old like most in Monta Clare.

She knew Dr. T like everyone in town did, because when she had strep throat it was his kind eyes she looked into. He was the man who came to their school and talked to the girls about menstruation, about changing hormones and bodies.

She walked lines of peach trees, plum, apple, and cherry. And in the dark breathed honeysuckle.

Saint heard a wild call and drew her slingshot, her hands already shaking as she thought of doubling back, climbing into her bed and pulling the sheet up high over her head.

She knocked on the door and waited, and as she did she willed herself to calm. She had borrowed **The Peterson Davies Book of Police Detection** from the library, and it told her she would have to play it clever, work around the tale he'd told and maybe find a way into his house so she could search for her friend.

At the side window she cupped her hands to the glass but saw little more than her own panicked eyes reflecting back.

Saint hammered the door harder, stood back and stared up at double-hung windows so dark she could not ever imagine such a place being a home.

At the rear porch she climbed the steps and shone her flashlight over the fading frieze beam and the columns and through the glazed door into an oak kitchen. Saint tracked the beam along dark counter-tops. She saw a dresser open to pots and herbs, and on the planed top a single ashtray, a cigar stubbed and balanced on the edge.

Along the tiled floor she could not see a dog bowl or bed, or a lead hanging from the bronze hare hooks by the door.

She rattled the door and found it locked, kicked it once and cursed. She tried the windows, and though the panes were single and thin and there was play within their frames, she could not prize them open.

"Patch," she called, though did not believe he

could hear her or reply, and maybe did not believe that he was being held there at all, just that the doctor had lied and no one had called him on it.

She cast her light back across the fields, and though her heart was heavy with another failure she began to slowly cross her way toward home.

And then she heard it.

A scream.

A scream so stark and desperate and utterly terrifying that she began to cry.

She turned back toward the house, and though her tears turned to sobs of fear she walked slowly back toward the sound.

"Patch," she cried out.

Saint ran back toward the front of the house.

And it was as she turned the corner that she felt a hand on her shoulder.

She screamed, and Dr. Tooms raised his hands, his face pale and stricken.

Saint moved back from him, keeping a good distance.

She did not move to wipe her tears or ask him to explain or lead her to her friend. Instead she raised her flashlight, and only when that blue-white beam met the crimson blood on his hands did she turn and run.

21

As cooling rains hammered the windows, Saint sat at the old piano and played Chopin's suffocation as her grandmother sat in the rocking chair beside.

Saint closed out the doleful notes, her fingers thin like her frame, her cheeks sallow and her skin paler. In the weeks that had passed, the realization that they had lost Joseph Macauley drowned her. She did not eat much or sleep much, and at school she sat mute, only now and then turning in her chair to notice the empty seat at the back of the class.

She had thought she was close the night she ran from the doctor. Norma had found her granddaughter sitting on the hardwood kitchen floor with the door bolted behind.

"It's him," she'd said.

Chief Nix arrived, and Saint had ridden in the back of his cruiser beside her grandmother, and then sat outside the Tooms farmhouse as the doctor walked from it and the two men spoke for a long time.

She heard Nix apologize and saw Tooms offer a sad smile directed toward the car.

Saint spent hours in the woodland behind her house, lying on her stomach and watching the Tooms land through Patch's spy telescope. Norma said he was a doctor and blood came with the territory. That the scream could have been mating wolves. Sometimes she noted a vehicle on the other side beneath trees that kept its color and driver in shadow, and she wondered if the doctor allowed house calls.

A further week and the reward money grew to two thousand dollars after Saint delivered handwritten letters to the folks on Parade Hill.

And the case began its slide from headlines to murmurs.

A bar fight turned into a murder in Cedar Rapids; a drunk ran a stop sign in Mount Vernon and killed an expectant mother. A group armed with placards torched a Planned Parenthood clinic in Columbia. Saint read of TRAP laws and crisis centers and broached the subject with Norma.

"We should have total control of our own bodies," Saint said.

"You would not be here if we did," Norma said, not looking up from her newspaper.

"But my mother would."

"It's a sin."

"Tell that to Jane Roe," Saint said.

"It's not your fight to take."

"Only because you wouldn't let me. I wanted to stand there with Misty and the other girls. I wanted to carry the placard and show my support on the front page of **The Tribune.** It's not fair."

"Fair has little to do with religion and politics."

Life in all its uneven fairness went on. As summer bled out, the fall air brought a chrysalis of calm. Greens ceded to browns and golds Saint did not notice. She took long searching walks through dimming woodland, her eyes straining the ground no matter how much she tried to force herself to look up. She missed curfew, walked close to the highway like bait. If the man was still hunting, she willed herself to be taken. Nix found her and drove her home, and her grandmother moved from anger to fear to desperation.

Norma wanted her to see a counselor over in Cossop Hill.

Saint told her she was fine, choked down a mouthful of stew but could not manage more. She lost more weight, her cheekbones high, her hair still thick and too heavy for her meager frame. She had no hips and still no chest, but she no longer cared about such nonsense.

Evenings crackled with bonfire smoke.

Patch's name was mentioned under people's breath that now smoked with cold.

Saint marked the change in Ivy Macauley each Sunday at church. How the woman's hands trembled as she prayed. How vodka now overpowered the perfume.

Saint watched the television screen as Ronald Reagan threw his hat into the ring, promising the kind of change not even a dozen lifetimes could boast. **This is it, you'll see.**

Saint was not sure exactly what **it** was, but the next morning as she watched the Ford flags stand defiant in frosting yards, she could think of nothing good at all.

22

In the woodland one fine frozen morning she found Chief Nix casting his rod out into the lake. She silently sat beside him because he was closer to Patch, her only link now, her only chance. Over coffee topped with brandy he breathed the steam.

"You need to check on Mrs. Macauley," Saint said.

"I do."

Despite the cold he had his shirtsleeves rolled back. Soft, dark hair covered his arms. Saint heard the women in town talk of him, perhaps the most eligible man in Monta Clare. She had not seen him step out with any one of them, and for some reason it made her glad.

"She takes drugs now," Saint said.

She watched his handsome face, his blue eyes and dark moustache. He lit a cigar from a silver case.

Saint flexed her fingers to bring the feeling back. "If Patch . . . if he's dead, I know I won't be able to—"

"You will." He spoke with such certainty as he

watched the bevel of ice clips felling reed tops like snow was due.

"Get on, Saint."

"I am—"

"You don't sleep. I pass by your place and I see your light burning no matter the hour."

She did not tell him she was studying her maps. That she knocked on doors, that she had filled her blackboard not with math problems but with names and addresses she had gotten by begging a Cedar Rapids cop, who had shown mercy. Everyone who owned a navy van. And that sometimes after school she went to watch houses and rotten timber garages.

"The newspaper said Callie Montrose came to see you a month before she was taken," Saint said. "Why?"

He licked the dry from his lips and watched the water. "That's between me and the girl."

"Even if she's dead?"

He reeled slow and she watched the bobber.

"Even then," he said, finally.

"Her daddy is a cop," Saint said.

"A good one, the way I hear it."

"Is he—"

Nix exhaled. "He's broken. Like Mrs. Macauley. Like you."

"And like you?"

He watched the bobber. "You believe in God, Saint?"

She did not hesitate. "Yes, sir."

"You pray for your friend. And you leave everything else to me. You promise me that now."

She did not speak.

"I mean it, kid. Your grandmother . . . you're all she's got. Swear it, that you'll let it go now."

She stood, and she lied, and she went on her way.

23

She passed dormant bulbs. Witch's hair hung from gables alongside dripping icicles caving to daybreak, and braids of poison oak targeted the Macauley house like it knew it would not be wrenched free. Three weeks into three months as winter undressed Monta Clare, tipping its way down the bare hillside, the naked arms of trees knitting a white sky without break.

Saint's grandmother bought her a shearling jacket she saw in the window of a Goodwill store, leaving her bus idling outside, the patrons moaning loud.

The collar was fur lined and the thing so heavy Saint struggled to put it on, but she no longer much cared what she looked like, no longer much cared when the other kids laughed at her, or said her grandmother was a bus-driving dyke. She pulled her hat down to the slaughter of winds and spent a moment looking at the rot of lattice that had once been wrapped with roses of different names and colors.

Saint did not go inside the Macauley house anymore. She had heard from her grandmother that Kim, the landlord, had been quietly trying to reclaim the house. Ivy Macauley no longer paid the rent, and, despite the promise of boom and regeneration and economic prosperity, near everyone was feeling the acute pinch of what would be that longest winter.

At the top window between drapes ruffled at one corner and yellowed from forgotten sun she saw the shape of Ivy Macauley. Skeletal, her body no more than a show of surrender. There had been the softest talk of another service. Chief Nix had said no; the old priest had stood in the doorway and clutched his book and looked around at the ringing phones and badges and holsters draped over chairs like he could not believe God's world needed such ardent protection.

Saint raised a hand to Ivy, who came down the stairs and opened the door.

She wore shorts and a vest, and her skin was the blue gray of the dying.

"You're too young for this," Ivy slurred.

And Saint did not say that so too was Patch.

Saint walked out to the woodland and tried to be mindful, to not trace the white canvas for errant tells, to notice the high sun melting a little of the season, the droplets that shivered down pines.

She found the girl sitting on hard ground staring at the water.

"They're going on," Misty said.

Saint watched a sandpiper test the water, then soar high and away.

"You think he's dead?" Misty said, hands deep in her pockets, her legs neatly crossed, her face drawn with the worry. Saint knew there was not always an exact moment when children turned to adults. For the lucky ones it was a long, hard-earned acceptance of responsibility and opportunity. But for her, and for Misty, the divide had been curt and fatal.

"Some people think he is," Misty said, like her words were not reaching Saint. "He's just a kid, like us. The other girls talk about boys, and movies and hair and . . . fuck. Goddamn motherfucking fuck."

Saint sat on the frozen ground beside her.

"What if he's cold? What if he's someplace and he's cold and he doesn't have a coat or gloves?" Misty said.

Saint looked at the branches, her eyes not meeting the girl's because she didn't want her to see it, that she had no right to worry about Patch because he did not belong to her like the rest did. She knew nothing about him.

"I keep trying to remember something. Even though my parents . . . they pay someone to make me forget." Saint watched Misty's tears. "Tell me something about him."

For a long time Saint was quiet. And then she talked. And she forget she was not alone, and allowed herself to be carried on the cushion of that memory.

24

The first time she played piano for him it was a cold Thursday in the reaches of the Super Outbreak of 1974. A hundred tornadoes in twenty-four hours and still he had shivered, surprised by thunderclaps so loud they rattled windows of the home and threatened to skin the roof from the honey house. Norma lit the fire and then moved to the porch where she sat in her rocker just shaded from hammering rain before trees stripped raggedy.

Patch had arrived soaked through, so Saint fetched a blanket while he stripped to his underpants and sat there in a puddle of rainwater as flames moved reflections in his eye. He did not smile that day.

"Why does your grandmother sit outside during storms?" he whispered.

"There was a storm the day my grandfather died."

When the rain broke and the wind died, he took her into the yard and in the small bag he had brought removed a heavy-duty Sportsman slingshot and a small box of metal pellets. He fetched empty Progresso cans from the trash and with five built a pyramid on sopping grass and stood beside her twenty feet from them, hitting each in turn.

"You can hunt with these," he said.

He stood behind her and taught her the draw distance, of muscle memory and the art of plinking. He told her to pull the pouch back below her aiming eye, and she got it then.

They practiced with stones.

The first time she whipped the top can from the tower she turned to grin but found him lost to her. She did not know that he worried they would not afford to heat their home that winter. That the refrigerator would remain bare. She did not know that kids worried about such things.

A couple of hours and she worked on her stance, accounted for trajectory and stone weight, and hit all five with ease. He taught her to stalk, of foot placement, to head into the wind, and of the magic hour. That last glimpse of daylight when rabbits venture out.

"You ever killed one?" she said, and held her breath till he shook his head.

"I could, though. I mean, if I had to kill. I could do it, you know?"

She nodded, and knew that she could not.

"You're different today," she said.

"I'm just tired, I guess."

"Tired of what?"

"Of being me."

He followed her inside when it was time to practice.

She sat at her piano and played, and at the first notes he drew his eye from the flames and watched her small hands as she played music.

Saint felt him sit beside her on the stool.

The heat from him.

And though she was certain he would mock her she sang of Mona Lisas and Mad Hatters, and how rose trees never grow in New York City.

He did not interrupt.

Did not laugh at her.

"This is the most beautiful music I ever heard," he said.

"Yes."

"My mother lost her job cleaning for the Parkers. They said she stole." He spoke while watching the fire.

His weight was now hers.

"You can come eat with us," she said. "And if you're cold you can come sleep here, too."

He turned, his leg pressed to her.

She spoke quietly, "I can help with your homework. And if your mother needs to borrow some—"

Patch cried then.

His small shoulders shook.

Saint watched him and felt it like a pain in her chest, like she had not felt anything before.

She reached her hand out and wiped his tears. "There's a place where the bees make purple honey."

He listened.

"The North Carolina Coastal Plain. The sandhills. No one knows for sure why they do it. But it's real purple. It glows. It's like proof, Patch. There's magical things out there just waiting on you."

He dried his eye on his arm. "Swear it."

"I swear it to God himself."

"Can we go see it one day? Where they make the purple honey," he said.

She nodded emphatically. "We absolutely can. It'll be our place."

"Where we can go hide from the world."

"We won't need to hide. Because we'll be brand-new there. We'll start over. I won't be the girl who no one sees. And you, well you don't need to change much at all. Because, I was thinking, to me you're kind of perfect. Even with the missing eye. You're the boy who—"

He kissed her then.

Her first kiss.

And his.

The next day at school Chuck Bradley took the slingshot from her bag and snapped it in two and shoved her down.

Patch had moved from the crowd and squared to the taller boy, small fist clenched as he threw the first punch. Always. And so Chuck's friends fell on him and beat him long after the fight was over.

"That was dumb," Saint said as she helped him to his feet and dabbed blood from his lip.

"You're all I've got," he said.

And she thought, I'm all you'll need.

25

They held the vigil in the town of Darby Falls, sixty miles from Monta Clare.

On the banks of the Hunter Bayou, where the cop's daughter, Callie Montrose, used to wade out with her friends and watch them fish bass with topwater bait before she was stolen from her life.

Norma had driven them on a cold afternoon in November.

Saint knew the story, like everyone within a hundred miles, how Callie had been walking home from school with her friends, said goodbye to them, and cut down a track of loose rock and tall trees and never showed up anywhere again.

Norma wore her husband's old deerstalker and thick mittens. It was nightfall, and beneath a smoky moon they stood on the edge of a hundred as a pastor led them in prayer.

Box lanterns were ignited and set to float on water so still the lanterns did not rush anywhere, just glowed there in a haphazard line.

The pastor spoke words Saint could not hear before the outline of lives touched so acutely by loss. Music played and a small choir of high school kids in winter coats misted the air with their song, and when it was done Saint left Norma on the outer edge and found Callie's father who stood there not crying like the others. Maybe a dozen cops stood around him in a guard of respect.

"I'm sorry," Saint said.

He wore a long beard and a ball cap and did not wear his uniform.

"You knew Callie?" he said quiet.

"I'm from Monta Clare."

"The boy."

She nodded. "I don't know why I came . . . I just . . . will you tell me something about Callie? Like, my friend, Patch. They never said what he was really like in the newspapers. They just made him sound . . . regular."

He paused a moment, and then took his ball cap off and smoothed greasy hair. "She is . . . she's full of spirit. To read the newspapers you'd think she was an angel."

Saint looked toward Norma, who stood there watching the lanterns burn.

"I caught her stealing smokes from my truck. And sneaking booze at Thanksgiving. It's the spirit, right. That's what we miss. It's the rough edges. The parts you know she'll grow out of."

He pressed his hat to his chest for a moment, like the true pain started and ended there.

"Mr. Montrose," she said.

He met the flash of her eyes against flamelight.

"Will they come back?"

For a long time he stood there, but he did not answer.

She turned back to the water, and then she noticed him, standing off to the side, through clusters of the departing. He knelt down and lit his candle and set it down in the lantern and pushed it.

Dr. Tooms looked over at Saint. She saw his tears. She saw so much in his face.

"Creep."

Saint turned to see the girl beside her, maybe a couple of years older, a head taller with an oval face and bobbed hair.

"He's a creep."

"Why?" Saint said.

"More than once I saw him sitting in his car outside our high school."

Saint stared at Tooms. "Doing what?"

"Watching the girls go by."

26

For Christmas her grandmother bought her a Nikon so old the lens cover was fixed with tape.

"You have one roll of film. Developing is costly. Choose your shots wisely."

Saint borrowed a bird book from the library, trudged white woods and fired off photos of house finch, waxwings, and one time a red-tailed hawk.

She watched 1976 being shepherded in beneath a canopy of yet more snow, at times so deep it fell into the tops of her boots, soaking her stockinged feet as she watched a street cleaner move through Main Street and slowly remove the posters of the boy with the eye patch. She took one from him and at home placed it on the high shelf in her closet. She read more, of trauma and amygdala. The Polson book of forensic science. Her head buried in books that would somehow keep her link to him alive. She read of a team in New Jersey that could lift fingerprints from tree bark, even leaves. She took it to Nix, who

27

On Main Street Saint saw Dick Lowell and a few others sitting out front of his hardware store and nursing the kind of sorry hangovers born of the tenth Super Bowl.

Saint did not understand how they went on with their lives like anything else could matter so much again.

That winter, so cold and colorless, she wondered if it would last her lifetime. Norma said she needed another hobby, or perhaps she might like to see that shrink because it mightn't be so bad to share her feelings. And so Saint borrowed a library book that taught her how to knit, and before long spent evenings sitting by the window just like her grandmother had. She made herself a scarf and hat and one for her grandmother and sometimes caught Norma watching her as if she were the oldest kid in history, like soon enough her hair would gray and her mind would slow.

Jimmy Walters knocked for her one Saturday

morning, and her grandmother let him in. Saint silently fumed. Norma fixed them hot chocolate, and together they sat on the back porch, Jimmy's cheeks flushing when he saw a cotton mouse head into the thicket.

"Little guy only lives five months on average," Jimmy said, standing.

"Less if I had my slingshot."

"There's marshland if you follow the line of woodland in your yard. Might be a painted turtle."

"Saint once saw a beaver heading that way," Norma said, joining them.

Jimmy's face lit up. "We could take a walk there."

Saint tried to smile, and did not tell him the marshland was where she and Patch once went to sail paper boats.

She stayed up into the night to watch George Foreman go to war with Ron Lyle. Norma climbed to her feet in the fifth round, hollering and boxing shadows, spilling her drink and making Saint smile.

Together they sat and watched the evening news as tornadoes tore towns apart, a car sat upturned, farmers held their heads, eyes closed in prayer as crops were lifted and taken and barns decimated.

"Lord," her grandmother said. "Three hundred dead and five thousand close to it."

Norma got up slow, because a stoop Saint had never noticed had grown worse, switched the channel and poured herself a finger of bourbon to watch the story of Randle McMurphy sweep the board at the Golden Globes. Norma reached for her dog-eared paperback and tossed it to Saint. "You need to escape more," she said.

Saint no longer knew how.

On a white Saturday, Jimmy Walters turned up with a clutch of frost flowers tied off with purple ribbon.

Saint told Norma she did not want to see him.

"He's resilient," Norma said, tugging her out of bed.

"So is influenza."

As they strolled in the snow Jimmy pointed to the stems and told her of crownbeard and dittany.

"Why did you bring these?" she asked.

"I just wanted to show you that sometimes things survive despite the harshest of odds."

28

At the first thaw, when icicles began to drip and the newest goldenrods broke out from beneath the white, Saint looked back and recalled little of that winter, or how she had noticed the first ephemeral flourish. The only evidence could be found on her camera, where choice shots captured pink wild geraniums, spiderwort, and the delicate white anthers of Jacob's ladder. She watched a disaster in Yuba City on the nightly news and wondered how there could be room for so much devastation, how Patch could possibly compete for attention from a God who planned with such grand abject cruelty.

On Patch's birthday she took to her bed and told Norma she was too sick to attend school that day. Norma offered to take her for ice cream at Lacey's, but Saint told her she was no longer a child. Norma bought her a thousand-piece jigsaw, and each evening a little more of Mount Rushmore was depicted.

Beneath a bluebird sky Saint sat on the bench

in the middle of Main Street, set back by a flash of coral roses that burst from hanging baskets beside her. She breathed spice as she waited for the bus.

Jimmy Walters sat beside her.

"Hey."

Saint did not reply.

"I see you at school and you . . . I miss seeing you smile." He nodded, like he'd said his piece.

"How's that fox you're feeding?" she said.

"Had cubs. Four show up now."

Saint tried to smile, tried to feel something else, even just for a moment.

"I see you with your camera. You know, if you wanted to see some whitetail I know a nice spot."

She glanced at him and wondered just how easy his life was, how small his troubles were. He carried an easy confidence her grandmother said came from true faith. Like he did not know that the other boys called him a church pussy, or if he did, he simply didn't care.

When the bus arrived Saint rode with her grandmother, on the plum leather perch just behind her. When she was small, Norma would let her push the lever, her face locked straight in concentration because her grandmother told her it was the most important job, that without her the good people of Monta Clare would not be able to get where they needed to go.

"You want to, for old time's sake?" Norma said, catching her eye in the big mirror.

Saint smiled and shook her head.

The bus shone. Though there was a team of cleaners at the depot, Norma brought an old leather cloth to catch the water marks. She made her inspection, tutted if she found an ashtray had not been emptied, sometimes found discarded comic books and brought them home for Saint.

People said it was noble that her grandmother went out to work like that. Taking the seat her husband had occupied back in the city, driving near thirty years. **The girl's got to eat,** Norma said in reply. Though Saint knew that purpose in its many forms was what kept the living just so. In quieter, shameful, moments she wished her grandmother was like the others, on those days when Norma would show at school and stand apart from the mothers, smoking a Marlboro and wearing her cap.

They eased up Marshall Avenue, the engine low and loud as Saint looked out over Edgewood Canyon, the emerald river buffeted by lime grass that fed the water's edge. Trees grew between slate boulders. An old waterwheel retired before the arc of a wooden bridge so faded it almost matched the gray bulwark that held off the blues. She leaned over and fired off a shot with her camera, and far above saw two men on horseback framed by that Missouri morning so crisp and beautiful she could not stand it.

"I miss the bees," Saint said.

Norma did not turn when she spoke. "We can order some more."

"No. I want my bees."

"Bees are bees. They'll all sting you if the mood takes them. I do wonder where they are."

"Dead. They'll be dead now."

A sheer cliff of limestone. Lichens and mosses and liverworts dropped to lush pediment, and the stunt of trees. And as they chased along she saw rogue cherts a million layers thick.

In the small town of Fallow Rock people climbed on and smiled at Saint like they remembered the girl she used to be.

Her grandmother had arranged to change over at Alice Springs, four towns from Monta Clare, and they stepped out and walked down toward the parkland and settled on a bench.

Saint removed their sandwiches from the picnic basket, unwrapped them, and set down two cans of lemonade and two apples.

"You want to talk about it?" Norma said.

"No."

"I miss him, too." Norma had been slow to warm to Patch, mistaking his smile for trouble, his pirate clothes for delusion. It had turned around on a late afternoon walk in the spring of 1974 when they passed the Macauley house and saw the street door ajar. Norma followed her granddaughter up the path; both stopped still when they saw through the window Patch cleaning the vomit from the floor beside his mother, who lolled back on the sofa. Patch laid her down, fetched a shawl and covered her over, then got back to work with his bucket and sponge.

Saint had moved to enter the house, but Norma had placed a gentle hand on her shoulder, smiled sadly, and led the girl away from a neglect Saint could not yet understand. They had finished their walk in silence. The next time Patch showed at their house, Norma baked banana muffins and said nothing when the boy took one for now and another for his pocket.

"Is this what happens? Kids get taken and never come back, and no one ever finds out what happened to them?" Saint said.

"You know that it is."

There had been no more missing since Callie Montrose. Whoever had started seemed to have stopped. Some nights Saint fantasized that Patch had killed him and was slowly finding his way back to them. That he had found his mean, like Edward Low. Sometimes he was sailing, leaning out over the bowsprit as his ship carved out a path toward her.

Far below she watched the wind of the river like a serpent threading trees and rock, its back so clear and startling blue. "You still pray," Saint said.

"I pray like I did when your grandfather died."

Saint wanted to ask what it was like, to lose the thing that defined you. But perhaps she knew: it left you someone else. A stranger you had no choice but to tolerate, and see each day and feel and fear.

"Will it go away? Because I can't—"

Norma took her hand.

"I want everything to mean something, to lead somewhere."

"I saw the Walters boy sitting with you," Norma said. "You might like to take him as a friend. You could get some more bees and make some honey and—"

"Jimmy Walters is dull."

"And how would you know that?"

"He just talks about animals. And God."

"Maybe if you just gave him a chance."

Norma removed her hat and placed it on her granddaughter's head, then took the camera from her and poked out her tongue.

When Saint did not react, Norma recalled the time Patch had tried to fix her up with the lunch lady at Monta Clare, who also wore her hair short.

"Of course, he later found out she had the cancer. And a husband. And that I'm not a lesbian," Norma said.

And at that Saint finally smiled. And Norma took the last photo on her roll.

It had taken her near two full seasons to fill that first roll of film, so sparing was she in what she deemed worthy to hold on to.

"If you ever get the chance to make someone smile, or better yet, make someone laugh, then you take it. Each and every time," Norma said.

"What about if it's at your own expense?"

"Especially then."

"I will hold on to him forever," Saint said.

Norma smiled, like she knew that a child's forever fell far short. Like it would not always be this way. Like she underestimated her granddaughter fully.

29

They strolled back into the town, and her grandmother walked over to a small café where a couple of drivers sat. Saint moved on, stopping beside the stone fountain as a cluster of kids balanced on the brim.

She shopped the windows of a dozen stores, almost stopped when she saw a replica colonial cob coin she knew Patch would die for.

In the Central Camera Store she spent a while looking over FD lenses, Super 8s, and autozooms. The guy at the counter wore a blue smock and a wide tie and talked aberrations and resolution, color balance and flare reduction with a customer.

Saint liked the smell, somewhere between chemical and new, the leather cases and brown canvas bags. When it was her turn the man noticed her camera, pointed to a name badge that told her he was Larry, and then flat out asked if she'd like him to take a look at her work.

"It's not work," she said.

It was as she waited for him to ring up her film

that she saw the noticeboard beside the counter, spilling with ads. People selling old equipment, just a series of numbers that meant nothing to her.

And then beside it.

She walked over, left Larry with his hand out as she stared at the poster.

ELI AARON PHOTOGRAPHY

Saint took it down and looked at the girl in the advertisement.

Misty Meyer smiling a little shyly, arms crossed over a long knit vest.

"Don't believe all that about making you a model," Larry said, wiping his hands on his smock. He cleared his throat, like he'd misspoken. "I mean . . . if you wanted your portrait done there's better on the board. I know girls like you, you all want to be models, right?"

Saint looked down at her overalls and her faded sneakers.

"You go try Sandy Wheaton, he's good."

Saint placed the paper on the counter. "This man—"

Larry shifted a little, uncomfortable. "We've developed for him a couple times."

"And?"

Larry dropped his eyes. "Listen, kid—"

"Please," she said, so tired now.

"No one made a formal complaint, but I heard some things. Not enough to give to the cops. Or to stop him placing his ads all over town. Put it this way, I have a daughter your age, and I wouldn't want her handing money to this guy."

Saint slipped the paper into her bag and walked out without her film.

Larry caught her at the door with it. "There's something else. Ain't really my place . . ."

"But?"

"He's the photographer for half a dozen schools around here. You tell your friends not to go wasting their money."

30

That evening she climbed the stairs to her attic bedroom.

On the wall was a series of spiderwebs Saint had built with ardent care. The newspapers said he was likely an opportunist and that Misty was beautiful, like the others, and that was enough.

She pinned the poster to her bulletin board.

In the hallway she reached for the telephone and dialed the station. She did not need to look up the number.

Nix answered like he was the only one still there on a Saturday evening.

"I think I found something," she said.

There was silence for a long time, just the crackle of the line as she sat on the floor with her knees pulled to her chest.

"I was in this store and—"

"You need to stop this now," he said, and she could see him there alone, as beaten as her.

"But you—"

"I mean it, Saint. For you this is over now. You go on, you be a kid again. You've already lost so much time."

"You don't understand. I saw this guy and then this poster and—"

She did not get to finish before the line cut.

Saint walked down the stairs, and through the window saw Norma on the porch, watching the street.

In the kitchen Saint found the bookshelf, and at the bottom in neat rows were the albums. She thumbed through them, stared at her mother for a while and looked into eyes like her own. She saw forgotten vacations, cities, and smiles.

Saint came to her school photographs, catalogued in an order where her progression was slow, her body clinging so resolutely to the protection of childhood.

And there it was.

A little over a month before it happened.

She looked at herself and wondered how she could have ever smiled so wide.

Saint took the photograph from its housing and flipped it over.

She did not flinch when she saw the stamp.

ELI AARON PHOTOGRAPHY

31

The gun was a high polish nickel six-shot Colt Python, a little over two pounds.

When Saint took it from the shoebox in the garage it felt like lead. She knew that it carried two bullets, that there was a box containing a dozen more hidden someplace else, and that if her grandmother caught her touching it she would likely execute her.

Saint wore faded overalls, a white vest beneath, and when she aimed the gun out her skinny arms hinted at biceps, her eyes at intent. On the back of her right hand was a skull and crossbones penned in black ink.

She found the address for Eli Aaron printed on the poster.

First light.

Night shining clouds began their scatter. She hooked the satchel over her shoulder and made the winding walk to Main Street. The police station lay in darkness.

The only light came from the church, where the

first candles were lit, the service booklets placed on their racks, and the bells readied to sound.

"Where are you going?"

Saint did not break her stride for Jimmy Walters, who stood by the church door, Bible in hand. "To see a photographer named Eli Aaron."

"Why?" he called to her back.

"To shoot him dead. And bring my friend home."

32

She rode the first bus of the day, alongside the shift workers, their heads down so they'd catch a little more sleep as the engine rumbled on.

Gray road burrowed a way through rows of browned wheat as tall as Saint, undulating like God had tugged the rug from beneath land farmers plied before it could settle. Pylons stood in slipshod formation like some grand steel army. A water tower of burnt red and no color in the sky at all.

At the town of Chesterwood she changed buses, the driver too interested as she sat alone behind him, watching fate loom, the horizon holding answers she was in no way ready to find.

Five miles out, a sign read 15 SOUTH as the world flattened and the grass yellowed and the verge turned to gravel the color of salt.

The bus crawled along, the gearbox ground out, the suspension bounced like a fairground ride.

She climbed out far from anywhere, the driver reluctant to leave, following her in his mirror till she cratered from sight; the dips and brows of hillside propped her from each side.

From the straight road she found woodland that carpeted a thousand acres, and she checked her map a dozen times before she found a hard yellow sign.

CAUTION MINIMUM MAINTENANCE ROAD

LEVEL B SERVICE

ENTER AT YOUR OWN RISK

She strolled down twin tracks, the grass between tall enough to fold beneath her sneakers. Crops tightly rolled to variegated bales checkered the fields haphazardly. A tractor sprayed with mud, its scoop left buried in the dirt. The track fed the mouth of woodland so dense she slowed as possum haw leaves slid to a gulley, their berries bright red against shadow behind.

Saint splashed through a stream crossing, her sneakers soon filled with the brace of cold.

She edged the bluegrass a long way, and in the distance were deer and raccoons and above ravens watched her like prey.

At the first fall of rain she looked through a canopy that stammered light as wind parted it.

The house came to view. Single story, a timber face worn till the browns bowed to chalk, a couple of shades darker where water fractured the seal. The roof was corrugated steel, and she counted three outbuildings, sloping like the ground was ceding to their weight. Another tractor with rusting chains that wrapped tires the height of a child. Another shack to the left, rotting, its frame exposed like charred ribs.

Saint moved with care. Loose leaves floated like snowflakes.

She discovered the first outbuilding empty as she peered through glass smoked by the haze of a dozen seasons.

She did not feel the kick of fear until she came to the largest barn, and through gaps in the wall saw the steel of a van.

Navy.

Chrome fender hanging from the front.

She heard something and spun, her breath falling short until she saw a fox squirrel head up the wide face of an American beech.

"Fuck," she spoke beneath her breath, glanced up, and the rain died as quick as it had begun.

She trod down braids of nettle, stepped onto a porch of russet boards, and stopped dead before the door and listened.

Inside her bag was her slingshot.

And beside that her grandfather's gun.

33

"Can I help you?"

Eli Aaron looked like he belonged in the wood-land. He wore a plaid shirt and heavy work boots and jeans slashed at one knee. Saint took a step back before fishing the poster from her bag.

"Can you make me a model?" she spoke quiet, the breeze stealing her words as he leaned down a little then studied the trees behind her.

"You came here alone?"

"I hiked from the service road."

"Ought to be careful. Wild snakes in the fields. I trap what I can . . . serpents rear up."

More than anything she noticed his size. Maybe six four and three hundred pounds. Heavy, sloping shoulders. His hands hung like meat by his side. His eyes were empty till he smiled, his teeth bright against stubbled skin, his hair long and parted with oil. She could not recall him from school, instead remembering someone entirely different. As if he shifted shapes when he had to.

He rubbed at his chin like it itched him. Saint had read in the biography of New York Detective Roger Gable of something called the feel, that it would later become his best friend, and under no circumstance would he ever ignore it. More than fear or distrust, it was a belief low in the bones, beneath the layers of skin and blood and guts, it was something that ached, it was something that told you soon enough you'd be drawing your gun, and you'd better be damn well ready to end a life.

Eli Aaron stepped aside and she walked in.

He took the poster from her and stared at it.

"You all think I can make you look like that. Jealousy . . . ain't becoming," he said carefully. "You have the money?"

She nodded.

"Nobody knows you're here?"

She shook her head.

The big man made small talk. Told her his grandmother had passed and left him a Leica and his passion was woodlands, but he took the school jobs because the price of gas had done nothing but soar. He cursed about embargoes and Israel.

She saw photographs in black frames of scenes she had passed walking in. Even there in sepia and black and white the despair could be felt, like the land used to be more in some uncountable way.

On the wall was a large crucifix of sawn timber. A single nail split the grain dead center. The kitchen was a single stove and pots that hung from wire, the windows behind blocked with sheets, bloating light through the thin of their thread.

Saint knew to keep him in front of her, enough of a distance away. Exposed pipework crawled along and up and through gaps in the wood to other rooms.

"Misty Meyer, the girl in your advert, she's in my class at school."

He leaned back against a hearth capped by thick cedar. A couple of candles burned halfway and disfigured.

"I saw it on the news." His eyes darted up once.

"You remember where you were the morning it happened?" she said, aiming for casual, but each word quavered.

"Brooks Falls. Bears come out of hibernation and pluck salmon from the river. I liked them since I was a kid. You see all the blood around their mouths like that."

"You stay in a motel?"

"Campsite."

"You live here alone?" she said, glancing around again.

He smiled like she amused him, like he skimmed every thought in her head and guessed her moves before even she knew them.

The sink was filled with pans, the dark metal sheared off to the bone of silver beneath. He pushed open a door and she glanced into a small bedroom with a bare mattress yellowed with sweat. He grabbed a couple of sheets from a dresser.

She saw books stacked floor to roof.

"Best education you can get," he said. "See through someone else's eyes and you understand more of everything."

He hauled on a leather shoulder bag.

Outside she imagined Patch there, maybe beneath the dirt she trod. The thought sharpened her.

Her eyes fell on the red barn.

"My darkroom."

"You develop yourself?" she said.

"I used to go into the drugstores. It's expensive."

"How about the store in Alice Springs?"

He bristled a little. "The guy in there . . . he doesn't understand art. He doesn't see what I see."

Eli Aaron trudged the leaves, glancing back every three steps.

Right then Saint longed to hear an engine, maybe sirens, anything that would tell her there was more than her, her grandfather's gun, and a giant in those Missouri woodlands.

She took a last, longing, look behind, and followed him in.

Inside the light was red and low. The corners of the room were lost to shadows, a maze of tables and machinery and the low whine of a generator. The smell burned the back of her throat.

She knew she was in trouble then.

Not the kind a kid finds themselves in, the kind

teachers yell at, the kind her grandmother could forgive.

This was the kind of trouble she read about in newspapers and saw on news bulletins.

The kind of trouble that no one recovers from.

34

In a room sectioned off with heavy drapes he dragged
a wooden crate out and told her to sit. She placed
the satchel on the ground as he readied continuous
lighting. He strung a sheet behind her, muttering
beneath his breath as he worked. She strained to
hear it.

And then the generator paused.

And Saint heard the words he spoke, her blood
icing as she recognized it.

He leads me beside quiet waters.

He refreshes my soul.

The same passage her grandmother had once
recited.

The Lord is my Shepherd.

A funeral prayer.

She was about to speak when the light died.

He flashed the camera, and for a moment she saw
him in front.

"Take off your glasses."

With a trembling hand she took her frames off and set them down on the floor.

"Don't smile. It hides you."

Another flash, this time she saw him to her left.

Saint drew a deep breath. "The high school girls that went missing . . . the college girl."

Another flash.

"I don't even know your name," he said.

She told him, and even in the darkness heard the joy reach his words. "You pray?"

"Yes."

"What do you ask for?"

Another flash. He blended with the shadows.

"A fit and just end," she said, the world around blurring, the edges soft.

He laughed. **"I am the way, the truth."**

"And the life."

"You know scripture."

She swallowed. "I know right from wrong."

"The Lord sent fiery serpents among the people. Don't worry, I won't bite you. You would be beautiful . . . one day you will be."

She felt her tears build. "The newspaper said those girls got dragged into a blue van."

"I have a blue van."

"Did you take them, Mr. Aaron?"

"Yes."

35

She did not know fear like it.

Fear that claimed her muscles, her blood and breath, her mind. Fear that told her to get up and break and run. That she had made a brave mistake, the same kind Patch had made.

Saint fell to her knees, scrambled for her glasses but instead found her bag, her hand meeting the cold metal as she raised the gun and aimed it into the darkness.

The gun was snatched from her hands with ease.

Another flash as he moved back into the shadows.

"You say you're a saint, but maybe you're a sinner like the others."

She found her slingshot and box of silver steel ball bearings.

Her hands shook so bad she spilled a dozen to the floor before she loaded one.

Saint cried as she fired off a single shot into the darkness, toward where he might have been. She stood, her whole body shaking as she felt the crunch beneath her shoes.

Saint picked up her shattered lenses, slipped them on and saw things broken.

A curtain opened and red light filled the empty room.

She moved toward it, out into the main barn, to long aisles of boxes stacked four high. The lights burned red.

When she came to the end of one aisle she turned and moved up the next.

It was only then that she looked up.

And when she did, she gasped like she'd been punched in the gut.

36

The photographs hung from chicken wire that crisscrossed above. Hundreds. She plucked a handful and saw the girls, wearing smiles for a stranger because their parents wanted a reminder at each stage.

And then she saw the marks on them.

Rough circles drawn above each head. Halos. She moved along, saw another row, unmarked. Saint felt her body chill as she looked at Misty. Saint counted a dozen photos. One showed Misty on the front of a newspaper. In another she was on the Sports page, her lacrosse stick loose by her side.

She heard a noise to her left.

Saint dropped the stack, moved on, quick till she came to the far wall.

It was only when she saw the bank of monitors on the wall, the grainy black-and-white video of a dozen cameras pinned around the house and the woodland, that she knew just what she had found.

On each screen she saw the rooms she had come from, the trees, a neater, nicer bedroom, and, finally, some kind of bunker, and there, on the mattress, a shape.

The generator died.

"I shouldn't be here," she whispered it, looking for calm in the sound of her own voice. "I want to go home."

Saint inched slowly past the boxes, staying low.

She found a door and moved through into another room just as dark. The chemical smell grew stronger.

In the pocket of her overalls she found her book of matches and lit one.

She made out shapes and shadows, and for a moment allowed herself to calm before the gunshot almost broke her, the echo vicious as a bullet snapped the wall above her.

She heard laughter, like he was toying with her. Like he was hunting her.

Saint crashed into shelving and heard breaking glass as she dropped the book of matches and ran.

She found steps down into a wide tunnel that ran back in the direction of the main house. Saint moved fast and quiet, through the tunnel and up the stairs, and then she was back in the living room.

Saint looked at the front door open to the woodland, knew right then she should break and sprint for the trees, make it back to the highway and call for help.

And then she saw another door. And she thought of Patch, and what he would do if she was in trouble.

Saint opened the door. Stairs led back down

underground like the whole compound had been built so Eli Aaron could move around without being seen. She hugged the wall as she descended into darkness, her slingshot up as she followed a tight turn.

She smelled earth and damp. The heat climbed. Sudden and humid.

Saint felt along the wall, found a light switch and flipped it.

For a moment she saw them.

A dozen tanks. The snakes looked wild, like he'd plucked them from the woodland only to keep them alive and captive. She knew some from her books. Copperhead. Massasauga rattlesnake.

The light flickered out.

"Patch," she called.

She heard Eli Aaron on the stairs, following her, and so she ran deeper into the dark.

Another gunshot.

The sound blunted around her. Saint fell to her knees and crawled.

She closed her eyes tight.

She prayed for it to be over.

37

Every cell in her body shut down with the fear.

And then she saw the light.

Only it flickered in a way that told her she was in a new world of trouble.

She smelled the smoke but could not see the flames that had chased her from the kindling of the barn back through to the wooden main house.

She cupped a hand to her mouth as she screamed his name.

At the end of the tunnel she looked up to see a hopper window, the glass painted black but cracks in the paint bled light.

Smoke constricted her chest, her throat.

She stood and hooked her fingertips onto the ledge, tried to haul herself up but could not find the strength.

She tried again, screamed as she found her footing on the rough wall and dug the toe of her sneakers in hard.

With the handle of her slingshot she cracked the glass once, shattered it twice.

Saint wriggled through, the glass tearing at her.

She screamed as heavy hands gripped beneath her arms and hauled her out fully.

She did not know whose hands they were, and she cursed with every word she knew, called him a cunt and a motherfucker and only when the flames met more chemicals and blew out the windows did she fall limp and dead in his arms.

"I've got you, kid," Nix said. "I've got you."

38

She sat on the back ramp of an ambulance as the fire raged.

She could not hear much when the woman spoke, shone light into her eyes and asked her questions.

A blanket was draped around her shoulders, up high at the collar, and she peered out through her broken lenses.

The cops fell back as fire kicked out and twisted and ran along dead leaves to the barns beside the house.

Saint told Nix what she knew, and before long they had a team and tracked blood far into the forest.

Saint gulped down mouthfuls of frigid air and wondered why the woods did not look different, why the sky still carried blue and the sunlight still sliced shadows through white elm. She moved behind a cruiser and puked. She would smell smoke for weeks.

Saint stood in the margin of nightfall and ignored

the stares as she watched and waited, as it took an hour to bring the fire under control.

And when Nix finally emerged and shook his head, only then did she run at him, and ball her fists and swing them at his broad chest.

She cried till her body caved to the past months, and she willed the land to cloud over and the colors to drain away.

He steadied her with an arm around her waist as she tried to head inside once more. To burn with him. To burn with them all.

"He's in there," she said, desperate, certain. "He is."

"There's no one inside."

"I saw—"

"You did good, Saint." He smoothed her hair and hugged her tightly to himself.

Cops fanned across unforgiving land, the soot marking their faces as the skeleton of the house sent embers into the air like dandelion seeds.

Moonlight hung deep in the east behind trails of white smoke sent up like a signal that it was over now, that they would surrender and admit a crushing defeat.

The rain came late and turned heavy, washing scrubland to mud so thick they could barely move. They found two bodies of water close to marshland swamp, their banks flowing over a ridge. One of the Ames County cops fell and twisted his knee, and they ate a couple of hours getting him out. By then

Saint knew what was coming but still fought back a scream when Nix called it a day.

They put out all-points bulletins, followed the usual protocol, and knew Eli Aaron could not have gotten far, also knew he had the land mapped better than they did. Also knew he might have died in there, might have burned till there was nothing but bone.

"I'll take you back. Your grandmother is waiting at the station."

With that Saint broke and ran.

She heard calls behind her.

Curses.

Saint lost them for near an hour, her clothes heavy, her sneakers dragging the earth with her, tearing her own track.

"Enough, now," Nix called, hair matted down by the rain.

She kept her head down as wind drove her back.

"Saint."

"Fuck you all," she said. "Fuck you. You all go to fucking hell."

She heard Nix call after her, then she saw the lights of a cruiser at the foot of a track, but they did not dent the pitch of that night.

She felt her blood too hot. She breathed dour dirt, heard the call of a barred owl.

She fell again and lay awhile, then clawed herself up, her overalls torn.

It was not until midnight broke that she crossed

daggers of nettles and a well of water that basined between mossed rock and inched up her numbed feet that she saw it.

Saint broke to running.

Her knees sunk in the mud as she cradled his head. His eye closed tight like he was holding onto the nightmare.

She clutched him, her tears falling hot onto his skin.

Saint did not notice the cops surround her.

"He's breathing," Nix screamed.

THE LOVERS,
THE DREAMERS

1975

39

That first day.

Patch shivered and cried, and reached up and felt his eye and it was open but there was nothing to see because he had found the edge of his world and was staring at its end. So dark he could discern no shapes or distance or silhouettes, no spells of light from the edges of doors or windows or gaps in the surround. He raised his hand and held it an inch from his face but could not make out his fingers or the blood dried in the lines of his palms. Wherever he was, whatever state he was in, he might as well have been blind.

He burned with cold, his life roils of dark and reds, his jaw locked so hard he rubbed until his teeth loosened and blood flaked from his mouth like paint from tape.

He wondered if he was dead.

Most in Monta Clare spent Sunday mornings in St. Raphael's, and one time Patch fell into step with them, sat at the very back and did not kneel or sing, just watched the man at the front as he lit candles and touched heads and told them they were failing but failure was expected.

Patch knew right then it was an act, and that death when it came was not light or confession, forgiveness or peace or fire. It was that cold piece of time before you were born, that glance into history books that told you the world went on before and would go on again, no matter who was there to witness it.

He reasoned the truest proof of life was pain, and he knew that the day the black car pulled up out front of his house and the two men with the stripes and military buzz cuts knocked on his door and told his mother that her husband would return on a plane with a hundred other bodies, all too young to even place Vietnam on a map.

At ten years old he realized that people were born whole, and that the bad things peeled layers from the person you once were, thinning compassion and empathy and the ability to construct a future. At thirteen he knew those layers could sometimes be rebuilt when people loved you. When you loved.

When Patch reached down to his stomach, he found stitches in long looping cotton bows that dove beneath swollen tears of skin.

Up higher he felt bruises on his chest.

And above that his cross hung from thin string around his neck. A cross Norma had given to him because she said it would keep him from harm. He did not believe in God, just in Saint and her grand-mother, and sometimes his mother.

He lay on something soft and beneath that was cement and the bestrew of dirt and gravels of sand like the top layer had been shaved off. The panic would come, even then he knew that, but time had deserted him so totally he drifted, and life was float-ing pieces unreachable, his mother's face, the Green's Convenience Store, Misty Meyer.

He heard screams but did not know they were his own.

Dark was his blessing and curse, and in lucid moments he wondered if he was in the hospital. An ICU where no one but Saint stopped by and watched his coma and held his hand in hers.

The pain came in such sharp savage bursts he would heave and retch and puke spume that would dry and crust at the corners of his mouth.

He did not know enough to be scared.

Patch felt a hand slip into his.

He lurched.

He was not alone.

40

Patch knew dreams were experience and anticipation, the trace of memories and proportioned acts.

The girl smelled of the outside, of sun lotion and cherry gum and woodsmoke.

"Open your mouth and swallow this pill."

He did not know her accent. Maybe it came from somewhere far south, where cotton grew and bourbon was drunk.

Her hand was smooth and warm on his jaw as she tilted his head back and placed a pill on his tongue and pressed a bottle to his lips.

"Tell me something I don't know." Her breath was hot and sweet.

He could not speak.

"I'll tell you something then. Shrimps' hearts are in their heads. So they're likely impulsive and practical. My mother said I'm all heart, but that simply isn't true. People talk about falling in love like a fall is ever a good thing."

The strain of trying to find his voice brought a sweat.

He heard the sound of her fingers against the floor, the walls, like she was mapping as she spoke.

"People say there isn't a grand plan. You know about serendipity? Maybe. You definitely know about fate and that whole sorry idea."

"What are you?" he said, finally, in a whisper that sounded wrong, like he'd forgotten the order of words.

"Just a girl trying to find her way through the darkness."

He went to speak again but she caught it.

"No names and no places. The big man listens. You're alive, right?"

"Yes." His voice was a croak.

"So maybe we don't do nothing that might alter that fact. If you're sick, you tell me. If you're hungry or you need more water. A bucket for washing, another for toilet. Fifteen paces to the door and you can leave it there and it'll be changed quick."

"How long have I been here?" he said.

"Ten sleeps."

"It must have been more than—"

"Your head is up in the—"

"Clouds," Patch said.

"The peak of the clouds, with the angel. Maybe you see the Misty Moon from up there."

"Misty?" he said, the confusion thick. "What day is it?"

"Days were named after the planets of Hellenistic astrology. Saturn, Sun, and Moon. Saturday, Sunday, . . . Moonday."

She moved closer until her bare leg pressed to his. "Are you real?"

"As real as this life is," she said, dropping her voice to a whisper.

"And the man, is he . . . the devil or something?"

"We're each our own devil, right?"

He felt the fever creeping, and when she placed a hand across his hand he heard her draw breath and curse lightly.

"Hotter than hades," she said.

"There were pirates in the Persian Gulf—" he squinted like he could see them. "The predatory. When they felt a fever coming they believed it charged them hot enough to sear their enemies, so they headed into battle."

"And got their sick asses handed to them," she said, and he felt a breeze as she sliced at the air with an imaginary sword.

"I need to go home now," he said.

She went quiet awhile, so he reached out and brushed her shoulder and found her like light during the bleakest winter night.

"What do I do?" he said.

"Pray." She gripped his face tight. "You want to

survive down here, you kneel and pray when he's around. And you believe."

"But, I don't—"

"There's a reason I'm still here and the other girls aren't."

41

She licked her palm and smoothed the hair from his face.

"My mother used to sing to me when she thought the world had stopped turning and she was lost somewhere dark. She'd tell it that when she sang about the place over the rainbow, God remembered everything good he'd created and he got off his ass and heaved the world going again. And before you knew it the sun reached you and lit the bad till it glowed so bright you couldn't look at it no more."

He spoke in a distant voice. "I think there's vents. I think they let in the air but not the light."

He felt the mattress dip as she settled.

Patch thought of the metal that pierced his stomach, that maybe it left something in him, something slow acting but something that might slowly change him. A rust. Burnt red and brown creeping through that healthy flesh till decay set in like rot through timbers.

"How long have you been here?" he said.

"Our universe is black. A galaxy and stars and dark matter, the planets and people and organisms. Everything is contained in this room with no light at all. Even when we get out, we'll take it with us, our own private black hole that'll swallow every good thing."

"I need to know your name," he said.

They heard noise.

She raised her voice and spoke in a clear tone. **"Be strong and courageous. Do not fear or be in dread of them, for it is the Lord your God who goes with you. He will not leave you or forsake you."**

"I have to go home now," he slurred.

Louder, **"Trust in the Lord with all your heart, and do not lean on your own understanding. In all your ways acknowledge him, and he will make straight your paths."**

He pleaded.

"Pray and stay alive," she spoke in a whisper.

"My name is Patch. And I was taken from—"

The key found the door.

Her hand found his.

He would not let her go.

Already he felt that way.

42

One day he could sit and trace the drywall. Painted black.

He searched the room, mapping each inch with the palm of his hand, looking for a gap, a loose board, something he could work with. He carried nothing in his pockets. Wore no shirt because it was warm. Not warm from his fever, just humid like he'd been taken so far south even if he broke free he wouldn't recognize anything.

No cuff on his ankle, no chain. No shoes.

No light came when the door opened, like whatever lay outside was just as dark.

The girl ebbed and flowed. Sometimes she answered and sometimes she hid herself so thoroughly he knew she could disappear when she chose.

At a time when he remembered his mother too clearly he sat upright and cried out and the girl eased him back down.

And when he hammered on the door and screamed to be freed she led him back to the mattress and told him to calm.

"Was I asleep?" he said. "It's hard to tell. I don't dream down here anymore. It's too dark. I don't know where I am."

"You think you're in hell. But God can deliver you someplace better."

"Why do you talk like that?" he said.

"I'm keeping us alive. And if I don't, then it's better to hedge our bets, right?"

"Tell me about the others."

"You're the first boy."

"But there were other girls—"

He heard her swallow. "And now there's just me."

43

He heard footsteps by the door.

"I can't breathe down here."

"You need to calm, and you need to kneel and to pray," she said.

"But I—"

"Fear not, for I am with you; be not dismayed, for I am your God; I will strengthen you, I will help you, I will uphold you with my righteous right hand."

They lay in silence until the footsteps departed.

She traced his stomach with her finger. And then she ran it over the bones of ribs that stood like fossils. At his collar she drew her finger along and dipped into the valley and then up and over his throat. His chin and mouth and teeth.

His nose.

She circled his eye and felt the lashes. It took the last of his strength to grip her thin wrist as she moved closer to the other side of his face, and even in the dark he wished he had the eye patch.

"Did you know that you're missing an eye?"

"The kids at school like to remind me."

He thought of Dr. Klein and his office of wonderful things in jars and models of the inner ear and the reproductive system. They did not have money for specialists, but then Patch was in no way special. **You simply don't have an eye whereas the rest of us do.**

"As sockets go, it's easily in the top three I've felt."

"Can he always hear us?" Patch said in a whisper.

"Maybe."

He clamped his hands beneath his armpits and fought a shiver that began low beneath his kneecaps before raging up his body, and at his nape he felt wisps of blonde hair rise. He did not get sick, not since he was a boy and his father died and he felt a flu descend that did not lift most of that year. His muscles resisting each morning when he walked down the stairs and slowly watched the emptying of their life. It was a slide toward poverty that he had not anticipated, that no kid ever does. Meals grew smaller and hunger larger till he noticed his jeans hanging loose from his waist as he notched new holes in his belt. His mother rose and fell like the seasons, sometimes warm as she hugged him and told him things would get better, and then sparse and bare as he asked what they could fix with stale bread, a bag of oats, and a couple of cans of tomatoes. She gained and lost employment so frequently he did not know if he would return to the smell of her Irish stew or to find the electricity cut or Dr. Tooms waiting at his kitchen table like he knew Patch needed so much.

"I'm not strong enough for this," he said.

He cried then.

"You're tough," she said.

"I—"

She placed a hand on his cheek. "You are. We sense our own kind. Kids dealt a losing hand. We look at others with fucking trivial problems, and we think how long they'd last with a taste of our childhoods."

He sobbed.

She smoothed his hair, her voice a whisper. "When you make it out of here no one will know how you lost everything, how you stared at an ending they can't comprehend. It'll give you power. It'll make them wish they never fucked with you."

44

"Are they looking for you?" she said.

"There's a cop that sometimes stops by." He thought of Chief Nix showing up when the neighbor called the police again because Ivy was slumped at the wheel of the Fairlane and Patch could not heave her inside in time. He didn't ever write it up. Just hauled her in and helped her to bed, then peeled a couple of bills from his wallet and handed them to Patch. He had not told Saint these things. He learned young that you could hide much with a smile.

"And your friends?"

"Saint."

He thought of her, small and smart and seeking out angles that brought them closer. How she mastered the slingshot a whole day quicker than he had. How she sat beside him when they did their math homework, guiding him toward answers that lay far beyond him, coaxing and leading till he was left with a single option that she beamed at like he'd figured it out alone. He thought of Norma, her heart and cooking and toleration. Of how he tried to exist in the shadow of their lives so they would not have to notice him much. He tried out his own angles, to be funny, to be charming and endearing. To make himself useful. One time he tended their yard when Saint rode the bus with Norma. Another time he painted the peeling window frame in the front bay of their large home. Those days he stayed for dinner so hot and filling he slept the night after, not even waking when his mother returned from her shift. Those days he stayed because he had earned it.

"She's . . . the best of me," he said.

"Tell me about her."

"She's smart. And she can play the piano so beautiful I stop and just watch her fingers. She's skinny and wears big glasses and her hair in a braid."

"What about her parents?" she said.

"Her mother died a couple days after giving birth. She was young. Saint said if abortion had been legal she wouldn't exist. Her father skipped town after. Didn't pay nothing to her grandparents. She found letters her grandmother wrote to him. Return to sender."

"This Saint, she loves you."

"No. She does it out of kindness, and maybe pity. I guess sometimes the two go together nicely. I'm not about to turn either down."

"You don't need charity. And I'll bet that's what

Saint already knows. She's being kind because she loves you."

He shook his head. "She'll see it now I'm gone."

"See what?" she said.

He spoke without intent, just a brutal and complete honesty. "How little I left behind."

He felt her bare arm against his.

"I need to know your name," he said.

Her voice dropped to a whisper, her breath hot as she pressed close and cupped her hands around the shell of his ear.

"Grace."

45

He knelt beside her, and she led him in prayer. Grace quoted scripture loudly until the man at the door left them.

"Maybe one day I'll be the first to see him after the Resurrection. And if I'm chosen, he'll send me back to the three persons. And they'll hollow me out. Watch my blood flow over black rock like I never even was."

"Amen," he said.

"Ready for the day?" she said.

He did not know if it was the absence of light that heightened her words or just the fact that she had the sweetest voice he had ever heard. She took charge and divided his hours into school and weekend. And on school days she set out a plan and both lay side by side and pretended they could see the chalkboard above them and her delicate cursive crawling across it.

"Monday morning," she declared, and Patch

wondered if it was actually the middle of the night, and also if the girl was a little bit insane.

She cleared her throat and propelled them back two decades. She spoke of the Channel that divides France from England and how on a Thursday afternoon leaflets rained from the sky and told the inhabitants of Paris to flee their city and head for the empty darkness of the countryside. She told of the bombers that crossed cauterized airspace.

"How can you divide up the air? It's air," Patch said.

"You can't just let any old Spitfire jettison right over your head," she said impatiently.

He did not know what **jettison** meant but stayed silent all the same. She did not like to be interrupted.

She told him how though Paris was burned once, its treasures remained intact because von Choltitz ignored a direct order. She pirouetted neatly toward Anne Frank and her bundle of contradictions. And when Patch learned of that fear, held in for 761 days, he felt the low knot in his stomach loosen a little.

"That's the Second World War done. Any questions?" she said.

"So did they—"

"Excellent. Moving swiftly on. From the ruins of Europe came our greatest artform, uniting the commies and the caps. I speak, of course, of ballet."

Patch sighed heavily and felt her scowl through the darkness.

She detailed the life of Pierina Legnani as she

climbed to her feet. "If you could see me now your eye would be wide with amazement. I am pirouetting with the elegance of Marta C. You might even mistake me for a swan."

"A swan?"

"A prima swan so purely graceful you would likely gouge out your working eye because you know it will never again witness such beauty."

"You talk about my eye a lot."

He felt the lightest breeze as she began to spin.

"The key is to focus on the same point as you twirl. It aids balance. I practiced as a young girl, and I rattled those wooden floorboards with my tap shoes until my heart soared and my legs shook like a shitting dog's."

"So purely graceful."

"With the speed I'm reaching now I could likely generate enough power to light the Christmas tree at Rockefeller Center."

Patch rolled his eye.

"You'll go to New York, Patch. And you'll watch Prince and Odette and Odile, and you'll feel every move they make. And at the end, when they're reunited in death, you'll be the first to stand and clap and whistle."

"Or the first to fall asleep during."

"Perpetual motion. They'll come from far and wide to watch the captive girl who went on to become the prima ballerina. The press will christen me the Spin Doctress, and I'll break the record for the most consecutive turns, never losing my balance."

With that she fell and landed heavily on the mattress in a heap.

"Grace falls," he said.

She took his hand and squeezed it tightly, leaned close to his ear like she was about to speak when they heard the lock turn.

46

"Hello, I'm Johnny Cash," Grace said, her voice deep and drawling.

She started slow, almost talking. She shot a man in Reno. And then she picked it up, and before long she was singing so loud and raucous that Patch almost smiled.

She moved from Folsom to Sue, walking the line before declaring they had five minutes to live.

"He wore black because he identified with the downtrodden. And there ain't no one more trodden down than you, Patch."

"Right."

"But don't worry, I keep a close watch on that heart of yours."

Patch moved silently, feeling his way. He counted nineteen paces by fifteen. He could not reach the ceiling, and for a while thought that might be the way. And for a while he'd tried keeping some kind of count between visits; how long until the bucket was changed, the water, the food was brought.

"Paint it for me," she said.

"What?"

"Your life. Or a piece of it. Paint it with every color you know, so I can see it, so we can see it."

He told her of the old house on Rosewood Avenue, of the day he started school and how the other kids had shied from him till his mother bought him the tricorne and the waistcoat, and made the eye patch with the skull and crossbones.

"She sounds like a good mom."

"She is," he said, and believed that fully.

"We never hear any other sounds," he said.

"I told you, there's no world out there. The door opens to outer space. A billion stars so close you can reach out and touch them. I need water otherwise I won't be able to do that encore."

"Where does the man go?" Patch said, handing her his bottle.

"Hunting."

"Hunting for what?"

She pressed her lips softly to his ear. "Bad people like you and me."

He thought of his mother then, and again felt the betrayal of tears.

"We don't cry anymore," she said, and wiped his eye. "He doesn't get our tears. No one does."

47

Against the far wall there was a brick rampart as thick as a small tree, and sometimes they sat on it and Grace told him they were facing the Pacific and pointed out bulk carriers and freighters and reefer vessels. She knew the names of sea birds he wondered if she'd made up. Crested Auklet. Erin Spencer. She told him sunsets were beautiful because the light took a longer path through the atmosphere so that it could scatter those violets.

"How do you know so much?" he said.

"I've lived a life."

As she spoke he dug his nails into the cement and worked on the groove he had channeled. And when she was gone he used the last of his strength to move the top brick back and forth, working it looser each time.

He scrambled when the man came. Though the dark was total he was not allowed to turn. The man did not speak, though Patch felt his presence, his power. Her fear.

He took his place kneeling beside Grace, who spoke with calmness.

"Behold, God is my salvation; I will trust, and will not be afraid; for the Lord God is my strength and my song, and he has become my salvation."

She nudged him lightly.

"Isaiah 12:2," he said, his voice strong, like they practiced.

Patch smelled things on him. Peach. Sweat. Cologne. Mildew.

And when he left them they breathed once more.

Grace made them exercise, so long and hard that he lost hours and days to flamed muscles. At first his stomach hurt so bad he waited until she slept to cry.

He felt her fingers guide something into his mouth.

"Peanut Butter Cups," she said.

"How did you get them?" He had never tasted anything so sweet.

"I'm wily like that."

They sat together, their backs to the wall.

"Tell me what you miss," she said. "I'll tell you what I miss. I miss when the moon slips underwater and turns everything blue. I miss the four faces of time. I miss yellow brick roads and tin men. I miss the fall."

"I don't miss . . . sometimes I don't even want to go back home."

"Why not?" she said.

"People say I'm a thief."

"Why?"

"Because I steal things."

She began to laugh, slow at first, and then her shoulders shook as the dam burst.

And then he started to laugh.

In that vacuum that sucked in everything before and turned it out, Patch and Grace laughed so loud.

This time his hand traced the contours of her face, the sharpness of her cheekbones, the shallow pits by her temples.

"Paint me," she said.

"I need to see you."

"I'm standing on a north shore, pink beneath my feet because nor'easters strip rhyolite so pretty I can't even bear it. Maybe it'll preserve me or something. Forty-two miles down with the crystals. Mummified in pink. I hope to hell I keep my looks."

"Are there people searching for you?" he said, and the question somehow made that room darker, somehow stole a little more of the air that they breathed.

"There's no one left out there. No one at all."

That night, after the man took her from him, he worked on loosening the brick.

He channeled the groove deeper.

His nail tore from its bed but he did not cry.

48

When she left, he saw her in acres of poppies, on blond sand or floating on dead sea. He could not make her a face or body so instead saw through her eyes. A vacation from the darkness where she walked among normal people. Those thoughts whorled around a darker stem he tried desperately to shield.

And when she returned fear bolted him to her side as he worked up the courage to move a little closer and to slip his arm around her shoulder. And, ever so slowly, she moved toward him and rested her head against his chest. He breathed her in. Her body molded to his.

"There's people searching," he said. "There's cops and locals and posters and TV appeals and helplines. And within that there's a cadre with guns and the right kind of training to ask the right kind of questions."

"Sometimes I want him dead."

He said nothing back because he wondered at which times she did not.

Patch knew that compassion was strength and at times weakness, and that it was what divided conscience. Sometimes he wanted her silent because he felt closer to her, and sometimes he longed for her to take him away with her stories.

"Tell me about the police chief," she said.

"When my mother works the night shifts, he idles his car outside our house." He did not tell her how he would wait for that sound, how only then could he lie down and relax enough to sleep. How one time he'd gone to the window and the cop had raised a hand then waved him back, saying go on, you go rest up because it's a school night and you're too young to stay in the big old house on your own.

"He cares," she said.

"But where we are now, and where he might be looking, could be they're not even close to similar."

"You have to think he's not the only one. The only good one."

"There's a doctor, too. Dr. Tooms. He's kind."

"When you're out you won't need any of them," she said.

When she was gone he prayed that she wouldn't come back. That she'd find her way home.

"When you leave here . . . this room," he said, and could not finish his thought, or sentence, or breath.

She pushed back into him, took his arm and

wrapped it around her waist and pressed it to her stomach. "When I leave here it's not what you imagine . . . what you fear. Those thoughts that make you want to—"

"To die," he said. "To kill him. To protect you." He felt the dip, the hollow place where her hip bones protruded. He felt the bottom cage of her ribs.

"We can't ever go back," she said. "It's not the same out there. Nothing is the same. The Rockies ain't snowcapped. The Colorado River runs dry, and the Apache Trail ain't in Phoenix. A church in Mesa Verde lost its god, so the people pray to each other like they ain't devils. It's different. Everything is different now."

In his mind her hair gleamed like spun gold, and for a moment he worried about what he looked like. That she might not like him because he didn't look enough like her painting.

"I have a gap between my teeth," she said.

"Oh."

"And those teeth are large. Rabbitesque. I could open a can with them. I imagine I'm quite adorable in the right light to the right hunter."

He smiled.

"Don't worry, I stared at those car barns instead of turning to notice the Charles River," she said.

"I never really know what you're talking about."

"I see what others don't."

The jangle of keys in a lock.

"So we go someplace else then," he said, into her hair. Later that night he would finally wrestle the brick free.

Heavy steps across the floor as he turned his back and knelt in prayer.

This time he smelled chard and metal.

It would not be until later that he realized it was the smell of gunshot.

49

She brought him things: a toothbrush and paste, a pair of nail clippers.

Sometimes she told him the date like she knew, like it meant something, like the two of them weren't all that mattered.

She moved through the seasons, taught him about the Galveston hurricane, the eight thousand dead. And the Dust Bowl drought, and how the prairies scorched and cracked till nothing would grow, not even wheat or barley.

"The gold rush. From California to summer in Colorado's Kingdom. Of course, it's not just precious metal buried in no man's land, but you get the idea."

She moved neatly to Steinbeck and the Joads and a thousand Okies chasing hope through depressed lands. She painted the Dust Bowl so vividly he could watch black blizzards turn day to night and feel them dry his throat and shroud his dreams.

"Maybe this is our great depression," he said.

She told him not to be so dramatic.

She taught French with such an accent he could scarcely make out a word she spoke. But still she went on, heavy through her nose, too deep in the gutter for her **r**'s, and when he tried to copy her she applauded furiously and called him her **chéri,** her **coquelicot,** her **chouchou.**

"Do you ever worry you're not okay?" he asked, after she had forced him to sing "La Marseillaise."

"Okay is the preserve of the uninspired, Patchwork. I'd rather live and die at the extremes than exist in the middle."

She let him dwell on the things she said. Tested him on her return, lighting the room when he remembered. And to his surprise he did, in a way he had not at school.

"It's my birthday today," she said.

"How do you know?" Patch did push-ups. Sweat dripped steady from his nose to the stone floor. He did not count, just kept going till his arms shook. He rested then started up again.

"I like to eat Christmas cake on my birthday. My mother stocked the pantry each December."

He'd not heard her mention her mother before.

"What's she like?" he said.

And when she responded that too was quiet. "Decent. Weak. I sometimes wonder if the two go hand in hand."

"Being decent takes more strength."

He heard her swallow and then she was closer than he thought.

"When we get out, I'll get you a gift."

"In a little blue box? We're too young and fucked up to marry, Patch."

"What would you like?" he said.

"I want you to find me. You can do that, right?" she said.

"You should do push-ups with me."

"I can't do push-ups on my birthday, Patch."

"I'll get us out," he said so quiet she leaned in close. "I promise I'll get you home again."

"You're tough now?" she said, and he heard the smile.

The key, the soft scratch of metal, the heavy turn as the man entered the room. She flinched, trembled in a way she had not before.

He had nothing to give her, no gift to make things right. But he knew there was something he could do to make her day easier.

Her fingers slipped from his.

He stood with her, felt his way along her as they knelt side by side in prayer. Patch reached forward and removed the loose brick.

Heavy and rough.

And ready.

"Do not take revenge, my dear friends, but leave room for God's wrath, for it is written: It is mine to avenge; I will repay," she spoke loud and clear and then nudged him gently.

"Happy birthday," he said, and he stood and swung, so hard and fast, the only sound the heavy crack of bone. And then the thump as the man hit the floor.

He lost her hand, scrambled for it but felt another around his ankle.

Her screams became distant as the man crawled up his body. A hand on his arm, dragging him down.

His eye closed.

He did not cry.

His life tasted of metal, and other bitter things.

50

"You're sick," Grace said.

He'd known it for a while, maybe hours or days. His skin was slick again, and though she said that his head and body burned, he could do nothing but shiver and huddle himself against the mattress. He tried not to show it, to talk without his teeth knocking together, his chest shuddering, his breath coming up short no matter how hard he tried to focus. The nausea was overwhelming.

"The ice rink. Rockefeller Center," she said.

"Is it night?" he said.

"Yes. And it's snowing. And we're the only two people in the whole of New York City. And we're full."

"Full?"

"We've been to Barbetta."

Sometimes she spoke of places he wondered if she had made up because they sounded right, or if in truth her world was a galaxy to his grain of sand.

"We've eaten so much pasta we can barely breathe.

You're wearing a white shirt and there's a spot of sauce, but it's on your blind side so you don't even know."

He frowned at that, and she seemed to sense it because she laughed.

"I'd lean forward and wipe it for you. I'd spit on my napkin and give it a scrub."

"And then they'd ask us to leave."

She laughed again and the sound was sweet. "I'd tell them they were in the presence of a pirate, and they should watch their step or he'd slice them with his sword."

"Cutlass."

"Fucken cutlass then."

He liked it when she cursed. It sounded wrong. Like a nun or a teacher cursing.

He coughed and tasted blood but did not tell her because there were more important things to say. "I was lost before."

"You're still lost, Patch."

"Two people are less lost than one."

"Have you considered writing poetry?"

"I can skate," he offered.

"I do not believe that. The one eye . . . you must fall constantly."

"I never really left Monta Clare much. I don't know where we are now, but it'll be the furthest I ever traveled."

"You need to see things. There's a wider world. Trust me and I'll show it to you."

"I trust you."

"Well then close your eye so I can paint you away."

He found a city he had never visited before. He saw ice and snow fall like ash from a white fire. Buildings so tall they leaned toward him. Refracted lights and glass and steel and steam rising from grates. She painted it all with her words, and he could feel the smoldering of that energy as it smoked from Wall Street and dazzled on Broadway. Voices and engines, the rustle of newspapers.

And music.

"Patch," she said it quiet. "You hear that?"

"It's real?"

She helped him to his feet.

The pain was too much.

"What do we do?"

He felt her looking at him, and he knew. There was nothing they could do. There was never anything they could do.

"We're on the ice," she said, focused. "We're on the ice and there's so many stars that we can't help but look up. We stop in the center and we lie on our backs."

"This song," he said, as he finally let himself hear it.

"You reckon that's where we are?"

"Where?"

"The dark end of the street."

He leaned a little, and she took his weight and pulled him close till his chin rested on the top of her head and she spoke words directly to his heart.

He did not know darkness could be so beautiful. He did not know that inside his chest one of his ribs had punctured his lung. That air was leaking into the pleural cavity.

Or that his spleen had ruptured, and slowly, internally, he was bleeding to death. "You ever danced with a girl before, Patch?"

She turned. He followed. And slowly they moved.

"We could dance on the ice, and people would see," she whispered.

"I don't like to be stared at."

"Well, then you picked the wrong girl to dance with."

For that one perfect moment they were almost nothing more than two teenagers falling in love.

"They're gonna find us," she said softly.

When the music softened and all they heard was the faintest crackle of the record, she tilted her head up and his lips found hers.

51

Grace told him it was dawn, the center of the sun eighteen degrees below horizon, its light scattered through their fragile atmosphere. She told him no matter what happened he had to breathe, to be brave, to be a pirate.

He drifted in and out of consciousness.

He dreamed he would emerge through some trapdoor into a woodland much like the kind he had been taken from. Or maybe a street in an unknown town in an unknown city, where they'd flag down a car and it'd take them to the cops and maybe the hospital.

He wondered at the furor, the flash of a dozen bulbs for the two kids long since buried. Most of all he worried about her, that she would be taken someplace else, that he simply would not survive without her.

"Don't sleep," she said and squeezed his hand too tight. "There's too much you haven't seen. The sky at Baldy Point, how Lake Altus-Lugert spills from the dam, crashing its way along the North Fork Red River."

"Tell me something real," he said and did not recognize his voice.

"I grew up in a big white house. A bedroom for me, my mother, and three more we rented to whoever was passing through. One time it was a girl maybe nineteen and she taught me the art of applying makeup. Decadence, Patch. There ain't a more decadent word. Another time it was a preacher on his way to Pearl River County. You ever seen Hemmsford Swampland? Man, that place needs exorcising."

He whispered, "Paint your house for me."

"A long driveway with tall trees on either side. Trees that reach over like they're linking arms to protect the people that walk under them. And grass so green it might really have been painted. And in flower beds beneath sash windows butterfly weeds glow like campfire."

He tried to smile.

"There's shutters at the windows, and a balcony that runs around the entire building. There's a staircase that winds its way from the yard to the bedroom, and in winter you can see it because the praying trees shed leaves till the house emerges like a snowflake on a summer day."

Grace made him finish his water, then she pressed her lips to his, and when she broke off he was breathless.

"You want to pray?"

He shook his head.

"Good, because the way I hear it praying involves asking for a whole lot of forgiveness, like that makes things better. But you know what I know?"

He shook his head again.

"Sometimes the only way to heal a wound is to tear a bigger one in the person that hurt you."

"I'm tired, Grace."

"Someone once told me you can hear a smile," she said.

"Bullshit."

"Say something and I'll tell you if you are."

"Though it's dark, I'll always find you. Though you're stronger than me, I'll always make sure that you're safe. To me, you'll always come first."

"You're smiling."

"Because it's true."

He did not remember falling. He did not remember her plan, or her cries, or her slapping at his face to try and wake him.

He did not remember the gunshots outside the door.

Patch did not remember smelling the smoke.

Or the heat of the fire.

He did not remember letting Grace go.

THE PAINTER

1976

52

The newspapers waded through the life of Eli Aaron but found near nothing at all. The devastation from the fire was total. Likely an assumed name; they found no record of his birth, of his life.

The cops worked the theory that he'd found the abandoned house in the woodland and claimed it. Squatting and fixing it up, making it his own. They also worked the theory he was dead, though rumors ran that there had been sightings and near misses; a clinic in Woodward where a man stumbled in with severe burns before discharging himself; a carjacking in Buchanan County where the description fit. What little was not destroyed by the fire was finecombed. They found charred press clippings about missing girls from as far as Oklahoma City. A hundred photos salvageable. One clear enough. Callie Montrose.

Cops went to each school Eli Aaron had visited, talked to a thousand kids who said much the same, that they didn't remember him. That he left no impression at all.

On the third day the dogs singled out a spot eight miles from the house, where they found the first girl buried in a grave so deep they hit an aquifer that slowed them.

The press pushed until Nix spoke choice words about fortitude, and the dedication the Monta Clare PD had shown, and the bravery of a young girl who led them to that woodland. He mentioned faith and heart, forbearance and extracting positives from tragedy. The reuniting of a mother and her fearless son. And then he confirmed that yes, they had now found the remains of three of the missing females, and that their families would be able to lay them to rest. They would continue the search for Callie. They did not know how many, if any, more victims were out there. There were no follow-up questions, just a settling of facts that left those there witness to tears in the big cop's eyes.

53

Saint slept in a hospital chair.

She ate her meals in the hospital canteen alongside night porters and junior doctors, and sometimes with Norma, who watched the girl with open concern.

"Please," Norma said, and tried so hard each night, but knew Saint had fixed on a resolution that could not be loosened with talk of missing school or church. No, she would stay. She would sometimes lay her head on his chest and wait for the press against her cheek because she did not trust the screen that made lines of his life.

I won't take my eyes off of you.

She would repeat that like the chorus to a song whose verses no longer mattered. He was hers again. She would not lose him.

For six days and nights, during which she left his side only when the doctors forced her, he breathed mechanized air and his skin lay cold and his eye untroubled by the hysteria he had caused.

Norma brought her several changes of clothes.

Saint held up the dresses and wrinkled her nose until her grandmother returned with her dungarees.

"I should look exactly the same as the last time I saw him," Saint said.

Norma touched her skeletal shoulder.

On the second night a code was called and an alarm sounded and Saint watched the doctors and nurses scramble into his room and lock her from it.

He can't die now.

She said that to them.

Her grandmother wrestled her into the prayer room, and Saint cried as she knelt and clasped her hands together once more.

"It strengthens your faith, now that you have your friend back," Norma said.

Saint looked up at her. "God started the fire. And now he wants the credit for putting it out."

54

Patch did not die that night.

In the waiting room she spread her jacket along two chairs until an orderly took pity and gathered blankets and a pillow. She breathed disinfected air, drank vending machine soda, her teeth furred, her skin dry and greasy.

Saint heard talk of another infection. A line in his veins would pump him full of powerful drugs now they had stabilized him, stemmed the internal bleed, drained air from his lung, and left a chest tube in to reinflate it.

A week in and she found Misty Meyer sitting like an apparition in the chair opposite, too polite to stare at the mess of a girl who graced the front pages of every local newspaper within a thousand miles. They called Saint a hero. Just like the boy.

On the chair beside Misty were flowers, and she looked deeply embarrassed about them.

"Is he awake?" Misty said.

Saint sat up. "Sometimes."

"Is he . . ."

Saint did not know what was coming next, but she spared the girl. "They won't let me see him."

"But he won't die," Misty said, her voice catching on that last word. She sat with her hands across her lap, her Mary Janes buckled over white tights.

"No," Saint said, with conviction.

"Did the photographer really do it?"

Saint rubbed her tired eyes. "Yes."

"He used my school photo on his poster?"

Saint nodded.

"He was creepy. He asked me a ton of questions, asked about stuff I believe in. If I had a boyfriend. But Patch—"

"Maybe he got free and got lost on that land."

Misty did not belong in that waiting room at that hour. It was reserved for the strugglers, for the uncertain and for the desperate.

"It said in the newspaper you might've killed him when you started the fire." She whispered the words, like they weighed so heavy they'd fall from her mouth and shatter Saint's chances of rejoining normality.

"Yeah."

"But they can't find him."

"No."

She stayed another hour, and Saint did not have the energy to speak, and so lay down and pulled her knees to her chest, and before long she slept. She did not feel Misty cover her with the blanket.

And when she woke to splinters of sun, she saw

Misty had been replaced by Chief Nix, whose hat lay on the table beside his belt and gun, his shirt unbuttoned at the neck, dark hair spilling from his chest.

Saint sat up as the fear shot her through.

Nix raised a hand, told her to calm, that he could not sleep so had driven over in the night and watched the kid awhile.

"How you holding up?" he said.

She did not reply.

"You need to see someone . . . what you've been through."

"I need to see Patch, no one else."

"You did a good thing, kid. I'm sorry I didn't listen to you."

Nix sipped coffee from a paper cup, prefatory, like he needed the caffeine kick before he spoke mindless words about the difference she had made.

"How's Mrs. Macauley?" Saint asked.

"Not ready for this. Dr. Tooms is with her. He sleeps in the chair in their den. I don't know if she realizes, with the pills and all."

"Will Patch be the same?" she said.

He stood and stretched and collected his things. And he touched her cheek as he left. "None of us will be, kid."

At the break of day eight, when she managed to slip past the night crew and crawl up onto the bed beside him, and curve her bony body around his and tuck herself neatly into his side, Patch woke.

And for a long time she knew he was awake by the change in his breathing and the ruinous realization that their world together would open till it was not them and them alone. And for that time she kept close and choked her tears back and would not let him see just how much the past months had undone her.

When she finally looked at him she sucked her breath deep.

"The cops took your **Playboy.**"

55

Chief Nix drove.

Patch sat beside Saint in the backseat of the cop car.

He felt the way she watched him, like she had done for the past week, looking for a tell, for something that would let her know he was or was not the boy who showed at her house to steal her honey.

She had been there when he screamed the name. Grace.

Screamed it until the nurses came and pushed a button, till memories shuffled and a new hand was dealt. Illuminations in darkness, his thoughts no more than the flare of matchlight in a storm. When it was all dark, he felt his bones disconnect as he floated down midnight rivers. He could not recall their last hours together. At times he saw the nurse and begged her to stop the drugs so he could make some sense, and other times he begged for more, so he could swim away again.

"I need you to find her," he said.

Nix met his eye in the mirror.

For six hours over three days the cops had sat with him and taken statements and looked at each other like they knew the girl down there with him was likely dead.

"We're all on it," Nix said.

"And I am," Saint said from beside him, her hand on the seat between them like an offering. He knew that he could place his hand on hers and give her back the friend she wanted. He turned from her and watched from too deep inside, his mind nylon strands pulled taut but holding. He would knit memories back together only for the drugs to unravel them once more.

They took statements, asked the same questions in different ways. He spoke of Grace and what he remembered, which was too much and not enough, the two state cops exchanging glances he could not read.

Afterward he would not be able to speak or eat or breathe.

Nurses lit his eyes with small flashlights, checking his pulse against their small silver clocks. He wrenched the tubes from his hand and watched his blood pool and drip till Saint noticed and screamed for the nurse to come repair him.

A doctor told him it was normal for his mood to be low. Brain fog, stress. Forgetting things. Weakened immune system. "We need light to survive," the doctor said.

"Not all of us," Patch said.

He watched the town appear, leaving and returning beneath blue sky. The past months might have
been a blink, if it hadn't been for her.

"She needs me," he said, as the forest flashed by,
and then corrected himself. "I need her."

He felt Saint beside.

"She saved me. She dragged me out." He said that
more than once. His knee bounced and he stared at
it and could not stop it, like he could control nothing at all.

"You remember that?" Nix said and glanced back
at him.

Outside the sky was raw now, the gunmetal stays
traced mountain curves. Saint had bought him sunglasses from the gift shop because light hurt him.
The doctor said it would take time. Time was a
thing again.

His fingers were scabbed, and his knees and el-
bows, and though they had cleaned him up he could
see the trace of dirt beneath his nails.

Nix cursed when they turned into his street, the
news vans idling across the drive. The neighbors
aimed smiles like he was the star of a parade, like
any of them had smiled before.

He pulled his hood up and hid himself as Nix
seared them a path with his badge and led them
down the side of the house and into the yard.

Patch saw his mother's face, and though makeup
hid much he knew when she pressed into him that
most of her had died.

"My baby," she cried.

He stayed limp in her arms.

She smelled faintly of Sweet Honesty and decay.

"The grass is cut," he said.

"Mr. Roberts comes across now." She wiped her eyes and nose and laughed gently at what he had noticed first.

56

Patch's bedroom was no longer his.

His clothes and bedcovers and wallpaper. His dresser and posters, his skull and crossbones. The flintlock pistol Saint told him she had borrowed and returned.

His skin was not his. It itched him, the wounds he would not let heal because he worried they would leave no scars at all.

That afternoon his mother walked in on him getting out of the shower, and she saw a body she did not recognize, and he saw in her that mix of fear and sadness and a little repulsion. She wondered, like the cops and the reporters and the other kids would. In how many ways was he not the same as them?

Later when she slept he unfurled the map he'd found in the attic. It covered the country in enough detail, each state colored from the pinks of Arkansas through Louisiana, to the steel of Michigan to the boldest green of Montana and beyond. "You could be anywhere," he said.

Outside he slipped by a single news van and walked down his street and wondered how the night could be so bright.

At the Palace 7 on Main Street he saw kids from school in line.

He saw the young couples and families dressing the window of Lacey's Diner. He watched through a long lens that would stay with him, like he existed a hundred miles from anyone.

And then he saw her.

Standing with her group.

He was about to move, to flee the scene like the crime it was, when Misty Meyer looked up.

He moved toward her on instinct, his legs working against his mind.

She slipped her hand from Chuck's, and then she broke into a run.

Misty hit him at full force in the middle of the road, wrapped her arms around him and buried her cries into his shoulder.

He did not feel the pain in his ribs, instead only the weight of her, so slight as she trembled in his arms.

Cars streaked by, leaning on their horns, but the two did not notice.

She held his face tight and stared into him like they weren't strangers, like they had ever spoken a word to each other.

She wore a white dress and sandals and smelled so sweet he almost could not catch his breath.

Another car blazed past.

And then Chuck took her from the road, pulling her hand tight. She looked back, locked onto Patch like he was some kind of ghost only she could notice.

He watched as she sobbed, as Chuck led her to the movie theater, and then he turned and walked slowly through town but hugged the shadows and saw life move on as he knew it would, as he knew it had.

He did not notice Saint standing outside the Green's Convenience Store. He did not hear her call because it was a whisper. He did not notice her follow at a distance until he was safely home, her bag on her shoulder, a slingshot inside.

He reached for the stack of newspapers piled high on the landing.

He worked without noticing headlines.

LOCAL BOY MISSING

He stuck pages to the window, one after the other until no hint of Monta Clare made it into his room. And then he closed the door and blocked the gaps with bedding, pulled the mattress from the old frame and set it on the floor.

He would not tell them he wanted to be back there.

They would not understand.

Only when the dark was total enough did he lie down.

And reach out his hand for her to take.

57

Saint did not see him that first week.

Each morning she stood before the old house on Rosewood Avenue and waited, watching his covered window, sometimes slipping into the yard and settling herself on a rusting lawn chair. Ivy came out and stroked her hair, told her he was sleeping, that he was tired. Saint spent hours making a pirate card, sketching the mast and body, detailing the rigging and casting a figurehead in his image, before deciding it was babyish and tossing it into the trash.

She suffered through school, endured whispered rumors that Patch had come back disfigured, that the bad man from the woodland had plucked out his other eye and now he wandered blind.

Misty approached in homeroom.

"How is he?" she said.

Saint did not answer though wanted to lie, to say he was not ready to see anyone but her, that she knew about his time away from them but it was not her place to share it.

"Should I bake him a strudel?" Misty said.

Saint did not know what a strudel was.

Jimmy Walters fell into step with her each day after school, often picking wildflowers for her, which she would clutch awkwardly until he departed and then toss into the Baxters' yard.

"Thanks for letting me walk with you," he said.

She shrugged.

"We could walk again sometime," he said.

She frowned.

"I could come see your beaver."

"You some kind of pervert?" Saint said.

Jimmy caught himself and turned a deep shade of crimson. "I didn't . . . I meant at the marshland."

"Where you'll expect me to show you my beaver?"

Jimmy began to sweat as he loosened his collar. "I just meant . . . I could help you photograph it."

Saint blew out her cheeks.

Jimmy looked toward the sky, then at his shoes.

And then Saint began to laugh. And she looked at his face, so open and honest and horrified, and she clutched her stomach and laughed so hard Jimmy could do little but dab the sweat from his brow and join her.

When they calmed she closed her eyes to the afternoon sun and could not recall the last time she had laughed. Or smiled. Or felt much beyond the agony of the past year.

58

Saint was summoned to the police station, where she stood beside Nix, who took her small hand in his and shook it firmly as he awarded her a certificate and a check for two thousand dollars. Daisy Creason took her photograph. Her grandmother, already bursting with understated pride, would buy a dozen copies and file them someplace.

Saint had her grandmother cash the check.

On that second Monday she arrived a little early and placed every dollar in an envelope which she left in the Macauleys' mailbox.

She found a box beside the trash, and inside neatly folded she saw his flag. She fished it out and beneath it saw his antique treasure chest and doubloons that glowed yellow.

And then she heard the street door open and turned to see her friend.

She smiled.

He wore jeans and a plain navy T-shirt. He was too skinny.

"What's all this?" she said.

"I'm not a pirate."

She studied the trash carefully. "The flintlock isn't there."

"That was a gift."

She lifted a little inside.

They walked to school mostly in a silence she tried so hard to break with talk of her bee mystery, of how she'd seen an Olds run into the back of a Chevy, and the two men get out and start yelling at each other. She told him her grandmother had stopped smoking Marlboro and moved to Virginia Slims, that Sammy the drunk had locked himself out of the art gallery and punched through the window, and then woke with no memory of it so reported the break-in to Chief Nix.

She barely took breath, but when she did Saint noticed the way he walked, quieter somehow, his chin a little lower, his mind far from her and the nonsense she spoke.

He no longer smiled.

The day after he arrived home she'd ridden her Spyder to the library and borrowed a book on trauma and psychological disabilities. She knew not to pry, that he was likely suffering nightmares, flashbacks, maybe physical sensations. Anger, shame. She had read through the night. She was ready for whatever he needed.

"I need to steal a car," he said.

She was not ready for that.

59

He walked through the school halls with his head down, his eyes not straying from the buffed floor. He took his seat at the back of the class, mute to the whispers. Teachers did not call on him or question why he sat for fifty minutes without picking up his pen.

The principal called him in and asked how he was doing, and then mentioned the war and how good men were forged from fear and bravery. This was his chance.

He walked out of the office and the school, and on Main Street he saw Mr. and Mrs. Roberts heading into Lacey's Diner for lunch. At their house he took their spare key from beneath the mat, stole into their guileless home, and snatched the keys to their mustard Aspen. He sat on cream leather seats and stared at his own home through the windshield.

He'd pulled his mother's Fairlane into the driveway more times than he could count, slipped the

Robertses' new car into first and eased down the street.

He drove to the public library in Panora.

An old lady peered over her glasses, mercifully offered a smile and some help using the microfiche. The screen was large, the case heavy, and the focus out a little. For two hours he trawled missing persons reports from every newspaper within a thousand miles, sorting by date.

So many gone and never found, and no one ever charged. Sometimes they ran follow-up pieces and Patch noted the toll taken, the parents who could not stay together in their shared agony, and so carried their infections and poisoned new partners but drank from their comfort, the only pain they had known so paling it did not count at all.

The girls outnumbered the boys fifty to one. They varied in appearance but were one and the same. Young. Mostly too young to realize they were birthmarked with targets that only boldened with time, invisible to begin with, taking shape through formative years and burning red hot through puberty and into their teens.

Saint slid into the seat beside him.

He noticed smells more now.

Flowers and mud and drugstore soap.

"My grandmother's route passes by here," she said.

He stared at **The Morning Star.** The girl was Callie Montrose. In the grainy black and white she was smiling, weight on one foot, hip pushed out. Everything to see but nothing he could place.

"She was taken after me?" Patch said.

"The girl . . . Grace, when did she arrive?"

He could not know.

"Callie Montrose. It could be her," Saint said.

He wrote down the name like he could forget it.

Patch moved to the next photo, and they looked at an Asian girl of thirteen. A couple of pages later were shots from her funeral.

"You came to the woods that day," he said.

She nodded.

"You stole your grandfather's Colt?"

Another nod.

"You got brave when I was gone," he said, and finally turned to look at her.

"I was . . . I was scared. There wasn't room for anything else."

"Tell me about Eli Aaron," he said.

She told him what he already knew, what he had demanded the state cops tell him. That the man photographed girls and maybe went after the ones he liked most. That they were still searching his land, but it was so vast they might never finish. That there were prints from a dozen vehicles. That maybe he didn't work alone. That the three bodies were found with rosary beads wrapped around their throats.

"That's the Robertses' new car out front," she said. "If I give Nix the keys, say I found them on the street, it won't be so bad. Maybe he'll think it was dumped and he won't look all that hard for who took it."

He reached into his pocket and placed the keys on the desk.

She breathed again.

"I have a camera now," she said and felt suitably lame. "I caught a shot of a barred owl. You want to come see?"

He did not reply.

"I mean, it was dead, but still . . ." she said, making it worse.

He finally looked up at her. "When you see Nix, you should tell him that if he won't look for the girl then I will."

Saint saw him then.

He stood. "And I'll burn everything in my path till I find her. I won't hesitate. I won't even look back at the ashes."

60

He found the envelopes in the ice compartment of the freezer.

FINAL DEMAND

There were threats of debt collection, legal action, eviction.

That afternoon he called the agency and told them his mother would work again.

That night as his mother lay dead to the world, he pulled on sweatpants and an old T-shirt and ball cap, and in the small garage beside their house he found her supplies and set off toward Main Street with her keys.

He'd tagged along once or twice before because some nights he could not fall asleep before she left the house and he did not want to sit up and hear the chirr of summer crickets or jump each time the trumpet creepers rattled the windowpane.

He started in the law office of Jasper and Coates, knew to use extra polish on the mahogany because his mother bitched that Ezra Coates liked to see the reflection of each bank note as he counted them out. Files littered each surface, spilling muted town secrets. Patch learned that Mitch Evans was suing the Missouri Ladder Company after taking a fall that Patch could only surmise was entirely his own fault, and that Franklin Meyer was involved in an appellate case Patch could not begin to understand.

"We look at others with fucking trivial problems, and we think how long they'd last with a taste of our childhoods."

He vacuumed the carpet, shined the windows and the brass of each switch and plaque, emptied the trash and wiped piss from around the toilet.

At midnight he moved onto J. Asher Accountancy and stood beneath towering binders stamped with an assortment of company names. He poured neat bleach down the basin because a note told him it was blocked. In the small kitchenette he ate a single biscuit from an open tin.

He hooked dust from cornices, brushed out a fireplace in an office bigger than the ground floor of his home. On a desk he picked up a photo frame and looked at the blue-eyed boy and girl. He did not dwell on fair and just as he emptied their father's ashtray of cigar ends, the plume of ash kicking up because he did not know to mist it first.

Four offices, a craft store, a typewriter shop. It was four in the morning by the time he finally made it to the last stop, his arms burning fiercely.

Monta Clare Fine Art occupied a double fronted stucco building at the head of Main Street.

Through large glass windows he stared at a painting of a Gettysburg battlefield, pressed his face so close his breath fogged the slayed, the smoking guns and frayed flags, a hundred shadows leaned like dominoes on Culp's Hill.

Patch took a deep breath and pushed the heavy door open into another world. White walls rose to lines of light that dropped stark bright without shadows to dull the heavy gilded frames. He stepped carefully, not wanting to cast an echo as he stopped before a series.

The floor was dark wood, shined deeply, the place so immaculate he could not imagine it would need cleaning for a hundred years.

"You're the boy that saved the Meyer girl," Sammy said.

Patch turned.

Sammy leaned on a cane though was not near old enough to need it. His shirt unbuttoned low, his jacket tweed and his feet bare and his hair a mess of curls. Handsome though he carried an air of fallen-from-grace.

His cuffs were turned back to show a thick gold watch. He held a glass, crystal facets catching the light as he sloshed brandy and fixed Patch with something like amusement in his eyes.

Patch looked past him, at a haunting painting, so large it took half the rear wall. Patch imagined the artist using a ladder to reach it. Up close he could not have seen what he was creating.

"The only good thing I ever did," Patch said.

"There's still time."

"Just not for me."

"People have short memories when you do something good, and long when you fuck things up," Sammy said.

"So—"

"So you either keep doing good . . ."

"Or stop giving a fuck what people think."

"You don't use chemicals to clean here," Sammy said. "You don't touch any of the pieces. You don't dust their frames. You don't breathe within three feet of them."

Patch glanced to his left, at to the small portrait of a girl no more than ten, her face streaked with surprise or maybe fear, like there was a difference between the two.

"The Memphis Girl."

Sammy did not draw his eyes from her. "Addison Lafarge painted her near two hundred years ago. She was to be sold to a merchant and knew this, and in her eyes you can see that she is about to be gutted of her childhood."

"It's—"

"Nothing on this earth more beautiful than sacrifice, kid. You'll do well not to learn that yourself."

Patch knew that look, sometimes worried that he now carried it, too.

He worked with more care, traced the baseboards with his cloth and swept imagined dirt and held his breath as he passed the little girl who watched each of his moves. When he was done he sat cross-legged. The floorboards breathed, and he closed his fingers over gaps to starve them. Behind him was a painting of an old ship wedged on stagnant water.

The memory came back startling.

"**Tell me something about pirates,**" Grace said.

"**In 1701 Sam Thompson captured the** Cursed Star. **He fitted it with twenty-eight cannons. A couple months later a storm off Cape Cod sank her. More than a couple hundred years later they found her wreckage. You can go see artifacts in Provincetown. We should do that one day.**"

"**If I'm still here.**"

He sidled close and felt her tears drop hot onto his bare shoulder.

Patch reached up and this time he gently felt through the dark and found her cheek and her tears.

"**I hate it when you cry,**" **he said.**

"**You take your hand away, and you paint me smiling then. In the dark we're always smiling. We're all the same. We're all well and happy and shining.**"

"**I don't know how to paint.**"

"**Art is feeling, nothing more. You know how to feel, Patch.**"

In a back room he found a set of pencils and an empty pad and stole both.

When he finally turned the key in his own door he was too tired to sleep and so sat and sketched.

She was fluid and rigid and lay just at the tip of his reach, his fingers bumping along the edge of her.

She was constellations he could not map.

She was beautiful and hateful, thunderclouds and summer rain.

He worked and reworked and discarded and built out, shaded and lightened. They would be the first sketches. He balled them so tight he felt pain in his knuckles as he tossed them into the trash.

The stars vanished as he climbed weary onto the mattress.

His alarm would wake him in one hour for school. He would switch it off and cut, his priorities shifting daily.

He hugged his knees to his chest.

He missed her.

61

It took a month of cutting school and riding the buses, placing notices on boards in far-flung towns and calling every hospital in the state of Missouri for Chief Nix to show up at his house. A little before eight, Patch opened the door and the big cop pushed past him and walked into the kitchen, opened a bag from Lacey's Diner and set a couple of cinnamon muffins on the table. Placed a second bag down and nodded toward it.

Patch peered inside, saw his old copy of **Playboy** and raised an eyebrow.

Nix raised his own in reply.

Nix sat.

Patch sat.

"Eat."

Patch ate.

"Harkness worked a late call, headed back in long after we closed up. Said he saw you cleaning the station." Nix took a large bite.

"Bullshit. I'm not old enough to work."

The linoleum torn at each corner, rutted around the stove and curling like butter. A stopped clock hung beside a calendar from a year past as if his mother had simply pressed pause.

"You look tired," Nix said.

"You can't find her."

"I also can't stop Social Services. School called me because I told them to keep an eye out."

"I'll go to school."

Nix took a bite of a muffin and did not speak again until he had swallowed. "How's your friend?"

Patch wore his tired entirely. "She's okay, like everyone is okay."

"Don't get many friends like that. The kind that would do most anything for you."

"I don't need friends. I need cops to do their jobs."

Nix stared at him, like he did not recognize the boy that had returned. "You and your life. I don't work another case again and you'll keep me busy enough."

"Find Grace."

"I talked to the state cops again. You were in total darkness for a long time. The strain that puts on your mind. Your body. You know what a mirage is?"

"Fuck you, Chief Nix."

"Your mind conjures something to keep you moving forward. It places salvation where there is none. You should speak with Dr. Tooms."

"He can't help me."

"He's the best man I know. He's—"

Patch cut in, "She's real. She's a girl lost. It's your job to make her safe. To make sure she's not hurting. To make sure she lives a life."

"This needs to end before you get yourself in a world of trouble."

"Tell me she's okay."

"I can't do that."

Patch met his eye. "If she's not okay, then it's not the end."

62

At lunch Patch sat alone on a fallen oak and stared at his map as Misty Meyer walked toward him wearing a navy jumper over a white turtleneck, her blonde hair scraped back tight. She took a large box from her bag and set it down beside him.

"You missed your birthday. When you were gone." She opened the box to reveal an iced monstrosity with several frosted protrusions fixed atop. "My mother sends me to culinary class each week."

He looked at the cake, took in the sloped crown, the deep cracks in each side. "Oh."

"It has a skull and crossbones," she said, and beamed.

He stared at a black sphere. The food coloring bled down one side.

"Chef Pierre said my ball-work is coming along nicely."

He frowned at that one as she took a silver cake knife from her bag and cut him a slice so large she needed two hands to pass it.

Patch regarded the dense, gluey streaks as she watched him intently. He took a bite and managed to swallow.

"Salt," she said.

"Yes."

"I like your patch today," she said.

"Satin," he replied with instant regret.

"My uncle works with pirates."

He took a little interest despite himself.

"He helps prevent copyright piracy."

His interest died.

She looked over at his lunch, the buttered bread and a single apple he'd pulled from the Baxters' yard on the walk to school. "Are you on a diet? If you are I can get you pills from Christy Dalton. I mean, you'll pass liquid shit, but—"

He glanced down at the bones of his arms.

She retreated quickly.

That afternoon he stole paper from the supply closet at school and made a batch of twenty posters that did not give much detail at all. Just a vague age and height and size and a name.

Saint caught up with him at the school gates and together they walked in silence.

She stayed by his side and boarded her grandmother's bus and took the seat next to him.

He slept on the hot leather seat, his head printing the glass with sweat as the bus made its route, Norma watching out for him like he was the last of his species. As he slept Saint looked at his hand and made to take it till she caught her grandmother's eyes in the mirror and the slight shake of her head.

They peppered surrounding towns, from Fallow Rock to Alice Springs, the Edgewood Canyon through the Coldwater Dam. He'd narrowed Grace's age to somewhere between thirteen and seventeen for no other reason than he'd pieced together particles of her stories and formed a kind of timeline that made little sense to anyone but him. He knew that when they were standing the top of her head nestled just beneath his chin. That sometimes her hair skimmed her shoulders, in other memories her chest. She was slight enough that he felt the bumps of her spine, that he could circle her wrist with his thumb and forefinger.

At a bus station they stared at the noticeboard where a single picture of Callie Montrose remained.

"Her father's a cop, and still they can't find her," Saint said.

"Just like they couldn't find me."

She slipped her hand into his.

And tried not to feel him flinch.

63

The next day Misty set down a Le Creuset dish, took sterling cutlery from her bag and handed it to him as she removed the enameled lid.

"Arroz de pato," she said.

He stared at the congealment with ardent fear, scratched his head and fussed with his eye patch as she watched him eat. "Can you get the moulard?"

He nodded and made a silent vow to find out what a moulard was and punish it. And he waited until she turned to notice her friends before he wiped his tongue on a hawthorn leaf.

In the distance a couple of kids tossed a football, now and then throwing glances toward Misty to see if she noticed. She did not, but Patch noticed Saint at the window of her applied math class. And she saw him and made an O with the thumb and forefinger of her left hand, before penetrating it with the index finger of her right.

Patch looked away quickly, his mind back in the basement.

"You know that means you want to fuck someone," Grace said.

"It does not."

"Think about it."

He did. For a long, long time.

"Jesus," he said.

"You were in the newspapers a lot. I made a scrapbook," Misty said, breaking him from it.

He wondered at her hobbies.

"Or maybe you just want to forget the whole darn thing and here I am coming to sit with you each day."

That smile again.

It was a smile all right.

"You don't have to do this," he said.

"I mean, I enjoy the cookery and all."

"You don't owe me or nothing, Misty."

She watched the sky, her eyes an even match for the blue. "I didn't sleep much. Probably get a mess of wrinkles soon enough. Probably look like a waffle. Pocked." She cleared her throat and looked at him. "We went to church and I prayed for you."

He wanted to get up and walk away from her, this girl who had too much. He wanted to walk out of the school gates and down to the police station and burn the fucking place to the ground.

"Is this cutlery real silver?" he said.

"Yes."

He made a mental note to feign choking and slip it into his pocket.

The school bell called, and he gathered his posters and walked away from the building, cutting biology.

Misty took a moment and followed.

64

That afternoon Misty Meyer climbed onto the bus with him, and Norma did not smile or nod, just let them take their seat and did not ask for the fare.

They bumped along, their legs pressed together as they watched the greens through the wide windshield, the road rolling past Kentucky bluegrass dried and tan before clapboard houses that clung to brittle shelves of hillside.

"I've never been on a bus," she said. "It's just a long car, really."

Norma frowned.

They got off at Branton, and Patch took the posters from his bag and tacked the first to a southern pine utility pole.

The heat climbed as they worked, and when they were done they sat at the bus stop on a bench carved from fluted cedar, their sneakers in the gravel. He plucked a dandelion, ran his fingers over the blowball as she pulled a soda from her bag, drank, and passed it to him. She talked. He learned she collected snow globes. She had no siblings but liked the idea of having someone to pass wisdom to. She had two dogs and thought they were related till she caught them mating.

"They still might be related," Patch offered.

"We'll know when the litter is born. Two tails and missing eyes and stuff."

He touched his eye patch.

She caught it. "Not implying you were the product of such . . ."

He scratched his head.

She bit her lower lip.

They rode back in silence, drawing the occasional glance from Norma, and in Monta Clare found their way to the edge of the lake. They lay out till dark fell, and Patch watched the stars edge into the water.

"My father can't talk about it. And nothing even happened, not really. He talks about you like you're a hero and a cancer. You came back taller, and people say you need sunlight to grow," she said matter-of-factly.

"Plants."

"You're kind of pretty, Joseph Patch Macauley. I mean, your eyelashes are too long. Maybe because your body gave them all to the one eye."

He frowned.

"It's damn wasteful on a boy." She quieted for the wave of cicadas.

And then she cried.

When her shoulders gently shook, he moved toward her and before long held her soft hand in his.

"We have this thing between us. This man and this thing. People keep wanting to know how I felt. I was just scared. And I left you there."

He watched ripples in the stillness. "You had to run. There was no choice at all."

"When Chuck took me to a movie. When Laurie Beth asked me to go to the salon. I wanted to fucking scream at them because you were out there, this person that kept me with them."

Patch kept hold of her hand. "The shrink they make me see, she taps her pencil and frowns at me. And she talks about how we construct our ideals out of our own past mistakes. And I wonder what exactly a mistake is. A thing we should not have done, right? But if learning is built on trial and error there can be no mistakes, only rungs on a ladder to someplace better."

He walked her to town and they stopped across from the Palace 7 where her group waited outside.

"Dustin Hoffman is a doll," she declared, as she pulled a pocket mirror from her bag and fixed her makeup, working the smears from her cheeks.

He saw Chuck watching them, and Patch imagined their future. It was then he saw himself fully, the smudge on their history, her time spent with him nothing more than penance.

"Are you okay?" he said.

She smoothed her pleated dress, and he thought of her sitting beside Chuck, taking his hand, laughing and gasping as she ate popcorn and the light flickered in her eyes.

She sprayed her wrist with a small bottle of perfume. "This is my Friday night. For a long time yours were spent somewhere so bad I cannot even imagine it. My nights and my days. Every bite of food. Every movie I watched or book I read. Every time I laughed or my mother hugged me. Everything, Patch. It was stolen from you."

He watched her turn to cross the street.

Right then Patch wanted to tell her not to waste her time. She hadn't stolen all that much. He never had anything to begin with.

65

"What's your biggest fear?" Grace said.

"Not seeing anything beautiful again."

"You will."

"Not leaving Monta Clare. Working someplace darker than here."

"There's no place darker, Patch."

"Someplace where I don't even have your . . . you."

"You'll see everything. All the beautiful places. You'll see them all. I'll make sure of it."

Patch woke drowning, the sheets balled in a knot. Slick with sweat he walked to the bathroom and christened his nightmares with cold water.

Her face came back to him.

He took the stairs fast, his heart drumming as he ran through the streets and let himself into Monta Clare Fine Art.

In the studio he found a ream of paper and started with a color chart and mixed everything from cadmium yellow through viridian to carbon black. Only two brushes, a Goldenedge size three and a Simmons zero, both a little chewed. A set of Pelikan Watercolors. All stolen from Goodwill as he swept their floor hours before. He dabbed them and smoothed the tip with his fingers.

He did not know to hydrate the pigment, to blunt with a spoon, to blot before selecting darker tones. From school he had learned basic mixing. His mind cast back to Miss Frey as she took them through masters, spoke of ink wash and stippling, cubism and Postimpressionism. He did not know the delicacy of contouring, to divide what was light from what was dark until dimensions were eked out.

Patch knew feeling and nothing more. He knew to close his eye until his world was her, and then reach through what seemed too dark until he could pull free the shades of her voice. The delicate way she formed vowels, the heat when she grew angry, the cool of her quiet. He raised his hand and remembered the soft trace of skin, the bow of her upper lip, the fine of her jawbone. He felt around each of her eyes, the soft brow above, the impossible rise of her cheekbones. And her hair, the gentle heat from her parting, the depth of her eyelashes.

And so he began to build her outward on each page. He gave little thought or care to structure, instead devoted thirty prints to each of her eyes, again and again until he could see what he had never seen.

He moved on to her hair, and in some she was lit with a fiery red and in others a dulcet auburn. A blonde that met white, a dark that mixed each of his blacks. Sometimes long and flowing, other times so short he could outline her skull.

As dawn broke his fevered night he sat back and looked at fifty or so pictures he had drawn. Abject, abstract, some consisted only of a single ear and the hair that fell over it. He gripped them tightly and slowly began to place them together. It took a long time, the pieces of a puzzle that had no completion. He knew nothing of creation, of how incomplete was often its own end. He could barely lift his arm, and he sat back on the hard floor surrounded by pieces of a stranger, and he tore at his hair and skin and cursed, and he took each piece and balled them in his fists.

66

Outside the bakery he smelled the sweetness as Mrs. Odell dressed her window with onion rye and Austrian pumpernickel. In his daze he heard bloodless laughter and saw the group led by Chuck as they walked up Main Street and ripped each of his posters down.

He gritted his teeth and stood in the center of the road mute to the horn as a Jeep ground its brakes, and he called out to the group that they were gutless.

They stopped and turned, five of them like an ordered army in their letter jackets, their general leading them back toward Patch.

"You're littering our town," Chuck said, so weak Patch almost laughed. Still handsome in that vapid way, a sweep of fair hair pushed to the side, an even tan and build, a good five inches taller. Patch glanced at Chuck's friends and wondered how they found each other, people so similar and lacking. Maybe on the football field, or maybe their fathers were the kind that worked in banks or insurance, and their mothers the kind who held coffee mornings and displayed fresh flowers in opaline vases.

Chuck held up a couple of posters. "This the girl-friend you made up, right?"

He glanced across into Monta Clare Fine Art and saw Sammy leaning in the doorway and watching, and beside him he saw the prints in the window. The wooden floor and the army of ornate girls in ballet pumps and colored ribbon. He thought of Grace spinning and what she had glimpsed for her-self and for them.

"Five on one," Chuck said.

Patch stared at him. "You want to fetch a couple more to even things up?"

He was not sure who shoved him, but he man-aged to stay on his feet, and maybe that was the wrong move because the shove was followed by a flurry of punches and kicks. He felt nothing as they landed, just dropped to the hard sidewalk and did not move to protect himself. He tasted blood and saw the flutter of her name as the posters came to land beside him.

He thought of Eli Aaron, how that was a real beating. They backed up a little when they saw him smiling at them.

He stood. Stretched. Raised his fists and grinned and beckoned them back for more.

Patch did not see the girl step in front of him until she pulled the sourdough baguettine from her bag and belted Chuck so hard the crack echoed.

Chuck clutched his ear, his eyes flaming.

The group moved again, but Misty severed their resolve with attitude alone, her eyes squint like she was choosing who'd be next.

A Coca-Cola sign spun as Patch carefully collected his posters.

Misty wore jeans flared at the ankle and narrow at the hips. Her blonde hair tied and sitting over her shoulder like a kind of luxurious throw.

A couple of kids stood watching on the redbrick sidewalk as Chuck carefully weighed things.

They stood there, the beautiful rich girl, the missing boy, the king of Monta Clare High and his followers.

They fanned out and walked away slow.

Patch reached into his school bag and took out a roll of tape.

Misty held the posters in place as Patch carefully taped them.

Together they moved up the street, from post to post.

"My parents want you to come to dinner," Misty said, focusing too hard on the task at hand.

"Why?"

"Gratitude. Or perhaps guilt."

She handed him the baguettine, so hard he winced

a little for Chuck's ear, and worried a lot for his own teeth.

"I made this for your lunch."

"It has some of Chuck's blood on it."

"The other day you didn't return the silver cutlery."

"I know."

67

Saint took her piano lesson early each Saturday, Mrs. Shaw tutting as Saint fumbled her way through "Claire de Lune," her left hand fucking up the quaver till Mrs. Shaw told her enough and sent her out into the morning air to clear her mind.

She saw Nix taking coffee beneath the okame cherry across the street. He raised a hand, his smile so sad she drew everything from the past year and returned to her seat and finished what she had started.

"Don't rush. Sometimes it's the notes you don't play," Mrs. Shaw said.

On Monday when he didn't show in class, Saint asked to use the restroom and walked down the faded parquet floors.

She peered in classrooms, ignored a smile from Jimmy Walters.

She found Patch sitting alone in a corridor. He looked slight then, the boy she had lost, the swelling by his eye already turning a shade of green against the delicacy of his skin.

She sat on the small plastic chair beside him and glanced up at the constant second hand as it rounded off another hour of their lives. She wondered if she would always straddle that confusing place between child and adult, if it was printed on her skin like a warning that she could not be depended on or desired.

"Was it because of what happened this morning? I heard about Chuck."

The principal's door opened, and he led Chuck and his father out. Chuck's nose crusted with blood, the dark already circling both eyes.

"What did he do?" Saint said to Patch.

Luke Bradley, Chuck's cornfed father, glared. "Chuck brought in a football trophy. Joseph stole it."

"Why would you steal his trophy?" Saint said to Patch.

"So I could fuck his mother with it. Apparently Luke ain't up to the task," Patch said.

"Jesus," Saint said beneath her breath as Chuck and his father took a moment to react. They might've gone for the kid had Principal Rodriguez not stepped in front of them.

Patch stared after them.

"Nice eye patch," she said.

Patch touched the blue star with an absent mind.

Saint spoke, "Hook-Handed Pete changed the color of his star each time he took a life. He cycled through most of them because he was a bad man. Then one day he drew his pistol and aimed at it a guy but was so drunk his bullet sailed by and landed in the heart of a girl named Nancy Blue. Hook-Handed Pete never took another life, and, for the rest of his, wore blue in tribute and feeling."

"I'm not a pirate," he said, as the principal led him into the office and told Saint to get back to class.

She waited the thirty minutes alone, and when the door opened once more she hid herself around the corner. Only when she heard the light steps did she join him.

"Suspension," he said.

She followed him out of the school, and together they walked back to his house in silence. He did not invite her inside, but she followed and saw Ivy sleeping on the couch, the blanket pulled beneath her chin though her legs were bare.

She followed Patch back out front and did not say anything when he opened the Fairlane and sat in the driver's seat and started the engine.

Saint opened the passenger door and sat beside him.

"You'll get in shit," he said.

"We'll get in shit," she said, as he eased from the house.

68

They drove through Monta Clare, and she did not ask where they were headed. Saint rolled down her window and rain fell for a while in tides through still trees till the streets made mirrors. He drove well enough, and she wondered how many times he had stolen the old car in the dead of night.

For a long time she risked glances at him and tried to see the difference but could not, not outwardly.

It was only at Eleven Valley Road as he turned down an unmarked track and eased the car onto mats of deadened pine needles that her breath shallowed as she realized where they were and what stood before them.

"Are we——"

"You can wait in the car," he said.

They climbed out together and she silently followed past stirs of poison oak and the tight knit of common juniper. He picked dark blue cones but stopped deadly still beside her as they stared down at Lake White Rock.

"Monta Clare might as well be our world, right?" she said.

Mountain rivers fed it with turgid darks that rippled.

In silence they made it to the burned remains of Eli Aaron's house. Police tape still hung but the cops had long departed. The dogs had traced near a hundred acres along with a specialist team that pulled three bodies from their fitful rest.

He stood small on the charr, the structure broken down, coarser, erodible, and repellent to the water it would need to recover. Saint was glad there would be no life at all there again.

"To find Grace, we need to find out how he chose her. And how he chose Misty. And the others," Patch said.

He pulled paper from his bag and held it up.

Saint stared at it.

"This is a picture of the rosary beads," he said. He had stolen it when he cleaned the police station.

She looked at the fine detail. The metal blues, the pardon crucifix. The beads larger at intervals, the marbling flowers so beautiful she knew they had been hand painted. She squinted but could not make out the exact saint or the engraving.

"Can I keep it?" she said.

She would later take it to the library and trawl archives and find nothing.

The house was gone. The barns still stood in a

crescent of growth untouched, and Saint did not want to follow but did not want to leave him.

"I didn't say thank you," he said.

"You didn't have to."

He stuck his head through a tear in lofting panels and saw nothing at all because the cops had removed near everything.

He climbed through and she followed, and soot marked her pants.

They scooped through debris.

Saint knelt and saw the rotting papers, the ink bleeding from rainfall and the fire hoses. The pages of books, the spines still intact. She made out odd words. **History. Art. Guide.**

"You think Eli Aaron is alive?" Saint said.

"Yes. Otherwise, Grace would have found me by now."

69

They came to the first grave maybe five hundred yards from the house, the land excavated and not replaced.

Patch knelt beside it.

Saint sat cross-legged on beds of silver-backed leaves. "Elk Rock, Roberts Creek, and Cordova Park. Thousands of acres we cannot even begin to map," she said.

"I wonder about this dead girl that was buried here."

"And around that is another thousand acres, and a couple roads. And a million places to hide."

"She would have had friends, favorite things. Maybe she kept bees," he said, and Saint smiled before realizing it was not said for her.

He tugged at the neck of his T-shirt.

"And I'm not just talking about our parks . . . our states," she said.

He looked at the grave, dug out far and deeper,

the sides stone, a sepulcher that no longer held its intended.

"Nix tells me to just stop. To just get on . . ." Patch began.

"I'm not—"

"Eli Aaron knew, right? He knew where she came from and where she was headed. I don't belong here anymore. I don't belong . . ." his words buried beneath the call of a goldfinch.

"People say . . . the world . . . it's wide open for us. But maybe you're closing it, Patch. You're blocking routes till there's only one left, and it doesn't lead anyplace good."

"I remember things. Sometimes in the middle of the night I remember something she said, and then I can't sleep after. Could be it's something that will lead me to her."

"Tell me and I'll note it down. I'll collate everything you have. I'm good at . . . being organized," she said, and sighed to herself.

"Tell me you believe she's real."

She thought of the way he described her. The long hair, the short hair. The voices. That there was no trace at all. "I believe she's real."

He dropped his head into his hands and buried himself so totally she reached out but could not bring her hand down onto his skin so let it hover just above, feeling the heat of his desperation. She wanted to see him smile at her again. She needed it.

Saint knew right then she was in trouble.

The same kind he was in. The kind they would likely never be free of.

"I saw you with Misty," she said, and God did she try and keep her tone neutral as she took her sneaker off and shook a stone free.

"She feeds me cake and rice and some kind of stew. She talks about veal bones and tofu and all kinds of shit I never heard of."

"She likes you."

"You haven't tasted it."

Saint wanted to go rockhounding, to dazzle him with Druzy quartz while he hunted galena, because in the right light he said it shone like pirate treasure. She wanted to sit beside him and watch Mister Rogers and Lady Aberlin, and Joe Negri show his accordion. And freeze when he tagged her, locking so still that after a while he'd poke her till she cracked. She wanted him to be a pirate once more.

"And now she wants me to go to her goddamn mansion house for dinner."

"My grandmother said you can come eat with us . . . even Sundays when she does the lamb." Despite where they were, and what lay around them, Saint still felt herself flush.

"I don't know how to . . . the Meyers. They'll say thank you, but I'm not sure what that means."

"It means you did a good thing, and sometimes in life you need to be reminded of the good things you do. Because if you forget—"

"Nix said you sat in the station every day so the cops wouldn't forget."

She fussed with her braid and did not look at him as she ran her tongue over her snaggletooth.

He reached out and covered her hand with his, and she exhaled like she'd been holding that breath a year.

"If it hadn't gone exactly the way it did then people might not know about Grace and that she's entirely brilliant and that she deserves to be spoken of and that she deserves to be found."

"Do you love her?" Saint asked, her small body tensed.

The question hung there.

The air cauterized.

He did not answer.

70

He took books from the small library in Pecaut. **Modern Art; Cityscapes; Realizing Portrait.** He studied them on buses.

The 74 took him to Lewisville, where he walked Main Street and placed his posters on each of the streetlamps. One time he tried to tape one to the white-washed windows of an old barber shop but drew angry words from a local cop. The guy softened when he saw the drawing; in this one Patch had made her hair lighter and her jaw softer. His posters listed the phone number of the Monta Clare PD. Chief Nix bitched about the number of calls they received from time wasters. Patch would have put down his own number, but the letters turned so red the people at Southwestern Bell finally cut them loose.

He rode the 50 to Le Masco, Saint beside him as they plastered the town.

Three buses to Afton, a township of no more than

a couple of hundred homes, some of them trailers. Rusting bottles of gas threatened to topple as they knocked wafer-thin doors and were met with blank stares.

He traveled alone to Saddlers Clay and Lenard Creek, Newton Bale, and near a dozen colonies. He shaded parts of a map so large he could no longer bear to unfold it fully.

"You know my granddaughter didn't sleep while you were gone." Norma skirted a pothole.

"I know."

"I'm guessing you also know she skipped school the other afternoon. She's all heart. Makes it easier for her to get it broken," Norma said.

"I know that, too."

"I'm not sure that you do," she said, and it was not unkind.

A small radio played Sinatra, the only music she allowed on the bus.

Norma dropped him at the corner of Loess Hills. "I'll swing by here at four."

"That's not on the return route," the old man behind said.

Norma scowled. "It's my bus and I'll take it where I please. And if that doesn't please you then maybe walking will."

In the town of Darby Falls he stood on the doorstep of the Montrose house. Richie Montrose let him in, and Patch followed him into a tired living room where a television played baseball and a couple of dozen empty beer cans made a tower beside it.

Richie sat and through red eyes looked up at Patch with a little confusion and disinterest. Patch saw his uniform laid over a chair, his belt and badge, his hat on the floor.

"You're the kid that keeps calling me?"

Patch nodded.

"You think you were held with my Callie?"

"There's a chance."

"I have to hope that you're wrong. I have to hope she . . . that this man didn't take her." Richie did not tear his eyes from the game.

"Can I take a look in her bedroom?" Patch said.

"Upstairs first door on the left. Don't touch nothing."

Pink drapes and bedcover, and a carpet burnt orange. Patch stood in the center beneath a low-hanging lampshade and looked at the order and the dresser and the posters tacked to the wall. Bowie and Hendrix and no one he could recall Grace mentioning. On her bookshelf was a framed photo, and he stared at her face and tried to recognize the shape of her, the flat of her forehead, the arch of her eyebrows.

Are you her?

He breathed deep and wondered if he would recall her. Her skin and hair and sometimes her sweat.

And then he heard it.

Patch walked down the stairs slow.

Richie Montrose was slumped in his chair, and in the corner the old record player spun.

Patch stood in the doorway.

And listened to the bass-baritone of Johnny Cash.

71

At school Misty delivered a goulash laced with steak so tough he worked a piece most of the afternoon, his jaw aching as she bent his ear about her technique, and how she'd likely open her own restaurant in the city. "Caraway seeds," she said, as if answering a question he had not asked. "I crush them by hand, no tools even needed."

He picked a large seed from his teeth.

Dinner with her parents loomed like an eighteen-wheeler on the narrowest highway.

Misty stared at the Graces, growing in number and detail and finesse. A boy possessed, he sat on his log sheltered from the rain as he smoothed out her skin with his pencil.

He fished something white from the stew and made a show of smacking his lips. "What kind of cheese is this?"

"It's turkey."

He dipped his head.

"It's payment," she said, running a brush though her thick mane of blonde hair. "For saving my life."

"I think we're even now. I mean . . . the goulash was real good. And the cake. And that thing with the fish heads—"

"So technically you owe me now."

He got home to find Dr. Tooms sitting in his kitchen.

"Where's my—"

"Sleeping," Dr. Tooms said.

Patch took the seat opposite and told the doctor he was fine. Tooms offered that sad smile, and Patch wondered what had happened to the man while he was gone. His bright eyes now dull and circled by dark. His shirt hung from his bones, and his fingers drummed the table like he could not relax.

"I'm worried about you."

"I'm fine," Patch said.

"I just . . . I wondered if the memories are coming back to you yet?" Tooms watched him with intent, his dark eyes fixed on Patch like he was seeking a tell, something that would show him the kid was drowning.

"Memories?"

"If you can remember more about the man."

Patch shrugged. "I mean, it's Eli Aaron, right? But I never saw him. I never even heard him."

Tooms sighed, then spoke of the therapy, of eating right and maybe taking gentle exercise.

"I've seen your posters in town," Tooms said. "I'll put one in the practice."

Tooms stood, tall, and moved to leave, but then stopped close to him. "You got out, Joseph. I worry you still haven't realized that."

Patch turned and saw his mother in the doorway, confusion marring her face till she placed the doctor. She shook a cigarette from her pack and offered him one, but Tooms shook his head, told her he'd never smoked but did not say it like a warning.

"This girl, you have no idea who she is," Tooms said.

"I didn't. But now maybe I do," Patch said.

"This girl . . ." Ivy said and tousled her hair.

"Tell me," Tooms said, leaning closer to Patch.

"I think she could be Callie Montrose. If I . . . could I have been unconscious a long time?"

Tooms smiled, his face written with pain, his eyes filled with so much Patch could not understand.

"I need a script. I'm running low on Quaaludes." Ivy cupped Patch's face gently.

Patch turned to Tooms but saw he was already out the door.

He did not look back.

72

That night he cleaned, so tired his body fought each movement with all it had, locking his muscles till they ached. He made it to the gallery at three. His back ached as he dropped to his knees and scrubbed the wood. And then he noticed a book on a glass table in the center of the room. Heavy and large, he flipped the pages, stopping at a woman lying on her back in water, one hand clutching wildflowers. Patch stared, mesmerized. The willows and nettles, the shades of green, the shape of her skull.

"Ophelia. You read **Hamlet** at school?" Sammy said.

Sammy wore brogues, no socks, his ankles tan. His trousers were tight, like the waistcoat. And beneath that a kind of necktie Patch had only seen in a book. In the right light, which was actually very dim, Patch decided the man could pass for a pirate. Perhaps a corsair, a privateer from the port of Saint Malo.

"No," Patch said.

"You even go to school?"

Patch said nothing.

They both turned as a woman walked down the stairs, slightly flushed. She clutched a handbag to herself.

"I'll be leaving then," she said, and smiled at Sammy.

"Your carriage awaits," Sammy said, and outside a taxi idled.

Patch watched her leave slow, like she was waiting on more.

"You won't clean here again," Sammy said as the door closed.

"I was just looking at—"

Sammy stared into the drink he held as he spoke on an exhale, like the disappointment almost matched the lack of surprise. "You can't steal from me, kid. You ever hear of honor among thieves?"

Patch stood there, the mop behind him, the bucket beside his sneaker. He wore a black eye patch, a T-shirt dogged with holes. "You're the only one I didn't . . . I didn't take nothing from."

"Locals would likely have it I'm duty bound to protect Monta Clare small business. I don't much give a fuck about anyone else. I look after myself and my interests and have done since I wasn't all that much older than you. I learned a hard lesson, yours will be easier."

"What did I take?"

"A ream of paper. You researched it, found out the

quality and the cost. Took something you thought I wouldn't notice. The skinny girl, the lesbian's granddaughter. She has it you're a pirate."

"I'm not a pirate."

Sammy softened a little, his shoulders sagging as he finished his drink. "Whatever you are, you're not my problem anymore."

"Will you tell the agency?"

"I have to."

Patch picked up the bucket and emptied it into the small sink beside the toilet. His mind ran to the bills, to the money that would be missed. His mother would take the call, find out she'd been fired from a job she had not been well enough to work. Maybe the last bridge burned. His stomach knotted tight.

"Most men find themselves at a crossroads at least once in their life."

"Fuck you," Patch said. He stopped by the door, opened his bag and pulled out the heavy paper he'd taken, the sketches of Grace on each sheet.

He threw them toward Sammy and did not stay to watch the fragments of his memory float down.

73

He found himself at St. Raphael's and stopped by the narthex. Hours from sunset and sunrise he felt as close to her when the town slept as he ever did. Right then as he stood in footprints of penitents he let the exhaustion and thorough failure lead him into the building that did not ever lock its doors. Patch could not understand such careless trust.

Candles burned, and the silence was a weight so familiar he drifted to the front bench and sat and contemplated asking for help when he looked across and noticed the man parallel.

"Dr. Tooms," Patch said.

The doctor knelt awhile longer and only when he had finished his business with God did he stand and walk over and settle close beside Patch.

He smelled of chard and metal, and his boyish face was drawn.

"You were praying," Patch said.

"I was."

"Is there a priest here?"

Tooms shook his head.

Patch said, "If I confess every bad thing to God . . ."

"Then you will still have done them, and they will still be bad."

"I don't want forgiveness." Patch looked at the altarpiece, at the relief of golds and creams and the sainted windows.

"So what do you want?"

"Help."

Tooms smiled like he knew of that ask and what the answer would likely be.

"When I was down there we quoted scripture to stay alive," Patch said. "And I repeat it back to myself, but it seems so vague."

"Some say the translation isn't literal. It's a set of rough guidelines that don't always fit."

"I fucked up, Dr. T," Patch said, desperate.

"Most people that come to church have."

"I don't know how to make it better."

"It's not your job to fix things, Joseph."

He thought of the sanctuary bells, how they rang during the liturgy, and people knew to focus on that part, to block out everything else.

"Why are you here now?" Patch said.

"To ask forgiveness for acts I know in my heart I will commit again."

Patch watched him awhile though the doctor seemed at peace. He wore smart shoes crusted with mud. His shirt carried a small tear along the seam.

"But you still ask," Patch said.

Tooms stared at the cross. "And he still ignores."

74

Saint helped Patch pick out clothes from the box of his father's things.

She looked away as he stripped from his T-shirt, his arms crossing loosely over his front, guarding the scene. In the window she caught the reflection of him, of the scar still risen, of a history carved so deep she had stopped trying to compete, instead gradually working to bring all of him home. She wrote the Federal Missing Persons Unit in Nebraska. The National Center for Missing Persons in Texas. She sat on the landing in the tall house when her grandmother drove the buses and dialed the Aileen Plattas Foundation in Arkansas, and she told the lady all she had, which was close to nothing at all. She found more agencies with large titles in the library and soon realized none of them was accredited or official, rather just small factions of society lost, trying to keep memories and hope alive as they collated information and shared it with police departments across the country.

"You don't have to be here," he said.

He did not notice that she wore a new tunic, the chevrons the same brown as her eyes.

"You're nervous," Saint said, her deflection accurate enough.

"I'm not wearing a tie," he said.

She tossed him a bright red bowtie.

He slipped it on and rolled back his shirt cuffs, and his hair fell over his eye. She took a little of his father's pomade and smoothed it back.

"I look like a greasy magician," he said.

"Like there's another kind."

She fixed the knot of his bowtie like her grandfather had once shown her.

"I missed you, Saint. When I was gone. I missed you."

She turned from him, so that he would not see how long she had waited for those words.

They walked together to the brim of Main Street, and in the Green's Convenience Store she chose a peach bouquet and paid for it with the dwindling honey money she had once hidden too well.

"I don't want to do this," he said.

"Don't steal from the rich folk," she said.

She watched the reluctance of him moving between tulip poplars that curved up and toward the big houses.

"I like your blouse."

She turned to see Jimmy Walters. He wore a smart

shirt and slacks, his hair brutally parted by a mother Saint had once seen clean his cheek with her spit on a handkerchief.

"I don't see you much now Joseph is back," he said.

Saint nodded.

"I prayed for it," he said quiet.

"I did too, Jimmy."

She stole a look at him, his eyes too blue and earnest, like he had never seen anything bad at all. Right then she longed to look at the world through his lens, certain it was simpler and purer, and easier to see everything good.

"I never said thank you," she said.

He faced her, and she noticed his eyelashes were as dark as his hair, his skin as pale as her own.

"For what?" he said.

She watched the cupid's bow of his lip as he spoke, noticed the finest hairs above it.

"That day . . . if you hadn't told Nix where I was headed."

"Then you would have handled it just fine without him."

She smiled at the lie, felt a surge of gratitude as he turned and left her.

She walked back to the tall house and changed into her dungarees and painted her face with greens and browns and blacks, and she felt the cling of her childhood as she waded through the thicket and took her place on a heavy blanket in the long grass.

Saint looked through the lens of her Nikon and watched the Tooms house.

She thought of Patch.

Each day she lost more of him.

75

Patch might've turned back but saw Misty standing at the foot of a winding driveway, the looming of a white colonial pressing him into the shade.

She wore a simple red dress, and on another day in another life she would have slayed him dead right there on the street.

Misty didn't look him up and down or notice his bowtie and creased shirt and slacks that shone at each knee.

He held out the flowers and she took them.

"She's been out here an hour worried you wouldn't show."

"Mom," Misty said, shooting her mother a look.

Mrs. Meyer was tall and severe and walked straight over to Patch and shook his hand lightly. And then she appraised him in a way her daughter had not.

"Do you like flowers, Joseph?" she said, as she led him toward the house.

She talked of yarrow and milkweed and cone-flowers. Pointed at an area she'd lost to ironweed. The borders bloomed with summer colors too bright for that fall evening, like the Meyers were rich enough to see them year-round, like they did not know the pallor of winter from their spot so high above.

Patch kept his eye on everything Mrs. Meyer pointed out, listened to stories of trees with diseases they'd brought back from the brink so they could preserve the landscape of the oldest house in town.

Mr. Meyer met them at the door and pumped Patch's hand too hard, like in that simple act he was trying to convey that he too would've taken a knife in the gut for the life of a girl that had not even known his name.

Franklin Meyer stood six two and wore cream slacks and a shirt opened three buttons. He looked Patch up and down but kept that smile on his face, his teeth large and white.

Mrs. Meyer dragged Misty into the kitchen to search out a vase as Franklin led Patch through to a formal living room.

He handed him a glass of something brown, and Patch drank and almost choked at the burn.

"Don't tell Mary I gave you this." That smile again, and Patch wondered if he could keep it going the whole evening before the muscles failed and drooped like the rich man was having a stroke.

In a dining room of heavy drapes and silk wall hangings, maple chairs and leaden china, Patch suffered through five courses, now and then looking to Misty to see exactly how you went about eating a lobster. He picked at it lightly, not wanting to fire out hot butter and take out an antique.

Misty talked of swim meets and track while her parents orbited him, Franklin aiming for sports, Mary floating the arts like she knew nothing of her audience. **Tristan und Isolde, Otello,** and **Tosca.**

"Misty wants to go into politics," Franklin said matter-of-factly.

"Because you were so proud when I campaigned for Jane Roe," Misty fired back, then turned to Patch and smiled. "I made the front page of **The Tribune.**"

"That's religion, not politics," Mrs. Meyer said.

"Yeah, I forgot. Which church did **Roe v. Wade** play out in?" Misty said.

Mrs. Meyer turned to Patch, asked if he'd ever been to Chicago or Boston, drank another glass of wine, and dabbed the heat from her cheeks with a napkin when he said he had not left the state.

Patch asked about **Swan Lake,** and Prince and Odette.

Mrs. Meyer lit up, took his hand and led him into yet another room where she rummaged in the drawer of an oak desk.

"New York State Theater, near six years back now." She found a small paper program and handed it to him.

"Cynthia Gregory was divine, though of course Franklin found her uninspiring."

Patch looked at the image, at the bold type and the running order. "Will they have a list of people that bought tickets?"

"I shouldn't think so," Mrs. Meyer said, still looking in the drawer. "I kept the stub . . . such wonderful memories."

She moved on to Dr. Coppélius and spoke of Franz and his toy girl, but Patch heard none of it, his mind instead finding Grace.

"And at the end, when they're reunited in death, you'll be the first to stand and clap and whistle."

She took command of his every thought.

76

Misty led him out into a yard that did not appear to have boundaries, just ran on forever, like they did not know limits of any kind.

There was a covered pool and a flowered pagoda and stone seats that faced a sculptured woman without arms. The two settled onto swings in the moonlit shadow of lush mountains beyond.

Her sandals lay in the grass, her calves gently flexed as she moved. He imagined the kind of parties they threw and the kind of boys she dated. He did not hate them, just did not dare to try and understand them.

"You want to come see me at dressage one time?" she said.

"I'm not sure what that is."

"I make my horse dance."

"Why?"

She shrugged and they sat quiet for a long time. "It's hard, right?"

"It's a dancing horse, Mist. Ain't going to be easy going against nature like that."

She shook her head. "I mean this part, the afterwards."

He did not tell her it had been hard before, just in a different, more manageable way.

"I never saw my father cry," she said.

He watched the geometric shapes of her, the cones and spheres and cylinders, and he wondered which might also belong to Grace.

"That day when they came to the police station and he saw my face . . . and then later, when they thought I was sleeping because Dr. T gave me all those pills. I sat on the stairs and watched his shoulders shake as my mother pressed her cheek to his back."

He said nothing because he knew that his role had already been played.

"It wasn't anything, Patch. Not compared . . ."

Her perfect world might've once cracked but was not close to broken. Right then he was glad. "You've done it now, Misty. You reached out and I'm grateful and all . . ."

"But?"

She had infinity to lose.

"Each time you come sit with me. Talk to me. Notice me. It's just a reminder that things aren't right with your world."

She shook her head.

Paint that clung beneath his nails.

"So what do I do?" she said, her voice holding.

"You eat lobster. And you sit on your swing."

She looked over, so beautiful. "And then?"

He stopped swinging. "And then you go on back to your side of the street, Misty."

Patch thanked the Meyers. And he told Misty good night.

And he knew that on Monday, when he sat on the fallen oak, she would not come and sit beside him.

77

Patch leaned on the bricked arches and clutched the paper program and traced a finger over the lettering.

Swan Lake.

He knew that Grace traveled, that she was cultured enough to go see ballets, educated enough to know about almost everything. That kind of girl goes missing and she leaves a void. He knew there'd be a record, parents and friends and a school.

He saw one of his posters on the noticeboard alongside wanted ads, the offers of piano lessons and gardening services, handyman services and a room to rent. The writing already bleached by the sun, the number of the Monta Clare PD so faded he could not read the last two digits.

He didn't feel the man beside him until he was dragged off.

"Follow," Sammy said, the word a labor.

Into the iced gallery air.

Inside a white office Sammy took his place behind

a desk strewn with the paper Patch had taken from him, smoothed out till he could see each sketch.

Sammy regarded him for a moment, frowned at his shirt, then his bowtie. "You've been practicing magic?"

Patch silently cursed Saint.

"These sketches . . . ," Sammy said, resting a hand on his stomach, the curls in his hair neat over green eyes. "You did these?"

"I thought maybe you might put one in the window," Patch said.

"Or I could just smear human shit on the glass. You're a problem, kid." His teeth were straight and white, his nails shined like he visited a salon. He smelled faintly of cologne, and ginger and mulled cider. Patch looked him in the eye and saw nothing but confidence, of acceptance and a violent self-belief.

"Maybe. But I'm not your problem," Patch said.

Sammy rolled his eyes quick, a move Patch guessed was forced on him often.

"You know about me?" Sammy said.

He had once asked Norma about Sammy when they rode the bus.

"People either drink like that to remember or to forget. I'd say both are true in Sammy's case."

"People say you're a drunk."

"I am."

"And a cad."

"You even know what a cad is?"

Patch shook his head.

"A cad is a gentleman cunt."

"I could see that," Patch said, and Sammy almost smiled.

Laid out were a selection of brushes.

Sammy picked one up. "Kolinsky Sable. The perfect backbone in the rarest of fibers. It will hold oil as well in fifty years as it does today. Wish I could say the same about your hair, kid."

Patch silently cursed Saint again.

Sammy selected another. "A filbert." And then another. "Cat's tongue." He waved a hand over the line. "A bright, a liner, two riggers, and a round. An assortment of sizes, you'll use a six for the finest of hair, a fourteen for swathes of skin."

Sammy flipped the latch on a pocked cedar box and turned it to face Patch.

"Sennelier oils. There is a store beside the Musée d'Orsay, favored by Matisse and Ernst and Monet and Picasso himself. Non-yellowing safflower oil, they will sit on canvas for a hundred years without fade or shine. They will be entirely wasted on you."

Patch said nothing.

"Old Holland canvas." Sammy picked up a small stack and dropped it onto the desk with a light thump. "One hundred percent Belgian linen. Two coats of gesso. Some will tell you the three-ply

Daveliou is superior. But then some will also tell you to go to church each Sunday." Sammy filled his glass to the brim.

"For portraits you'll paint with oil. On canvas. Under natural light. Hog brushes. Ventilation. Turpentine if you want to gas me . . ."

"I definitely want to—"

". . . Walnut oil if you don't. Linseed if you must."

Patch rummaged in his bag for paper to make notes. As he did he dropped his brushes to the floor.

Sammy inspected them like they were entirely foreign. "You use these for cleaning drains, yes?"

"Did you say turpentine seeds?"

"Jesus. I have display easels that will be adequate. And a room behind this one. Northern light. The diffusion is everything, you may come to learn that, or you may produce the same dogshit as you would under five thousand k. Time will tell."

"I don't understand," Patch said.

"You'll paint here."

Patch shook his head. "I'm not taking—"

"You will not take. These are loaned. At some point you'll ply a trade, likely in some kind of factory or pit, and you will settle your debt, of which I will keep exhaustive note. A real man settles his debts."

"I can't—"

"Did I ask you a question?"

Patch shook his head.

Sammy walked out and Patch followed.

He unlocked a door hidden behind a large sculpture, a jagged piece of rock fifteen feet tall, its face a curve of smooth dark.

Inside, the room was white. The floor and walls and ceiling. Empty but for a single easel. No stool. Nothing beyond a window, lightly screened by some kind of paper.

"I will give you a single key. You'll work here when the mood takes you. You will not speak to me or anyone who visits. You will leave the studio in this condition. You will place your belongings in a small locker I will provide."

Patch looked around. "Why are you doing this? Why didn't you tell the agency I stole?"

Sammy leaned in the doorway, and for a moment looked at Patch like he knew him, like he knew the quiet agony of each passing minute. And then he shook it off, glanced past him and let his eyes settle on the promised girl. "Each day I take a walk up Parade Hill to remind myself why I didn't leave this nothing town a lifetime before. You saved the Meyer girl. And for that I will always be grateful. You want to find your Grace?"

Patch nodded.

"Bring her to life then."

78

"Will you come find me?" Grace said.

"I won't have to. We'll walk out of this place together. And we won't leave each other's side. Because no one will realize. No one will know like we know."

"They'll think they do, Patch. They'll think they can imagine it. And they'll tilt their heads to one side in sympathy. They'll make us see shrinks who've sat in fancy libraries in fancy universities and read stories like ours. They'll reference Charcot and Freud, and William James and Pierre Janet. They'll read the same books I do. And they'll draw the same conclusions. Eventually."

He took her hand. "What conclusions?"

"That people like us exist in a state of crisis. That it will be a miracle if we die of natural causes. We'll turn to drink or drugs, and we won't form close relationships because we'll keep too much from others."

"We don't need anyone else," he said.

"**We do. You just don't realize it yet. Unhealthy pursuits. We'll exist at the extremes because the middle is where the healthy pass their time.**"

"**Will we be okay?**" he asked, and could not stop the words from leaving his lips.

"**Not one part of us.**"

The memory veered him from a light sleep.

His stomach was hollow. Exhaustion cloaked him. He knew he could not keep it going much longer. Something vital would break.

He used his key and pushed the door and half expected the call of an alarm. Sammy lived in the apartment above, and Patch was light enough on his feet.

In the back room he turned on a small lamp and saw the restored industrial storage locker and inside found the oils and brushes, and in the center of the room was the easel, and a canvas lying in wait.

He spent an hour growing familiar.

He wore logger boots because though they were two sizes too large, they were close to new. He stuffed the toes with newspaper to cut the slip, and wrapped both heels with cotton to stave off the blistering. The day before he had walked eleven fruitless miles through Ellis County to a trailer park because he read it did not have power nor telephone lines and he figured they ought to know a girl was missing out there.

A light dew clung to the glass as he found a flat

pencil and began to sketch. The paper was thick, and he felt each mark forge. His hand shook as he clutched the brush.

"Hold from the end."

Sammy stood in last night's suit and shirt and tie and watched him but said nothing more.

An hour later Patch saw a woman pass and linger at the door before stepping into the street where she threw a longing glance at the upstairs balcony before leaving.

"Was that the Sampson widow?" Patch asked as Sammy descended.

"I heard a rumor she fucked her last husband to death," Sammy said, shirtless and barefoot. He carried a wine bottle, green against his tanned skin.

"Was it true?"

"Well, I'm still here, aren't I? If I'm honest I'm a little disappointed."

"I think most of the town is."

Patch had painted eight strokes in browns and reds. Her hair burnt. He thinned with acetone and circled Grace's eyes. He darkened the soft lines with ochre, titanium white over before he momentarily lost her.

He turned and paced before blocking the window with sheeting he found in a small closet. Only when the dark was total did he stop and find her again.

He heard the door open and then close, and when he finally pulled the sheet down and went back to work he noticed a small cup of coffee on the floor. He drank it down and his heart raced for the next two hours.

At the window he saw the steel fire escape from the building beside, the ironwork chewed with rust, and he took that color and made her hair.

He used the paint too sparingly.

He knew it was madness.

All of it madness.

He cursed.

"Patience," Sammy said from the doorway.

"I don't have the time for it."

79

Over three weeks his Grace emerged.

Sammy came and went, one time told him of Caravaggio in the early hours of the morning, speaking into his brandy as though he were reciting a play to a captive audience of one. A new woman came, and Sammy sent her upstairs and stayed with Patch, who worked as he listened, from sketch to engraving, from Caravaggio at work to his hedonistic evening.

The next night, another woman was ignored as Sammy told Patch of Frans Hals.

"And with those same hands he would later go home and beat his wife."

And Paul Gauguin.

"To hold absinthe as a day drink and keep wine for the evenings." Patch noticed the note of awe in Sammy's voice.

Each time a little more competent, each stroke still deemed an insult to the canvas, a shame to the brushes used to create it. Sammy drank no matter the time or day, once finishing four bottles of wine before an evening showing, so drunk he took to his bed as the cluster of visitors formed their own line in the street, waited an hour in the rain before retreating, muttering their curses.

And, when Sammy thought he was progressing, Patch took the canvas and tore it in half.

"It's not her. It's still not her."

Through a mild fall and into a heavy winter that smothered all but the color in that small room, Patch settled into a life of stringent purpose. He would sleep in the studio on a small sofa that had appeared a day into the New Year, a heavy blanket and light pillow folded neatly atop it. Sammy did not mention the new arrangement, and Patch made sure to be a ghost around the building, not disturbing the lady callers. Some nights his mother noticed and he told her he was staying at Saint's. Most nights she did not.

He trudged the ice through January, shook snow from himself like a wet dog before he removed his boots and worked in his stockinged feet for a couple of hours before and after school. His fingers taped where the brushes left them so raw he could barely hold his pen.

He passed Misty in the hallway, their eyes met, and he would fight the urge to let her know that he thought of her often, that he was glad when he saw her running track, or laughing with her friends, or even that she seemed to have made things up with Chuck. He would be a small scratch in the record of her life, no longer deep enough to alter the perfect rhythm.

He took weekend walks with Saint. She would show at the house with plates of food and tell him she was heading across the Baker fields because she wanted to photograph the frosted crop lines. They would walk mostly in silence, though sometimes she would tell him how she wanted her grandmother to stop driving buses after a minor collision at the apex of Masterton Avenue. Patch did not notice when she wore a light shade of lipstick or a new coat, or curled her hair. He did not notice that she wore a retainer, new glasses with a lighter frame, that she'd grown two inches, that she finally had call to wear a bra.

In the first folds of spring Sammy told him he would need to quit the cleaning and begin helping around the gallery. His tone left little room for negotiation, and one week later Patch was given new slacks, a couple of smart shirts, and a pair of polished wingtips. The debt deepened, though in the immediate term he was able to cover the rent and the bills. Sammy bought a small grill and would barbecue fine cuts of meat on the balcony, seasoning with saffron and cardamom and insisting Patch take dinner with him, pretending not to notice when the boy wrapped cutlets in napkins to sneak home for his mother.

Sometimes Saint showed at the gallery and stood

by the window, hoping to glimpse him inside till Sammy scared her away with a narrow stare.

"That girl," he said, and Patch did not understand at all.

Sammy took a trip to Cuba the week after the ban was lifted, brought back a case of cigars and a deeper tan, and told Patch of a collision of old and new. "Salsa dancing, kid. I tell you, my cock didn't soften the entire trip."

In the darkened room Patch breathed turpentine until his nose ran slightly and his head craved the cold and fresh air. Sometimes he made coffee for the visiting women and would sit with them.

"Does Sammy talk about me?" a young blonde asked, her smoky eyes expectant.

"All the time," Patch said, as he caught Sammy descending the stairs, seeing the blonde's presence and quickly retreating.

"Do you know if he wants to marry someday?"

Patch nodded. "And he talks about having children."

That last comment added a penalty charge of a hundred bucks to his tab.

Under that barbed tutelage Patch dry washed backgrounds, underpainted each tone of her skin, layered and lifted and bloomed and feathered. In his contouring Grace gained dimensions till her face floated clear of the canvas. He learned to sketch first with a heavy 4H pencil, from general to specific, difficult with his small rigger, but he gained in confidence and technique. He blocked in the dark values, burnt ember and cobalt, squinting as he worked, the light areas still untouched, her skin cooled with feathered pigments. He glossed her hair by leaving a lighter wash visible, loose and gestural, and she emerged from the night with a vagary that took his breath away, sometimes a stranger and sometimes so exacting, so perfectly **her** he would turn his back and leave and lock the door and not return for a day such was the agony.

There was no praise from Sammy. His skill was nascent, but undeniable. Patch would not think of it as a gift. A gift was given. He ground his competence out. Slow and hard.

And then, as glimpses of summer blessed the town of Monta Clare, ten months and countless failures later, as Reggie Jackson slugged another into orbit on the small television, Sammy marched into the room and took the brush from Patch's hand.

"You're done," Sammy declared.

Patch stepped back and stared.

"Whether it's her or not," Sammy said. "This painting is complete."

80

Inside the small police station Sammy placed the painting on Nix's desk. "**Grace Number One.** Copy it."

Nix might have said something, might have unloaded the sheer madness of it all, but for the painting, when he glanced at it and it took all his attention so fully. In that harsh light he saw nothing drawn from imagination, a print so clear and forensically detailed it was like looking at a photograph. Had he not known of the haunted provenance, Nix might have guessed a young girl had sat for some aging master.

He did not move for a long time, transfixed as he stood and looked down at the face. "You did this?"

Patch nodded.

And beside him Sammy simply looked bored with the awe in the chief's eyes.

"It's her?" Nix said.

"**Grace Number One,**" Patch said.

Nix handled it with great care, hovered the heavy

lid of the old copier above it so as not to make contact.

Patch watched closely, knew the mechanics involved because he had read of powder imaging, negative charge, and photoconductors. When the machine spat out image after image, he held one up and was pleased with what remained.

Nix ran fifty copies.

"We'll circulate them. Send one to police departments in every state in the country," Patch said.

Sammy drew a small flask from his pocket and sipped from it.

"I'll do it," Nix said, still staring at the girl. "I'll make sure it gets where it needs to go."

Patch walked back into the gallery and sat, stared at his Grace and lost himself in the cleanest contours of her.

Misty appeared at the door, only noticed because her sweet perfume lilted over the chemical air and snapped Patch from his trance.

She stood there in a green dress, hair tucked back behind a white band among the littered corpses of near a hundred Graces.

Misty stood before the final canvas. "She's so . . . she's so beautiful."

He looked down at her feet buried beneath the lake of canvases.

"It should be on the wall . . . in the window or something. In a big gallery."

She knelt and picked up the lost girls and thumbed through them, the difference between each almost invisible, but Patch knew his circumspect progress would one day bring her closer, till he was certain he saw her before him, heard her voice and felt her fingertips fathom him entirely.

"There's so many," Misty said.

Last count Patch owed Sammy an even thousand bucks. Patch was not sure of the mathematics involved, only that an errant stroke could somehow add much to the tally.

He set the brush down gently and turned and finally saw the delicacies of the girl that stood beside him, the fine strokes and boldened shades. He saw Misty in mixes, her skin titanium and singed umber and alizarin. Her Prussian eyes. Her hair would be lain darks softened with sienna before light layering.

"I see you at school. And I miss you," she said.

He stared at her and saw cadmium steeled with Winsor Violet and Phthalo Blue.

"You look at me like no one else," she said, and her cheeks reddened.

In her hand was an envelope. She handed it to him and turned and left.

He stood in the doorway and watched her walk away.

Patch knew it then.

He could use each color he owned painting Misty Meyer, and they would still not come close enough.

81

They drove to the Castor River Shut-Ins, and through the lens of her Nikon Saint captured the pink granite. She bent her grandmother's ear about the formation as they watched a Saint Bernard wade out toward plunge pools so beautiful Saint drained a whole roll of film before they even made it to whitewater.

And there her grandmother took her hand and the two crossed the flat path through the Amidon Memorial Conservation Area. In the hardwood forest Norma slowed a little.

"How much do I need to worry about you?"

Saint looked up at her grandmother, and she saw the worry lines, the watery blue eyes, the fine hair graying more each day.

She changed film and shot shortleaf pine and moss and scrub oak. Beside lichen that glowed deep green her grandmother sighed.

"You can't save him," Norma said.

"I can."

Saint aimed her camera at water so clear she would later see the shadow of sculpin and smallmouth bass.

"Saint."

Saint finally lowered her lens. "I'm okay, Grandma."

"He leaves messages on our answering machine. Sometimes in the middle of the night. He rambles about a dream he's had, a line he remembered the girl saying."

"I told him he could. I'll keep the tapes and one day they'll lead me to her," Saint said.

"Lead you to her? You're . . . you don't smile anymore. Not in the same way. His life isn't yours."

Saint drew a deep breath. "He's my best . . ."

Norma looked on. "We'll come back for the wildflowers in spring."

"Why don't you like him?"

Norma closed her eyes. Some said she was severe, the way she cut her hair shorter, the awkward way she wore her height. Her slender arms carried muscle, and when Saint was small she would ask if one day she would be tall and strong and Norma told her yes.

"When I . . . if I look at him now, like I looked at him then, I don't see much the same, Saint. And I know he won't . . . and for you I want everything. And I can't be sorry for that."

"It's not fair," Saint said, sudden, abrupt. She did not want to cry and tried with all she had. "I notice pebbles and things he might like. But he doesn't like them anymore."

Norma watched the rushing chutes. "I ran into Dr. Tooms in town. He said he sees you out there, watching his house. Sometimes late into the evening."

"He lied that night," Saint said.

"He—"

"I heard a scream. I saw blood on his hands. And when Nix went back there, he'd washed them clean."

"You got the man, Saint. You saved your friend's life. You don't owe—"

"It's not about debt."

"In two years you'll go to college, and Christmas you'll come back and I will still be driving the bus. But I'll smile, each day I'll smile when I think of you out there. And I'll break a little when I think of Joseph, really I will. But you're mine. And he is not."

"He doesn't have anyone. He doesn't have enough."

"He's running a fool's errand. This girl isn't real. I see it in Nix's eyes, hell, I see it in your eyes."

Saint gripped her camera tight. "I'll find her for him."

"And you'll lose yourself in the process."

They drove back in silence.

Outside the tall house Saint found the invitation that had been left in their mailbox.

Saint looked up and down the street like she expected someone to jump from the neighboring yards and reveal the joke.

"What is it?" Norma said, as she took to her chair and watched the fume of distant smokestacks.

"Misty Meyer is turning sixteen. There's a party tonight."

Norma did not mention the eleventh hour, but then Saint knew an afterthought was still a thought.

"You'll go," Norma said.

"I don't have a nice dress."

"Joseph will be there."

Saint shook her head though she did not know. Their time was now spent solely on the hunt.

"You'll go, and if Joseph is there then I suppose you'll remind him."

Saint stared at the paper, at the fanciful lettering and the word **cordially.** "Remind him of what?"

Norma took her small hand and gripped it tight. "That he didn't lose everything when he was gone."

82

Outside a couple of girls in peasant blouses passed by.

Their hair fell in waves to flared jeans and dizzying heels, thickening the air with perfumes stolen from their mothers.

Patch sat on the curb beside his bag as a sun-dashed Monta Clare eased toward closing day. Boys along the sidewalk wore jackets and florid shirts, unbuttoned to slivers of pale skin, their hair mostly long.

A dozen signs spun in the breeze. Hanes Jewelry and Rewalt Autos; Braybart Coffee; the red, white, and blue of Pepsi-Cola. More girls in dresses smiling beside shell-shocked boys intent on making the night count in a way that both thrilled and terrified them.

Outside the Town Clerk's Office he leaned against the glassed floodplain map and stayed there until darkness fell totally and light from the church hall shone up.

In the pocket of his jeans was the invitation Misty

had delivered, his impromptu promise to attend a regret that stuck like a lump in his throat as the day neared.

He carried a small box, inside a snow globe he had seen in the window of a craft store as he postered the hamlet of Wellbray Creek. Inside the globe was a miniature snow-washed town so delicate and detailed Patch took to staring at it each night as he lay down to sleep. It had cost him a dollar. He lamented the waste.

In a cluster by the door Chuck's group passed around a small bottle of liquor. Inside streamers hung from rafters and neon balloons floated up toward a glitter ball that ricocheted chinks of light.

Groups of girls danced, their feet moving in unison, and right then he wondered just what he had missed. And what Grace would miss.

Patch had almost made it through the crowd when the box was snatched from his hands.

He heard laughter. Talk about his clothes, his old sneakers, the length of his pants. He tried to move forward but was blocked, tried to head back out but was shoved to the ground.

And for the coldest moment he felt his eye patch tugged from him.

That was when the laughter died, and maybe something in the way he looked up at them finally stopped it, and someone tossed it back to him. He quickly looped it over his head and pulled it into place.

And then the box was thrown toward him.
Patch heard the glass shatter as it hit the ground.
He stayed there kneeling as they left him.
Right then he longed to be back in the darkness.
Beside her.

83

Saint had spent an hour in Miss Kline's store on Main Street, the lady keeping the place open past business hours because she read the pleading in Norma's eyes as Saint disappeared into the fitting room with a cream corduroy puffed-sleeve midi dress.

"I look like a tartlet." Saint's voice came from behind the curtain.

Miss Kline fetched a watercolor house dress.

"I can turn up looking like the birthday girl's mother. That would be nice."

An abstract red psychedelic print.

"I feel a little nauseous."

And, finally, a red and blue maxi dress with a deep V neckline.

"Do you also sell tits to fill this thing out?"

Miss Kline glanced at Norma, who gazed longingly at the door.

They settled on a black floral dress with white collar.

Saint paraded back at the tall house.

"It's a little long," Norma said, as Saint gathered handfuls of material to keep it from dragging on the floor.

"I'm a little short," Saint fired back, in no kind of mood.

Saint rummaged through her grandmother's makeup box and scowled. "I think these have gone bad."

"Makeup is like wine," Norma began, stopping when Saint held up a separation of foundation from 1955.

Ten minutes later Norma fetched Mrs. Harris from across the street. Saint took in the woman's beehive, powder-blue eyes, and industrial makeup box and shot her grandmother a panicked look.

"Relax. Mrs. Harris does the dressing for Mr. Nathaniel," Norma said.

Saint's eyes widened in horror. "Mr. Nathaniel . . . from Monta Clare Funeral Parlor?"

Mrs. Harris pushed her back into a chair with a heavy hand. "If I can bring a corpse back to life, I can handle you."

"And the freak show is complete," Saint said.

"You want me to do something with this braid?"

"Yes. Leave it the fuck alone."

"This is why I don't work with the living."

Twenty minutes and a couple of curse words later and Saint walked down the stairs. Her grandmother took a dozen photos as Saint fought the urge to flip the camera off.

84

She drew looks at the party as she skirted the edge of the dance floor, found the gift table, and set hers down. A pink sweater she'd knitted while he was gone, the pattern a little large for her, so would likely be a little small for Misty.

"Is he here?"

Saint turned as Misty stunned her into silence in a white dress that skimmed her knees, and matching heels. Her nails were painted, her hair piled in curls, her eyes touched with the lightest shadow that told Saint the girl had likely not been beautified by a corpse handler.

"I don't know," Saint said.

Misty looked around, drawing looks from every boy in their year, and most of the girls.

"Happy birthday," Saint said.

Misty smiled but it was empty. "So he didn't come with you?"

Saint shook her head. And then she got it. And

as she did, she felt the air leave the church hall. She knew then why Misty had invited her.

"Don't take him," Saint said, and she felt the flush in her body, the shame of her words.

Misty looked down at her.

"I know how that sounds. But you . . . you can have, you already have everyone." Saint watched the flash of lights and looked across at Misty's grand family.

"I'm not sure what you—"

"Please, Misty. If it's pity, if it's some kind of obligation, then . . ."

She did not get to finish what she started because the music slowed and as the guitar strummed Chuck grabbed Misty's hand and tugged her toward the center of the floor, where she belonged.

And through the open doors Saint saw him, slowly walking away from them.

If she had her time over, she might've called out, but standing there in her dress and makeup she felt so foolish she could do nothing but look on as Misty shoved Chuck away and stepped out into the warm evening air.

"You look beautiful."

Saint turned to see Jimmy. He wore a blazer and slacks, his father's tie.

"I didn't think you'd be here," she said.

He shrugged. "My mom knows the Meyers."

She turned.

"Saint. Would you like to dance?"

She shook her head.

Jimmy smiled, and it was warm and kind. "When Joseph was gone . . . and I told you that I prayed for him . . . I wanted him to come back safe, of course. But as much as that, I wanted you to be okay. I needed it."

"Why?" she said.

He kept his blue eyes on hers, this time did not blush or shy away. "I see you, Saint. I see the way you care. I see the way you close your eyes for a couple of seconds before you laugh. I see you try and hide your tooth when you smile. But you don't need to, because you're . . . because it's a perfect smile."

"Jimmy—"

"I know that . . . I know I'm not your first choice. But still, dance with me."

Saint glanced back once more, outside, to where Misty walked toward Patch.

And she took Jimmy's hand.

85

"You're late," Misty said.

Patch turned. "I . . ."

"I was worried you wouldn't show."

"What did you get for your birthday?"

They stood side by side and looked back at the hall as the music slowed and pairs were made.

"You think it'll always be this hard?" she said.

He saw her parents, her father with his back straight and his arms stiff, and her mother elegant in her long dress and heavy pearls. He wondered what it was to have your future painted just so, to have your perfect world so closed. Maybe he already knew. Just in a different way.

"I worry I'll never find her," he said, and could almost not bear to speak such a truth.

"You can keep looking," she said. "But you might miss what's right in front of you."

He would not look up.

"Maybe what happened to you . . . you're not like

them, Patch. Everyone is . . . no one knows you. Not really."

"This song," he said, in that moment, beneath that perfect sky in their small and perfect town. Though she took his hand his feet would not move, and so they stayed rooted there.

"You think it's true, only love can break your heart?" she asked.

The moon was too bright. There were too many stars above. Sometimes he wanted to blot them all.

"If your world should fall apart," she spoke.

She slipped his arm around her waist and placed her own on his shoulder. And gently kicked off her heels and let her bare feet sink into the grass.

It was not the first time he had danced with a girl.

He breathed her in. "You didn't tell me what you got?" he said.

She looked up at him with eyes so blue and deep he knew he would likely drown. "Exactly what I wanted."

"And what was that?"

In barely a whisper, "I got to dance with the boy who saved my life."

THE BROKEN
HEARTS

1978

86

Misty waited for the 42 bus each day after school let out.

And when Patch stepped from it, a little over six feet now, overalls tied off around his waist, white T-shirt hinting at new muscles and his golden hair tied back beneath a dark cap, she ran across Main Street, jumped into his arms, and wrapped her legs tight around his waist. The two alone in their kiss, the other girls looking on.

At sixteen he had left school and took a job at the Bell Lewis Company, riding four buses each morning to the foot of the pits, where he collected his vest and hard hat and worked alongside men twice his age. The first time he traveled down through dolomite rock to the mine face he'd leaned against a pillar and stared up, the room clawed out to the size of a high school gym. Induction was swift and tough. He shadowed men loading ore onto haul trucks, got too near the crushing house and by the time he made it back to the hoists his ears were ringing. It took a couple of days to get used to the smell, and the damp and the cold. A couple more till he remembered to cross himself in front of the small Saint Barbara plaque before he went down. Patch spent eight hours each day below ground, often in the kind of darkness punctuated only by the shimmer of ore and his memories of Grace. Drilling, blasting, and hauling. The men groused about steel prices over sandwiches they ate side by side on wooden benches beneath the flicker of orange bulbs.

"You got a girl?" one of the men asked at the end of his first week.

Patch nodded. "Yeah, I've got a girl."

Patch moved through life girded by a girl who was fast becoming the most beautiful young lady. While adolescence printed much of her class with pimples and awkward angles, Misty rode that breaking wave with impossible grace and purpose.

They spent white winters tramping woodland; on fine spring mornings they braved the cool lake and trod the undercurrent, sometimes lying on their backs and floating. The first time Misty stripped down to her bathing suit Patch had looked away, only to find her eyes rolling on the return of his gaze. Her confidence as a cook grew, if not her skill, and he gamely choked down such wonders as rabbit bourguignon, crab kebabs, and a signature chili so fiery he spent much of that fall sweating.

On television they watched a blizzard send New England into chaos. Misty pushed her bare feet beneath his leg like she could feel the cold seep through the VIR television. The Meyers regarded their burgeoning romance with something like amusement, certain their daughter would pay down her debt soon enough.

Patch spent Saturday mornings at the gallery, frowning as Sammy openly wept the day Larry Flynt was shot in Georgia. **He's given us so much. So, so much.**

In the fall of '78 Misty got her license, and that winter the two drove across state to the snow globe town of Petra in Marion County. They coasted down white highways till they saw the rise of the Cupler Windmill. Patch left Misty in the warmth of her Mercedes and met with a lady named Carol Birch whose daughter had disappeared four years back. He'd found her details in the **Marion County Herald** and letters had been exchanged. Together they huddled in their winter coats and trudged the iced streets by the Nine Fork Canal. As Carol told Patch about her daughter, they watched a couple of swans grace the frozen water. The girl's name was Melinda, and there was nothing at all to suggest she was or was not Grace. Carol carried that sense of dread with her, as if for four years she had been watching for the doleful knock on her door. Patch wondered if hope was its own kind of punishment, sometimes worse than certainty, than the long and closed-off road toward healing.

He left with a photograph of Melinda taken before

a Mount Vernon sunset. They drove back in near silence, and when he got home Patch pinned the photograph to the noticeboard in his bedroom while Misty climbed out onto the flat roof. Patch followed and together they held hands and waited for the stars so that he could tell her stories of ancient Greeks and lasting legends.

"What's it like in the mines?" she said, and wrapped his arm around her.

"It's fine, Mist."

"I worry a rock will fall on your head."

"I wear a hard hat."

"Did you share my cupcakes with the other boys?"

Patch thought of the cakes rotting down there beneath the breccias and nodded.

"Good. That's how you make friends, Patch."

While Misty's grades soared, he chased leads all over the state. Most came to nothing. Sometimes people didn't show or answer his calls, and sometimes he felt that pain in his stomach, that he would not find her, and, perhaps, that she was already gone.

87

On a fresh morning in the town of Huntersville he met another mother and collected another photograph, and then he sat with Misty at the back of the basilica. She knelt while he looked at the blue columns and starred ceiling.

"I struggle to pray now," she said.

"Why?"

"I've been given enough already."

She kissed him.

When they broke apart she kept hold of his hand. She would not let go of it again.

She did not notice him compare the rosary beads that hung from the wrought-iron robe hooks by the door against his memory of the ornate kind Eli Aaron had buried his victims with. There would not be a single moment when he forgot her.

He spent much of his free time in the public library, working his way through a decade both torturous and prosperous. He skimmed past news he wondered how he had missed; A Buffalo blizzard;

Harvey Milk and Mayor George Moscone; a black-
out in New York City; a science fiction movie with
lightsabers; a dead king and 75,000 people on the
streets to mourn his voice and the indecorous way
he moved onstage.

He widened his search to surrounding states and
grew his collection of names and faces. He made a
copy of each at the Xerox place two towns over, then
made sure to drop them on Nix's desk. The chief no
longer acknowledged his plight, instead taking the
copies from him and filing them in his desk drawer.

Sammy perfected elaborate marinades, and each
Sunday night the two would barbecue together on
the large balcony that overlooked Main Street. Patch
sipped a soda while Sammy talked **Roots** and Kunta
Kinte. "I get the tribal rite of passage and all, but do
they really need to take your foreskin?" Sammy said,
a protective hand over his crotch.

"A woman came to see you this morning. Said her
name was Nina," Patch said.

Sammy pinched the bridge of his nose. "Must not
have read the memo."

"I took her number."

"And I sent her an actual memo thanking her for
her service but making it clear she would no longer
be required in my bed."

Patch waited for him to laugh.

Sammy did not laugh.

For Misty there was tentative talk of prom. She
did not outright ask to be asked, but each time they

passed Miss Kline's on Main Street she would stop before the yellow dress in the window, with the lace detail and waistcoat, and sigh so heavily he eventually worked up the courage to take her to Elion Point, where he went through expected motions and she hugged him tight enough to cause damage.

He did his best to care for his mother, made sure to pick up her pills and fix breakfast and dinner and make damn certain Misty never stepped foot over the threshold of his house. Between what he made at the mine and forcing Misty to take gas money, and placating his mother's landlord with just enough back payment, what little was left did not cover utilities. More than once each month his mother would call into the gallery to say the power had died, and he would return to a dripping refrigerator and a growing sense of unease.

Sometimes he passed Saint in town and she would offer a small smile and he would return it. He took comfort in the fact that she would leave him behind fully soon enough.

And so he existed in that altered state, that middle ground between living and not, moving on and stalling.

If the travel became his scream into the void, his paintings became true north, his skill so heady that Sammy no longer guided, just stepped back and watched in quiet reflection.

He painted the Birch girl, then the Huntersville girl, each took months, and when he was done he had Sammy pay the freight and shipped the work to their mothers. A week later Carol Birch made the long drive to Monta Clare, pulled up out front of the gallery, took Patch in her arms and sobbed.

And then he painted Callie Montrose.

In such fine and skilled detail locals stood outside the gallery window the entire day Sammy displayed it. None for longer than Chief Nix, who stayed rooted there, his hair cut a little shorter now, his kind face still so utterly troubled.

The painting was duly shipped to Richie Montrose, who sent it right back.

"What will you do with it?" Nix said one afternoon as Patch cleaned the glass front of the gallery.

"Sammy said we can hang it here until she's found. Why didn't her father want it?"

Nix kept his eyes on the girl. "Sometimes it hurts too much."

88

Patch spent more time at the big house on Parade Hill. One time Misty's mother took them to the Lakeland Mall. Mother and daughter led him into a department store where they browsed rows of Oxford button-downs, plaid sweaters, and polished dress shoes.

Misty grabbed armfuls, thrust them at the clerk and told Patch they were an early Christmas present. He flat-out refused, Misty close to tears as they left empty-handed, her mother looking on like Patch had failed some kind of test he had never agreed to take. He tried not to see himself as their project, an extension of her mother's charity work.

Spring '79 and Saint's grandmother drove her last route. She'd wanted to go on, though the DMV held stringent rules on age and necessity. Norma had bitched them out, then bitched out Patch who rode with her each morning. She threatened to sue, took a meeting in the law offices of Jasper and Coates, who told her the case had no merit. Norma threatened to sue them as well.

He grew to know everything about Misty Meyer. The way she laughed when he wore a flat cap. The other girls began to notice him, perhaps it was the feted company he kept, the consensus he was now a man in a sea of boys, the eye patch he wore, or the fact that he had once risked his life to save another. Whatever it was, the cocktail proved heady enough for Anna Blythe, Christy Dalton, and Heather Baxter to show their hands, each making their play within days of each other, appearing at the gallery while a bemused Sammy looked on. Misty dispatched them with a barrage of curse words so profane Patch almost flinched.

"You don't fuck with a honey badger," Misty said, as Heather fought back tears and sloped away.

"Pretty sure that makes you the honey," Sammy whispered to Patch, who carried more than a little fear in his eye.

Some days they took her old red Sting-Ray and rolled the sloping twists toward Pike Creek, the sun cropping a pretty horizon as she sat on the handlebars.

They sunbathed by the lake, where he worked up the courage to remove his eye patch because the cotton frayed and bothered him, only for a breeze to send it into the water. Misty balled up her dress and waded in after it, stood there dripping wet and slipped it back over his head before kissing him.

They spoke of Grace often, but never in the kind of terms that threatened Misty. He knew that Misty wondered in what way she had to compete with a girl so much of ghost.

And after he chased another dying lead and withdrew into the place she couldn't reach him, he knew that she fretted, though perhaps also drew comfort from his failures. And so the wretched circle was completed.

They had their first fight on a frigid May afternoon. She'd bought them tickets to a movie at Palace 7. He'd taken a call from a lady over in Loess Hills who'd seen his poster. He knew deep inside it was nothing, but he'd gone all the same. Misty had worked herself up, that he did not react at all only made her madder. As the bus moved away she chased it down and kicked the side of it so hard her father had to write a check to city transport.

"She's full of fire," Patch said.

Sammy raised his glass. "Just like her mother."

They sat on the balcony, facing Main Street.

Sammy had lost a little weight and credited it to seeing three different women at once. "That last one stopped by, and I'd run clean out of fluids. I had to feign orgasm. And people say I'm a misogynist."

Patch completed another painting, conjuring images from every word he could recall her speaking.

"So that's the house?" Sammy said, staring at the

painting. The white house beneath soft morning light, loose swirling brushstrokes meeting dapples of unblended color. Yellows of a meadow behind, the beginnings of a rolling hill. The sense of place was staggering, the detail, the fabrication of Grace's family home.

"I'm showing your paintings," Sammy said.

"To who?"

"My empty nut sack. Buyers, moron."

"They're not for sale."

Sammy topped off his glass and drank a little more. "Don't make me remind you what you owe me."

Patch cleared his throat, his eye anywhere but on Sammy as he spoke. "You know there's an art school in St. Louis. I figure if I'm good enough then more people will see the paintings. That's got to be a good thing, right?"

Sammy waved him off, sending a glug of bourbon down his forearm. "Fucking art school is the scourge of origination. You might as well take those hundred-dollar brushes and wipe your—"

Patch raised both hands in surrender.

"What about the blonde? She doesn't mind you working in a pit?" Sammy said as he calmed.

"She'll finish school. And then college. And this thing will meet its end."

"And until then?"

Patch placed the cold soda to his head and closed his eye. "What the fuck am I doing, Sammy? Pretending to be normal. I've got a girl. We go to the movies and grab burgers, and I pretend it's not a clear waste of my time. Each second should be devoted to finding her. Instead I'm—"

"You're pressing pause, kid."

Patch nodded, though knew a pause by its very definition was a temporary thing.

89

Saint played Liebestraum No. 3.

Her small hands a blur over the keys, the fast cadenza bringing sweat to her forehead and a level of concentration that did not allow her to notice her grandmother enter the room.

Spring rain made mirrors on the street, kaleidoscopes that reflected the bow of white trillium.

As she neared the middle of the piece, the series of octaves before the arpeggios, her grandmother came to stand right beside her, an act unheard of when she was practicing.

Saint glanced once and saw the large envelope she held.

"It has a Hanover postmark," Norma said. She had taken to wearing glasses, lighter than her granddaughter's.

Saint slowed and rolled the suspension chord. She told her grandmother to open it.

Norma's hands shook not from anticipation but because she could not stop them.

Retirement had aged her overnight.

"My god. You got in, Saint. You got in."

Saint thundered the keys.

Norma stayed for the entirety and lightly applauded when it was over.

"That was perfect," she said.

"I lost my counterweight," Saint said, and stared at her right hand like it had somehow betrayed her.

"You got into Dartmouth, Saint."

"I don't want to leave you."

Norma pressed Saint's head to her. "Silly girl."

"You're all . . . I ever had."

"Come, I'll take you for ice cream at Lacey's Diner to celebrate."

Saint turned back to the piano.

She would try it again.

She did not know how to give up.

90

Weekends Saint worked in the public library in Panora, leaving her bicycle leaning by the black railings as she adhered herself to library work like a swan to a lake.

Handling inquiries and loans, orders, and even simplifying the antiquated card system. And in quiet moments, of which there were many, she searched.

She wrote letters to a hundred coroners in as many jurisdictions, spoke with thirty-seven hospital receptionists in a thousand-mile radius of the Eli Aaron house. She gave the description of the girl in the painting, swallowing down her own protestations and her grandmother's.

"He can't know what she looks like," Norma said over lemon muffins one afternoon in Lacey's.

Saint had not replied, just looked out across the street as the 42 bus drew up and he climbed from it and into Misty's open arms.

She knew from Norma that Patch worked his own angles, seeking out the parents of missing teens, making notes in a red folder as he rode toward the St. Francois mines each morning. Saint spent a year searching public and state records. She focused on death certificates. The work was painstaking and exacting, though most could be discounted by age bracket alone. She worked with the baseless assumption that Grace could be three years older because it gave her a little more to go on, and so she searched professional licensing. Nursing, therapy, law, and medicine. When she found possible matches she made a note and then began to delve into their lives. She made close to three hundred calls to bewildered women, mothers and fathers and grandparents. Saint worked on her approach, to begin with softening the ask, before long just leading with the question, **Do you know a boy named Patch.** Sometimes they hung around for a little of the background, but others simply cut her off.

She looked into requesting federal records, though with only a first name to go on she gave up quickly.

Saint lost interest in Dr. Tooms after a year of watching his place. Whatever he had hidden, she was certain it was not Grace.

Patch still called in the middle of the night, and he had filled three tapes with his ramblings. In some he was frantic, muddled and confused. In others he spoke of the way Grace smelled on what might have been a winter morning in the basement they were held in. He recalled lemon on her skin, peppermint on her breath. He mentioned the sky at Baldy

Point, how Lake Altus-Lugert spilled its way from the dam, crashing its way along the Fork Red River. Each night Saint covered the telephone with a blanket so its ring would not wake her grandmother. It was madness. It was her link to him.

She did not coast at school, rose clear to the top of the class, mute to the excited talk of college and prom. She no longer wore her braid, instead tying her long hair back and mostly ignoring fashions and the passing trends. Layered blowouts, platinum blondes. She wore corduroy overalls and looked on as Misty dazzled in cape collars and lace yokes.

She woke one day to see a line of roses leading from the street door to Jimmy Walters, who held a large bouquet.

"He wants to ask you to prom," Norma said, from beside her.

"I know that."

"I hear Patch is going with Misty," Norma said, like it needed saying at all.

"I hear that, too."

Norma softened. "I also hear Sammy is showing his paintings next weekend."

"Oh."

"Give Jimmy a chance. For me. And I promise you, if it doesn't work out, I'll take full responsibility."

91

Saint spent the next week placing calls and dragging her grandmother to faraway towns. From Camden County to Dade, Jasper to Ozark, she asked and harangued and outright begged until a couple of local news reporters agreed to come see the pirate kid who painted the life of a girl who might never have existed. For those on the fence she used the library machine to fax over copies of the prints, and so taken were they with his talent they agreed to run something.

In the small office of the Monta Clare **Tribune** Saint sat in front of reporter Daisy Creason, who kicked her feet up onto the desk and chewed on a pencil as she looked at the print.

"This is the girl?" Daisy said.

"I mean, it might be."

Daisy furrowed her brow.

"If you run it, I'll get the pirate kid to quit bothering you," Saint lied.

Daisy nodded quickly in agreement.

On the fateful night Saint arrived an hour early and saw Patch through the window sweeping the floor as Misty hung lantern lights from a makeshift bar that Sammy propped up. The works hung on each wall, a half dozen in number, no variation in their brilliance.

Saint waited the hour in the churchyard and when Norma finally made the slow walk up she met her at the gate and the two walked in together.

"Is his mother coming?" Norma said.

Sammy stared into his brandy. "No point anyone coming. The idiot's decided he won't sell any of them. And I've got a guy heading in from the city."

Saint hid at the dark end of the gallery as it began to fill with locals, a couple of reporters and city folk she did not recognize. Misty's parents held center, for that night content that their daughter had selected such a promising artist to court.

She did not notice Jimmy Walters until she smelled the cologne, light and fresh.

"I have a ferret," he said, by way of an opener.

"And I suppose you want to introduce it to my beaver."

Jimmy blushed but managed to add a laugh. He wore a satin shirt that clung to his chest. Saint sometimes saw him running by the old railroad.

He cleared his throat. "The ferret's heart beats two hundred and fifty times each minute."

Judging by the shake in his voice and the dark patches beneath each arm, Saint guessed Jimmy's was an even match.

Sometimes she allowed him to walk with her when she headed into the woodland with her camera. He mostly knew to stay silent, though she felt his eagerness like a constriction, his need to be something that she would notice. She did not know why he cared, why he saw something in her that she herself knew was not there.

"Saint," he said.

She turned back.

"I know you don't look at me like you do Patch. But I'm here asking you to prom, and he isn't." Jimmy smiled again and went back to join his mother, who stared at Callie Montrose.

Saint glanced around for him, then saw the back door open and found Patch sitting alone on the terrace, the night sky washed with stars so bright they filled their own canvas.

"You're famous now."

He looked up and smiled for the first time that evening. "Hey, Saint."

"Hey, kid."

He stood and for a moment she thought he was going to hug her, but he stayed back by the railing.

"Sammy is pissed with me."

"He's a drunkard idiot."

"How have you been, Saint?"

She tucked her hair behind her ear. She had worn a retainer for eighteen long months, and when she smiled he did not notice her tooth had straightened. She was still small, her face told she might have been far younger, the freckles still crossed her nose though she wore lighter frames now.

"I've been . . . I've been here."

He smiled. She tried not to feel it in the pit of her stomach, in the ache of her chest.

"You work in a mine."

"I can't sell the paintings."

Saint looked to the sky. "The more people that see what you see . . . you hang them here or maybe you send them on their way, maybe they end up on the right wall at the right time and something happens."

Patch looked out across the lights of Monta Clare. "It's not real, is it? This can't be my life, Saint."

Saint looked back in through the window, where Misty stood in conversation, though her eyes scanned the room for him. "You got the girl though, Patch."

"Some nights I lie in the dark and I can't find her anymore."

She wanted to tell him she still searched. That when she looked at him she knew she would never give up.

"Is my mother inside?"

"Could be. There's so many people, you know?"

He saw through it. Smiled.

"You think I should sell my paintings?" he said.

"Maybe you put some of her life out there. And see what comes back."

Inside Patch found Sammy at the bar and words were exchanged.

Saint found Norma standing alone before the painting of the white house. "It's so beautiful," Norma said.

Sammy introduced Patch to a lady named Aileen who had stood staring at the street scene, **Grace's Main Street,** for near an hour. She told him it was a thing of beauty, that it would hang in her husband's office, like a window to someplace nicer. Sammy told her a price and she shook his hand lightly and thanked him kindly and reached for her checkbook. His very first sale.

Saint stepped out for a moment and saw Dr. Tooms across the street.

"You coming in?"

He smiled, shook his head. "He's doing all right?" Tooms strained his eyes to make out Patch among the crowd.

"He's still looking for the girl."

He turned.

"Dr. Tooms. I'm sorry. For what I did."

"You were looking out for your friend."

"I was. But I'm still sorry."

"The girl in the painting. Grace. I hope he finds her. She deserves to be found."

"They all do," Saint said.

She turned and saw he watched the Callie Montrose painting. "Beautiful," Saint said, though when she turned back he had gone, up the street, toward the church.

Saint spent a long time moving from piece to piece with Norma clutching her arm. Once again she stopped by the white house, rooted to the spot.

"It's like where my mother grew up. In that photograph you have," Saint said.

"A damn sight grander."

"But still, it reminds me of her."

"You did a good thing for that boy, Saint."

An hour later all but a couple of paintings carried a small red sticker. Patch stood guard over **Grace Number One,** and though a man from St. Louis offered a decent sum, and Sammy cussed something awful, Patch would not sell her.

Another hour and the booze ran low. Nix showed late and stared at Callie Montrose.

"How much?" he said.

"No price. Says she's not his to sell," Sammy said.

Nix smiled at that, tipped his hat to Patch and headed out.

"I'll pay you back," Saint said, smiling widely.

"You never ask for anything," Norma said.

"I once asked for bees, Grandma." Saint kissed Norma's cheek and hugged her tightly.

The next day they would take delivery of a single painting.

Saint would hang the white house above her piano and watch it as she played.

Outside she found Sammy lighting a cigar.

"He's brilliant," Saint said.

Sammy stared at **Grace Number One** through the glass. "He isn't, not yet. Too many touch-ups. The boy doesn't know when to let go."

92

The late afternoon sun was too blinding, Monta Clare woodland unforgiving in its beauty. Saint aimed her camera at a distant whitetail, its foot in the air, head tilted as she fired off a shot. It waited a beat then moved on, like it knew. Above, a summer tanager watched her. Her grandmother had once told her the bird was a symbol of patience, of the universe letting you know you were being guided, your path laid long before.

And as she wound the film and strolled back through the trodden walkways, she breathed summer and felt as close to calm as she had in a long time. The bad dreams, which she told no one about, the haunt of Eli Aaron's face, had slowly begun to fade.

She took the small roll of film from her camera.

And as she stood in line at the drugstore to deposit her film, she noticed a couple of boys standing nervously in the opposite aisle.

"Condoms."

She turned and saw Ivy Macauley behind her. Her face gaunt, eyes red.

"Senior prom," Ivy said, rolling her eyes at the boys, who scanned the shelves with fear in their eyes.

"It's nice to see you," Saint said.

Ivy reached out and gently touched her cheek. "You look the same as . . . I call it before. You look like the child I remember."

Saint smiled.

"You're going tonight?" Ivy asked.

"Yes." Saint thought of Jimmy Walters, how he had asked another half dozen times before she finally crossed the church the Sunday before and told him yes. His mother had smiled as wide as her son.

"Joseph is going. The school said he could."

Saint thought of Patch wearing a powder-blue dress shirt and almost smiled. Then thought of Misty on his arm. They fit. Somehow, against the longest odds, Saint would look at them and think how beautifully they fit. She told herself she could do that now.

"I can't remember if I thanked you," Ivy said.

"You did."

Ivy looked into her eyes, seemed to read her but smiled it off because whatever she had said or not said had been so totally buried. "You have children, and you don't realize that your whole becomes too big."

"Have you seen his paintings?" Saint asked.

"I wonder where he gets it. No one in the family. I like the idea of God given."

"I do, too."

"Being a mother, there's no practice for it. Just because you can do it, because you're able, doesn't mean you're good at it. And if you're not, it's not just your life . . ."

They watched the boys make their selection, then the taller looked over, saw Ivy staring at him, and dropped the pack. The two hightailed it back into the street.

"Looks like someone's getting pregnant tonight," Saint said.

Ivy laughed and dragged a hand through her hair, bleached blonde now, the roots dark and greasy.

"They wanted to have a funeral or something. Back then. I can't shake the memories now. Father Adams wanted to bury my boy without a body. Put an empty box in the ground so I could move on. Or maybe so he could. So he didn't have to mention us each week, you know. Sometimes I think that's real, and this, right now, this is the dream. Like maybe I'm dead and this is some kind of purgatory."

They drew a couple of glances now.

"But you're real, Saint. You brought my boy home."

"Yeah, Ivy. He came home," Saint said softly.

"The wait in this place," Ivy said, her hand shaking a little. "Still can't sleep without the pills. Goddamn nightmares come for me."

Saint stepped aside, let Ivy go in front.

Ivy moved to the counter, and Saint tried not to listen as the girl told Ivy she could not give her any more pills. That there were no refills left on her prescription.

"Call Dr. Tooms and check," Ivy said.

The girl told her sorry.

"I don't need apologies, I need to fucking sleep." Ivy grabbed the girl's hand. "Please."

The girl snatched her hand back as Ivy righted herself, cursed again as she walked back out into the street.

Saint gathered the papers the girl had dropped. She glanced down at the name printed across the top.

Martin Tooms. His personal prescription.

She wasn't sure if it was curiosity, or that gut feeling never leaving her. Saint stood and scanned the pages as the girl and the pharmacist followed Ivy out to check on her. Broad spectrum antibiotics. Painkillers. Sleeping pills.

She glanced around, and then she slipped the papers into her pocket and left.

Saint waited until she was home, and she had climbed the stairs and seen the doll blue pleated hem dress hanging in her room.

And then she took the scripts from her pocket,

sat on the bed, and held her breath as she checked when the refills began.

Saint checked twice.

Her blood rushed.

September ninth.

The day after Patch was taken.

93

Franklin Meyer handed Patch a heavy crystal glass filled with brandy, poured one for himself, and walked them out onto the stone terrace.

Way out in the distance a gardener tended the grounds. A wooden walkway ran through trees toward a body of water punctured by a large fountain. A long line of lavender scented the air, the sun just beginning to drop as hidden lanterns flickered on.

Behind, the white stucco loomed with hip roofs of blue slate and flowered headers on each of the fourteen windows and pediments.

Franklin led him over to a long, smoked glass table and they sat on cushioned wicker chairs. For a moment they enjoyed their drinks and the sound of the evening approach.

"So tonight is the night?" Franklin said, crossing a leg. He wore a white shirt opened three buttons.

"Yes, sir."

He looked at Patch's suit, navy, expensively cut

and borrowed from Sammy. It was a little large, but a good way from the ruffled blues and creams he'd seen on the walk over to her place.

A limo idled in the driveway, beside it a photographer sitting in his car, waiting for the signal to come capture the most beautiful girl in town on the night of her senior prom.

Franklin smiled. "Makes a change from the movies, right? I forget who she likes now . . . the boy with the sideburns."

Patch's mind ran to Danny and the T-Birds, Sandy and her Pink Ladies. He'd been made to sit through five showings now. The Saturday before they'd caught the return matinee before Misty pouted her way through her burger and fries till Patch relented and they caught the evening show, too. Not just caught it; Misty sang through each of the numbers, before declaring herself hopelessly devoted to Patch on the walk back up the hill, her voice so screeching, so awfully at odds with the rest of her.

"How's work going? You're over at Bell Lewis, yes."

"It's good."

His last shift. In the depths. Floor to underside five feet seven so Patch spent each of his nine hours stooped. Straightening up afterward had almost brought tears to his eyes.

"It's honest work, Joseph. Important work. The heartlands . . ." he trailed off. "Senior prom," he said, a note of wistful in his voice, like Misty's childhood had passed by too quick. "You know we wanted more children. A son. I suppose all men think about it at one time or another. It wasn't in the cards for us. So, you see, Misty is everything. And I don't mean that as a throwaway comment, Joseph. Misty is everything we have."

"She's a special girl, sir."

"You've tasted her cooking?"

Patch nodded.

Both men stared off into the distance wearing matching frowns.

"The pair of you have grown close. Of course, Misty will be heading off to Harvard in a few months."

"Yes, sir."

It was both spoken of and unsaid, looming on their track like a freight train headed toward them. Patch knew the damage would be severe but also knew it had been on their horizon since the moment she sat beside him on the fallen oak. For her part Misty deflected whenever he brought it up. He imagined her there, her fit tailored, among girls like her and boys entirely unlike him.

"She says she doesn't want to leave," Franklin said. He drew out a large cigar, offered one to Patch, who shook his head. He lit it and fanned the smoke with his free hand. "If I'm honest I thought it would pass."

If he were honest, Patch did, too.

"I understand about origins. The two of you . . . there's romance to it. I'm not too old to see that. Like it was written in the stars."

"You all think I saved Misty. But she's the strong one."

Franklin smiled at that. "But you must know she feels—"

"Obligated."

Franklin held up a hand, steadying, cooling though Patch remained calm.

"Sometimes when you're in my position, when you have so damn much . . . it's easy to be painted as self-serving . . . as righteous and pompous and, well, everything I used to think about my own father. We're custodians of old money. My main job was not to lose it, maybe grow it a little. Preservation of place."

Patch glanced back at the house once more as lights manifested through the glass. The slow smoke of one chimney, the gray lolling above before dissipating. An upstairs window opened to music. The easy guitar, the promise of childhood living and wild horses.

And he sat there and waited for what he always knew would one day come.

"We have to want more for our children, Joseph. Otherwise we restrict them only to mirror ourselves. That's not how progress is made. We strive. My daughter is brilliant in most ways, but none more so than her desire to claim everything she can. Every misstep her mother and I have made will be realigned by Misty."

Patch stared into his glass, cutting a dozen tones as he held it to the lantern buried in the trees. He wondered if the person who made it knew it was a perfect thing. He looked around at their world and saw so many perfect things. And only one thing that could never belong.

"I'll talk to her," he said, quiet.

Franklin smiled gently and finally looked over at him. "I don't think talk is enough at this point. She dodged one bullet that morning . . . I'm just trying to help her dodge another."

Patch smiled, not because he did not understand, but because he did.

And with that Franklin reached into his pocket and took out the check and placed it on the table. "I will die grateful to you, Joseph. There's so many things I can give you, but my daughter isn't one of them."

He stood and touched Patch's shoulder, and then he went back into the house.

Hues of dusk caved in that placid summer day.

They stood at the foot of the grand staircase as Misty made her descent. Patch remained there in the photographer's strobe, dazzled not by the flash but by a girl he could not possibly have dared to hold on to. A floor-length gown, the same yellow as the band in her hair. She met him and took his hand.

Her parents joined them.

He had never seen Misty smile so wide.

"You look so beautiful," she said, as she ran her hand through his hair.

"Stealing my lines."

Nothing about them fit. Nothing about them worked.

She loved him entirely and absolutely.

94

The Tooms house lay in darkness, the moon no more than a sash of white.

Saint stood before it in her prom dress.

She had been to the salon, and her hair fell in chestnut waves. She had applied her makeup carefully, lightly sprayed herself with perfume and carefully buckled her Mary Janes.

Norma had said, "You look beautiful, Saint. Your hair is—"

"Brushed."

"And your makeup is—"

"On."

Norma quit while she was behind.

And then she had left ten minutes before Jimmy Walters would knock on her door, carrying a smile and a corsage.

Saint crossed the vegetation and stood on the blockwork slabs and looked out over a thousand acres.

She thought of the girl. Grace.

Maybe she was out there somewhere. Maybe she

was breathing, or maybe she was buried so deep not even the dogs would find her.

At the farmhouse she climbed through a downstairs window and moved through the darkness, her dress trailing on the floorboards.

In the kitchen were cans. Campbell's soup and Van Camp's Pork and Beans, condensed milk, and Hunt's Sloppy Joe.

Canned food did not perish.

Everything except dog food.

She did not know what she was looking for, but she was too exhausted even to feel the prick of fear.

Out the window, far out across the woodland, the light of her grandmother's house burned.

Upstairs she saw the door to the attic.

And then she heard it.

She pulled the chain and watched the steps unfurl. "Dr. Tooms," she called.

Her knees shook a little as she climbed.

She coughed dust. Her dress tore on sawn rafters.

And then she heard it again, close behind her.

She turned, her muscles tight as she choked back a scream.

95

They drank spiked punch in the school hall, which had been transformed. Streamers ribboned from the ceiling, a glitter ball hung low in the center as light cut over couples who moved slow on the dance floor. Chuck and his group stood together, occasionally throwing glances at a boy who now stood a head taller than all of them. The girls stared because he was no longer one of them.

"And now you need to dance with me," Misty said.

"You know I don't dance."

And then the song died and the one that took its place sank his heart as he sighed and her eyes widened.

She dipped her head a little, pouted until he took her hand and led her to the center. A space cleared, and she clutched his back and pressed herself close.

She took his hand and held it aloft, slowly spun before him and sang of how hers was not the first heart broken.

She nodded toward him, imploring, begging.

Grumpily, he told her his eyes were not the first to cry.

"Eye," she corrected.

He frowned and she laughed.

She whispered the words, devoted herself so hopelessly that he lifted her clean off her feet and spun her in his arms, her hands looped around his neck.

"I love you," she said.

The check weighed heavy in his pocket.

Heavier still on his heart.

96

"Goddamn, kid," Nix said, lowering his gun.

He helped her down.

"Breaking and entering," he said, his big frame illuminated by the window.

"It's Tooms."

"This again."

She looked down at her torn dress. She thought of Jimmy Walters as she moved from room to room and began opening closets and tossing out clothes.

"Enough," he said, and she barreled past him and went into another room.

Her heart racing as she dumped drawers out onto the carpet.

She went to pass him again, but this time he barred her with a strong arm around her waist.

"Get the fuck off me."

He held her firm, said nothing and did not react to her curses.

She couldn't stop the tears then.

The frustration of the past years, of losing her friend, of the stranger that came back to her. How he didn't smile. Most days didn't even notice her in the street. Of Patch and Misty. Of Jimmy Walters.

She sobbed it out.

Nix held her, did not tell her things would be okay, and for a moment she loved him for it.

"I'm sorry," he said, and she knew that he meant it.

Outside they met the moonlight.

She breathed and calmed.

"I saw you in church when he was gone. You prayed for this, kid. Take the win."

She looked at the Tooms house.

He cleared his throat. "To hold on to your faith . . . when you do this job. It's something I never managed. God is a first call and a last resort, from christening to death bed. In between is where faith is tested. The mundanity. Anyone can drop to their knees when they're facing crisis, but doing it when everything is steady . . ."

"I made a promise. I think about it every day," she said, and did not know why she was sharing it with him on that night.

He watched her.

"I promised God that I wouldn't sin. If he'd bring back Patch."

Nix did not laugh or mock. "You'll do the best you can. You'll take your plaudits and head forward. Norma tells me you'll go to Dartmouth."

"Grace is out there," Saint said.

"And you're here. And you're missing your senior prom. Come on, I'll take you back."

She was about to turn when another cruiser pulled up and Deputy Harkness got out.

"Ain't nothing," Nix said, waving him back, but Harkness took the moment to light a cigarette.

Saint stopped in front, keeping the cops with her in the mad place she existed in. "I know he did something bad. Please. Just for a moment imagine there's one more girl out there. One more set of parents. You all said Eli Aaron might've worked with someone else."

"The town doctor?" Harkness said, raising an eyebrow.

"Don't do it because I ask, or because most of Patch is still missing. Don't even do it because you're cops. Do it because she should be somewhere now, standing in her prom dress and smiling for cameras. And—"

"We already searched the house," Nix said.

Harkness crossed the gravel and stood before a pile of firewood.

"What?" Nix said, following him over.

Harkness frowned. "I used to come up this way when I was a kid. There's a trail that leads to the back of Adler land, we used to race through the corn, get ourselves lost and scared."

He began shifting the wood.

Saint bent and helped him.

"There was a storage cellar. Right here, I'm certain of it."

The car lit the mountain of firewood, leaves, and gutter mulch. By the time they reached the base layer they were sweating hard, her dress streaked with dirt.

"We don't have a warrant," Nix said.

At that Harkness finally stopped.

Saint pleaded, said it could be something but saw in both of their eyes it was over, that she was chasing the last lost cause.

Nix led her to his car, let her ride up front as Harkness started his engine.

The two cruisers eased up the track.

Saint reasoned Nix was right, that her friend had come home. However distant, whatever remained of him, he was back in Monta Clare. And each night she thanked God for that.

"You want to go change? I can take you to prom," Nix said.

Prom. Saint thought of Grace. She thought of Callie Montrose. Maybe they had no one like her, no one fighting hard enough.

Saint popped the door open as Nix hit the brakes.

She heard him curse as she sprinted back toward the firewood.

She fell to her knees and heaved sheets of rotten timber from the ground, laid there like cover.

"Goddamn, kid," Nix yelled.

Both cruisers turned and drove back, pulled up like a V, their high beams crossing over her.

And over the old wooden doors she had bared.

Saint heaved the double doors open.

The steps led down into deeper darkness.

Saint went down before they could reach her.

The steps shook a little, the wood soft, the frame bowed and ached.

Harkness aimed his flashlight down.

It gave them just enough light.

Saint cried then. A hand over her mouth.

Harkness lay on his stomach, not risking the steps.

He cast light over the scene. "Jesus."

A single mattress.

And a lot of blood.

97

Patch and Misty walked back up the hill, and she slipped off her shoes and carried them, complaining her feet hurt till he leaned a little so she could climb onto his back.

When they reached her house they stopped out front and watched Monta Clare; the land fell away so sharply, like the town had fallen from heaven and cratered its place.

She held his hand, her head on his shoulder. "It's so beautiful."

"It is. But there's a big world out there, Mist. At least that's the way they tell it."

"Yeah, but sometimes people go out searching for something they've already got."

"Boston. The city, all those smart people. You can walk the Freedom Trail . . . I mean, you might have to pay someone to carry you the last mile but still."

She did not laugh.

"Faneuil Hall, it's beautiful, right. You can ride the Swan Boats, you seen them? They got the Old North Church, and the water, and Copley Square. And you know in the museum they got the **Grainstack.** Sammy said it's a sight. And that's before you even get to Harvard Square."

"What are you doing?" she said.

"I saw a book in the library. I wanted to know what it was like . . . where you're going."

She looked down at her corsage. "I'm not going. I already decided."

"Bullshit."

She stared up, her eyes quick to blaze. He reached out to touch her cheek, but she turned her head.

"You can't just throw this away," he said.

"You sound like my parents."

"Maybe they're right."

She laughed. "You hate my parents."

He slipped his hands into his pockets. "I don't, we're just . . . we're so different."

"What's wrong with you? Why are you being like this?"

"I just . . . I don't know how this is going to work."

"It'll work because I love you and you love me." And then she caught it, like she hadn't before, like the music and the dancing glossed over it.

He turned, framed by a moon too heavy, by starlight that was not wanted.

"You can't compare to her," he said.

He felt her hand on his shoulder. "You don't mean that. You're just saying it so I'll go to Harvard."

He felt a dull pain deep in his chest.

"If you mean it. If you do. Why can't you look at me then?"

"She needs me. You don't. Go be your real self in Boston. You won't have to play at being dumb anymore."

"That's not—"

"I didn't say it back." He gritted his teeth. "When you told me you loved me. I never said it back. Because I—"

She shoved him. He stepped forward. She shoved him again and he turned. And she slapped his face.

"You don't break up with me."

Another shove and he fell into the dirt.

"I can't compete with her because she isn't real. She's a fucking ghost. Everyone knows it. Grace isn't real."

His pants were torn at the knee.

"I decide it's over. Someone like you doesn't leave someone like me." She stopped then, stunned by her words, broken by them.

"Honesty, Mist. Never feel bad for it."

Her parents came out onto the driveway. Her mother held her daughter tight and tried to lead her toward the house, but Misty looked back at Patch sitting there in the dirt, kicked herself free and rushed toward him.

He stood and she fell into him and grabbed his shirt.

Franklin took her from him.

Patch stood and walked from their lives.

He did not look back.

COPS AND
ROBBERS

1982

98

They drove out across Route 9.

At a gas station miles from anywhere Saint took down a statement from the old guy who worked the pumps and then watched security tape so grainy she could not make out much beyond a blur pulling a gun and making off with just under a hundred bucks.

Nix stared at vacant lots and half-built homes. "They say we're out of recession. Couple million jobs lost. The way I see it they still haven't been found again. All that talk back then about oil and Bretton Woods."

In a diner of red booths, the leather split and the padding bulging out, a fan spun, a milkshake machine rattled, and truckers drank endless refills and stared at day-old newspapers like they were always a step behind.

"You did good," Nix said.

Saint wore the navy uniform, the shirt the smallest

they carried but still, the sleeves ended halfway between wrist and elbow. "Taking a statement isn't catching a—"

"Fundamentals," he said, and bit into a grilled cheese. "Ain't a better meal on this earth."

She sipped on her soda.

Nix dabbed at his moustache with a napkin. "How's your grandmother?"

"Same."

"There isn't any shame in wearing a badge."

"I know that."

Nix stirred another sugar into his coffee. "You heard from the kid?"

"No."

"He's out there looking?"

Patch had bought their rental house as the decade eased to a close, giving his mother the kind of security she had chased for much of her lifetime. Saint did not ask where the money had come from.

After prom she had watched him climb from the 42 bus at the end of each day, overalls tied at the waist, his long hair pulled back with a bandana, his jaw strong. Sometimes she caught the girls watching him and whispering and giggling in that way they did. And for a while she saw Misty, if possible even more beautiful as she stood apart from her group and sometimes stole looks at the boy who had once saved her life and broken her heart. After graduation Saint heard Misty took a year out to travel, to put some distance between herself and Monta Clare and the memories it stirred. Her grandmother told her first love was the most terminal of ailments.

"I filed another request for visitation with Tooms," Saint said.

"He won't see anyone."

"But you go there each and every weekend."

Nix shrugged. "I just need to see him. I need to look into his eyes."

"Maybe we'll never know why."

That fall Martin James Tooms pleaded not guilty to the murder of Callie Montrose, bringing to a close a year of trial prep, during which the DA leaned and Tooms's savings eroded. He lost the farm, but through it all kept the kind of undignified silence that led Saint to pray for his demise each Sunday.

Saint had sat beside Nix and the DA when they ran through detail in its minutiae, and they promised to keep the Macauley boy from showing at the prison gates armed with a dagger and a promise to gut the man if he didn't tell him where the girl was. A promise they failed to keep on so many occasions the Ellis County cops had no choice but to arrest Patch, keep him overnight, and set him free beneath the flotilla of sunrise.

Patch wrote close to sixty letters to Marty Tooms; Saint read each before delivering them. Sometimes he rambled for pages about his life and where people said he was headed. Other times he begged, pleaded, offered to go see Judge Heinemann and ask for his captor's salvation ahead of sentencing. And on dark days he cussed the man out, speculated on what kind of hell was waiting for him, on how he could have worked with Eli Aaron to bring such horror.

They worked on an impact statement. Saint wrote while Patch spoke of the kind of empty horror that kept him awake each night, wondering about Grace, hoping to God she was not real. She did not bend his words or salt the wounds; for three pages she simply detailed what had happened to him: his life before, his life now, and what might still come. A lifetime of therapy, of sleeping on the floor in the darkness. Of chasing a shadow of a girl who, if she was out there, was likely dead or wishing she was.

Tooms did not speak, even to his lawyers, who moved to have him declared insane for that very reason. The judge noted his level of forethought and promptly threw it out.

The case strengthened when hair samples taken from the remains of Eli Aaron's house matched those of Marty Tooms. Saint and the DA connected dots that weren't all that hard to join together. And then came the blood.

Eight samples were taken from the mattress in the underground store of the Tooms house.

All eight were matched to Callie Montrose.

Saint had looked to her left as Nix shook his head in despair, then closed his eyes to it all.

Behind them, in the gallery, Callie Montrose's father screamed and cursed and kicked as he was dragged from the room by the same cops he used to work beside.

The only emotion Tooms showed was when they asked for the location of Callie's body, so that her father might at least have the scarce comfort of laying her to proper rest.

Tooms remained silent through his tears.

Records were pulled, and it was put to the jury that Marty Tooms had written out prescriptions for himself for a large amount of painkillers and sleeping pills, and supplied them to Eli Aaron, who would use them to subdue his targets. Saint had watched those twelve men and women dab tears from their eyes.

The night before sentencing Patch followed Judge Heinemann back to his colonial in Elion County. The judge called the cops. While he waited to be hauled away Patch sat outside, leaning back against the door and speaking of Grace, of the kind of girl she was, of the life she should have been living. He did not know if the judge or his two daughters heard him, only that the next day Marty Tooms was sentenced to death. A punishment that rippled through the state as Heinemann had always leaned liberal. Saint watched as the reporters speculated that it was a ploy, that the sentence would be reduced to life if Tooms gave up the location of Callie Montrose, and the rumored missing girl. Saint marveled at Patch, who kept true to his word.

He would burn everything and everyone in his path.

99

"Norma thought it was a phase when you turned down an Ivy League college," Nix said.

"You did, too," Saint said.

"Year on the desk before you could even start training. Not that you listened."

"Still made me your partner," Saint said.

He frowned. "Partner? You're a rookie under my watch, don't even have a badge yet. I promised your grandmother I'd look out for you."

Her first day she'd begun looking into the life of Marty Tooms. And she did not stop until the following winter, when on a frosted afternoon as they watched Reagan sworn in and the hostage crisis in Iran come to close, Patch took the Fairlane across the state to chase a lead so tepid he did not even give details, only asked her to check in on his mother, who remained in that pregnant pause while the world spun around her.

Saint knocked on the door and stood awhile then tapped on the glass but could see no one inside.

Maybe it was instinct that led her down the side of the house and into the yard. She walked up onto the rear deck and peered through the French doors and saw Ivy Macauley sprawled out on the kitchen floor.

Ivy was pronounced dead at the scene.

Patch took the news evenly.

He did not cry at the funeral. She had died so long before.

The next day he left the town of Monta Clare behind him.

"You ever wonder how Tooms and Eli Aaron came to work together on this?" Saint said. "I've tracked as far back as I can. Tooms lived his whole life in Monta Clare. Med school at the U of M. Maybe they met there, but I didn't get the vibe that Aaron was educated."

Nix stared at his hands, at the lines of his life.

She fished the ice from her soda with her fork then remembered where she was and set it down. "I guess bad people have a way of finding each other. A death sentence without a body though."

"We all get death in the end," he said.

"And what of Grace?"

"You've read the case file. The report from that shrink. You tell me what you think." Nix signaled the waitress who topped off his coffee and added a smile.

Saint fussed with the saltshaker. "As his friend or as a cop?"

Nix watched her, like she needed to ask.

She took a breath. "He conjured her from that dark place in his mind that told him he was a thirteen-year-old kid trapped in the room with a monster who did God knows what to him. He wouldn't take the evaluation. Not fully."

"You know that yet you missed your own prom to chase down a local doctor. You gave up your place, a place you earned, at one of the finest colleges in the whole damn country. And you tell me you're not doing it to find this girl?"

She watched a couple at the counter.

Nix said, "You heard the interview tapes. You've listened to them a thousand times."

Saint thought of them, of the recordings made with the state cops, with Nix himself, with the psychologist. Their aim had been to build a picture, to recover clear memories that might lead them to the girl. She did not tell Nix she had made copies, that Patch's words sent her into a fractious sleep every single night.

"Details," Nix said.

"He gave a lot of detail because each conversation was still fresh in his mind. And when new memories come to him, he calls my house, fills up my answering machine. I keep the tapes. I keep everything."

"But the details change. One time she's got a drawl, the next she's all Bronx. He thinks she's a Texan blonde, sometimes a West Virginia red. She's older. Sometimes his age. She's tough—"

"She's always tough. That never changes."

"She's tough because he thinks he wasn't. Dissociative identity disorder. It's when—"

"So he's the girl now?"

A family pulled into the lot. The woman carried a baby, and Saint watched them all the way in. "That level of trauma. Doesn't mean he made it up."

"Let's say he didn't. Tell me what we have to go on. So many cases, so many people doing bad things. They outnumber us a million to one. And that's assuming we're all good. Giving a man a badge and gun doesn't mean you've given him the moral code to use either correctly. Masks, Saint. A suit and tie. A lab coat and scrubs. They're just dressing."

"So we're all flawed," she said, as he pulled off a ten and left a decent tip.

"Some of us assign greater merit to those flaws. If we're ten percent bad does that make us good?"

Out in the sun she placed a hand on the hood of the cruiser. "It depends on how bad that ten percent is?"

"Heat of the moment, I shoot a man dead over a gambling debt. Am I worse than the man who lays into his wife each week? The law says I am."

"The law is bullshit."

He laughed. "Now you're starting to sound like a cop."

Beside the diner were a couple of stores shuttered, and on white-washed glass she saw a poster long since faded.

MISSING GIRL.

"Move forward, Saint. It's not our place to deal with what's left."

"What if she's out there?"

A breeze towed clouds till shade covered them.

"If she is, she's dead," he said.

"You don't know that."

"But I know the kid wouldn't believe it anyhow," Nix said.

"It's noble."

"It is. Noble acts . . . they don't always end anyplace good. But wherever that kid is, I hope to God he's not getting himself into more trouble."

100

Patch stood in line at the First Union Bank.

The place was grand and tired. Marble pillars flocked with dark veins held up a ceiling of flaked paint and sat on gray carpet so thin it rucked up like waves crested beneath. A line of areca palms, the plastic leaves browned with dust.

Behind him a woman and her daughter stood; in front an old man clutched a checkbook and a couple of twenties. Through large glass windows heat swirled over distant Rockies, capped by snow and fogged by a city's breath like smoke waiting to be exhaled. He wondered if it was the painting, if Sammy had seared his brain into exchanging what was plainly beautiful for something more.

His '72 Celica was parked three streets away.

He'd packed what little he owned and left Monta Clare an hour before sunrise, opened the window and heard the faint quake of an airplane as he drove out of the only town he had ever lived in.

He had not met traffic until Des Moines, noted the passing time by changing light, the ambers waving from Kansas. His mind on Misty as he traded the interstate for two-laners, concrete for Flint Hills and tallgrass prairies so lush. He parked up at Cottonwood Falls and strolled with ranchers and their families toward the red-bricked downtown where he looked in windows of cloistered galleries.

A couple of miles on he'd stopped by the Chase State Fishing Lake and walked its shoreline toward the mudflats where fishermen pulled saugeye and bluegill. He met with a husband and wife named Drew and Sally and they held hands and sat on a bench by the north shore and showed him photographs of their daughter Anna May who had wandered from her life near eight years prior. It could not be Grace.

He'd left them with a promise, and in turn they left him a photograph of their daughter, so precious a commodity Sally gripped it for a moment longer as she handed it to him.

Thirty miles up the byway he found a spot and unfolded his easel and canvas and painted Anna May backdropped by land unchanged in a thousand years, the spirit of the Kaw and the Osage steeped in the dirt as he slowly chased north light.

He spoke with Drew and Sally, who instead of asking for the painting wondered if he might display it somewhere. Where it could be seen. Where their daughter would not be forgotten.

A month later he pulled from the Sacred Heart Trail and in a small post office carefully packaged his canvas and scrawled Anna May and the date she was last seen on the back. He sent the photograph back to her parents, along with a note telling them that the painting would sit in Monta Clare Fine Art, where Sammy would do what he could to highlight her.

He'd stuck to Interstate 35, immune to the lights of Oklahoma City. Slept in the car, opened the window to a Texan night sky, the stars his blanket. He ate grits in roadside diners, one meal each day because what little he had was spent on gas. He washed in their bathrooms and filled his flask with water from their faucets.

A week in the sweep of Texas, endless as he crawled mile on mile only stopping to meet with two families he had tracked through newspaper archives. In Corpus Christi he saw the ocean for the first time in his life and spent a day watching its folds and breathing salt air so dry and perfect he placed a call to Sammy and told him exactly how the water had felt when he found a deserted stretch, stripped from his clothes, and waded out deep.

"Stop calling me," Sammy had said, though it was only the first call.

For eight weeks on that very beach he painted Lucy Williams and Ellen Hernandez. Cars backed up almost to the road as trucks opened their beds and families built canopies and spent the day in such unassumed luxury.

Patch brought the missing back with practiced strokes of his brush, heading into town when he was done, the canvases scrolled.

"Are you a pirate?" a small boy asked, as Patch headed past him into the post office to mail his work to Sammy.

"I was," Patch said, his smile reaching his words.

That evening he walked through the bustling port as the sun dipped and cannoned color across the ocean. And then he saw the boats.

Patch lost that whole night to the gleaming decks, bowriders and catamarans and cabin cruisers. The walkways fed small islands, and Patch hopped a barrier as skippers guided their vessels toward the marina, his hands in his pockets, a wide smile on his face.

The heavy chug of engines, the glass-fronted watchtower a mirror of wonder. His eye locked on the twin hulls of a pontoon that glided with such elegance he thought of Misty. He slowly walked toward and watched it moor as a boy no older than him hopped from it barefoot onto the wooden deck to rope it off.

Patch studied him intently, certain he just might be the luckiest kid he'd ever seen.

As the sun drowned, the marina chorused with people sitting on their decks, drinks in hand. He was not sure if it was the water, or maybe the gentle sway, but as he noticed a woman with the right shade of hair, hosing down the hull of a towering sailboat, he felt that low ache, not quite pain, just a feeling that he would chase her until the day he died, and that he would always feel less without knowing she was okay.

For ten months he pinballed from state to state, chasing down the weakest links, the slightest hint he was tracking something live, and he moved. He lived from a single bag, bought only what he deemed essential. He ran when he could and ground out a couple of hundred push-ups each morning.

He read newspapers in bus seatbacks, saw color photos of troops too young being sent to a place they could not pick out on a world map, fought under a sun entirely foreign, against an enemy they would train hard not to understand. Deaths were victories. Patch knew those kids, like his father, history not so much doomed to repeat itself as just plain doomed.

He met a dozen families looking for a dozen lost girls, and sometimes they were hostile because they had already mourned and did not wish to again, and other times he sat with empty mothers who clutched their photos and trinkets, and both hoped and dreaded that his Grace was theirs.

In a Kansas hamlet he spent a week at a small farm with a father. Patch knew within a few hours that they were not searching for the same lost soul, but the man leaned heavy on him because those closest were not strong enough to speak of the girl. Over bourbon they sat on a porch swing and watched the twilight prairie. Sometimes there was just enough beauty to temper the pain.

He worked on a farm for a month in Louisiana, the end of the season, the clouds so low and heavy he could almost touch them. And on Sundays he skirted Lake Martin because in the archives he found a picture of a girl that might have been Grace who'd gone missing when her father was fishing. The man was long dead, but Patch thought maybe he'd feel something as he headed through swampland, cut the trails, and watched the egrets and the bullfrogs and the ibis.

A month later he hugged the Texan coast, met a man on the Galveston Strand and walked the seawall, and as the man showed him a photo, in the shade of Moody Gardens, Patch contemplated his own sanity. Searching for a girl he could not place, from a time so distant he was met by only the most desperate.

And then he ran low on funds, called Sammy who bitched about the bite of recession, cursed out stagflation, and slurred through a story of a couple who wanted to buy a missing girl and made an offer so derisory he'd had to chase them from the gallery with a cane just to cauterize the insult. Nix had come, threatened to arrest him, and he'd responded with an invitation to duel.

And so, in that Tucson bank, Patch waited for the old guy to pass before he strolled up to the mahogany counter, pulled a gun from the band of his belt, and aimed it squarely at the teller.

It took a moment to register, for the smile to drop and the fear to kick in. Heavy fans spun thickened air as sweat broke out and dripped from the man's nose.

"Fill the bag," Patch said. He wore jeans and a dark T-shirt and dark glasses, and on his head a bandana tied back his hair.

The man glanced around to catch the eye of a sleeping security guard but decided his life was not worth the trouble.

The mama with her little girl stood just far enough back, and as Patch turned he caught the girl's eye and smiled. Her mother returned it with one of her own.

"I'm sorry this happened," he said to the teller.

The man wiped at his sweat. He wore short sleeves and a navy tie with a gold clip and a digital watch. "I've got a wife and two children."

"This gun isn't loaded."

Patch took the bag and walked out into the street, climbed into his car and drove.

Behind him there was no alarm or chase.

The next day in **The Post** the teller would claim Patch had threatened his life and the lives of his wife and two children. By then Patch would be under the open skies of Utah where he would see about a girl, knowing deep in his heart it would not be her. On his way he would donate all but a couple of hundred bucks to the Destiny Missing Persons charity.

101

They ate dinner with Norma, who mostly ignored her granddaughter and instead smiled at Jimmy Walters as she piled his plate with pork steak, fried potatoes, and steamed greens.

"All that studying must make you hungry," Norma said, as she buttered a roll and set it down on his side plate.

Saint pushed her potatoes around as Jimmy told Norma about his studies, and his weekends assisting at Culpepper Zoo.

He went on to run her through a wolf with canine distemper, a tortoise with poxvirus, and a hippo that needed a tooth extracted.

"Sounds tough," Norma said.

He shook his head. "Tough is sexing a dormouse."

"Pretty sure I could arrest you for that," Saint said.

Jimmy smiled at her, but Norma did not.

They finished with butter cake, Norma cutting Jimmy a slice at least double the size of Saint's. And when they were done, after Norma thanked Jimmy for saying such a wonderful grace before they ate, Saint followed him out and together they walked to Main Street.

They shopped the window of Monta Clare Antiques where he pointed out a walnut chamber ogee wall clock, a Carolean wingback, and a three-pint cocktail shaker.

"I could spend my whole paycheck in an hour," he said, as he took in a dulled Costello globe so beat up she could not even read the detail.

It wouldn't take long, she thought, and bit her tongue because she knew studying for a DVM while working weekends took a toll. And that in the long run, when he qualified as a veterinarian, he would earn a decent wage.

Beneath the canopy of Monta Clare Hardware store he took her hand. "It'll get easier, with your grandmother."

"Only if I hand in my badge and go back to school," she said.

"Would that be such a bad thing?"

He kept his eyes on the windows, on a passing couple, on the high church tower.

"I mean, you'll have to stop one day, when we start a family," he continued. He wore a beige sweater and white pants and boxy shoes she tried not to notice. Most evenings they ate with his mother opposite a wall dedicated to photographs of Jimmy that detailed how little he had changed since kindergarten. Though broad and handsome, he stood only a couple of inches taller than Saint. People at church said they made a cute couple.

"My mother asked if you wanted to come eat with us on Saturday night. She's making her famous Sloppy Joes."

She had tried them at least a dozen times before, still trying to figure out the reason for their fame. "Sure, Jimmy."

He squeezed her hand, then lightly kissed her cheek.

"I love you," he said.

"You too," she said.

"You could wear the green dress I bought you."

She thought of the dress, how it skimmed her ankles and buttoned high on her neck.

"Not too much makeup, you know how my mother is," he said, making to roll his eyes.

She laughed.

After he walked her home, Saint retired to her attic bedroom and sat down with her copy of the Joseph Macauley case file and flipped the pages idly. She settled on Eli Aaron and the rosary beads. She had visited each church within a hundred miles, each Chinese supermarket, small gift shop and jeweler and Catholic bookstore, consulted with a dozen priests who scratched their heads and reasoned there were a million types of prayer beads, each a little different, each carrying the same weight of promise. And once more she ran over what they had. Photos of half a dozen girls. One of them Misty

Meyer. One of them Callie Montrose. She'd traced Eli Aaron back across a dozen states where he had taken photographs at two dozen schools. She could not put names to the other girls. Marty Tooms had worked with him. Maybe Tooms lured them sometimes. Aaron snatched them other times. It was messy and altogether uneven.

She fell asleep with the file across her chest.

Every night.

102

His name was Walter Strike. He walked with a cane and limp and told Patch of his ancestors, Revolutionary War patriots and a secessionist government that spoke of fierce independence.

The backdrop of mountains rolled toward Virginia, a vein so ornery Patch felt the fight in the man as they walked beneath the patterned shade of palmetto.

"I used to think we didn't need anyone," Walter said.

Patch smoothed his hair beneath his cap and buried his hands deep in his pockets.

"Cops can't do enough. My Eloise was fifteen, and they acted like that was of age. Like she wasn't a child at all."

They passed a woman with four children tangling around her, speaking a language fast and loud and sweet.

"Gullah," Walter said, nodded to the lady and

smiled at the children. "Friends say she took off with one of them, but I know she wouldn't."

Patch listened intently to these stories, trying to build Grace from their memories and always missing necessary materials.

"My wife still jumps out of bed when we hear a car slow at night. Like she expects her to roll in, maybe a little drunk, rattle the cabinets as she fixes a sandwich like she used to. Play my Johnny Cash records and start wailing." He laughed.

They spent the afternoon at Middleton Place, an Ashley River Plantation, the gardens so elegant Patch wondered how anything bad could have ever happened there. Walter told him of the day she vanished, how the cops followed a trail so long it led to black water swamps.

They slowed by a gazebo, stood well back as a couple posed for photographs, the bride flushed in her simple white gown.

Neither said it. Walter's daughter, Eloise, was likely dead. He would not get to stand at her wedding and watch her smile, give her hand to someone, see his wife's tears.

"I have a son, Coop, and he lost his way when Eloise . . . he works in a library now. He lives quiet, because the world lost its sound and taste and . . . It's a hard thing to do."

The day faded out and the last Carolina wren sang.

"What?" Patch said, quiet like he was afraid.

"Say goodbye. How many people have you seen just like me?"

Patch thought of the noticeboards in his old basement. The faces. The map dotted at Wild Basin, Kitt Peak, Chesapeake. And so on. He knew the first names of two dozen charity workers that dedicated their lives to finding the missing.

"Too many," Walter said.

"Not enough."

The man extended a hand, held on a little longer and pulled Patch close. "I know you've been told this before and will likely hear it again. You get a single shot . . . doesn't seem fair, but aim right and it's enough. I won't ever forget you coming to see me, just to hear someone speak her name awhile has been everything. If you learn from the times you go wrong, you can revel in the times you don't."

103

The next morning Patch walked into a South Atlantic Bank, put his gun in the face of a kid not all that much older than himself, and filled his bag. As he turned onto Interstate 95 a cop tailed him for near three miles before passing. Patch figured if they caught him he'd go down with a single regret. He reckoned that was better than most.

He gave close to every cent to the Harvey Robin Foundation, which covered several southern states, their work tireless and vital.

Another two families, he painted their girls and packed the canvases off to Sammy, didn't call in much, didn't think of home because he did not know where that was. He still owned the house in Monta Clare, thought of selling up but knew it was all that tied him down, that gave him the smallest link to the town where it all began.

A month later he moved from Silverton to the Red Mountain Pass, through Calf Creek Falls till he reached Bryce Canyon. His feet stirred the dust, his brush rarely left the canvas as he met parents and grandparents and friends who could not ever let go. He watched grainy home movies in empty dens, sat on sofas and strained to hear their daughter's voices, his heart sinking each and every time he could not place her.

In the early hours he called Saint, waited for the beep of her machine, and recounted a memory so sharp it cut through his doubt.

"Everyone in the world has a voice unique to only them," Grace said, as she lay top to tail beside him, her own voice coming close from the darkness.

"Like a fingerprint?" he said.

"The length and tension of your vocal cords. The depth of your lungs. Your resonating chamber."

"Sometimes I think you know too much."

"I take comfort in it," she said.

"In what?"

"In the screams I hear. That last cry in this world. So personal it will never be heard again."

He took a route from the Colorado River down to Sedona, from arid to lush, dunes to pine. And at Phoenix he joined the Apache Trail.

He watched the sunrise as he threaded his way through the Rockies, the Million Dollar Highway soared, and at Mesa Verde he stopped at a small church and joined the morning mass and dipped his head and spoke his apology. As the plate came round he stuffed a hundred dollars into it; the

woman beside took his arm and gripped her gratitude like she knew nothing of the bandit and the
taint on each bill.

Beside the church, a woman sat in a rocking chair,
her hands working on a macramé wall hanging. In
her basket were a dozen more, and beside them on
a table were trinkets and rosary beads.

Patch looked through them quickly.

"A chain of roses," the woman said. Her skin
was dark, and her white hair peeked from beneath
a scarf. Her apron was faded and her eyes sunken
deep, her view of the world narrowed.

"They count prayers," he said.

"And remind us of the three mysteries history
cannot teach. From the joyful to the glorious.
Christ's birth to the resurrection. My son was buried with his."

"Why?" he said, caught himself and offered his
condolences.

"We place them on the dead and then cut the
rosary to stop another death following."

"The joyful and the glorious. That's only two. You
said there were three," he said.

She squinted up, the sunlight blinding. "The sor-
rowful. Suffering and death."

"The dead. What happens if the rosary beads are
left uncut on them?" he said.

She crossed herself slowly and continued her work.

104

Saint took the call.

A streetwalker in St. Louis, sounded young, but Saint kept her guard in place. She did not give a name, only said that there was a new girl being pushed, couldn't have been more than sixteen and maybe looked a little like a faded drawing she'd seen on a poster as she passed through Alice Springs. She gave a street she'd work that night, in itself not usual though Saint checked the clock, thought of Jimmy and his mother waiting so they could have dinner together. She grabbed her keys and headed out.

An hour till she saw the high-rises, the Gateway Arch and the white lanterns along Herald Street. People emptied from bars, loud and raucous.

The lights were out on North Street. Cars lined up facing the road, the white buildings behind so run-down. Electrical cables fell from the roof like bowels tied off. A group of guys stood together, watching her pass, each of them locking eyes on her as she pulled over beneath a busted streetlight.

She checked her gun, always, saw the guys lose interest and go back to their game as a girl moved from the shadows. Late teens, despite the heavy makeup. A skirt skimmed her ass; her eyes were young though Saint could only imagine what they had seen.

Saint rolled down her window, and the girl tossed a piece of paper into the car. She carried on walking past before disappearing behind a steel door, so bent out of shape it did not close behind her.

Saint found the address on the paper, a mile out of town.

Right then, as she watched the old house on the corner of Fairshaw and Brooklyn, she got a feeling so strong it shook her knees as she climbed out.

She called it in and gave enough details for a dispatch.

Saint did not want to notice the upstairs light cut out, or see the shape of a young girl pass by the window, the big man following.

The music was loud.

Behind the street lit blue.

Local cops took control as Saint sank low in her seat while the arrest was made.

They led the girl out.

Saint followed to the St. Louis PD.

The girl, Mia, was sixteen years old and had fallen in with a group she could not break from.

Saint sat in the lot till dawn, when the girl's fraught parents arrived, took her in their arms and sobbed.

She drove home in sunlight.

It would be the first time Patch saved a missing girl.

105

Beneath a steel sky so foreboding Patch might have known, he strolled into the Merchants National and did not notice the extra guard posted by the side door, sitting back behind a newspaper. And when he pulled his gun he did not see the man pull his own.

The teller shoved bills into an envelope, then glanced up once, over Patch's right shoulder, as he handed him the money.

The shot sounded like a cap or a firecracker.

The glass divider shattered.

The screams dropped him to the floor with the rest.

He crawled his way across the carpet as hell broke loose around him. An alarm rang out; sprinklers washed the panic from him as he settled behind a desk and breathed deep.

There was hollering as the guard moved forward, trembling gun held out in front as he fired.

Patch did not know the background of the man, but did know that the Model 36 carried six bullets, and he'd counted five shots.

So when he heard the sixth thud deep into the desk behind, he climbed to his feet and sprinted for the door.

Until then it had been a game. A redistribution of wealth to where it was needed most.

He mailed the money to the Forever United charity. The bills still wet as he sealed the package.

106

Patch didn't breathe again until three days later, when he met the cool of Washington, D.C.

They ate an early dinner in a downtown steakhouse so fanciful Patch could not decide if the 77 scrawled beside the filet mignon was the price or the number of years it had been aging.

Patch flagged down a waiter and tried to order a Coke and a footlong.

"Why do you do this every time I take you someplace nice to eat?" Sammy said, as Patch bit his lower lip.

Sammy ordered two bottles of Chateau Palmer, asked the waiter to hand over the corks, and then gave one to Patch and kept one for himself. "In thirty years you'll find this someplace and remember the day you drank it was the day some dumb Washington lobbyist paid ten thousand bucks for one of your lost girls."

"Send the money—"

"Half to the family, half to some obscure missing persons charity. I know, kid."

Patch picked up a breadstick, gripped it between his teeth, and asked Sammy for a light.

Sammy sighed. "They all want to know about you. The collectors. I give them a little . . . just enough flavor. The pirate hero who mourns his lost love. Hell, I'd consider buying them if they were much, much, much better."

Patch raised his glass, pretended he could taste the black fruits, the tannins.

"Long finish," Sammy said, and smacked his lips.

"Not the way you drink it."

Over heritage chicken, scallions and confit potatoes they talked art, the progress Patch was making, each piece he sent now so valuable Sammy sent a courier service to package and collect.

"We need another showing. We need people to see these girls," Sammy said, as he cussed out the chef for leaning too heavy on the vadouvan.

Patch wore a black shirt, three buttons undone, the smartest sneakers he owned, which weren't all that smart. He caught the eye of a waitress, his interest in the angle of her jaw, the S of her clavicle, the hint of red in her hair.

"I have a friend in New York and she's—"

"I'm heading to New England," Patch said.

Sammy sighed once more, ordered another bottle, his cheeks red. "And where are you getting money from? You pay taxes on a house you don't live in. You should sell **Grace Number One** and—"

"My mother dreamed of owning that house."

Sammy might have told him what he already knew, but instead turned back to his plate. "I see Saint."

"Still can't believe she's a cop?"

"Are we playing the game where you pretend you don't know why?" Sammy's hair was neatly parted, his tan deep and his teeth white.

Patch ignored him, focusing on the waitress.

"She's got herself a boyfriend."

Patch smiled at that. "Jimmy Walters."

"Churchy Mama's boy pussy bitch motherfucker." Patch sighed.

"He critiqued Callie Montrose. Said her blouse was cut low in the painting. I believe he used the term **immodest.**"

"But he loves Saint."

"What's love got to do with it? In other news, I fucked Trisha Mason." Sammy stared into his glass with remorse.

"From the dairy?"

"Suppose I'll have to find someplace else to get my Gruyère. . . ." He shook his head, like it was no fault of his own, went on to talk of a supplier in the city as Patch tuned him out.

Patch looked over at the open wood oven, the chefs in brown aprons, the suited men around.

". . . Fucker tried to sell me dry aged Jack. Like I don't know the pH. Like I didn't already tell him I wanted to melt it onto Bellota."

As the waitress passed, Patch reached out and took her hand. She spun, about to curse off another power broker with wandering hands when she saw his face and smiled.

"What's your name?" he said.

"Melissa." That smile again. He noticed her teeth, the way she formed her words, and he lost interest as soon as the familiarity died.

"You'll get arrested grabbing girls like that," Sammy said.

"The voice of experience."

"I liked you better when you were cleaning piss from my toilet."

Sammy called for a fourth bottle, and Patch settled back in his chair and allowed in the warmth of the place.

"You want dessert?" Sammy said.

"Anything with honey."

Sammy ordered ricotta brûlée for himself, "And a jar of Manuka for Winnie the cunting Pooh."

"You ever see Misty Meyer?"

"I see her mother."

"How are they doing?"

Sammy smiled drunkenly. "The one that got away. Misty is at Harvard."

"All is right."

"Not all. The girl also tends bar now."

Patch raised an eyebrow. "Bet her parents love that. Not like she needs the money."

"Place called the Boatman. Same place her mother used to drink way back when. I reckon slumming it with you has broadened her world. That family."

"You know them well?"

Sammy waved a hand. "No one knows anyone well, kid."

When the last diners settled up, and Sammy threatened to add the tab to Patch's servitude, the waitress brushed past and slipped her number into his pocket.

"Tell me you'll use that," Sammy said.

Outside Patch tossed it into the trash.

Patch was about to turn toward his car to sleep it off when Sammy bundled him into a taxi. He watched the streets blur by before they pulled up outside a beaux arts building, so grand Patch dizzied as he stared up at the arced windows.

A doorman was about to step in front when he saw Sammy, moved aside, and tipped his hat to Patch, who bowed low.

"Don't fucking bow," Sammy hissed.

Patch took his arm as he staggered toward the elevator. They rode to the top floor, where Sammy occupied the penthouse.

Patch helped him over to the bed. Sammy lay back and let the room spin as Patch looked around at the opulence. "How do you have so much?"

"Painting," Sammy slurred.

"You painted?"

"I bought a painting. I was a little younger than you are now. Rothko. I saw the state of his mind where others merely saw the color."

"You bought a Mark Rothko painting?" Patch said.

"I was poor. A poor kid like you."

"You don't act like you were a poor kid. You went to Harvard."

"I went to Harvard to see a girl. Nothing those cunts could teach me anyhow."

"Right. And you were so poor you had money to buy art." He pressed his forehead to the glass and marveled at the monument.

"I sold my soul to a rich man. Lost love, there isn't a pain so exquisite."

Patch turned to look at him. "I don't understand."

Sammy spoke on an exhale. "When the rich have a problem they throw money at it to make it go away."

"I understand perfectly."

"There's a minibar."

Patch picked a miniature Johnnie Walker, and by the time he made it to the bed Sammy was snoring loudly.

At the window he looked out over the city lights to the country beyond.

And he thought of how much his world had widened.

.   .   .

He watched a full moon shine over the city, closed his eye as the memory stole his breath. He dialed her, waited for the machine, and spoke of the peak of the clouds, of Misty Moon and ten sleeps. It made no sense at all.

He would find her.

He would die before he quit.

107

She found Jimmy waiting on her grandmother's porch, laid out on the swinging seat, his jacket for a blanket. Saint had worked late, taken a call with Harkness and ridden to a burned-out car on old Eastern Avenue, close to where Patch had been taken. Saint had shone her flashlight over the dirt like she could still see his blood seeping in.

She stood there and watched him sleep.

She'd been to see him the day after their missed prom, took a little shit from his mother as she led her into the house where Jimmy's suit hung, back in its rental bag, a sight that still caught in her throat sometimes.

He was six months older, knew most things about most animals. He voted Republican because his father did, went to church because his mother did, and because he believed in a way that dazzled even her grandmother.

She had sat in his childhood bedroom and noticed laundry neatly folded, the bed sheets freshly made. His mother had knocked on the door with oatmeal cookies. He was the kind of boy who would become the kind of man that needed tending.

"There isn't another kind of man," Norma said, one evening as they ate barbecued chicken before a St. Francois sunset.

Patch was another kind, Saint thought, spilling barbecue sauce down her shirt.

"Joseph is different because he did not have a woman to do things for him," Norma said, reading her mind as she dabbed at her shirt with a napkin. "Just like he does not know how to care. How to conduct a friendship. How to be a man."

"Women teach men how to be men?" Saint said.

"Of course. How else do you think they learn?"

Jimmy had kissed her, but nothing more. And it was not the open-mouthed type of kiss she had seen Misty and Patch share, the kind of kiss that led to the kind of sex she saw in the movies, the kind that had once made her blush but now made her wonder at the deal she had made with God. Never more so than when she wore a dress, drank two wines, and placed the flat of her hand against Jimmy's muscled chest, lightly pushing him toward the bed she slept on. His breath had been raggedy as he broke the kiss and stepped outside to take some air.

The next Friday he had taken her to the Palace 7 to watch a movie. The leading man was so handsome in his navy suit that Saint had found herself pawing at Jimmy before he could get through the door. He had sat her down and told her he did not believe in sex before marriage.

"He stopped by last night and asked me for your hand," Norma said.

Saint took a moment. "But I'm only—"

"You've been dating awhile. You know what Jimmy is, how he dotes on you."

Saint sipped her coffee, her mind on the young streetwalker. "Is sin a real thing?"

Norma sat opposite.

"I saw a girl the other night and she had done things, . . . and I know he's not a vengeful God and all, but surely she can't be judged."

Norma took a moment. "Is she the girl Joseph is looking for?"

Saint shook her head.

"We're all reaching, Saint. Some people stand on others. Some people give you a boost when you need it. You know which kind Jimmy is?"

Saint shook her head again.

"Sometimes ordinary is more than enough," Norma said.

"He wants to live a life like his parents'."

"They seem happy."

"What did you tell him?"

"That your hand isn't mine to give or his to take. Only yours to offer."

"I'm not sorry I didn't go to college," Saint said, a challenge in her cyc.

Norma stood behind Saint and placed a hand on her shoulder.

Saint leaned her head to the side and met the warmth of her grandmother's skin. "What should I do?"

"I'd say follow your heart, but in that way madness lies. Do you believe in fate?"

Saint took a moment and then nodded.

"That day, when you took your grandfather's gun and headed into the woods—"

Saint still saw the pain on her grandmother's face. "I'm sorry—"

"If Jimmy hadn't told Chief Nix where you were going, if he hadn't cared enough to do that, then maybe I wouldn't have gotten you back. And Ivy would not have her son back."

"So I owe him?" Saint said.

Norma shook her head. "No. But I will say that there's a grand plan for all of us, and Jimmy Walters is part of yours."

"How do I know if I love him?" Saint said.

"When it comes to marriage, love is merely a visitor over a lifetime. Respect and kindness, they are the true foundations. If I'm honest, I think you should marry him."

"Jimmy is a good man," Saint said, swallowing, her eyes filling with tears. "But he's not—"

"I know."

108

After the mess at the Merchants National Bank, Patch sold his car and spent a month hauling freight. At four in the morning he would pull on a hooded sweatshirt and load frozen meat into the backs of trucks that would cart it across the state.

As he walked, dawn stalked him like a reminder that sooner or later time would push him on. He took a room at the top of an old house, paid the cash up front because the old lady looked at him like she knew his kind.

The days grew longer and harder, and only when it was truly dark, when he blocked the bleed of streetlamps with duct tape and pressed newspaper over the glass five pages thick, when he'd cleared everything from the small bedroom, ripped the carpet from the floor and taken down the prints of the water lilies, did he pull the mattress to the floor, close his eyes and sleep. He didn't know which nights he would find her, but they were lessening now.

He noticed a couple of girls with the right kind

of hair, almost the right way of speaking. Girls that emerged from the steps of fabled schools, drank in college bars, and soon grew weary of the same kind of college boy. They'd glance his way and mistake the light in his eye for something that might reflect onto them. He'd probe at their past, find nothing but symmetry, and slip from their dorm rooms before first light.

After a long day he returned back to find his bag on the stoop. The old lady told him she did not care for the remodeling of his room.

For a month he stalled his hunt because he knew what little luck remained could not be ridden so hard, so at a Gloucester marina he stopped at each trawler and asked if they needed someone to do the kind of jobs rising lobster prices meant they could farm out.

He cleaned algae from the metal lines, blood and guts and sinew. He set traps, hacked bait, and measured lobster from eye to rear. He sifted through, pulled out new shells, notched breeders, and banded the unlucky.

"Steady, kid," Skip said, as they rode billows. He stood beside the center console and held the wheel and watched Skip's men haul yellow traps from the seabed as evening mist surfed swells. Behind, the New England coastline hid towns and mountains after white sand beaches.

A couple of men gave him shit about the eye patch, like he was playing at being a pirate. The first time he'd sat on the gunwale, his throat dried from the salt air and his face ached from the smile. And after, when they reached the marina, he'd unload and begin his cleaning while Skip reached for a cooler and handed out beers.

Patch stayed on the boat and drank alone, watching the setting sun.

At night he slept on a piece of beach bracketed by low bluffs, his shirt rolled up to make a pillow on the fine sand. Tired out from the day, he did not eat near enough, kept what little Skip gave him because he knew soon enough he would move on, toward her.

109

Two weeks in and a couple of the younger crew dragged him out. The cab smelled of cheap cologne and desperation as they passed around a bottle of Jim Beam and speculated on the lure of real men to college girls. Fifty miles in an old camper, a couple of hours till he saw Boston lights loom.

They crawled along JFK Street, Patch wearing his old jeans and leather boots, so faded he could not recall exactly what color they were supposed to be. In the first Irish bar a few girls smiled his way, one came over, made small talk, her hand on his chest as she tossed her hair back and laughed at something he did not recall saying.

"Shit, got to get me an eye patch," one of the boys said, as they piled out into the street and moved on.

In a bar called the Boatman he scanned the faces of every girl inside and wondered if some stood the way she might have, smiled the way she might have. He caught the edge of conversations and heard the shape of her words, the pitch of her laugh. Grace was everywhere and nowhere.

Patch sat alone on a barstool, saw a couple of cops walk by, his fear rational but without merit. His world was small. No one knew him at all.

As he threaded his way through the throng he heard a voice a little louder than the rest, clear enough the girl was struggling. He glanced over, saw a couple having some kind of domestic, the girl tall and blonde, her back to him as the man she stood with put a hand on her ass.

She pushed at his chest firmly, but he laughed it off, pulled her closer as she tried to undo the knot of his hands.

Patch saw a couple of the guy's friends laughing at what was playing out.

The guy was tall and broad; his light hair flopped to one side. Patch noted the signet ring, the gold watch. He was almost to them when the girl stepped back again, wresting herself free. Patch threw a hard punch.

It was over quick.

The big guy a mess on the floor, the girl still tumbling as Patch leaned forward and caught her in his arms.

It was only then that he finally saw her.

She looked up at him, her mouth slightly open.

The guy's friends gathered.

Beside him, Patch saw his own crew, fists ready, smiling.

A bottle sailed by his head and smashed on the table beside him.

Through the chaos of a Friday night bar fight, Patch scooped Misty Meyer off her feet and carried her out into the balm of a perfect Boston evening.

110

Misty kept hold of his hand and led him through the common, the Brewer Fountain keeping watch over the Park Street Church.

"They used to hang pirates from the Great Elm," she said over her shoulder.

"Doesn't sound so great, Mist." He followed her, soon enough lost in the noise of Chinatown, the smells and lights and bustle.

Down a side street opposite the park they sat on upturned crates and drank warm sake from wooden cups, her cheeks a little flushed as she ran her fingers over the swell of his knuckles.

She took the flat cap from his head and placed it on her own, grinning up at him, her eyes still too much. She looked different, but he was not sure how, still everything most were not, but maybe it was being out of Monta Clare; she seemed worldly, if possible even less attainable.

"You still look like it's 1975," she said.

He took in her bleached jeans and silk shirt, heels and light makeup.

"But you got muscles," she poked at his arm.

"I work on a boat."

She lit up. "A pirate ship?"

"We pillage the Casco Bay for lobster."

Misty laughed, a sound that took him all the way back.

Beside them neon signs spun. A basement beauty salon beneath a grated fire escape, the trash piled in the thickening glow of streetlamps.

They skirted Grace, the reason he had left, her parents and the drag of everything they had shared, and for a few blissful moments they were two young people getting to know the shiniest parts of each other in a city that blazed without limitation.

As they drank she became a little louder, a little more impassioned when she told him about her course, her lectures and professors.

"I mean, people like my father voted for him because he knows I'll never struggle to find work. He wants that layer of insulation to grow thicker. You should have seen his face when I told him I was tending bar, that I wanted to earn my own money. Like you did when you left school. The New Right isn't all that new, Patch. I mean, he's pulled us out of recession by plunging us into debt. Trickle-down economics only works if there's true translation, right?"

He sipped his sake and hoped and prayed she did not expect some kind of reply.

"Did that sound smart? I got it from a book," she said.

"You're at Harvard, Mist. Not sure you need to dumb it down, not even for me."

While they could still walk, she led him through a string of streets and pointed out sights.

He tugged her back to a Bay Village busker who warmed the night with her guitar and the soul in her voice.

The city slowed for them, and he reached out and placed a hand on her lower back.

He took her other hand, and they stood facing each other.

"I thought you didn't dance?" she said and stepped close. The busker smiled and sang as she felt the earth move in her hands.

Misty took the deepest breath like she was preparing to drown but wanted to stay conscious throughout.

Together they moved, and she pressed her cheek to his chest. "You didn't just break my heart."

"I'm sorry."

"You chose her over me."

"Everyone will choose you. Everyone."

"But not you."

He leaned down and pressed his head to hers.

"Look at us out here, Patch. In the world."

Above them stars shone like it was written.

And around them people stopped and watched

because the music was beautiful, or maybe because they knew the two kids dancing together were torn from some kind of tragic history book.

He lifted her gently, her hands wrapped around his neck as he slowly spun her. In the distance he heard sirens and wondered if this is how they would end.

"I don't know how to forget you," she whispered it, right into his ear, her words tunneling into his brain and forging their own place in him, to call on in case there were moments of doubt, moments of weakness that told him he might be good, beneath it all, what he had done and what he would do, he might just be good enough.

"You close your eyes, Mist. And when you open them again I'll be gone. And you'll live this . . . this fucking wondrous life. You'll go to your classes and talk to other kids who've got shit to say, who've got opinions and ideas. Soon enough you'll forget my face, and the sound of my voice. Because you'll realize I never had much to say. Not really."

She shook her head fiercely.

He hated it when she cried.

111

Afterward she led him along the dark of the Charles River, Eliot House so grand he stared at the exalted white windows, and when she finally dragged him across the checkered floor and up the paneled stairs to her room, he was dizzy at the thought that she got to live in such a place.

She kissed him and he kissed her.

She pulled his T-shirt from him and stepped back and stared at him, her eyes tracing the spareness of him; the scars borne for her. He stood back in the shadow of her dresser, like wherever he was he lamented the space he took up in her world.

Hours from morning he woke and slipped from the bed where she slept, and through the window he watched the sky flare over the Charles. He took a pencil and paper from her small desk and sketched the shape of her in a detail he knew he would not ever forget.

As he scrawled his name and placed the picture

down for her, he saw from the window the rise of the cupola and beyond it JFK Park.

And as he stole from Misty's life he followed that view and stood where he knew Grace had once stood, his steps in hers.

He knew then he would not go back to Skip.

He knew then things would get worse and maybe not ever better.

112

On the morning she sat at her piano in her robe, her glasses lying on the lid, the fallboard propped to the reveal of simple gold lettering. Outside a strong wind blew and broke the petiole of russet leaves till they freed and fell, and Saint wondered if anything died a more beautiful death.

"What is this?" Norma said.

Saint did not turn to notice that her grandmother wore a navy dress with a gorse flower hat, like she could not decide whether to celebrate or mourn.

"It's a song by a frog with an introspective soul," Saint said, and watched the season like it was her last, like it would not be so noteworthy again.

"It's sad," Norma said.

"It isn't. It's for the lovers and the dreamers."

Saint stared at the painting of the white house as she played, and she thought of the way his fingers delicately grasped the brush, the way he breathed as he brought color into her world. The night before she had sat in the hallway and listened to the telephone ring, fought the urge to answer, and instead listened to his voice on the machine as he talked of a gold rush, a summer in Colorado's Kingdom. She had woken her grandmother and made her promise to keep the recordings after she moved.

Saint and Norma ate breakfast together for the last time. It had been decided that Saint would move into the small house on Alexander Avenue, a gift from Jimmy's mother as his parents fled Monta Clare for retirement in the warmth of Florida. A house where reminders of everything before sang so loud she forgot her own rhythms. He told her they would decorate together, that they would head to Monta Clare Hardware and pick out colors she liked, and they would rip out the old bathroom and kitchen.

Saint dressed in an ivory gown with a lace bodice, simple and unfussy, but when she walked down the creaking staircase her grandmother's smile told her she had done enough for him, for the church and the townspeople that would fill it to witness the rookie cop marry the rookie veterinarian.

"I thought you would wear your French braid," Norma said.

"Not today."

She had wanted to get a car, but Jimmy had balked at the expense, and so grandmother and granddaughter set off toward the church together, walking slow to take in a morning already beginning to turn.

A few neighbors came out and smiled, and a little

girl waved and clapped her hands. And when they met the crossroads with Rosewood Avenue Saint breathed deep.

The church was a fade of variegated gray; the pinnacles rose, and before them Saint took Norma's hand at the far end of a winding pathway she had walked a thousand times before, in anticipation and fear and, mostly, relief.

"And these are happy tears?" Norma said, and carefully dabbed at Saint's cheeks. And then she knelt and used that same handkerchief to clean the mud and grass from Saint's flats. Norma stayed down there, her knee on the damp ground as she looked up at her granddaughter backed by a church they had spent the better and worst parts of their lives looking to.

"He will be kind to you. I promise," Norma said.

113

Inside, half the town showed, and when it was time her grandmother led her before their eyes, and she stood opposite him in his two-button suit, his satin lapels and sage paisley tie.

She did her best to smile, to speak her vows, to make far-reaching promises from a limited vantage point. And only when all was nearly said and done did she make the fatal mistake of glancing to the back of the nave.

Patch sat alone, and for a moment she met his eye.

She took Jimmy's hand. As the applause rang out and he led her down the aisle, she looked for him again. And saw that he was gone.

Outside in the break of rain as the photographer readied and the locals gathered to throw confetti, Saint slipped from her husband's hand and moved back down the pathway.

"Hey," she called.

And she took a breath before he turned.

"How did you—"

Patch smiled. "Sammy."

"Right."

"You're not staying for the party."

He shook his head.

Soon enough his hair matted down with the rain, but for a long time they stood there, so familiar and foreign.

"He seems—"

"He'll be a veterinarian," she said.

"You always liked animals."

She smiled, and she wondered if he still saw that girl with the crooked tooth, the overalls torn at each knee.

"He treats you well?" Patch said.

She wanted to tell him that Jimmy said there wasn't room for her piano. That sometimes she fixed his dinner and he forgot to thank her. That he was not silly in any of the good ways. She wanted to tell Patch that Jimmy did not like her being a cop. That he wanted to have children right away, and that when they did he expected her to step out of her life and into a mother's. Most of all she wanted to tell him that she was scared. She was a cop who had done so many brave things. But she was scared.

"He treats me well."

He took her in his arms and she felt the strength of him, the heat as his hands pressed the small of her back, her chest against his.

"I miss you," she whispered into his ear.

"Every day," he said.

"There's so much to say, Patch."

"But nothing that will change much of anything."

He wiped her tears.

"You be good, kid," she said.

And then she walked back to the church, where Norma found her and took her into the side room and dried her off, fixed her hair and the little makeup she wore.

"You look beautiful," Jimmy said.

"Thank you."

"I was worried you were going to wear that braid in your hair like when we were kids," he added with a laugh. "Where were you, before?"

"I had to say goodbye to somebody."

Saint managed to smile for the photos, managed to shake the hands and kiss the cheeks, and make small talk with everyone who filled the church hall into the evening.

And it was only when the dance floor cleared, and the spotlight fell, and Jimmy took her in his arms that she felt the smallest stab of relief that Patch had left before the reception.

The small crowd gathered at the edge and smiled as the speakers crackled with the opening notes.

"Why did you choose this song?" Jimmy asked, as they gently swayed.

"I just like it."

Saint moved with him and did not meet his eyes, instead closing hers tightly.

She sang in a whisper, of Mona Lisas and Mad Hatters, and how rose trees never grow in New York City.

114

Nix sat, his line in the water, face shaded by his fishing hat. He pulled catfish and walleye, his creel so full he tossed a couple back as he nursed a cold beer.

"You wanted to see me," Saint said.

"You came all this way. You should be on your honeymoon."

"I got the message. I came here."

The sun fell low over the Glenn Hook Reservoir, straddling Calder County and Winton. Saint watched fingerlings break the surface as she tossed bait between slips of reed and saw black bass hunt down shad.

"I told Norma it could wait till you were back," Nix said.

"I never . . . we didn't go anywhere. We're saving to fix up the house. And Jimmy has exams coming up."

He'd made the drive out in the RV, parked back at the campground by the Crook City Causeway.

"So what do you need?" Saint said as he made to pass her a beer, but she shook her head.

He set it back in the cooler. "Let's talk awhile."

The past years Saint worked seven-day weeks; a vague sense time was passing only by the changing seasons and nothing more. She watched the harsh bite of winter but did not feel the cold. Trampled the foil green woodland in spring and threw herself into the mundanities, the patrols and forced entries, the parking tickets and misdemeanors.

She stared down at the simple gold band on her finger and thought of the wedding night. How Jimmy ejaculated before she could take his pants off. And how he got mad and walked out of their cheap motel room and smoked a cigarette in his car. When he came back in he slept, and she watched the ceiling and imagined her life and the contours of missteps. At first light he climbed on top of her and grunted into her ear. It was over almost as quick. She had thought it might hurt. She had thought she would at least feel something.

"You like being married?" Nix said.

She spun the ring, a size too big on her slender finger. "It's good, Chief."

"And I'll bet Norma is happy."

Saint smiled. "She wanted me to marry Jimmy. She believes he's a good man."

"You think that's the only reason why?"

Saint turned to him.

Nix smoothed his moustache. "You marrying Jimmy, maybe means she won't have to be so fearful of Joseph."

"How do you mean?"

"Every time you did something reckless, every time you deviated from your path, it was because of him." Nix smiled.

"She's protecting me."

"You're all she's got. And you're worth protecting, Saint."

She blushed a little.

"You love this guy?" he said, and he did not meet her eye because it was not a comfortable question for him to ask.

"Love is a visitor."

He laughed, but it was not unkind. "Well, then I hope it comes to stay soon."

"You were never married."

He sipped his beer. "People talk about one life . . . one chance. But I reckon a single life is made up of a dozen or more roles and responsibilities. I can count the versions of myself like friend and foe. Mistakes are the detours that remind you of the true way, Saint. To love and be loved is more than can ever be expected, more than enough for a thousand ordinary lifetimes."

"I don't know if that's true."

"I hope one day you will."

She batted blackflies. "You didn't ever want kids?"

"That responsibility. I'm in awe of people that take it on. Plan to bring another person into this world."

"It's not always planned."

"A million and a half terminations last year. Each

clinic you got some goddamn ghoul with an opin-ion and a placard."

She watched the water. "Heading in the right direction."

"Too little, too late for some."

"This might be the worst honeymoon anyone ever took."

He laughed deeply. "I did have a dog growing up. Loved that mutt like it was human. Maybe more. That sound strange?"

She nodded.

He laughed.

"There's women in town that want to date you," she said.

"The idea of me, maybe. The real me, well he lost his heart thirty years ago."

She smiled. "What happened?"

"What always happens. One of you leaves the other one alone." He raised his beer toward the water, and she could not imagine a woman that would ever leave him.

"Where will you head next?"

He reeled and cast and sat and drank. "Long drive to Severy City. Maybe I'll fish from a kayak. Got my eye on those sunfish."

"My grandfather was a bass fisherman."

Nix whistled and followed it with a wide smile. "Alabama River. All spring in the north, maybe the finest largemouth I ever pulled out."

Saint did not say that Nix seemed sadder since.

She could not say why, just that something indelible had been written for him the day Joseph disappeared, or maybe the day Marty Tooms lost the remainder of his life. Like he could not begin to understand the things he had not questioned before. How a murderer lived in his town.

"Sometimes I think we've come a long way," she said.

"And other times we haven't taken a single step."

"I think of Callie Montrose," she said. "I heard her father took early retirement. Also heard he caused a little trouble the other night."

Nix pressed the bottle to his forehead. "Maybe we all should've stopped after. Just shut down and gone home. Richie Montrose will see out his days at the bottom of a whisky bottle. Can't say I blame him."

As the air cooled he leaned back and watched the light ease.

"The FBI want you," he said. "I got a call from a man named Himes. Executive something or other. They want you to fly to Kansas City and meet with them."

"Okay."

He lit a cigar.

They stayed till the sky made mauve of the water.

At her car she hugged him tightly. She did not know a better man than Chief Nix.

115

Jimmy picked at the chicken she had roasted.

"It's bad enough I can't sleep at night worrying about you in Monta Clare." Dark rings circled beneath his eyes. He did not shave on weekends, and blue-black stubble peppered his cheeks and neck. Most nights he studied till late, surprised by his own limitations. He had made good grades at school. He had never questioned his own future, his abilities, his faith in himself and in the fact that everything would be just fine. It was one of the things she admired most about him.

"You don't need to worry about me."

"You're my wife."

"It's my career, Jimmy. It's important to me."

He sipped his water. "You don't think I know why you do it."

"I want to make a difference," she said, and ate a mouthful but could not swallow it down. Behind him the wallpaper had been stripped but left in wet piles.

She stood and made to clear the dishes.

He pulled her onto his lap, and she smiled.

"We've got each other. We've got our faith. I'd do anything for you," he said.

"I know that. I'd do anything for you, Jimmy."

"Except show up for prom." He pinched her sides and she laughed and he laughed.

He kissed her. "Don't go to Kansas. I've only just about got my head around being married to a police officer."

"Jimmy, I—"

He reached for her breast. "We should try again . . . tonight. Now."

"The dishes . . ."

"You can do them after."

He tugged her hand and led her up the stairs.

116

Saint pressed her face to the window as her stomach dropped with the engines of the 720.

She had not flown before, politely declined drinks and did not fuss about the heavy smoke from a dozen cigarettes, the man beside seeming intent on fogging her view.

Mercifully she was in the air less than an hour before they taxied and she stepped down into Kansas City.

A car took her to the federal building, and inside she joined seventy-three agents and forty-three support personnel covering the Western District of Missouri and the entire state of Kansas. She cleared security, rode the elevator, and stepped into a rush of noise. People worked phones in small cubbies with gray felt walls like a view would be surplus to the task at hand.

A noticeboard showed faces, names, and crimes ranging from murder to drugs to jail breaks. Rewards ran into the millions. She thought of Nix, of Monta

Clare PD, a nervous flip in her stomach as she was led into a glass-walled office.

She met with Himes, two decades older, with a title so long she lost it after **executive.** Plaques lined the wall, framed photos of him with various dignitaries she did not know. He ran a little history, from Eberstein to Bonnie Parker and Clyde Barrow. She wondered how many times he had told it, how many rookies had sat in her seat all wide eyed and burning ambition.

He homed in on the massacre in 1933, four lawmen dead at the hands of Adam Richetti and Charles Floyd as Frank Nash was being transferred back to Leavenworth prison. He moved on to Ollie Embry, tucked a napkin into his shirt and broke a bagel in two and offered her the smaller half.

She shook her head.

"Thing about this job, you consume when you can. You never know when you'll be called out."

"With all due respect, sir, I still don't know what I'm doing here. You talk about being an agent, but I'm two years shy of your age requirement."

"We can recruit from wherever—"

"So you're offering me a job? I think you might've made a mistake. You see I'm a new—"

He set the bagel down, stood and dusted crumbs from his trousers. "We don't make mistakes. It's not a job . . . more like an assignment. And you can start—"

"You're assuming I want it."

He smiled at that. "I pulled your record. Quite some background. The Eli Aaron case. I saw the photograph."

Saint knew the picture. It had run on the front of **The Post.** She stood there small before the flames of the Aaron house, her cheeks dark with soot. A few hours later she would find Patch and save his life.

"And you graduated valedictorian. Turned down the Ivy Leagues."

"Is there anything you don't know about me?"

"You're married."

"Yes." She thought of Jimmy, how he had left the house before her, didn't wish her luck because he didn't want her to go.

Himes picked up the bagel again, bit it, a piece of lettuce hung from the corner of his mouth. "Most of us were at some point. You're studying still. Correspondence course. Major in psychology with a minor in behavioral science."

She had not told anyone but Jimmy that she was studying, and that was only because he found her papers.

"Why?" he said.

"For exactly that reason. I'm interested in why."

"Nothing to do with a missing girl. Name of Grace."

He tossed a file onto the desk, and she opened it, saw the body, or lack of it, just the bones.

"Found by the Tensleep Creek. Up by the Misty Moon Lake."

"But—"

He turned the page for her. Her eyes scanned it and then settled on the photograph. She felt her blood cool as the air left her lungs.

The rosary beads.

"Angela Rossi. Can't accurately date the death. One of yours though, right?"

Saint thought of Eli Aaron.

Himes wiped his mouth with the back of his hand. "We can help you. And I think you'd make a good addition to the team."

"Doing what exactly?"

He tossed another file onto the desk between them. The lettering bold and black.

BANK ROBBERY

"I don't understand," she said. The first page. The picture was grainy. The man wore a ball cap and sunglasses.

"How much did he take?" she said.

"Couple thousand bucks."

Himes handed her another three pages. "Six banks now. From Lawton to Austen to Kingsville. Almost got himself shot in the Merchants National."

She flipped through interviews with tellers who all told the same story. He was calm and polite.

"Might not be the same guy," she said, the locations so far apart.

"It is."

"How?"

"He pulls the same gun."

She frowned. "I'm sorry, but I'm still not making the connection here. Why you flew me out here when, all due respect, I'm green as they come. You've got people here, likely people that know something more than nothing about robbing banks. And—"

"He pulls a one-shot flintlock pistol," Himes said, leaning back on his chair and watching her intently. "Likely a replica. Real unusual."

Her breath quickened a little.

A pirate gun.

THE HUNT

1983

117

She breathed the city deep, went to the theater and watched a murder of Hamlet, and afterward sat alone at a grill and ate barbecue chicken. She flew back each weekend and saw Jimmy, who had not spoken much since failing his exams.

When she had told him she would be spending her weekdays and some weekends in Kansas he had argued. When she told him why, he had punched the refrigerator, the only damage done to his hand, which Saint had bandaged.

"He gets angry," Saint said.

"Anger is misplaced fear," Norma said.

"So he's scared of the refrigerator? You wouldn't think that if you saw him without his shirt on. His tits are now bigger than mine."

Norma bit her lip and turned away.

Saint took to exercise, running at first light, pounding morning streets till she gained in speed and distance. She found a salon in the east of town and had a little blonde added to her browns. She watched changing fashions, big hair and big shoulders and parachute pants. She saw neon and sportswear, each trend only highlighting that she had paused a decade before.

Sundays a farmer's market took over the corner of Bleaker Park, and Saint spent her time picking through greens, folding back the leaves and tutting at their shade in a move that would have pleased her grandmother. She weighed okra with her hands and prodded at watermelons to gauge their insides, her sterile apartment soon filled with the rich smells of home. She cooked enough for a month, ate alone at a round table, and when she was done began the long cleanup. She took quiet comfort in having her own space, and if she were painfully honest, she would note it was mostly because Jimmy was not there. Sometimes she called and would get the machine; other times she would ask about his day and he would fall mostly quiet and would not ever ask of hers.

In the evening she settled onto her new sofa, closed the blinds, killed the lights, and placed the tape into the stereo.

She listened to Patch's young voice on the interview tapes.

"I miss her." His voice echoed around her apartment.

The trade had been simple enough. Saint would search for him, because Himes said she had once found him when no one else could. And in exchange she could use the vast resources of the FBI to look for Grace.

She would train with Himes's team.

"Robbing banks is serious business," Himes said, each and every morning, unsmiling as he ate a bran muffin.

At lunch Saint had finally asked why Himes cared so much about finding a man who did not take all that much.

"Some cases reach you. I have a daughter. I would hope if she were ever in trouble there might be a boy like Joseph Macauley to help her."

Saint looked up from her sandwich. "And?"

Himes dipped a French fry in barbecue sauce. "If we get him now, there's still a chance for him. He's ridden his luck. If you don't bring him in, someone else will put him down."

118

Saint drove eighty-five miles along Highway 177, past tallgrass hikers as she headed toward the red-roofed limestone Chase County Courthouse. She parked her sedan in front of the First Kansas Bank and saw Cottonwood Falls locals glancing her way.

She was ushered through to a back office where she met with a girl no older than nineteen. Toothy smile and thick brown hair, her name tag read DAWN, and her nails were painted bold red like her lips.

"You mind if I eat lunch while we talk?" Dawn said, unwrapping a sandwich so thin it couldn't have held much filling. She took a bite and frowned. "Sticks to the roof of my mouth so I might lisp my way through this."

A tall man returned with a tape and handed it to Saint, threw a glance at Dawn and headed out.

"He wants to date me," Dawn said. "His family own farmland, which he'll inherit. Fuckin' smell of those cows."

"Can you tell me what happened?" Saint said, meeting her eye and trying to keep it.

Dawn set her sandwich down and smiled. "Now that was a boy I could date."

"A bank robber?"

Dawn clutched her chest, all theatrics. "He didn't rob nothing but my aching heart."

Saint rolled her eyes.

"I mean, it was a while back now, but I think about it each and every day. He came in and I was alone, which ain't unusual on a Wednesday morning. And he walked up to the counter and he smiled . . . and this wasn't no ordinary smile. I mean it lit the place. He wore this cap, kinda like a flat cap, sort of khaki."

"And what did he say?"

"He said he was going to rob the bank," she said, smiling wide.

"You weren't scared?"

"You could tell he was decent, and I know how that sounds. He didn't even draw, just opened his jacket a little. And this gun was . . . like it was beautiful. And his jeans were tight and—"

Saint held up a hand. "What else did he say?"

"I opened the cash drawer and there weren't many bills, so I was scrambling for the key to the other, and then he looked past me at the photograph on the wall. You see it? It's my parents and me when I was small, the day they took the bank over from my grandmother. And this boy, he starts asking me about it."

"Asking you what?"

"I told him it was tough, you know. We're a family bank and we only hold local money, and the farming community, the slaughterhouses and feedlots, they're producing, but no one's buying. Wheat prices and all that. Kansas farmers don't feed the world no more."

Saint saw the first hint of sadness beneath the glitz and the ditz.

"He just listened as I talked. And it . . . you know how boys just stare at your tits. . . ." Dawn glanced at Saint's chest and winced a little.

Saint sighed.

"I mean this boy was listening to me. And he had this skin, kind of like gold, and his hair was a little blonde but darker, and I'll bet behind those dark glasses his eyes were—"

"So you handed him the money and then called 911?"

Another smile, this time knowing, considered. "That's the thing. He didn't take nothing. Just left the bills on the counter and walked out."

"He left the money?"

"And me."

Another sigh.

"I wouldn't even have reported him neither, but they check the tapes, you see."

She followed Dawn into a small back office where the tall guy fed a security tape into the machine.

"Y'all about to watch the beginning of a love story," Dawn said.

When she saw him, Saint couldn't help but smile. She reached a hand out and stopped short of touching the screen. Her heart heavy, her mouth dry at the realization. She had known it, but seeing him, like that.

"What the fuck did you do, kid?" Saint said, quiet, to herself.

119

She slept in a motel along Highway 33. Payne County and miles of green fractured by white-domed crude oil storage, the pipeline crossroads beneath her as she lay in a bath so hot she breathed steam.

Outside her sedan cooled, the engine ticked. Already she felt a little like a traveling salesman peddling the illusion of safety.

The phone lay beside her, the cord stretched as she dialed.

"Hey," she said.

"Hey," Jimmy said.

"How are you doing?"

"I'm doing."

"You can retake."

He did not reply, and she could see him, sitting in his recliner. She asked after the animals, his parents, and if he had eaten. Saint heard **SportsCenter,** heard the ring-pull of a beer.

"I miss you," she said.

"Come home then."

"The house and us. Is it how you thought?"

"Did you find a church yet, Saint?"

"I'm still searching." She had not yet searched out a Kansas church to join.

He breathed through his nose. "I love you so much. And I know that I've let you down. And my parents, and your grandmother. But I—"

"You didn't let anyone down. It'll be all right, Jimmy. You need to focus and—"

"You don't think I study hard enough? Or maybe it's because I lay awake worrying about my wife, and why she isn't home."

"Jimmy."

For a while she listened and waited. And then she heard the cold of the dial tone.

A minute later the telephone rang.

Her calls were forwarded wherever she went, mostly so her grandmother could reach her. Norma had taken a fall, said it was nothing, but Saint had Nix pay a visit when Jimmy wouldn't. The two sat on the porch and drank so much brandy Norma had taken another fall.

"Jimmy?" she said.

"There was a pirate named François l'Olonnais."

Saint sat up.

"I mean, this guy was bad. He had a hatred for the Spanish that bordered on crazy. And I know crazy."

Saint fought a smile.

"One day he captured a Spanish fleet and pulled the still-beating heart from the captain, and he ate it. And he spared one of their crew so he could tell people what he saw. He sailed for maybe a decade before he was captured by the Kuna tribe. They tore him to pieces. Rumor has it parts of him were eaten."

"Lovely."

"There's poetry in karma, right?"

She closed her eyes as the water dripped from her. "How you doing, kid?"

"I feel like I'm getting closer to her, Saint."

She breathed deep. It hurt.

"Where are you? Do you wear the flak jacket with the yellow letters and the ball cap, or is that for the movies?"

"Sammy told you."

"It makes me feel better that you're out there, on the right side, Saint. How's Jimmy treating you?"

"He's . . . it's good."

"You know you deserve the world, right? Anyone that tells it different, I'll smack them in the mouth."

She smiled and almost cried.

The tap dripped. "Today I was in Cottonwood Falls. At the First Kansas Bank."

Just the crackle of the line for a long time.

"Right," he said, and she imagined him in a phone booth on the edge of the world, his forehead against the cold glass as he stared out at emptiness so vast he could not know if he was floating or just falling.

"Dawn make you smile?" he said.

"You need to stop."

"Yeah."

"You can't run forever, Patch."

"I'm not running. I'm searching. I give people the means to search, too. The net widens each time. Not just for her. For every Grace lost."

"Are you eating?"

She imagined his eye roll.

"Yes, Ma. I ate a hog just last week."

She sat up, the rivulets gathering, her mind on the clearing, on his small body that clung to life so resolutely. Her grandmother would now say there was renewed purpose for him.

"I saw Misty," he said.

"How is she?"

"She's . . . she's perfect, you know."

"I remember."

"She told me you wanted to talk to me," he said.

"I asked her mother . . . she told me Misty had long forgotten you, but I made her promise, just in case."

"Covering bases."

"I need to see you. I need to talk to you in person."

"I'll bet you do, fed."

Silence.

And then he spoke, and this time he was quieter, less sure, the Patch only she got to see back when they were kids. "So this is it. It's you . . . it's you looking for me."

She held the receiver away from her because she did not trust her voice.

"You know I can't come see you, Saint."

"And why's that, kid?"

"They say I'm a pirate. And you're a lawman."

For a long time she matched her breaths to his, and when she finally spoke she closed her eyes to her tears. "When the time comes, I'll take you down."

"I know that."

"It will kill me."

"I know that, too."

120

A little over a thousand miles away Patch walked past opulent Charleston mansions, stood before each and looked at the detail, imagined them in the right colors, maybe before they'd been altered. He buzzed the gates and strolled the allée, breathing the heaven scents. He was met by a housekeeper who told him the same blessed family had lived there near a hundred years.

"I got a letter from here a few years back. A girl named Mya Levane's parents wrote it."

The housekeeper hustled him out into the street and closed the door behind herself. Told him that Mya's body had been found six months before.

"What happened to her?"

She softened a little, smiled and touched his arm. "Nothing you want to know about, son."

He spoke a little about Grace; she stopped him and told him that Mya was not his girl, that she had been across the border in Mexico at the time.

An hour later he walked into the Bank of South

Carolina. He left with a thousand bucks, gave all but two hundred to a cluster of homeless people by the Ashley River. A girl no older than fourteen hugged him for a long time.

He rode a bus through the night, through a landscape that morphed from sunset burned over the Blue Ridge Mountains to a night sky that chased every hint of life from lush hills.

He did not sleep, just kept a hand on his scar, his mind drifting back from one lifetime to another. His eye, when he caught the passing of lonesome trucks' light, saw through a fifteen-year-old lens, like it did not carry the haunt of the hunt, the hungry stab of a million fruitless hours. He wondered how it would end. What would be his last role, when the curtain would fall, the interested long since departed. His mind settled on Eloise Strike, her father Walter. Something about the man, maybe the strength, told Patch they might have been searching for the same girl. It was a hunch. It was all he had.

121

Heavy doors unlatched, the chambers between big enough for two.

Bars sliced sunlight as she waited on the waxed floor in the kind of silence she had not imagined possible in such a place. Saint shivered a little, steeled herself, and was led into a long, thin room, empty but for a table and two chairs.

Tooms was waiting, shackled at the hands and feet.

Still, he smiled.

"You wanted to see me?" Saint said. The letter had arrived at the tall house. Norma had called her right away.

He had lost so much weight. His skin dull. When she looked into his eyes, she did not see the man that had once scooped her up when she fell from her bike.

"I got your letters," he said.

"You ignored them."

"The future starts today, right."

Above, the light was too harsh, the bulb caged

behind black wiring. She smelled it, that captivity, beneath sweat and detergent and vinegar.

"You're a police officer," he said and managed to smile. "I always thought you might make a fine doctor."

"Why?"

She stared at his mouth as he spoke, a slight cut on his upper lip, a welt on his neck.

"I saw you married Jimmy Walters. I remember when you used to eat your lunch beneath the oak. Always smiling. Feels like another life. My house—"

"Gone," she said.

He must have known, but still she caught the flinch. "Memories lie in people, not places and things."

"You wanted to see me," she said again.

"Joseph writes to me."

"Do you know where he is?"

He shook his head, closed his eyes. When he opened them again she saw something.

"Tell me," she said, quiet like it would stay between them.

"I see the postmarks. He's traveling. Last one came from Baton Rouge. He's south now."

Sometimes at night she would close her eyes and see him on a beach, maybe with kids his own age, a girl on his arm.

"He's looking for her," Saint said, holding his eye. "Not just looking . . . he's dying without her."

"I wanted him to be okay," he said.

"You know how that sounds?"

"You ever feel like you're living someone else's life? Paying for mistakes you don't even remember making?"

"The missing girl. Grace."

"His medical reports back then, they all came to me as his family physician. His mother, maybe she wasn't fit to care for him. I had a duty to report it. I weigh these decisions. Each night when I don't sleep."

"He can't move on from this until he knows. Give him his life back. You've taken enough already."

Tooms looked at her, pleading in his eyes, in his voice. "I can't wash the blood from my hands."

"Tell me where she is. Do it for Patch. Let him go now. My grandmother said we're all capable of compassion. It's not too late for you."

"There's no way he'll let this drop?"

She heard such desperation, such pain as she shook her head.

He took a deep breath and talked.

If she had known she might have braced, might have held her breath, grit her teeth, not crumpled for Patch, not run out of that room, past the warden and his men, just keeping it together till she made it outside and vomited in the dirt.

122

From the beat of late summer through the flames of fall, Saint tracked his movements like he was a pawn in a game he could not possibly understand.

She split her time between her sullen cubicle in Kansas, a decay of motels, and her navy sedan, now littered with wrappers and cans from a dozen meals eaten on the road. Nix told her to stay fit, so she woke at five each morning and ran wherever she was, through Wichita woodland that recalled Monta Clare; through iron streets in downtown Dodge, Hell on the Plains; her gun never left her side.

After the phone call, Patch disappeared entirely. Saint worked with Himes's team, growing in skill and stature, her senses so sharp Himes pushed her onward.

She sat in an unmarked car outside a drab apartment block thirty miles outside the city. She'd tracked a Missouri man from Lee's Summit through Kansas City and on to Odessa. Micky Hubert had walked into the Summit Ridge Credit Union, waved a Smith & Wesson 9 mm in the face of the teller, and walked out with a little over three thousand dollars. He dropped all but seven hundred as he climbed into a waiting minivan, whose license plate a lady in the salon across the street took note of. Five thousand dollars from the Central Bank of the Midwest, and two thousand from the Bank of Odessa.

She traced the plate to the apartment, spent a couple of days watching on rotation, and wondered if all her cases would be so simple as Hubert and another man climbing into the same minivan.

Her heart didn't even kick as she watched a sedan head them off, drew her gun and directed Hubert out and onto his stomach. He wore a robe, and in the pocket she found a stack of bait bills, their serial numbers logged. Hubert was out on federal supervised release after a prior felony conviction for bank robbery.

"What the fuck else was he going to do?" Saint said to Himes, who shook his head at her French but nodded at the sentiment.

She worked background on a Southhaven man who robbed the bank he worked security for, missed the take because the Federal Bureau of Alcohol, Tobacco, and Firearms grabbed the guy a day early in the parking lot of a 7-Eleven.

"Haven't those motherfuckers got bootleggers to chase?" Saint said, as Himes tried to placate her with a croissant.

She drifted further from Monta Clare, from the life

she was supposed to lead, from Jimmy. Sometimes they went days without speaking. Jimmy's mother called her, told her she was worried about her son. Told her Jimmy had missed church, that he wasn't used to failing at anything, and that maybe it was a little because of Saint, because he could not keep his focus while his wife was not living in the marital home. When she did return, he alternated between attentive and sullen, passionate and cold. She saw flashes of the boy who loved her, of the man growing tired of the woman she was still becoming.

She settled into the rhythm of the unit, slept with files at the foot of her bed, and took each case so personal it was as if every dollar had been stolen from her own checking account. She leaned on a pusher pulled in on the floor below, who gave her the name of seven others who were casing the Standard State Bank in Independence. She flexed muscle and budget, and under the eye of Himes set up two surveillance vans and bugged the back room of a bar on Southwest Boulevard. The night before it went down she did not sleep, in her stomach that cold pain she'd been searching for. All seven taken, she made page two of **The Kansas City Star.**

"Half a million bucks saved, and they gave the front page to motherfucking golf," Saint said.

"Closest since the tie in—"

Saint shot him a look.

Himes turned back to his burger.

123

Thanksgiving she went home for two days, sat in the back of the church as her grandmother attended mass.

With Jimmy watching football at the tall house she roasted a turkey, mashed potatoes, candied yams and baked green bean casserole, corn and dinner rolls, fed cranberries with muscovado sugar and orange juice. She laid the table, and the three of them ate together among the mountain.

"You want buttered biscuits?" she said.

"If I eat a tenth of what's already here, I'll likely die," Norma replied, and then cast an eye over Jimmy, who wore the reddened eyes of a man who drank a couple of beers before lunch, and then a couple of vodkas during. He had gained weight, blamed it on Saint not being there to fix his meals so he had to order in most nights.

Norma yanked the plug from the radio before the news played out and took her brandy to the back porch where Saint wrapped herself in a blanket and sat beside, her head on her grandmother's shoulder as she warmed the frigid air with the float of cigar smoke and swirl of her glass.

"You don't call," Norma said.

"I'll do better."

"Come back one weekend and I'll take you for ice cream at Lacey's Diner."

"I'm too old for ice cream."

"I'm worried about you," Norma said.

"I carry a gun, Grandma."

"I worry about Jimmy and what is happening to him. The male ego is—"

"Fragile."

"An affliction. They know how to find the good in themselves, the decency and the respect, but sometimes they lose the compass."

"Love is a visitor."

Norma took her hand. "Did you marry him because I told you to?"

Saint did not meet her grandmother's eye. "I don't do anything you tell me to do."

Through the starlight she saw the shape of the hive. She remembered that time like each moment was a pearl of summer, perfect and without blemish, light till so late, beginning so early, like there was scarcely room for the dark.

"It was hardly night when I was a girl."

Norma smiled. "Must take its toll, being surrounded by everything bad. I pray for you. You know that."

"I do."

"He gives us the tools to be better, to build better. And if we turn around and use those tools to hack at others, to undo whatever good has been constructed, then we may turn back and accuse him of not doing the building for us."

Saint took Norma's glass and breathed in the warmth and the spices.

"I pray for Joseph," the old lady said. There was so much written in each line of her face, so much pain and sadness hid completely by the greatest smile Saint had ever known.

"I need to see him," Saint said.

Norma wore an old purple sweater that Saint had once knitted for her. "I wish the newspapers hadn't called him Patch all those years ago. I keep the cuttings. When they said you were a hero."

"I wasn't."

"Hush now." Norma took the glass back. "When you kept the bees, I used to come out each morning before you woke to check for the dead and remove them. Their friends used to get together and attack me."

Saint smiled.

"And you know why I did it? Because your day would be ruined. Because you take the problems . . . the flaws in design, and you take them so personally."

"He's still a kid."

"And what does that make you? He knows right from wrong. And . . ."

"And?"

"And he knows how to paint. God, that boy knows beautiful."

Saint looked up.

"You haven't seen it?"

124

They left Jimmy sleeping on the couch. Saint wore her old fur-lined hiking boots.

They walked past a cluster of revival Colonials, and in the window of each Saint saw Christmas scenes straight from the front of a greeting card. Big trees and candelabras and the soft hue of fairy lights as they headed up a frozen Main Street.

Only one store carried no decoration at all because it was not needed, and Saint smiled as she saw his new painting in the window.

Saint spent a long time just as lost as the girl in the painting, unable to move away.

Sammy came to the door. He wore a tux, his bow tie loose. "Special Agent Saint Brown."

"How are you, Sam?"

"Warm and wealthy."

Norma walked on slowly.

The two stood in silence awhile, staring at the colors.

"Can you just leave him be?" Sammy said, for a moment clear eyed, like he knew the weight of the ask.

"Do you know where he is, Sammy?"

Sammy said nothing.

"Maybe I'll have someone take a look at your taxes, see if that jogs your memory."

He shook his head disappointed. "You're bringing shit to a pissing contest?"

"Do you know where he is?"

Sammy nodded at the girl in the heavy gold frame. "Her name is Eloise Strike, and most nights when I lie down to sleep I see her face as soon as I close my eyes. Do you know where she is, Saint?"

Saint kept her eyes on the girl.

Sammy spoke quiet and without challenge. "Anna May. Summer Reynolds. Ellen Hernandez. You know where any of them are?"

"No, Sammy. I don't know where any of them are."

"So maybe you and the rest, you look for them first. And then after you find the girls, you look for those soulless ghouls that took them. And if there's anything of you left, then you go after the boy. But I hope I'm long dead before that happens."

"Do you know where he is, Sammy?"

Sammy looked at the canvas. He had turned down thirty thousand dollars from a Deerbank collector who traveled halfway across the country just to view it. "I don't."

She too kept her eyes on the painting. "But if you

did . . . if you did . . . then I'd be the last person you should tell."

He nodded and might have told her he understood her pain, but she did not need his compassion. So she followed her grandmother to St. Raphael's, and in the cemetery she stopped beside Ivy Macauley's grave for a moment before heading into the cold church, where she lit a candle then sat beside Norma on the front bench.

"Last time you prayed here," Norma said.

"I felt just as desperate as I do now."

"You don't ever need to feel that way."

Saint closed her eyes. "But I sit here, and I don't feel anything but fear. I don't hear anything but silence."

"The bad are the few, but often they shout louder than the many. Don't mistake silence for weakness."

And so, beside her grandmother, she gave herself over.

Saint closed her eyes and prayed to God that she would not catch Joseph Macauley.

And when she opened them she turned to her grandmother.

"I'm pregnant."

125

People came and went. Hitchhikers bummed a ride from a driver too kind for the route. An old couple bitched quietly, seething at the interloper. Patch closed his eye to Hamilton County, opened it to the midnight lights of a Tennessee paddle wheeler. At the break of a new day he watched a woman on horseback, the sun behind her.

Another bus and he made it to Stillwater, and from there the bus filled with so many Patch gave his seat to a girl not old enough to carry the life that grew inside her.

He traveled five days across three states and more than a dozen counties. In Oklahoma City he sat the whole night at a bus station, found a pay phone and dialed.

"I was thinking about Callie Montrose," he said.

"Yeah," Saint said.

He leaned back against the glass, cool through his shirt. "She was like us, right. Same age. Could be that she had a friend like me. And they hung out and hunted and fired cap guns in white woods."

"I'm begging you to stop now. You're getting reckless, kid."

"And Marty Tooms just killed her. For what?"

"I don't know."

"And Eli Aaron. All those girls just like you, just like Grace."

"I need to see you. I need to see your face and talk to you and tell you something."

"Is it good?" he said.

"It's . . ."

"Are you pregnant? You'd make the best mother, Saint. Better than mine, you know. You'd raise a good kid."

"You're a good kid."

"I'm not, Saint. No matter how you look back, before and after, I was always on the edge of something, always close to falling in. You held on to me, right. You and Misty. But I was always going to fall."

"You're my friend, Patch."

"Sammy says I'm a hustler. But, like, it's not a bad thing. It just makes it harder for people around you to know if they're being hustled."

"Are you hustling me, kid?"

"I think maybe I did with Misty. I let it happen because it was nice. It was a nice thing to see what she saw. For a while at least. You find anything on the rosary beads?"

"Not yet. I'm still looking. I still look."

"Thank you, Saint."

"You don't ever have to say that to me."

He closed his eye, and though he heard something else in her voice, a longing maybe, or a warning, he listened to her talk awhile. And she told him of Monta Clare and Norma and Chief Nix. And then he told her good night. And she could not find the words to say it back.

He did not know that at the other end, Saint had traced his call.

He crossed the town limit on foot.

He carried a map covered thick with his scrawl as he sat on a bench before St. Joseph's Cathedral.

"Are you a pirate?"

He looked to his left and saw a woman pushing ninety, her sunhat low.

"I used to be. Now I've got a wife. Grace."

Another smile.

"We live out west, small house but a lot of land."

"I'm glad you have someone."

"She's all I need. I knew it right from the start."

"When you know, you know."

"I also know pirates wore eye patches to adjust to the light and dark above and below deck during raids."

She rested her hand on his and gave it a gentle

squeeze. "So you're in the light now, but you've come from the dark."

That afternoon he robbed the MidFirst Bank.

Saint arrived only fifteen minutes after.

The net was closing.

126

The Derry Younger Center. The kind of nondescript name that did little to keep it hidden.

A two-story building, painted a shade of pink, the roof mottled green. On another day Saint might have faced placards, maybe a couple of men who laid claim to women and their bodies like rapists champing at a noble cause. Your body, my choice.

Inside Saint gave her name and took her seat and did not look up to notice the others.

Two hundred miles from Monta Clare, from Jimmy and his bloat, his tired eyes and the pitch of his disappointments. Sometimes Saint would clean the small house and Jimmy would not lift his legs for the vacuum cleaner.

She had booked him an appointment to see Dr. Caldwell. Thought maybe he needed some pills to redress the imbalance since he failed his exams. He had not gone.

"Docs it hurt?"

She looked at the teen beside her.

Saint wanted to tell the girl that she guessed it would, at some uncalled for time in the future, when she could look back from a different vantage point and not feel that retaining cord stretched so taut. The cord that tied her to him and that life where she was not the lead or even a bit part. Perhaps it would ache come Christmastime. Or when a friend fell pregnant.

"You'll be fine," Saint said.

On a small black-and-white screen she watched the channel 9 news as cops tracked James and Linwood Briley and four other death row inmates who bunked from the Mecklenburg Correctional Center.

"There's something romantic about a prison break," the girl said.

"Spree killers running loose, be still my beating heart."

The girl laughed, and Saint wondered at her life.

"I don't know how I got here," the girl said.

Saint smiled but guessed she did know. Like they all knew.

"Is there a difference between a mistake and a regret?" the girl said.

"If you learn from the mistake, it's less of a regret."

"I'm never having sex again."

"That's the spirit."

Saint heard her name called.

At the desk she handed in her form. Behind the

tired receptionist she saw a photograph, and in it she saw a line of people the first day the clinic opened. Dr. Tooms stood slightly away from the rest. He did not smile.

Saint kept her eyes on his as she was led through.

127

She found Jimmy sleeping on the couch.

The TV played a hockey match, though the sound was muted.

Three empties on the glass coffee table. He did not clean when she was away, so she would spend most of their first day together tending to the house. She wiped his piss from the linoleum in the bathroom. Washed shirts stained yellow beneath the arms. She had suggested they get someone to help, to come wash and iron once each week, but he would not hear of it.

Saint clutched a hand to her stomach and watched the rise and fall of his chest.

She bagged take-out cartons, did not balk at the smell and the congealment. She emptied the ashtray and did not wonder when he had begun to smoke again. Cream drapes with an autumn flower print. A wooden TV stand filled out with magazines and a few of her books. A VCR, a stereo, and a lamp she did not recall purchasing.

The kitchen was cream cabinets and veneer handles. She had wanted the white, but Jimmy said the cream reminded him of his mother's.

She jumped when she felt the hand on her back.

"I thought you were sleeping," she said.

He wore sweats and the glassy eyes of a drunk. "It's good to have you home."

She fixed them sandwiches though it was night.

He sat at the table and watched her and did not pass comment when she set the plate down in front of him.

The drywall was unpainted because he had been busy, but she did not know what with. She asked after his day, and he told her how a group of schoolkids had visited the zoo, and one had puked so much he had to fetch two buckets. She pushed her sandwich away.

"You caught your boyfriend yet?" he said.

She sipped her juice. "He's not—"

He raised a hand. "I'm kidding."

"Did you stop by and check on my grandmother?"

"I will."

And so it went. Until she heard the knock at the door, and instead of inviting Nix in she decided to step out, and they sat side by side on the front step.

"Saw your car," he said.

"Glad you came."

He smiled, and she had missed that. In his eyes she saw reflected pride and also the drain of the past years. No matter what he said, how he tried to preach of caring just enough and then switching off, something about the Macauley case had dragged him in deep.

"The FBI," he said, and let out a low whistle. "Anything on the Macauley kid?"

She shook her head, felt her breath leave her for a moment that still hurt.

"Daisy ran a piece on the gallery, on the new girl in the window. You ever think something good can come out of something so bad?" she asked.

"Something beautiful, maybe. A dawning. A realization. But nothing good, kid. The price is too great."

Streetlights flickered on, and distant church bells called. Saint remembered a time when contentment had settled over her each night like a comforter.

"I checked in on Norma."

She touched his arm.

"She's not taking it well. You being away," Nix said.

"I know."

"She said female FBI agents will likely turn barren through stress before they reach thirty."

"Barren?"

"As the Mojave. No chance of a clutch of eggs for you."

"A clutch? Like I'm a goddamn animal."

He reached for a smoke, and she saw a slight shake in his hand that she had not noticed before.

"I fucked up, Chief."

"We all fuck up, Saint."

She shook her head because he could not understand, and she loved that he would not ask.

"How do I fix things?" she said.

"You're not always able. But you take a moment and remind yourself where your north is. But I've got a feeling you already know that."

They stood by his cruiser. "Why did you stop by?" she said.

"It's not only the old lady that misses having you around."

He hugged her.

"I went to see Tooms," she said.

"And?"

She looked him in the eye, smiled, and shook her head.

Nix smelled of cigars and cologne, and maybe of everything before.

"What do I do?" she said.

"Do something meaningful. Or maybe just mean everything you do," he said.

128

"I fell pregnant."

There was a moment before Jimmy reacted, and she kept her eyes on the television because she could not bear to see more.

He stood and moved to cross the room, his smile lighting him up.

"I went to the clinic in the city."

He stopped then. Just short of her.

"I went there to make it go away. I'm sorry. But I have to be honest. Because if we're not honest then—"

She was not prepared for the punch.

During her training Saint had worked a placement in Uniform Crime Reporting, another in Victim Assistance. She'd shadowed an agent named Dana Cowell over three of the most harrowing weeks. Nights spent in the emergency room watching shells of women condemned to a life of eternal shock. Sometimes there were blackened eyes and swollen lips, handprints in blues and reds. Sometimes there were drugs and alcohol, more often than not there was sexual assault. She saw the subhuman levels of men, those who took so much, not realizing how little they left behind. And she saw the toll it took on Dana, who had once told her all men had to diffuse their guilt before the crime had even been committed. Capability was enough. Trust was the hardest of earns.

As Jimmy knocked her to the floor in a fit of blind rage and she curled herself up.

As he followed his flurry of punches with kicks.

Saint closed her eyes and found Patch's face.

And through her tears she cried out for him to help her.

Like he did when they were small.

129

He woke in a cold sweat, cried out into the darkness as she told him to paint her.

That she was standing on a north shore.

He reached for the telephone and dialed.

Patch tried to slow his breathing as he waited for her machine.

"Hello."

He stared at the receiver, knew the voice on the other end so well, yet still, for a moment he was too ashamed to speak.

"Joseph?"

"Hello, Norma."

He heard her sigh, imagined her sitting awake while the town slept around her. He could still picture her face so clearly, her smile, and, more often, her frown.

"Please, Joseph. Give yourself up."

"I can't," he said, and knew that she would hear the pain in his voice.

"You're a good boy." And he heard the pain in hers.

"I wanted you to . . ."

"Tell me, Joseph. What did you want?"

He swallowed. "I wanted you to be my family. You and Saint. I wanted—"

"It's not too late for you. You come back and I'll take you for ice cream at Lacey's Diner."

He smiled. "I miss you both."

"You're breaking my granddaughter's heart."

His voice caught. He wound the telephone cord around his finger, blinked back his tears, and tried and failed to answer a statement he knew to be true.

"I'm sorry," he said.

"You have to let her go now, Joseph. Saint doesn't need you anymore."

130

Saint sat in her small apartment and stared at the map.

It was large, covered half the floor, and she stepped carefully around it with bare feet. She had not slept or eaten, just climbed into her car and made the drive back to Kansas, where she stepped beneath a warm shower and did not dare look in the mirror.

"You didn't come see me?" her grandmother said on the telephone that evening.

Norma could not see the swelling around her eyes, the torn lip and the cut by her ear. The way it hurt to sit, to speak, like Jimmy had dragged from inside each thing that made her.

She still tasted blood. "I had to get back to work."

"You don't sound like yourself."

"I have a cold coming."

"You work too hard."

"I know, Grandma."

Saint looked at her nails, short, functional. In her bag she kept mascara and lip gloss and a light perfume she'd bought for her last birthday.

She thought of her tree in Norma's yard, how she would sit beneath the threadbare canopy and let the rain speck her coat. Where she had once jarred her honey and completed her schoolwork and dreamed of other kids coming over so she might dazzle them with her facts. She tried to see it but knew now that nothing would be alike. No memory would be clean because her path had led her so far from home.

She knew of cognitive dissonance. She knew that negative associations could be unlearned and unlinked. She knew so much.

"Are you okay?" Norma said.

"I am."

"When you come by, I'll take you for ice cream at Lacey's Diner."

Saint smiled and felt the sharp ache in her jaw, her tooth still loose. "I'm too old for ice cream."

131

Saint did not leave her apartment for two weeks. She checked in with Himes and told him she was tracking the pirate. She listened to hours of interviews, pored over transcripts and tapes from her grandmother's answering machine, and plotted his route like there was some kind of method in reams of madness. She ate little, slept on the sofa, took comfort in Patch's voice as she shut out all the light and cranked the volume on the small stereo beside the television.

"She told me about the sky at Baldy Point, how Lake Altus-Lugert spills from the dam, crashing its way along the Fork Red River."

"You think she's from that way?"

"I just know that she saw it. She knew places I never heard of. How could I know this if she wasn't real?"

Saint brought her knees to her chest and took her pen and marked the spot in Oklahoma on her map.

"She told me how the sun sits on Fort Sumter

before dropping into the Charleston Harbor. In White Point Garden you can smell peach and violet. You know it's haunted, right? They hung thirty pirates in the marsh beside it. Stede Bonnet. She even knew more about pirates than me."

Saint marked that point in South Carolina.

She ate cans of soup. Did not let the sun in at all. Just broke from herself and moved into his world so she did not have to face her own.

Forty hours. She was back there, her mind in Monta Clare, Patch fourteen again.

"She made it so I could see the mining villages, those elegant Victorian buildings. I could hear the stampede of bison, see the view from the mile-high step at the state capitol."

Saint marked Denver.

For another five days she sifted the crumbs of Joseph Macauley's memory, listened to talk of Cottonwood Falls to New York City, New England to Montana. She marked the map and drew her routes.

And then, thirteen days after she'd begun, she listened to the final tape, checked it against where he'd mailed the last girl from, and drew her circle in bold red.

"She told me you could see more of the universe over Tucson. The Pima County dark sky code . . . Kitt Peak, it made us feel smaller, you know. You don't know. You don't know shit because you're

**looking at me like I'm some crazy kid when you
should be out there finding her."**

They had thought his order random.

She paced a little, and then she picked up the
telephone and called Himes.

"The pirate. He's seeing what the girl saw. I think
I know where he's headed next."

132

A week later, in the shadow of the beautiful mission church of San Xavier del Bac, the trail led her across tracts of hardened dunes, mesas, and buttes, the oranges and grays of the saguaro.

She saw in bruises and blood, heard in screams and cries, smelled Jimmy's cologne so opened the window to drown it.

She aimed the sedan over land laced with silver she had learned of in school, the rowdy frontier life, the miners and farmers and the Salt River. She checked into a small hotel in the town of San Carlos, opposite the Chase Bank. For three days she sat by the window, the sun deadened by the faded awning. She gritted her teeth, slept in fits in the old armchair, sometimes saw Jimmy's face so real she rubbed at her eyes till only colors remained. She checked in with Norma, said she was busy when Norma read between her small talk and demanded to know what was going on with her.

And then, in the vacancy of a Tuesday morning,

as she stepped from the misted bathroom, her radio blasted. She sprinted down the stairs and out onto the street.

Saint made it there clear ahead of the local cops, spoke to a shaken teller who told much the same story she was used to, only this time he had followed the kid out front, watched him climb into an aging Chevy and head in the direction of the Apache Trail not five minutes before.

She climbed into her sedan and gunned the engine, climbed through the gears, and opened the window to the lore of the Superstitious Mountains. Saint gripped the wheel tight as the road twisted and climbed drop-offs so steep her stomach flipped.

Her radio crackled as she passed a steamboat on Canyon Lake, but she tuned it out, her eyes locked on the trail. Through Tortilla Flat and the spirit of outlaws, the smooth of the road ended at Fish Creek Hill, and she bumped away, slowing little despite the sheer falls, the barriers missing.

And then, ten miles from anywhere at all, she pulled off the track and parked in the dirt behind the pickup.

He stood in the sunlight, the world unfolding in front, his back to her, but she stayed far enough from him.

"The road drops a thousand feet up ahead. A couple switchbacks," he said, and then turned. And for the first time in so long, Saint looked into the handsome face of the boy she had given everything for.

He looked taller, tanned, his hair touching gold. And when he smiled it took all she had not to return it. Absolutely all.

"Hey, Saint."

She drew her gun steady, her mind on her training. "Hey, kid."

He stared at the barrel, the smile replaced by such sadness she almost broke again. "I like it when you call me kid. It makes me feel like there's still time."

"There is."

"I'm getting closer," he said. "Eloise Strike. I think she might be my Grace. The name, and the look in her eyes. Her father listens to Johnny Cash."

"Just like Callie Montrose's father. And a hundred million more," she said, feeling the cold of her words, but still he smiled.

In the distance, green hills erupted through the orange face of rock formations, the sky a blast so clear she almost could not breathe in the awe.

"You see those families at the lake, Saint?"

"Sure."

"Kids with treasure maps, looking for Dutch gold. I notice smiles. Maybe I didn't see them before. I need to see her smile. Just once. And then I'll get on, I'll keep my head low, and I won't trouble anyone again. I just need to see the smile I used to hear. Because if she can manage that, just once for me, then I'll know, right."

"I have to bring you in, Patch."

He stared past her. "I didn't take more than they'll miss. These charities, Saint. That don't have enough. They won't find her if they don't have enough."

"Doesn't work that way, kid."

The sun gilded him.

"I saw you a couple miles back . . . this road," he said, and scratched his head, his shirt riding up, the stomach muscles lean. He wore a blue eye patch.

She did all she could not to see the child, how they had run together the day he taught her to track whitetail tracks. Her badge burned hot.

He took a step toward her.

"Please," she said.

He saw her face then, closer. "Jesus." He spoke with such care, such worry.

She found she could not lie to him. "I told Jimmy I aborted his baby."

He looked at her, the bruising and swelling so stubborn, no matter how she numbed it with ice, like her skin was too fragile.

"And he did this to you?" She saw that dark in him, raised a hand to call him back.

"I deserved it. The apportionment of dues. It's what keeps our world in check."

"Saint—"

His hand rested gently on the back of her neck. She felt nothing but warmth.

She stepped into him and closed her eyes, and for the first time since felt close to something, to home.

They stood there together, and she let him hold her, and she thought of what she had done and sobbed into his chest. Above them a red-tailed hawk circled, and as it called she pushed him back.

"You have to turn around and put your hands behind your back." Her voice held.

"The track gets bad. You can't drive it fast, not if you give a damn about your life. You deserve everything good, Saint."

"Turn around and put your hands behind your back."

"I can't do that."

"She's dead."

He watched her.

"Tooms killed her. He told me. He buried her in Thurley State Park. Won't say more than that."

"You're lying."

Her tears fell. "You know that I'm not. They'll add it to his sentence. He's dead anyway."

He shook his head. "Liar."

"Please, Patch."

"I can't leave her again. I won't."

"Please," she said under her breath. "If it's not me, it'll be someone else. Someone who doesn't see you. Just the things you've done and might do again."

"You're strong enough. You do what you've got to do."

He smiled again, this time it was less, and in his face she saw so much that he had lost. She thought of Misty and the kids in their class, kids that had gone on to college, to jobs, to family and everything he deserved.

She whispered, "Please God don't make me do this."

And then he turned, and he broke for the car.

Saint held her breath.

And pulled the trigger.

FATE

1990

133

Saint stood in sunlight despite the frost, crystals that sheened the lot like jewels on that most precious of mornings. She drove a year-old Bronco, the thing so big her grandmother told her she looked like a raisin atop a monster truck, but it made shorter work of their white street as record snow fell.

The James Connor Correctional Facility sat in tracked soybean fields, built low so it could not be glimpsed from the highway.

Heavy locks turned and he appeared.

She smiled.

He smiled.

Patch walked with a slight limp. The bullet had passed through his thigh, nicking the bone but missing every nerve and major blood vessel. The surgeon had said he was lucky. Patch knew that luck was born from her hours spent at the shooting range, hitting nines with her eyes closed.

"Hey, Saint."

"Hey, kid."

He opened his arms and she stepped into them, pressed her head against his chest and squeezed till he called for mercy. He wore a khaki shirt, his hair close cropped, his eye still bright.

She wore perfume, a little makeup, her glasses exchanged for contact lenses.

They rode those miles on Interstate 44 with Patch watching passing trucks and gas stations, leaning water towers and distant silos iron against a pale washed sky. Now and then she looked at him and fought the urge to ask if he was okay, because she did not know how you could spend six years caged and leave without bearing some kind of difference.

They ate lunch in a diner of ragtag patrons by the Will Rogers Turnpike, where they ordered burgers and fries, and she could not help but think of every major and minor thing he had missed. He had lost a little weight, still so handsome the waitress added a smile as she fetched their order.

"How's Norma?" he said.

"Still there."

Saint had tried to visit him more than a dozen times, though Patch would not see her, or return her letters, though still she wrote them. A hundred pages of nothing, of telling him of her small life, of how she had moved to supervisory special agent, which didn't mean all that much more than she could afford to rent a bigger apartment to rattle around in. How she had moved departments, worked fraud for two years, wrapped a major case, handled dozens of indictments and pleas. How she walked up the stone steps and into the courthouse on State Avenue and watched a young judge hand out sentences that would lead many to die in prison. How she knew she had done a good thing but felt a cold detachment.

She wrote of how she thought of getting a pet, maybe a Maine Coon or a Ragdoll, but settled on a small aquarium. How she played piano again. Looking back she was not surprised he had not replied.

A couple of hundred yards from the Kansas line they broke the swells of a snowstorm that slowed them into Missouri.

"I saw you in the newspaper," he said.

"I saw in you in a couple, too."

He smiled. "They called me a pirate."

"They did."

"The Gower homicides. You work murders now?"

"Yes." She hadn't leaned all that hard on Himes, just told him she wanted to do something meaningful. He saw through it. That she wanted to stay better connected to the missing dead girl.

"There was a television set," he said, and she glanced at him though he kept his eyes on the drift of snow.

"I got to see it, you know. Hubble breaking the sky. Couple guys hollered when that wall came down in Germany."

"How come?" she said.

"Prisoners don't like walls, Saint."

"Right."

"I thought of Monta Clare a little, Misty and . . . damn we were so young, right? When it all happened we were all so young. I see all those boys heading to Iraq, like didn't we learn nothing from . . ."

She touched the brake for a tractor, knew his mind had found his father.

"And then I was sitting there when the reporter cut to a courtroom . . . the man was shackled, Bible resting across his lap. We were all watching it because something was shifting, you know. The people that said they were innocent, which was most of them, they sat there quiet after. Tommy Lee Andrews."

She could not keep the concern from reaching her face.

"DNA," he said.

She was quiet a long time.

"We can go back," he said.

She lightly cleared her throat. "I once told you no good can come of any of this."

"Is the Tooms farm even still standing?" he said.

"It's empty. No one will buy it, after they heard. The bank owns the land."

He leaned back and for a moment he was fourteen and Nix was driving them back from the hospital, his hopes still clinging to the margins.

"The color has gone," he said, and she waited for him to go on. "When I look back. I know there were summers, but I don't remember a time when it wasn't cold, when it wasn't winter. I wrote Tooms again."

"You wrote the judge, too," she said, because Heinemann had called her. "Rare that a victim testifies on behalf of the perpetrator."

"Almost as rare as a cop testifying on behalf of a bank robber, after she shot him."

Saint smiled.

"If Tooms dies he takes her with him," Patch said.

"He doesn't know where he buried her."

"Bullshit."

"If we don't find anything new, what will happen?" she said, and he could hear the way she lightly held her breath.

"A strand of hair. Something that gives us a shot. Eloise Strike. Her father, Walter, he wrote me in there. Said his wife passed, so now he doesn't have a reason not to start looking again."

"What will he find?" she said.

"Maybe nothing. Maybe it's what keeps him from dying, too. Hope is—"

"Hope is expectation. Anyone that tells you less is lying to themselves."

As they drove into Monta Clare he stared at the streets like he expected something to have changed.

"My grandmother tended the yard . . . and we painted the windows last summer," she said, quiet as they pulled onto Rosewood Avenue.

He took her small hand in his. "What you said during the trial and all, and after what you'd been through. Getting me moved closer. I wouldn't last in a Texas jail."

"Charles Vane set fire to one of his own fleet and sent it toward Governor Rogers's forces during a brutal dogfight. Pirate blood. You go down swinging."

He smiled. "We go down swinging, kid."

"Stealing my lines."

She looked up at the old house, still standing, the only blight on that street, in that town.

"What happened to him?" Patch said.

"The same thing that happens to all pirates."

"I don't like my chances, Saint." He climbed out, then stopped and turned. "Edward Low. Fearsome. Some reckon he was hanged in France. But one story has it he escaped to the Caribbean and saw out his days on the beach, in paradise."

She stayed at the bottom of the path as he walked to the door, and felt it each time he limped.

"Patch."

He turned.

"What I said about hope . . . I still hope you'll find your paradise. Entirely and absolutely."

134

Winter washed Monta Clare with resolution; white sky met white treetops, and the town existed in a bauble where snowflakes drifted no matter the hour.

That first week he did not leave the old house, just removed the dust sheets and opened each window wide to air so frigid he took to wearing his father's gabardine overcoat, deerstalker, and fingerless gloves.

"What the fuck do you look like?" Sammy said, as he pushed his way in and decanted a bottle of Glen Grant he'd been saving into two glasses. In the tired living room Sammy looked around. "It's so fucking dull in here, if I had a gun I'd blow my brains out just to color the décor."

"I'll go fetch my father's Smith and—"

Sammy sat on a wicker garden chair and crushed it fully, cursing as it imploded, his feet kicking up as he landed on his ass, while he made a decent production of keeping his glass level. Patch laughed so hard he had to head into the yard to ease the pain in his stomach.

"You need to buy yourself some furniture." With that he pulled a check from his pocket and placed it on the kitchen counter. "I sold a painting."

Patch moved to protest, but Sammy held up a placating hand, the middle finger raised in case there was any room for discourse.

"You said take care of the house. Taxes."

"What did you sell?"

"Relax. None of the girls. I sold the ice."

Patch closed his eye and saw it, the two figures shapeless, Sirius casting the only light on the frozen lake as a dozen colors rained around them, the brightest emerald to the coldest cobalt, though the two could see only each other.

"Who bought it?"

"Same woman over in Jefferson City. I had seven bidding."

"You reckon one day I can buy it back?"

"No. You paint another."

He shook his head.

"Then you at least come collect the mail."

"Sure, Sammy."

"And this shit." Sammy nodded toward the two large bags he had carried in. Video tapes. News taken from the past six years.

"You made these?" Patch said.

Sammy waved him off. "I was fucking the girl from channel 7. Archives. Had to take her to dinner. Jesus."

"Thank you for your sacrifice," Patch said.

Sammy stood, rubbed the base of his spine, and aimed a curse at what was left of the chair, another at Patch.

"How was prison? Your asshole still intact?"

Patch frowned.

"You get the package I sent each Christmas?" Sammy said.

"Guards took the cheese."

"Beaufort d'été. The prince of Gruyères. What about the sashimi?"

Patch shook his head.

Sammy threw up his hands in despair. "The fucking Wagyu then?"

"You know they don't let you cook your own—"

"Fucking warden. I furnished his feast six years in a row. Almost feel bad for adding it to your debt now."

"Almost."

Sammy drank three glasses.

Patch followed him to the door.

Sammy cleared his throat. "It's good to—"

"I know."

"I mean. This town without—"

"Yeah."

135

Patch strolled when the town eased quiet and soft snowfall froze solid. He avoided Main Street, kept his head low, and breathed that free air so deep his chest burned with the cool. In prison he'd sat with an old man named Terrence Roots in the weeks leading up to his release, might have served the full fourteen years had Saint not shown at the parole hearings, smart in her suit, impressive with her title. Patch had not left his cell, but Roots broke it all down, and then prepared him for re-entry, like he was about to tear through an atmosphere so inhospitable he would likely seek solace in a return.

He was taught of seeking mentors, core relationships, locating resources, and serving others. Roots spoke of developing daily routines, like the couple of thousand days of habit had not ingrained. Finding help, avoiding trouble. Patch nodded when he had to, wrote down what needed writing down, did not tell the man, or the judge or the parole officer, that they need not worry about him, that his purpose had died hard that first year, as he lay awake each night on his bunk, reached out his hand but could not find her at all. He had mourned her death quietly and completely.

Saint phoned each evening, and he made enough time to tell her he was doing just fine, smiled as he spoke because one of the men he bunked with agreed you could, in fact, hear a smile.

He worked the driveway, cut a path in the ice then began cracking it down with the heel of his boot.

Saint stocked his freezer with dishes and clear instructions of how to heat each of them. He ate fried chicken, salmon patties, meatloaf, smothered pork chops, and banana pudding.

Sammy showed with another bottle, this one a 1950 Martell Very Old Pale. He poured two glasses and drank both down, then opened a bottle of Courvoisier for Patch and finished off the Martell himself.

"You wouldn't taste it right with your waxen prison tongue."

So drunk was he, Patch helped him back to the gallery, his first trip onto Main Street, which had not changed all that much since he had been away. A couple of stores exchanged for newer models he did not know. He pulled his collar up and stepped through the door as Sammy collapsed into a scroll wingback and passed out cold.

It was only when Patch turned the harsh lights on that he saw them.

Each girl against the brickwork, framed and hung with such care and flair for a long time he did not move, just stared like they had been dredged from a long sunken shipwreck of memory. He walked around, afraid to cast an echo, fourteen again. Sammy had not parted with them, had not made space for paintings he could sell. Patch moved from Anna May to Lucy Williams, Ellen Hernandez to Mya Levane. Only at Eloise Strike did he stop and stare into her eyes and search out his Grace. And at Callie Montrose did he reach out and stop just short of stroking her hair.

For two hours he moved through prints that spoke of more than a decade of his life. And then he saw the sack of mail, sent to the gallery that held his paintings, from the parents of the missing, desperate to reach him.

He grabbed a silk twill blanket, the diamante print from some fabled Italian archive, and gently draped it over his friend.

"You did a good thing, Sam. But it's over now."

136

In the old house he sifted through a collection that screamed of his madness, items he had not seen in ten years, that used to bring him closer to Grace.

The shelves bowed with **Time,** local newspapers and cuttings. The walls papered with old maps, streets colored in marker pen, and beside them clippings from a dozen catalogues, Junior Bazaar, Misses Fashion, Sears. Outfits cobbled together from snippets of conversation that had come to him mostly in the dead of night, when he'd wake with such urgency, pad down the stairs, and write in journals that numbered near fifty. Words that did not run together. Plaid, cut loose, emery, vanilla. He interpreted them in different ways on different days, sometimes sounds or smells and sights. He cut faces from magazines, joined them to hairstyles from newspapers, sometimes changed the eye color with the shade of a paintbrush.

He did not know if it was that leaden certainty that she was gone, or that he looked back at his folly from a mind recused, but he gathered the assemblages, tore everything from the walls of his old bedroom and filled a metal trash can in the yard. He fetched a can of gasoline from the garage and doused it all fully and lit his memories on fire.

As he breathed the smoke down and closed his eye, he found himself back there, the flames lighting another time he had thought forever confined to darkness.

"Wake up," she cried. "Fucking wake up, Patch. I'll try and pull you out. I'll try and keep you with me." She coughed and choked and tugged his arms. "I'm not strong enough to save you. I'm not strong enough to do any of this without you."

And only as the smoke twisted on its rise did he look up through his tears and seek out a night sky he had not noticed in so many years.

137

Saint returned to Monta Clare and dragged him out of one old house and into another, where he sat with her grandmother on the porch and listened to the old woman alternate between blowing her harmonica and sucking on a cigarette, one time losing her rhythm and sending a plume of smoke through the mouthpiece. Norma coughed as hard as Patch laughed, till Saint came out onto the frozen porch and ripped into them both because the neighbor girl had a new baby and did not want a geriatric and a jailbird waking the thing.

Sometimes he sat and listened to Saint play the piano, and only in those moments did he feel anything at all.

That first month his life hummed along, not reaching a roar, but Saint and Sammy keeping it from falling to a whisper. The snow remained, and before long they were closing in on the '78 record; kids pressing their faces to windows each morning, praying the old heating system at Monta Clare High was not up to the job. The terms of his parole meant he had to find gainful employment, so he took to sitting at the gallery in a reflection of time past, only now people wandered in and stared at his work, sometimes inquired as to the price, which he answered by pointing them in the direction of another gallery fifty miles south that carried better pieces.

"I'm adding each lost sale to your debt," Sammy said.

"What's the count?"

"Two hundred and forty-seven thousand dollars."

From deep in the lungs of the gallery he watched the first shoots of spring as the great thaw began.

In Green's Convenience Store he picked up coffee Sammy ordered in special, and beside him watched a small blonde girl swipe a candy bar and stuff it into her pocket.

"You'll get caught doing that," he said.

She tilted her small chin up. "Fuck off."

He crouched low. "You want to go up the sleeve, kid," he whispered.

She watched close as he demonstrated, noted the ease of his technique, and watched him stroll out.

He stalled at the alley beside, the memory catching him so sharp he pressed a hand to his stomach. As he walked on he saw a cluster of purple beardtongue sprouting from a tear in the concrete and noticed the violet trumpets, the white throat that called summer.

And then, through the window of the dressmaker, he saw her.

She stood beside her mother, and though she wore a cream shearling bucket hat, he saw the nape of her neck, the pale white of her arms, the pinch of her waist.

He stood mesmerized, not hearing the pass of traffic.

And then she turned.

And he had almost forgotten how Misty Meyer's smile could slow his world.

138

Her wipers could not clear the deluge that morning.

Hammering the roof of her truck as she pulled up outside the small house. Saint ran up the drive and saw him on the bench, the tree's canopy doing enough, though still, rain dropped steadily on his shoulders, wetting his shirt dark.

"You know it's raining," she said, sitting beside him.

"It's today?" Nix said.

"Yes."

"And you hope to find . . ."

"I don't even know. Something of hers. Something that gives us a name. A past. An identity."

Nix sipped his coffee, staring at the tree and the roots like they were something sacred. Saint looked around and even in the rain it was beautiful, like a haven from the outside world.

"How do I deal with this?" she said.

"You always know, Saint."

"And yet I always come back to you."

"You find something, and the kid goes off chasing

for her story. Her background. You don't, and he'll find some other way of keeping it spinning. I used to think it was crazy."

"And now?"

"Now I think . . . if he loves her, if he cares that deeply, ain't even a choice to make."

"You ever get lonely?" she said.

He watched the sky through the trees. "The memories are enough. Maybe you tell the kid that."

"My grandmother says you pray an hour each week. Before the service begins. What do you ask for?"

He sipped his coffee, and she smelled caramel and flowers and bitter smoke.

"I ask for understanding."

"For what?"

"The bad things I do."

She could not imagine him doing a single bad thing.

"I don't see you at church anymore," he said.

She smiled, but it was small. "I'm not sure that I'm ever welcome—"

"Jimmy Walters doesn't decide who belongs, Saint."

Jimmy's mother had told the town of Monta Clare her secret. That she had terminated a life. That she had broken a pact with God. Norma had not spoken to her much that summer.

"I pray at home. Sometimes by the lake. I don't kneel or clasp my hands, but I say what needs saying," she said.

He reached out and patted her knee. "You're a good person, Saint."

"Tell that to my grandmother."

"She loves you."

"She does. Just less now."

"That can't—"

"I test her faith," Saint said.

He smiled. "The great ones always do."

139

At the mud trails Saint saw a single white van.

Three women stood pulling on forensic suits.

Patch showed though she had told him not to, and he stood far back between trees still sparse from the hangover of winter.

The old Tooms farmhouse stood strong; it had weathered greater storms than errant owners. Built a year before the 1896 St. Louis tornado took a couple of hundred lives. Saint had pulled the title for no better reason than Tooms seemed to care so damn much for a building, and so damn little for human life.

Distant land had grown wild; florets spiked; in the distance big bluestem reached seven feet before thinning to white birch, trunks like milk that raised arms already beginning to color.

Saint stared at the house in wonder, the grain boards dark like they'd been freshly stained. The immediate acres still appeared tended, like someone was waiting on the return of life to ground made fallow by the saddest story.

She did not follow the team into the house, stayed back and let them work. She knew of a rising tide of convictions being overturned; seven on death row had their futures reinstated thanks to strings of sequence she did not fully understand. Himes told her of double helix, genetic instructions, and molecular markers.

They worked the best part of that day before moving to the underground store.

Saint sat in the Bronco, glanced in the mirror and saw him still there but did not summon him, his presence alone a flag that could one day be raised should anything come. She did not know how they sifted through so much human debris, allocating hairs to heads, skin to bodies.

When they were done, she watched the van press the gravel deep as it followed the trees and curved out onto the road.

"You stood there seven hours," she said, as he walked over, that slight limp still catching in her throat.

"When will you hear?"

She shrugged because she did not know. It was an act built on favors she would one day have to repay.

They sat on a slick rock, knees touching as she poured coffee from a thermos, black and bitter and drying their mouths.

She leaned down and picked up a magnolia leaf, inspected it and carefully placed it into her pocket.

It rained too lightly to trouble them.

"This could be it," he said.

"If she's in the database. And if not . . ."

He cupped the plastic and breathed its steam. "I just want to say goodbye. Maybe find her family. I don't know."

"I understand."

He needed closure to a chapter already too long.

140

Patch looked at the house for the first time up close. Looked for cracks that seeped blood, strained his ears for the echo of their screams. "I can't see any of it. And I know how that sounds . . . but I just—"

"Have you seen Misty since you got back?" she said.

"We're going out tonight."

The week before his release Saint had sat in the salon as the woman lightened her hair. She had been to the nail salon, bought new makeup and perfume and even some new dresses. She was fit, her body lean, her face clung to youth. She drew looks from men, comments from assholes.

"I look out for her when I'm in town. Maybe she doesn't walk into Main Street anymore. They've got the department store in Palmer Valley now, fancy dresses and all that."

"Sammy told me what Jimmy's mother did."

"I'm the first woman to divorce in Monta Clare."

"Norma must be proud."

Saint thought of her grandmother. Of how she had stopped asking her to attend church each Sunday. A move that hurt more than that fateful day. Saint thought of the summer after, how she had not returned to Monta Clare, refusing to let her grandmother see the bruises, the way her jaw clicked when she ate, the way her body had emptied. How she had taken a six-month sabbatical, only left her apartment to take a stroll each morning. She had read, watched television, and cooked. Spoke to Norma on the telephone and told her she was too busy to come back. The hardest summer of her life. And there was much competition.

"We're still young," he said.

She plucked the head from a black-eyed Susan and wondered just how it had survived.

"You know that this is the first flower to grow after a fire or natural disaster," she said.

He took it from her and admired the rays. "We're tough, right."

"Buy a boat, Patch. Go sail the Indian Ocean."

"Why can't I feel her . . . here. Why can't I feel anything at all?"

"Circadian desynchrony. A failure of light information. The blind don't have heightened senses."

"I was blind down there."

"Grace wasn't. She saw what she saw. He let her out and put her back and she carried that with her.

And what she saw . . . people say unimaginable horror, but we can all imagine it. You suffered. You survived."

"In part."

He picked moss from the rock with the blunt of his nail.

"I've known you, what, more than twenty years," she said. On a tree beside were holes forged with a heavy hatchet, the sap dried like fingers of varnish. The catkins of black alder circled the base like peppercorns at a giant's table.

"You ever see Jimmy?" he asked.

"He left town. His mother told my grandmother he couldn't bear the shame."

"Do you think of the baby?" he said. No one had asked her that before.

She could not speak, so nodded.

He kissed the top of her head.

For a long time they let the wind blow over them.

He moved toward the store before she could stop him. Before she could call him back, tell him it was not worth it, it could never be worth going through it again.

She slipped in the mud, cursed the rain, and climbed down the steps behind him.

He stood silent in the center.

Beneath his feet was the concrete he might have once lain upon.

Saint knew it then.

He would die once they knew how Grace lived.

"Shut the door," he said.

She shook her head.

"Please, Saint."

She heaved the heavy hatch door closed and held her breath.

And she stood beside him.

And she saw the look, for a moment confusion, and then something clearer. She saw it because the room was not dark at all, because light splintered from a thousand gaps in the surround, slicing through everything they thought they knew.

For a long time he walked around the area, tracing the walls with his fingers. He paced it out, her eyes on him as he counted aloud.

"It's so much bigger," he said.

He knelt and touched the ground, stared around like he could see what he had not been able to see.

He stood and turned to her. "You think Tooms took me and gave me to Aaron."

"I never said that."

"So tell me what you think."

"I don't know what to think. Nothing is clear. Could be that Aaron took you right to his farmhouse. Maybe it was just Callie Montrose that was held here. Or maybe we'll find DNA that puts the other girls here. There's still questions we might not be able—"

"But Tooms was there that morning I was taken. Those same woods. Not a hundred yards from where it happened."

"Searching for a dog," she said. And even then, to her it did not sound right.

"Grace wasn't here either," he said.

She looked at him and was about to reason but knew that it would do no good at all.

"I can't feel anything, Saint. I've never been here before."

141

Misty wore a blue dress and pearls, her hair pulled up, cheekbones high beneath feline eyes that seemed amused as she glanced his way.

"The bank robber himself," she said.

"You tell your mother who you were dining with tonight?"

"She told me to watch my purse."

He trailed her into Lacey's Diner where they took a booth at the back. He looked around at the green leather stools, the chrome counter and checkerboard floor.

"I can't decide if this place is different or I am," he said.

"New light fittings," she said.

"The place then."

Lacey herself came over, told him it was nice to see him, though did not back her words with a smile.

He ordered a banana split, which Misty rolled her eyes at as she picked at low country shrimps and grits.

He stole looks at her face, thinner now. Her skin paler.

She told him how she had dropped out of college, how life takes turns you do not see coming.

Patch told her he was sorry.

She told him her father died a year before while playing golf beside the Ozarks. That his heart had not been as strong as his principles, his belief in a greater good sometimes only he could see.

Patch told her he was sorry.

"I only moved back to Monta Clare recently. Spend some time with my mother. Sometimes it feels like you can slow life a little in this town," she said.

"And that's what you want?"

"It rushes by so quick."

She settled the check before he could, and outside the sun had fallen and the sky glowed ink.

"Good night," she said, and he didn't catch up with her till she reached the top of Main Street. Before the silhouette of the St. Francois range, the outline shorn from a horizon he once longed to cross. A new clock fixed to the old building that housed the law offices of Jasper and Coates told him they had sat only an hour.

"I'm sorry," he called.

Misty stopped, her back to him. Beside him the window lights of Monta Clare Books pushed jackets he did not know.

She turned. "This is how you always wanted it, right. Me on my side of the street."

Patch walked out into the middle of the road.

"Why are you sorry?" she said.

"Because I left you."

"You think I regret that night?"

He wondered how she could not. He wondered how she could not regret each skeletal moment she wasted on him, each time she held his empty hand, fixed him inedible food, and joined his search for a dead girl.

"My mother . . . when she saw you were back in town. When she heard I was meeting you tonight. She told me what my father did."

Behind her was a new store that sold ironstone bowls, earthenware plates, and metal skillets. He saw organic dishcloths and oatmeal linen and imagined the couples that came there seeking to upgrade after their starter sets. Slowly making the exchange from temporary, from light to substance. He knew then that what he had taken from the Meyers was more than money, more than a chance to give his mother what she chased.

She stepped down onto the road.

"Tell me you're married now," he said, because she wore a plain band on her ring finger. "Tell me you live up in the hills, and you take morning walks with your Lab. Your husband is kind and decent. You've got two children, but one day you'll go back to school and—"

"My life is just fine, Patch. But my mother thought telling me would make me see you."

"Did it?"

"I always knew I couldn't compete."

"It wasn't a—"

"You're right. It was a shutout. I see that now."

"I mean, technically we both scored that night."

She finally broke a smile. "Ugh. How can I stay mad at the boy that saved my life?"

142

Misty bought a bottle of wine from Green's, and together they walked up the hill to the edge of the road, sat back on the grass, and looked out high over the light of Monta Clare to the dark of the mountains, lined up like an audience waiting on their encore.

"I know it was a long time ago, but we loved each other, right? I need to know that."

Above, they watched the showers, the lumps of rock that had traveled a million miles only to die in their world.

"Sure, Mist. We loved each other."

She shivered and he slipped his arm around her, his finger in the gulley of her ribs.

She asked him about his life. He spoke for a long time. She gasped when he talked of being shot at by a guard in the Merchants National Bank, limping into prison and staring down a twelve-year sentence. How he might not have made it through but for a prison guard who stopped it before it began,

a man big in every way. He told her of life impris-
oned. Some nights he saw flashlights beaconing the
new toward isolation chambers because they'd tried
it and failed and would now be watched so they
could not try it again. At eight he would leave his
cell and see an old man mopping blood spilled from
that freshly cut wrist. Into the communal bathroom
where forty men washed up, cleaned their teeth,
tried not to breathe shit from the toilets.

He told her how he ate oatmeal then worked the
penitentiary's industrial laundry. Eight hours each
day; each month tending a million pounds of linen
from surrounding hospitals and institutions. He
learned the machinery, checked the filter screens
and fill hoses, changed frayed belts and blistered
brushes, and wiped down gaskets.

The menu changed with the seasons, food nothing more than fuel after a couple of rotations.

And then he talked of Grace. Of those first years
when he mourned, when each evening he read the
books she had spoken of. From Heathcliff and lost
love to Holden Caulfield and his rail against pho-
nies. He would close his eye and drift by the tropical
island watching the scraps of Ralph's savaged ideals.
Laugh at Scout and hear Atticus Finch in Grace's
noblest rants.

But it was then, when the lights cut and sleep
would not come, that he truly missed her, and Saint,
and, of course, Misty.

"Did you paint?" she said.

"I lost my reason to."

"I'm so sorry she's gone."

"I think about it, and I can't see it. Tooms and her. Thurley State Park . . . Saint took the dogs there. A team. She drove back each month. I want to go there. And I don't. I don't think I'll find her or nothing, but I need to see it."

"So let's go see it then."

143

Misty drove an '85 Mustang, gunned the engine as they pulled onto Interstate 35. She wore boots, a raincoat, her blonde hair buried beneath a cream woolen hat. She slowed by the Gold Run River as he opened the window to soaring bluffs and heard nothing, the katydids months off.

They pulled off the road beside a box canyon so deep and narrow he imagined Grace down there, her body long since given back to the ground.

Misty reclined her seat and closed her eyes, and before long he heard her sleeping.

Patch lay awake till morning broke around them, climbed from the car and stared into woodland blanched, the trees thin in places, the ground mulched leaves like a blanket laid atop her. Patch knew it ran over a million acres.

Misty took his hand. Trees leaned with a hill so steep they took a longer route, crossing fallen joists as thick as his waist. Tooms could give no more detail than that he had taken one of the couple of hundred tracks till it grew too thick, and then stopped and dug, and hauled the body of a young girl from his car, left her in the dirt, and dragged earth over her skin.

Above them a great oak held bronze sky in its trusses. Patch sought a stream that shone like polished glass shattered over rocks that humped from the bed so the sandpipers had a spot to fish from.

Saint's instruction had been clear and vague enough.

Patch moved through shortleaf pine, Misty a step behind.

They stopped by the rusted sign.

"This is it."

She breathed hard, so they stalled awhile, boots in the all-weather gravel road that had long since closed. Saint had mapped the area, relayed everything Tooms said and guessed at the route he'd taken from Monta Clare, the likeliest place he'd pulled into, the next access road near seventy miles along highways he would not want to travel.

"The rooftop trail," he said.

They walked slow.

The track rose steep, near five hundred feet above dolomite glades ringed by American smoketrees that opened for a horizon of thick oaks, hickories and walnuts.

"No way he carried her this far," Patch said,

without emotion, the thought so cold Misty pulled her hat low over her ears and hugged her raincoat around her.

From there they walked back down, Patch stopping at each break in the trees, each tableland before it rode the cascade of mossed banks slick with morning dew and knots of joe-pye weed.

For hours he stopped still in places, looked at the dirt like there was method to his madness. It was only as they came back in sight of the access road that Misty stopped.

"This is the road by Turners Breach?" she said.

He nodded.

"There was a storm . . . when you were taken. Took down tracts of woodland. I remember they didn't clear it till fall because the Danby Dam burst. My father owned land further up and took the Department of Natural Resources to court. It was in **The Tribune.** So if the road was blocked—"

"Then he can't have buried her here," Patch said.

"No other way into this area. The next trail is an hour north. He'd risk driving that with a body in the trunk?" Misty said, the words not sounding quite real as they left her mouth.

They drove back in silence, Patch contemplating what he knew.

In the old house he picked up the phone and dialed.

Saint answered like she'd been waiting.

She made her checks and called him back. "Doesn't mean—"

"He lied, Saint."

"Maybe he got the spot wrong. It was night."

"Or maybe she's still alive."

144

They spent the summer drifting toward the kind of friendship both needed. Each Sunday morning they set off early and hiked river scene trails, the Meramec River laid down like a gold path choked green beneath trees that swept out over banks. Misty told him of hydrotropism, her hair pulled back, her cheeks blush from the gradient. She told him how her father used to bring her to the mountains, their bicycles loaded onto the roof rack. The two would ride miles that felt untouched since the resort era.

They stopped before the bottomland, the flood-plain forest drained. She unpacked Tupperware, cutlery, and napkins.

"Sausage and hash brown casserole."

He felt a little bile rise.

"My mother made it."

He swallowed it down.

They ate beneath a sullen sky, and she asked him about Tooms. He told her he had made another dozen requests for visitation, written again, offered forgiveness, an avenue for atonement. Saint had done similar, though her belief waned, certain that Tooms had killed the girl and enjoyed toying with them, the last vestige of power for a man who had been stripped back to bone.

"Will you keep looking?" Misty said, as she sipped coffee from a thermos and watched starlings move to an orchestra so tightly conducted.

He watched her, outwardly so stoic it was like something or someone had robbed her passion fully. "Hydrotropism. When did you get so smart, Mist?"

"I also know that a group of ladybirds is called a loveliness. I like how some things are just perfect, you know."

He looked at her, and knew.

145

Sometimes Misty stopped by the gallery and sat on the stool beside the window like a living display as he sprayed the glass and wiped it down, the sun warm on his skin as the missing girls watched him.

Saturdays he took breakfast with Saint and her grandmother at Lacey's Diner. Saint watching Norma with tender concern, despite the barbs she lobbed at her grandmother when she asked the waitress to Irish up her coffee. Norma asked Patch if he had seen the riots in Los Angeles, the looting and shooting, told him that civil disturbance implied civility to begin with.

"She's getting preachy in old age," Saint said, to a scowl.

The Palace 7 had closed its doors in the fall of 1986 and remained empty while Sammy, the new owner, wrestled with **the cunts at the town council** over a change of use. It had the high ceilings and broad windows he craved. For years the battle had raged. And then Walt Murray, the projectionist at

the Palace 7 for over thirty years, neared his nineti-
eth birthday. Walt's wife, a hard-faced dame named
Mitzie, approached Sammy about opening the old
doors for one night only as a surprise for her husband. Caught in a Remy Martin haze, Sammy read-
ily agreed, only to clean forget the next morning. A
week later, when a poster appeared on the window of
the 7, so horrified was he by his act of munificence,
Sammy headed over to the law offices of Jasper and
Coates and threatened all manner of legal action.

"The old bitch blindsided me. Everyone in this
goddamn town knows I celebrate the death of Jackson
Pollock on August eleventh. Fucking drip technique."

Patch hauled him back from across the street, the
two standing outside the empty movie theater as
Sammy steamed away.

"They might look on it favorably. You're giving
back to the town," Patch tried.

"I do nothing but give. People can walk by my
window and transport themselves away from this
bastard place with a single glance."

"Everyone misses the 7."

"The place ran at a loss."

"People would love you if you reopened it. Good
karma, Sammy."

"The day I give a fuck what people think about
me is the day I see hard proof that karma is real.
That good things do happen to the good."

"Just for one night then. You can't back out now,
Sammy. You just can't."

Sammy shook his head in despair. "What are they showing? It better be something with Catherine Deneuve."

Patch looked at the window, and then he saw the poster. "Oh, Jesus."

146

"They're showing **Grease** at the old Palace 7," Misty said, at least a dozen times on their next hike. Patch deflected with talk of alluvial, glacial meltwater, and piping plovers.

"You know I still know all the words," she said. "Want me to prove it?"

"A lot of people mistake the Bell's vireo for a wren."

"I reckon I can still fit into that yellow dress I wore the first time I saw it."

"One time in prison a man shat himself in protest over the poor hygiene standards. The irony of it, Mist."

She did frown at that one.

"I do love that movie, though," she said.

He fussed with his eye patch, cleared his throat, and longed for a mudslide to sweep him away.

Misty raised an eyebrow. "Probably have a big cake for old Walt. Maybe Mitzie will make it. She used to own the bakery at number fourteen. My mother said her cakes were a slice of heaven."

"Sammy said she has the psoriasis. So bad he has me sweep the floor after she visits. Likely be a lot of skin in that cake, Mist."

Her eyebrow dropped.

They hiked another mile. Misty kept her head down, not looking up for the butterfly glade, the roadrunners, or the lush pastures.

She did not touch her English muffins, even though she had not baked them herself.

And then, finally, back at the car, he took a deep breath. "So, I was thinking, this movie at the—"

"I would love to go. Thank you, kindly."

147

The town was Breckenridge, and Saint stood outside the old lodge in the shade of the Tenmile Range while Summit County cops guarded the scene in the kind of stone silence that accompanied only the death of a child.

It was held for her, frozen in place by six uniformed cops who closed down the surrounding streets and taped off the woodland behind. She met the local chief, skinny with a horseshoe moustache, his pallor a little green like he'd spent the early hours bent over a toilet trying to purge the memory. She did not tell him it would not get easier. It would not fade.

She wore gloves and zipped herself into white coveralls. Bags over her shoes as she ducked beneath the tape and followed him down a steep slope to a flatland of felled trees, machinery and workmen a good way back, hard hats in hand as they watched her.

"New homes," the chief said.

Saint saw the rounded aggregation of large stones and beside it hills of damp earth.

The clothing had held up well enough. Beneath it were bones.

And the reason she had come.

With gloved hands she carefully removed the rosary beads.

Saint held the marbled blue to the light and stared at the medal.

The girl had been buried in her clothes and shoes and with her schoolbag. Saint plucked a purse from the debris and ran her thumb over the polyester shell and then carefully unclasped it.

"You know her?" the chief said.

"I know all of them," Saint said.

148

That night she called him from a pay phone outside her motel, breathing the lilacs that grew ten feet high. Lights sailed up high toward her as cars followed roads that circled the base of the mountain. She had spent a long afternoon in the Summit County PD, called Himes and faxed him her report, ate bad pizza and ran through her notes till the ink blurred and then made the call.

"It's midnight," Patch said.

"Sorry."

"Are you okay?"

She could see him sitting there in the dark, not a single light on in the old house.

"I'm at a town the locals call Breck, and from where I'm standing I can see a mountain that would put ours in shadow. If it just fell . . . if it . . . it would crush us all."

"I think Misty has a husband or something."

"Why?"

"We just see each other early on Sundays. I don't

know much about her life now. We talk about the past but nothing beyond."

"You meeting the parole officer?"

"Yes, ma'am."

She laughed.

"I worry about you," he said.

"Stealing my lines."

"I thought about you every day, Saint. I thought about Jimmy and what he did."

"It was a long time ago now," she said, like she did not think of it, too. Like she did not still ache each time she saw a mother pushing a stroller. Like for a long time after she had not avoided the children's section in bookstores, had not sped up when she passed playgrounds. She did not imagine a different life, where she could be what she did not deserve to be. Where Jimmy had passed his exams, and not raised his fists. Where though he could not be the man she wanted, he could be a father. They could be the kind of parents she herself had not known.

"You remember Summer Reynolds?" she said.

"Fort Worth. Her hair is cadmium and ochre and violet. Viridian eyes that told her parents she was one step ahead. I remember her mother said she was trouble, but said it with a smile, you know."

She told him.

And heard the click and the dial tone.

149

The next morning she woke early and strolled downtown past painted buildings that dated back to the first gold rush and to the Blue River diggings. She raised her camera to the Chinese Laundry House, the Pollock House, joined a trail and captured the Iowa Hill Boarding House, wondered to herself what those miners would make of it all. They were laying the bedrock for a town that would shrug off wildfires, a call to modernize, a place where a young girl would lose her life at the hands of a man who remained out of reach despite all they knew about him. She found a horse chestnut case and split it, removed the glossy conker and placed it into her pocket.

In a small toy store she looked at a wooden train and studied it carefully. She stared at shelves of books on subjects as varied as outer space and fine art, American history and wildlife. And, of course, storybooks from Dr. Seuss to Rudyard Kipling. Saint watched a mother and her son, the little boy aiming a smile, and Saint smiling back. They selected **Where the Wild Things Are.** Saint made a note of the title.

At her motel she saw the old Buick in the lot, Patch leaning on the hood.

He looked beat, like he'd grabbed his keys the moment their call ended, driven through the night and much of the day.

"Are her parents here?" he said.

There was so much she could have said. Instead she simply nodded and led him back down Main Street to the police station. He carried a large package, and when he saw Mrs. Reynolds she broke from her place beneath the old clock and met him. Though many years had passed she hugged him like he was family.

She left them alone in the back office, where Patch unwrapped the painting of their daughter and gifted it to them. Saint had heard the numbers from Sammy, that it was a gift worth many thousands of dollars. She also knew it was a gift they would not ever part with.

Over a long afternoon she sat with Patch in the Blue River Café as he mourned the memory of another girl he had not ever had the honor of knowing.

"I got the DNA results from the Tooms farm," she said. "Lot of samples but none of them matched. Doesn't mean she wasn't there. It was such a long time ago. It was likely cleaned with bleach . . . I don't—"

He hit the table with the flat of his fist so hard the cups smashed to the floor. Saint held a hand toward the waitress as she led him out.

And as the afternoon burned off she made him promise to drive straight back. He had broken the terms of his parole. She would not offer the truth, nor would she lie for him if asked.

"Summer Reynolds. How long had she been there?" he said.

"A long time."

"Callie Montrose. Nothing on her?"

"Nothing," Saint said, her mind on Richie Montrose. Last Saint heard a bar fight had gotten out of hand and Richie spent the night in county jail. Only got it squashed because of who he used to be, and maybe because everybody knew.

"How many more of them, Saint? How many more of these girls I paint are buried out there?"

150

Patch drove for seven hours, so tired at times the old Buick veered across white lines till he opened the window and allowed the humid air to sober him. Fifty million acres of darkness.

He carried an old ordinance map, but most was lost to the marks he'd made. He glanced into the river but found nothing like those old miners had, no glitter in the silt, just a reminder that if his story had an end it would not be the kind he hoped for, where he found Grace, where she had lived a life filled with everything she deserved. He pulled off from Interstate 70 and slept fitfully.

At the first sign for Monta Clare he remembered, his heart sinking.

He passed by Rosewood Avenue and drove up toward Parade Hill, left his truck across the street and walked over.

"I missed the movie," he said.

Misty nodded.

"I'm so sorry. Something happened."

"It's nothing," she said. "Just a movie."

He wanted to tell her but guessed that she already knew. Whatever the reason, she had come to expect it. To expect less from him because all those years ago he had emerged as less in every way.

"I can . . . we could go out someplace—"

"I need to stop now, Patch. Wherever we might have been heading, I can't anymore."

"Of course."

"I'll see you, then," she said and leaned forward, stood on her toes to reach up and kiss his cheek, and held there awhile, like the moment meant something he did not fully grasp.

When he turned he saw it at the foot of her path. A yellow hairband discarded in the bushes. He remembered it from all those years before.

He bent and collected it, then turned and walked back up her path, not knowing exactly what he would say, just that it needed to be more.

Patch was about to knock when light hit the window beside.

And there, through it, he saw her.

And he saw who she was with.

There was a moment before the pieces aligned. Before the world once again turned without him.

151

The girl's name was Charlotte, and she stood in front of a large television set.

Her hair was gold and reached her waist.

Misty left them.

Patch looked at his daughter, and she stared back coldly.

"Do you like Muppets?" he said, noting the stuffed toys.

She wore denim dungarees, her feet bare on wood floor that caught the shine of the morning sun.

"You're friends with my mom," she said, holding his gaze so intently he knew then that she was blessed with her mother's confidence. That way of looking at the world like your place was warranted. Deserved. He felt the relief acutely.

"Yes," he said.

"How come I don't know you then?"

"I've been searching for someone."

"Who?"

He cleared his throat lightly. "A girl I knew."

"What's her name?"

"Grace."

Her eyes belonged to him, he noticed then. The lightest brown and the heavy dark lashes.

"Mom said she was friends with a pirate, but I thought it was BS."

He watched the bow of her lips as she spoke.

"She also told me you're the bravest boy that ever lived, which I also think is BS."

She moved so close he could smell the lotion on her skin as she studied his face. "The girl you're searching for, maybe she isn't real. That's what my grandmother said. Which I think means you're crazy."

He smiled, but she did not.

"She is . . . she was real," he said, matching her whisper.

"So she's it," Charlotte said.

"What?"

"Your rainbow connection."

"What's that?"

She rolled her eyes in a move that echoed her mother. "Everyone on this earth is placed here for someone else. You follow your dreams and find them, and you make a match and nothing else matters. Haven't you heard the frog sing it?"

He shook his head.

She stood beside him and together they watched the green frog clutch a banjo.

She mouthed the words, told him someday they'd find it.

At the door Misty stood.

Patch could have stopped then. Right then, at that point he could have pressed stop and their world would have shuddered and groaned and finally come to a close.

"The lovers, the dreamers and me," Charlotte said.

152

"That's why you dropped out of school," he said, as they sat side by side on the swings.

"Yes."

"You could have told Sammy."

Misty laughed, but it was not cold. "And drag you back to handle a responsibility you were clearly not ready for. Shit, Patch. I wasn't ready for it. My mother . . ."

"Does she know?"

"She doesn't want you around Charlotte."

He could summon no reply.

Misty took his hand. "I wanted to tell you. But I wanted to know you again first."

"What's she like?" he said, daring to ask, like he had a right to.

Misty smiled again; this time it was whole. "She's . . . I don't even know where to begin. She's tough. Smarter than me. She likes animals. Her favorite place on earth is the Culpepper Zoo. She curses, which makes me laugh and my mother die a little. We don't even know where she picks up the words. And she . . . steals things. We don't know where that comes from either."

He frowned.

"Candy bars mostly. Sometimes trinkets. I used to sift her pockets and find it all."

"Outrageous," he said, keeping his eye low.

"I think it's just a phase since I haven't found anything of late."

He would not tell her to try the girl's sleeves.

"She's you, Patch. Sometimes she's so you I can't even bear it."

"Don't tell her," he said, sudden and desperate.

She squeezed his hand. "She needs certainty, not a father who drops her each time a letter arrives, or the telephone rings, and then heads halfway across the country, her not knowing when she'll see him again. She needs roots she can take hold of. Stability."

"I have no . . . I'm not anything she can be proud of."

She went to speak, but he shook his head.

"That's not anything but the truth, Mist. She's this perfect thing, with this perfect mother, who is everything. Please don't tell her." His breath came short, so he looked to the sky. Right then mammatus clouds sagged like pockets of rainfall, the framing sky detonated like it could no longer hold blue.

Misty called to Charlotte, who came out and stood beside her mother, their heads tilted back, the gardens so beautifully tended, the house painted a new shade of yellow.

Patch knew a storm would come, and for a while they would have to hunker down and ride it out, waiting on a break.

153

That night he sat with Sammy on the small balcony above the gallery. Distant thunder rolled in from the St. Francois Mountains as they waited on the gales that would twist through the state, plucking trucks from the roads, roofs from farmhouses, the families beneath hunkered in their shelters. It would kill ninety, injure a couple of hundred more, and fade only fifty miles from them.

Patch did not dare think of Charlotte as his daughter, because she was only in the way that counted least. He had told Sammy, who opened a bottle of Rhum Clément 1940 to **wet the baby's head.**

"She's seven years old," Patch said.

"Dalí started at six."

The first rain fell. They sat unmoving as the heat still clung. Sammy protected his drink with the flat of his hand. "You're worried."

"I don't have a right to worry. To know her. To speak her name."

Sammy smiled. "How long have I known you?"

"Too long."

"And I never paid you a compliment. Agreed?"

Patch thought a little, then nodded.

"I won't start now. But I will say this. The little girl, she's got a father I've watched turn from a boy into a man. And I don't know many of them. You already made half your life a search for someone who needed you. Maybe now is the time to take a little of it back. Not for you, but for what you could give to her."

"Misty said she needs stability. She needs roots."

"So you give them to her."

Patch watched the rain. "I don't know how."

Sammy drank. "You do. You're just afraid to let go."

"I think of her genes, of Misty's father and how he looked at me."

"Franklin Meyer was a cunt, and not the gentleman kind. Franklin's father was a cunt, too. As kids they were cuntlets. A line of cunts, each one cuntier than the last."

"I wonder what the collective term for—"

"A cuntet," Sammy said knowingly.

Patch took a drink and watched the rain. "Grace needs me. More than Charlotte needs me."

Sammy reached over, placed a heavy hand on his shoulder and let it rest. "Don't worry too much. I never knew my father, and look, I turned out just fine."

The next day Patch instructed Sammy to sell half a dozen paintings.

He would put down roots in Monta Clare.

154

Summer climbed as Patch stripped off his shirt and began hauling furniture out into the front yard. The sofa and bookcases, small dining table and sideboard. It took less than an hour to rid the ground floor of their lives, his mother entwined in each object, the shape of her in cushions, the smell of her in the kitchen cabinets.

He boxed utensils, dragged the refrigerator through and onto dead grass.

Upstairs he stripped bedding, bagged clothes and towels and makeup and perfumes. A bottle of something fell and smashed, and memories the scent carried blazed at his throat as he worked.

In his bedroom he boxed the pirate memorabilia. He was not a pirate. He was a thirty-year-old man with a criminal record.

At lunch he fetched Saint's grandmother, who stood in the front yard as a small van came and collected what could be used. Norma talked of housing projects and charities.

She lit a cigarette and watched as Patch returned from Monta Clare Hardware with a sledgehammer and began to swing it. He tore doors from frames, ripped out baseboard and rolled up carpet. His muscles tight as he ran roughshod through the old house, heaving it up and down with brutality; knocking banisters from posts; splitting the kitchen counter to a dozen fractures. He smashed the porcelain bath and sink, took aim at himself in the large mirror and swung.

The old house fought back, an errant nail catching his shoulder and tearing the skin, the drywall coughing out so much dust that by the time he walked back out into the afternoon sun he was gray.

He stood there sweating and bleeding, caught his breath then headed back inside for a second round.

Saint joined her grandmother.

"I think he's gone mad," Norma said.

"You're implying he was sane to begin with."

That night Rosewood Avenue glowed with flames as smoke rose from the yard of the old Macauley house. Patch sat on what was left of the porch and watched the timbers he had stripped charr and soot.

Misty and Charlotte walked down from the tall hill and watched the show, along with Sammy, who wandered from Main Street, decanter in hand, offering slugs.

"Château Léoville—Las Cases Saint-Julien Deuxième Cru," he managed.

"She's a child," Misty said, slapping Charlotte's hand away as she moved for a glass.

Patch stood before the flames and watched his daughter. It was not only the heat from the old house warming him that night.

155

The next day he drove a large track excavator down the street and straight into the front of the house. Neighbors gathered and watched as the scoop reduced what was left to rubble.

He stood atop the small mountain for a moment, then brought in a bulldozer and began to strip the land back.

Patch slept in his car, did not shave, washed up in the lake, and ate his meals with whoever would have him, more often than not Saint and her grandmother.

"What do you do now?" Saint asked, over a dinner of fried chicken, macaroni and cheese, and cornbread.

"I build," Patch said.

Saint glanced at her grandmother, who shook her head like the bearded man had mislaid the last of his marbles.

He did not hire an architect, instead worked from

paintings, from a memory he knew could not fully be trusted.

Wood was delivered on the back of tractor-trailers that rumbled the town and shook the neighbors awake at ungodly hours. To make amends Patch promised to throw open the doors for a party the second it was done.

"It'll likely collapse if more than two people climb the stairs," Sammy said, from his place on the lawn, where each afternoon he would sit on a folding chair and drink and watch the mad man, complete with toolbelt, handsaw, various hammers, chisels, and drills look through a series of sketches and scratch his head beneath the fearsome midday sun.

When funds ran short he would walk around the gallery and select another painting to part with, each time losing a piece of her world he could not reclaim.

Misty brought Charlotte to the gallery, and Patch told her of the missing girls and a little of his plight.

"Batshit crazy," the girl said to her mother, who could do little but agree.

He spent a small fortune on a lathe, a bigger fortune on timber and glass.

He dug foundations by hand, from sunrise to down, one time bringing in industrial floodlighting and attempting to work through the night before the neighbors got together, led by a nervous looking Mitch Evans, and told him not one of them could sleep. Patch scratched his beard, then offered to black out all their windows with newspaper and tape.

Soon enough Misty stopped by daily with Charlotte on their walk back from Monta Clare Elementary, and the two would look at the beard, now dropping almost to his chest, the mess of hair and the tanned skin, and they would tut at each other.

Sammy, tiring of the spectacle, brought in several architects from the city, who looked at Patch's drawings, frowned, and shook their heads. And several builders, who Patch allowed to assist on the condition that if they suggested a single design change they would be made to walk the long plank that jutted from beneath the towering gable.

"You can't threaten contractors," Saint said, over burnt ends and slaw.

Patch nodded.

"Real fine looking house though," her grandmother said, as the portico took shape, the colonnade so tall Patch took to hauling tiles up with a system of pulleys that often failed and sent Sammy running for cover as slate rained from the Monta Clare sky.

He took such a deviation from building codes that he held his breath when the building inspector, a man more wire than flesh, his limbs like spindles fixed to a rake of a body, peered over the top of his spectacles and shook his head several times.

Saint took the man by his arm and told him a

little of the story of how the house had come to be. A couple of amendments and a token fine, and Patch was back to work that same day.

Work slowed each winter as the ground froze. The sky whitened, and Patch wore a woolen hat Charlotte gave him for Christmas. In return he gave Charlotte a portrait of her and her mother as they stood before the burning house. Charlotte accused him of making her eyes too large, then quietly hung it in her bedroom when she learned of the monetary value.

He accompanied Misty and her mother to Charlotte's piano recital, the frost beginning its thaw across town, though not between Patch and Mrs. Meyer, who did not once acknowledge him.

He put down tools whenever the weakest of leads presented itself. Sometimes in the dead of night his battered Camaro would pare the street and aim for the highway, cross a thousand miles so he could speak with aging parents clutching at slim chance, less sagacious, more hopeful. It was a compromise of sorts. He would not let Grace go, but he would prove to Misty that he would always return.

156

When the framing was completed and the stucco dried, he spent an entire week painting it white, the shutters a shade of Aegean that changed each time he lay in the darkness and plucked memories like peacock feathers that fanned his craze.

"And I rattled those wooden floorboards with my tap shoes until my heart soared."

Patch deciphered a code that was not there, decided he needed heart pine floors and so spent another month scouring reclamation yards until he found a shade that matched his mind's eye.

"A bedroom for me, my mother, and three more we rented to whoever was passing through. One time it was a girl maybe nineteen, and she taught me the art of applying makeup. Decadence, Patch. There ain't a more decadent word. Another time it was a preacher on his way to Pearl River County. You ever seen Hemmsford Swampland? Man, that place needs exorcising."

Five bedrooms for a man who would live alone. A

cavernous den and kitchen, a dining room because Grace mentioned the formalities of Thanksgiving dinner. An orangery, which Saint named, because Patch did not know what the fuck an orangery was, only that the glass roof shed morning light over the white walls.

The external staircase was a labor of hatred that brought him to his knees when it would not join, or float, or fix. In the end he accepted help from Saint's cousin Patrick, a carpenter from Brookfield who fixed it over Labor Day weekend. The end result so close to his vision he'd hugged the man so long Patrick looked to Saint to free him.

"Stop scaring people," Saint said, over Brunswick stew and corn muffins.

Patch nodded.

"Real fine looking house though," her grandmother said.

157

The following fall Patch was as good as his word and threw the doors open to his vast and empty house. Norma took care of the invitations, and near three hundred turned up, including Daisy Creason from **The Tribune,** who ran a front-page piece, which Patch only allowed because it might somehow find its way to her.

Sammy declared himself the only dignitary worthy of cutting the ribbon, and he stood there in his tux and tails and slurred his way through a speech so rambling people checked their watches and shrugged at one another. He spoke of red tape, bureaucracy, and the cunts at the town planning office. There were tuts, an outright gasp, and the raucous laughter of Charlotte, who drew a scolding from her mother.

Sammy decreed it the Mad House, at which Patch almost broke a smile.

Misty took charge of the catering herself, leading

locals to scratch their heads at creamed shrimp vol-au-vents and turkey pizza.

Sammy had decided to hang a couple of paintings, which generated a little buzz and led a handful of single ladies to seek out the artist and ask him if he might get lonely rattling around such a large house on his lonesome.

"Oh boy," Misty said, linked his arm in hers and took him out through the French doors into the yard where fairy lights had been threaded through hands of ninebark.

They sat on a bench carved from a single piece of oak with a chainsaw Patch had discarded afterward for fear he might one day regain his sanity and begin hacking at the foundations of the Mad House.

"This house," she said, looking up at the turret.

"What do you see, Mist?"

"A purity of execution. It looks like the painting."

"Somewhere out there is a house just like this one. And inside it she lived."

"You think people like my pizza?" she said.

"How could they not?" he said, the couple of slices she'd thrust at him now mulching in the flower beds.

"Half our lives, now," she said.

Through the grand window they saw Chief Nix talking to Saint and her grandmother.

"Why did you come back, Misty?"

"So Charlotte could have what I had. So my mother could know her. Why did you come back?"

He placed his empty beer bottle on the grass. "It's too big out there. If you lose someone, you'll likely find them again if they stay in one place, right. But both of you moving . . ."

Patch stood.

"There's something else," she said.

He turned and from her face he knew that something was not good.

"I'm sick, Patch."

"Sick?"

He looked at the shape of her, at the colors he knew better than any other. Beneath the moonlight he saw the delicacies that made her, the fine strokes and boldened shades. He saw her in mixes: her skin titanium and singed umber and alizarin; her Prussian eyes; her hair would be lain darks softened with sienna before light layering. In all her blinding glory. She could not be sick. The world would not allow such a tragedy.

"The kind of sick you don't get better from."

He took her in his arms and knew he could use each color he owned painting Misty Meyer, and they would still not come close enough.

158

The Quartz Mountain State Park.

Saint was met at the Cedar Creek Trail by a sheriff's deputy who wore a wide-brimmed hat and led her in stone silence. The sun-baked scrubs of wild land by Black Jack Pass Trail trodden down.

In the distance the granite face of Baldy Point rose. Three hundred feet out. She had passed through Hobart and Lone Wolf, and in her stomach was low-level dread because the deputy was skilled and could make no determinations at all.

She saw a couple of climbers in the distance.

"It'll be unbearable once the heat gets up," the deputy said.

She could not read his age from his face, though guessed he was a veteran as he did not react when they reached the burial site.

They had guarded it as best they could.

Getting trucks in would not be possible.

Saint knelt in the dirt and fell into the shade of the deputy.

"A dog found her?" Saint said.

"Yes, ma'am. Wichita Mountain Climbers Coalition were setting new anchors. Figured they'd worked on clearing a new trail."

Saint stared at the skeletal remains.

"Guess he couldn't bury her deep enough. Lot of rock. Maybe hard ground when he did it."

No clothes or bag. No litter. Just a single item remained intact alongside the bones.

She looked at the fine detail. The metal blues, the pardon crucifix. The beads larger at intervals.

"Same guy?" the deputy asked.

Saint nodded, calm, because she had felt it long before she knew for certain. "Same guy."

159

Patch was not prepared for the speed at which the cancer ravaged Misty's body.

In the summer of 1993 he heaved her bed across the room to the large bay window so that she could watch the fall approach before winter swept colors into memory.

He spent his time at the big house on Parade Hill, where he existed mostly in the background of scenes that began their dim. Charlotte curled beside her mother, sometimes reading from her schoolbooks, other times listening to Misty speak of their shared past, how Patch had once stood up to a bully near twice his size.

"Chuck Bradley? Is he the bald guy who works in the Ford dealership?" Charlotte said.

Patch nodded. The same dealership where he took his new F-150 to be serviced.

The television ran a background of an Amtrak train derailment that would claim forty-seven lives and leave more than a hundred injured. Patch stared at the wreckage of the Big Bayou Canot Bridge. The reporter was young and stood before the tragedy in a shock that quavered her words, but in them he heard something so familiar he held transfixed till Charlotte yelled at him to fetch her grandmother as Misty's fever spiked.

Through the coldest summer and colorless fall, those hard-bitten months chased the promise of a Christmas where he could buy his daughter a proper gift, though by then Misty was in such pain that Patch would take a brooding Charlotte down to the gallery each evening while the nurses came. The damage to Misty's nerves could be dulled with morphine; the prescient mourning in their daughter could not.

He taught her to paint, locked Sammy out of the small studio and encouraged her to find her center and work out from it. In the locker he found brushes he had not used in near twenty years.

As she washed up, Sammy emerged, looked at the canvas and shook his head. "Fucking awful."

Charlotte scowled and he flipped her off, almost causing a smile to form on a face so resolutely troubled.

They turned when a woman emerged and walked down the stairs, glanced quickly at Charlotte before leaving.

"Was that my choir teacher?" Charlotte said.

Patch looked to Sammy, who shrugged. "She could certainly hit a high note."

"Jesus," Patch said.

"Mentioned him at one point, too," Sammy said.

"As in Jesus get this old bastard off of me?" Charlotte said.

Sammy turned and both watched his shoulders shake as he tried hard to stifle his laughter.

At the turn of the new year the three sat on Misty's bed and watched the Monta Clare sky light with fireworks. Charlotte pressed her face to the glass as rockets streaked their paths and fountains glowed from a Main Street display Sammy had agreed to fund during a drunken stupor, to commemorate the first anniversary of the death of Audrey Hepburn, **the first lady I blew my load to.**

A little after midnight, when the sky cooled and only starlight remained, Patch left mother and daughter sleeping and found Mrs. Meyer on the sweeping terrace.

"Joseph," she said, and he walked up the stone steps and joined her.

The grounds lit, the same spot he had once sat with Misty's father all those years before.

"You're good with her . . . with both of them."

"I'm not, but thank you."

She was so much her daughter, elegant and dignified though altogether iced. Her hair still blond, her skin alabaster, like she deflected the harmful rays with her cold. "Will you stay . . . after?"

"Yes."

"But will you really? Will all of you stay, or just

the part that belonged to my daughter? I wonder that. I wonder what you can ever be to someone else. Does that seem harsh?"

He shook his head.

"I don't miss him. Franklin. I know how that sounds, but the way he saw the world, and the way he chose to deal with problems. It's a Meyer tradition: throw money at it and make it disappear. . . ."

"I was a problem," Patch said.

"Oh, the biggest," she said, adding a smile. "He never made me laugh. And I knew, before I met him. I knew love and laughter and how sweet life could be."

"You still married him."

She looked at Patch like he was a child, like he did not know how the world kept turning. "Sometimes people reserve so much of themselves. It's like saving a fine wine for an occasion that never materializes."

"So just drink it then. On a Tuesday when the sun is shining, or when a storm cloud hovers, just drink it," he spoke, thinking of Sammy.

"For so long it was just the three of us. Charlotte is everything, she has to be."

"I know."

"I'm not sure that you do, but I hope in time that you might."

160

They drove to Lake Pine the day the freeze set in. Patch helped Charlotte with her ice skates and huddled beside Misty as they watched the girl turn pirouettes, picking up such speed Patch worried she'd corkscrew right through and he'd have to head in after her.

"Thank you for not asking if I'm okay every thirty seconds," Misty said.

"It's because I don't care all that much."

She laughed, a sound he would commit to a memory already fleeting, his grip on their time fierce and loose. Charlotte grew taller, more beautiful and inquisitive and angry.

"I want to tell her," Misty said, trussed beneath layers of blankets and a pink woolen hat.

"No."

"Soon though. She'll love you. She'll see how brilliant you are, Joseph Macauley."

"Hush now, you're too sick to make any kind of sense at all."

Each week they drove to a facility in Alice Springs, where Misty had access to the finest facilities. A hundred acres of Missouri greens. The sign told it was a private palliative care center. Misty would stay at the large house in Monta Clare, but she liked to visit the friends she had made during her therapies. Patch would sit outside, Charlotte attending school, Mrs. Meyer taking some time for herself. He bumped into Chief Nix, who gave up his Sundays to volunteer now. Nix smiled as he pushed a young woman in a wheelchair. Of course, Patch knew of cancer and the rising tide, but until then its reach seemed boundless, secular.

On the drive back they stopped at St. Raphael's.

"I'm scared," she said.

He hugged her tightly.

161

One crisp morning he answered the Meyers' phone to discover Charlotte had cut school. He covered for her gamely, told the teacher she had come down with a cold, and then he set out through Monta Clare to find her. He remained mostly calm, reasoned she could not have gone far as he roused Sammy and sent him out to cover the higher streets.

Patch found her by the lake where she sat alone and held a few-leaf sunflower, her fingers small around the short lance of the bract as she stripped toothless leaves and floated them on the water.

"Mind if I sit?" he said.

"Always."

He sat far enough away to keep from touching her knee with his. "I used to cut school and come here when I was your age."

"I'm not cutting. I chose not to go. It's not prison."

"Are you scared . . . your mother."

"I'm not scared."

"I am."

"That's why Sammy calls you a pussy."

He frowned.

"I've seen pictures of my mom when she was young, and she's beautiful like she is now. But she chose you," she said, like it was a challenge, like there could not be a thing less fathomable.

"Because you saved her. My grandmother talks about pity. Because you were poor. I saw it in the photos you're in. You're all skinny and your clothes don't fit. Your mother didn't love you enough."

"I was hard to love."

"You were bad."

He nodded.

"But she gets sick and you don't."

"Do you believe in God?" he said.

She took a moment and then shook her head.

He fought the urge to reach out, and she sensed it and stared at him with such heat. "I'll never want you as my father."

"I . . ."

"You all think I don't know."

Behind her a bufflehead dove and concentric circles crowned until they grew too large, until there was no trace left at all.

"You should know I'll never hold your hand. I'll never hug you. I'll never be yours in any way at all."

He nodded.

"It's not fair," she said.

"It rarely is."

She walked back toward home.

He waited awhile and followed, keeping her just within sight, far enough away so that she did not have to feel him there at all.

162

As Misty weakened, her mood soured despite her resolve to keep things steady for her daughter. At her grandmother's asking, Charlotte decided to put on a show and act out her mother's favorite movie on the grand terrace. An idea that struck Patch with a new kind of fear when she told him he would play the role of Danny to her Sandy, and that he better well fucking try.

Patch spent a week rigging lights, building a crude set, and gathering props from the Goodwill store on Main Street. Charlotte wrote a script and berated without mercy when he could not recall lines she changed daily.

On a perfect evening Patch redefined shambolic, missing cues and falling over his feet while Misty laughed so hard her mother further worried for her health. Mrs. Meyer took the role of stagehand, aiming a spotlight as her granddaughter expertly belted out songs, moved between costumes and changed hairstyles.

When it came to the final number, Patch swept Misty into his arms, tried not to notice how light she was, how his fingers nestled between her perfect bones.

"You know I'm still hopelessly devoted to you, right?" she said into his ear.

Another week passed.

Misty was there.

And then she was not.

163

Patch sat with Saint on the rear deck as the charcoal cooled and a breeze he could not feel kicked up white ash from the grill.

That morning Patch had walked into the law offices of Jasper and Coates, both now moneyed with their navy suits, salt-and-pepper hair, gold cufflinks and watches. He was unsure of why he had been summoned, and he sat beside Mrs. Meyer, who reached out and took his hand in an act of such unexpected compassion it could only have been born of tragedy. The days since had robbed her of something vital. Thoroughly beaten, she looked a woman who had outlived her child.

The reading had been brief. Misty had left her estate to her daughter, of course. A small amount to charity, her trust would be nullified and eventually redirected and repurposed. She left a picture to Patch.

And then Jasper had straightened a little, cleared

his throat, and removed his gold horn-rimmed spectacles. "Charlotte Mary Grace Meyer will be left in the sole custody of Joseph Henry Macauley."

Patch sipped beer, crossed his legs, and watched Saint in the kitchen, scraping their plates into the trash. She returned and settled beside him on the swing seat, her feet folded beneath her.

"I'll bet Mrs. Meyer had something to say," Saint said.

"She already knew."

"She's old now. Not as old as the woman inside the house." She glanced in through the window to where her grandmother dozed in a leather wingback. "She can't give Charlotte the life you can. The girl needs to get out and see the world outside of this town."

"That's why she did it?" Patch said.

"We both know the answer to that one, too."

"The kid, she steals."

Saint bit her lower lip.

"Not like I stole," he said.

"Kids do stupid things."

"Like the time you fashioned me a new eye out of papier-mâché."

"That wasn't stupid."

"The protrusion."

"So you could see around corners."

"You can't think the kid would be better with me. You've seen the Meyer house, the life . . ."

Saint chased the errant flutter of a bat with her eyes. "I saw it. And you saw it. But seeing and—"

"Knowing?"

"Understanding. We all see you, Patch. We all tell you to move forward, but where exactly is forward? There's no other place we can go. To face the past is to momentarily turn your back on what is now. And when you do that, you miss so damn much."

"So what then?"

"Misty is setting you free."

"And if I don't want to be free—"

"Then you see out your days in that basement, trying to make sense of the dark."

Patch exhaled. "Tell me about the Oklahoma girl."

Saint exhaled. "Not on your list or ours. No way of knowing exactly how long she lay there. Mother is dead. Another of Eli Aaron's. I looked into her life as best I could. No reason. Nothing."

"We need a break. In all of this, we just never caught a break."

"A parking ticket. A stolen car."

"Anything, Saint."

Saint yawned and stretched. "Breaks tend to happen when you call off the search."

"This girl could be Grace," he said.

"Yes. But you don't believe that."

"No."

164

They buried her in the small cemetery beside St. Raphael, on a day when mist eddied in the hills and the sky unfolded somber grays toward the Cedar Valley; where only smoke from the John Deere factory over in Pecaut reminded Patch people still went on during such a hateful day.

Charlotte wore a navy dress and did not cry. Her shoes were patent-leather sandals. He looked at her toes and her ears and the fine blonde of her hair. He thought he might take her to the Clear Spring Lake, to walk the villages and maybe head out on the water to fish for walleye and white bass.

She asked pointed questions about his life and his past, and he answered too truthfully, which pissed off her grandmother, who sometimes looked at Patch like he could do little but break her granddaughter's heart in the same callous and understood way he had her daughter's.

Patch noticed women who were once girls he had

gone to school with, and they dabbed at mascaraed eyes. When the tall men lowered the polished casket, Misty's mother finally cried out.

He wanted to tell Charlotte it would be okay.

He did not want to lie.

Patch followed his daughter, and in her small hand she clutched petals and tossed them onto the wooden box that held the body of her mother.

"You don't cry because it's over, you smile that it happened," she said.

He thought of Charlotte's books, but still, he could not muster a smile.

When it was done and Charlotte was led toward the small hall, Patch walked over to Chief Nix, who stood to one side alone.

"This day," Nix said. He wore sunglasses but they could not hide his sorrow. It was still his town, the people in it under his care. "It's good to see you, Joseph."

Patch finally smiled and the two men shook hands. The chief's grip was loose, like he carried no strength at all. Saint had told Patch of the stroke, how it came on when Nix was fishing. They said it was minor.

They looked at the ground. The flowers in their abundance. A grosbeak called and both men watched it.

"Monta Clare . . . any other day it would be beautiful," Nix said.

"I don't think it can be again. Not in the same way."

"How are you, Joseph? Tell me you did something good. That it didn't bury you."

Patch wondered at his directness and thought maybe it was the stroke. He had no time for small talk.

"I'm still looking for her."

Nix closed his watery eyes and nodded, and when he opened them again a tear fell but he did not move to wipe it away.

"Saint said you won't ever give up."

"Did you?" Patch said.

"I never gave up on you. I never stopped hoping you'd find your way into another life. A better . . ." He swallowed.

"My mother . . . she always spoke highly of you, Chief."

"Just Nix now. I haven't been chief since that day, Joseph. Not really."

Nix glanced back at the grave, crossed himself and turned to walk away.

"Will I find her?" Patch called, and felt like a child.

Nix turned. "That day, when it happened. You came out different. You were strong, and focused."

Patch thought about that often. The divergence. Sometimes he played an alternate version, where he heard Misty scream and did not intervene. He imagined himself and the life he led parting ways. His mother still alive. The pieces of their lives gathered up like a broken vase, rebuilt so tightly that afternoon barely left a flaw.

"But your old self, who I used to come see sometimes . . . Maybe it was him you left in the dark. And only him."

"I don't even remember myself before that day."

"You came back so fucking hot, kid. So burning hot there was only one place you were heading. I was sad when I heard, but surprised? No."

Patch looked back toward the town of Monta Clare, saw what Nix must have seen, a lifetime of decorous order, of being invited in for coffee, turning up at the elementary school and letting the children hold his badge. And then that day.

"You think people are good?" Nix said, and there was nothing mocking in his tone.

"We're all capable of goodness."

"Yin and yang were born out of chaos to exist in perfect harmony."

"That's a fable," Patch said.

"People think maybe the good and bad find a way to coexist, to keep balance, the bad reminding everyone of the need for a line."

"So Marty Tooms was just placed on this earth as a cautionary tale?"

Nix softened then. "Marty Tooms is . . ." he cleared his throat. "Have you ever been to Yellowstone? A town called Cody sits in the flatland . . . frontier image. The North Fork of the Shoshone. You go there, you see something so beautiful, you meet certain people and you just, you feel it."

"What?"

"That there ain't a god up there. It's all so perfect there's not a way he'd let us all loose down here to ruin it."

"I'm tired, Chief."

"You've got a daughter now. Take a little time for her. And when she doesn't need you so much, you go on back to your search. And I wish you the best life. There isn't a single person more deserving."

165

Charlotte arrived on the doorstep of the Mad House with a small white suitcase decorated with blue butterflies. Her grandmother stood at the end of the pathway and nodded to Patch, and in that simple gesture he understood the exact weight of his responsibility.

She walked into the hallway and cast a critical eye over the detail. Down at the parquet floor, each strip laid by Patch in exacting lengths.

Charlotte did not touch anything, kept her pink coat buttoned and her case clutched to her chest. She looked at artwork, which coated each wall, then at the chesterfield, the hide rug and the heavy drapes.

"Do you want to see your room?"

"Nothing here is mine."

He followed her up the stairs.

The bed was white, the frame ornate with carved roses and leaves. A pink canopy hung above in case she wanted to shut out the world. And to that end the white shutters he had made himself, adapted to louvers because her room faced south sky. He worried it would get too hot in the summer, so vented the frames; too cold in the winter, so tore down the drywall and added another layer of mineral wool before building it up again. He had painted several times, varying shades of pink that seemed right going on and wrong on reflection. A reading sconce because Misty said she had lots of books. A triple closet because Misty said she had lots of clothes. A dozen soft toys because she liked animals.

She turned and headed back down, and in the yard she saw a large oak and from it hung a swing. She walked over to it, running her fingers over the larch seat. "My mother's swing?"

"Yes."

She sat there in cool sunlight.

He did not know how to be around her.

It took near three hours for her take off her coat, another to take off her shoes.

166

That first night they ate pizza that he made himself because he worried there was too much salt in takeout.

"You cook like my mother," she said and pushed it away.

He fixed her orange juice but did not know to dilute it a little, so she left that too.

"You want a sweet? I could fix banana splits?"

"What the hell is a banana split?"

He peeled a banana and added two scoops of ice cream for her and watched her frown and push it away. "You might want to call it a banana shit."

He ran a bath for her, then called Sammy because he did not know what time she went to bed.

"Midnight."

"Is that not a little late?" he said.

"Eleven-thirty, then. Fuck. What do I know?"

He had picked up a new television.

"You want to watch TV? You have your own television in your bedroom."

She stood abruptly and went up the stairs.

He waited fifteen minutes then found her in bed, her small body turned away from him.

"You want me to tell you a story?"

"Stories are for children."

"You want me to tell it anyway?"

She did not reply.

He told her a story of a mad man who drove the backbone of California, from Lake Tahoe through Mammoth Lakes to the boutade of the Badwater Basin because a lost girl had once told him of tufa towers and a bristlecone pine forest that held the oldest living things on earth. And of a hundred hours on the Alaska Highway, sleeping outside of gas stations, waiting for them to open because the next fill-up was more than a tank away, and because that same girl once told him that the Muncho Lake was the exact same emerald as her eyes.

He took a small wooden chair and placed it outside her door, sat and strained to hear her breathing change.

Patch might have sat there all night had it not been for the knock.

He opened the door to Sammy, who walked through the house and out into the backyard, where lanterns fixed to the double skin of brick, lighting the coping warm.

Patch knew the routine well enough to grab a glass from the kitchen and follow him.

They sat together as Sammy poured from a bottle of Blue Label.

"You're not joining?"

Patch nodded toward the upstairs window.

"Ah yes, the princess hath arrived."

"Is there a reason for the Blue Label?"

"New York calls."

Patch sighed.

"**Grace Number One.** You don't want to hear what the offer is? Humor me."

"I don't much care, and you know that."

"Does it stop now?" Sammy said.

The question hung in the cool evening air.

"I see myself in the girl," Patch said.

Sammy blew out his cheeks. "So you've got some parenting to do."

"I don't know how."

"You once did not know how to paint."

"You showed me."

Sammy laughed softly, still disarmingly handsome though the years had added grays. "You must know that isn't true."

"But you don't believe anything is God given."

"To do that I would have to believe in God." He lit a cigar, and Patch looked up to make sure Charlotte's window was closed tight. "Do you ever think of Marty Tooms?"

Patch knew the appeals were running out, the stays, the pleas. Before long the only person who could lead him to her would be gone.

"They got a new governor today," Sammy said. "His name is Mark Conrad Bracklin. People are tired of walking their dead men. It'll be a bloody time under him."

"Tooms should die for what he did."

Sammy smoked. "I don't know where I land on that. It changes depending on how much I've had to drink. Will you paint again?"

"No."

"Well then I won't ask again."

That night Patch climbed his stairs and saw the low light from his daughter's bedroom. She slept deeply, the remote in her hand. He was about to cut off the TV when he saw the news of the young man who took a Mak-90 into an air force base hospital and opened fire. Four dead and more than twenty injured.

Patch stood there and felt the acute weight of keeping another person alive against such ruthless and random odds.

167

They found the body at Iona's Beach.

Saint took the call late, still at her desk, Himes on the other end. She heard the tap of Newton's cradle, the sip of coffee, and, finally, Himes biting into something.

"You can always eat," she said.

"I can."

"Doesn't mean that you should."

"Or that I shouldn't."

The fax took a while, Saint pacing her office as the images slowly emerged.

"Pink sand," she said.

"Something to do with the rockface and waves and blah blah blah."

"I like it when you get technical."

Eight pages. She sat back on her chair and stared at the site, dug out far and deep. Nothing but bones. In time they would find out the girl's name was Crystal Wright.

Saint stared at the preservation of rosary beads.

"He traveled," she said.

"He did."

"How many more?"

At that Himes finally stopped eating. "One is too many."

168

Charlotte did not speak much that first month.

He took her to the small public library, surprised that such a reader had not been before.

"So other people have touched these, maybe even read them on the toilet, and then you just go ahead and take them home?" she said.

His surprise waned.

She watched other kids with their mothers, awkward until he crouched beside her and made selections and ushered her over to the beanbags where she sat straight backed for a half hour, the book closed beside her.

He chose four books, from Louisa May Alcott to Robert Louis Stevenson, remembering Grace's favorites.

At the Mad House she left them on the kitchen counter, and he took to reading aloud each afternoon. At first she declared him insane, told him to use his inside voice, to shut the fuck up. He continued, bringing Jim Hawkins and Smollett to life, the mutineers and the **Hispaniola.**

Charlotte would not sit near him; instead he caught her reflection in the window as she curled behind the sofa and listened. The next day he placed the fine woolen rug down in front of the blazing hearth as snowflakes floated outside the window. She lay like a cat, unmoving, eyes closed, trying not to gasp when the murderer, Silver, struck.

She would rise early like he did, and before breakfast they would walk down to the foot of their land in silence where she gathered the ash and he chopped it. They filled a wheelbarrow so big he struggled till she took a side and together they wheeled it back toward the house.

She decided she liked the smell of birchwood better, though it burned quicker and the gum deposits were a wretch to clean.

After breakfast they would walk to Main Street and spend a little time at the gallery, where Sammy would stare at the girl as if she were some kind of bull, flinching each time she aimed her horns in the direction of a painting, insisting she remove her boots before she came in, one time even suggesting she might like to wear white handling gloves after returning from the bathroom. Charlotte dispatched each request with a savagery that left Sammy quietly impressed.

Patch set her up in the studio, lowered the easel

and stool, and ignored the glowers as he squeezed a little oil paint onto the board and gave her his first brushes.

"Jesus," Sammy said, biting a fist before topping up his glass.

"How else will she learn?"

"Fucking Crayola," Sammy hissed.

Patch had not worked in a year, despite the calls, the endless haranguing from New York dealers desperate to maintain a long distant wave.

They took lunch at Lacey's Diner, where Charlotte tucked into new delicacies each time. Pork patty breakfast sandwich, home fries, corned beef hash, biscuits with sawmill gravy.

"She has food around her mouth," Sammy said, a hand to his own at the horror.

"She's a kid," Patch fired back.

"I don't think I like this," Charlotte said, looking up from her beef chili.

"And yet you licked the plate clean," Sammy said, still smarting from his attempt to teach Lacey how to prepare a croque madame. "I think the béchamel is mayonnaise," he said to no one in particular.

Each afternoon Charlotte would spend time with her grandmother while Patch sat in the yard beneath the cover of an ornate gazebo Misty's mother had once imagined her daughter marrying beneath.

Sometimes Charlotte would head up to her mother's old bedroom and nap, leading Patch to question whether she was in fact allowed to stay up until midnight.

Mrs. Meyer would pour them coffee, and they would sit in the grand kitchen, looking out over the snow-topped St. Francois.

"You're doing well," she said, quiet.

"She still hates me," he said, quiet.

"She's angry. I'm angry."

"I worry that she doesn't talk about Misty," he said.

"Have you tried?"

"She changes the subject. She doesn't cry. She doesn't want to visit the grave."

"Time changes our ability to view the things that hurt us."

"But not the pain."

"No. Not the pain."

169

Evenings Charlotte sorted through recipes in a stack her mother had left for her, and he tried his best to work out exactly why Misty so taunted him from the beyond.

Patch stood at the stone counter and scratched his head.

Charlotte wore an apron and scratched her head.

"So you bake it, even though it's ice cream. And it doesn't melt. And you make a sponge. And then you light the thing on fire," he said.

"Yep. And it tastes like Alaska."

Near two hours later they sat at the small oak table, a spoon each, and ate from the charred wreckage.

"Turns out Alaska tastes like crap," Charlotte said.

"Maybe we should store these recipes in the basement. In a locked box."

"I didn't even know there was a basement," she said.

He led her down and she stood before the walls, each covered in sketches and paintings and newspaper cuttings, letters and maps and postcards and photographs. He said nothing at first, just let her find her way as she walked around and took in the height of her father's madness.

For an hour she thumbed through the past two decades of his life, said little before telling him she was tired and that she wanted to sleep.

He gave her a while then headed up, and in her bedroom she lay curled away from him, only the Day-Glo of the starred ceiling keeping the darkness from total.

"You want to come back down? We watch movies every Saturday night," he said.

"The girl," Charlotte said, without turning.

He settled onto the floor beside her. Above he noticed Polaris a little out, throwing off The Bear.

"You remind me of her," he said.

"I know that you saved my mother's life. That's a noble thing, isn't it?"

"I don't know."

"Why don't you know?"

"Because I didn't choose it. If I had weighed options and made the decision to go . . . to help her out, then maybe people could say it was brave. But if you just do something, if it's some kind of innate reaction, can we be sure of its intent?"

"She said I should be proud of you."

"I think I have to earn that, Charlotte."

"I wanted you. Before. I wanted a father."

"And now?"

"Now I know you won't stick around. You can build a house and take me in. But it's . . . it's not real. You don't have a life, you don't have friends or—"

"What about Saint?" he said.

"The woman that shot you."

"Sammy?"

"Mom said he's your pimp." She turned over. "You know what else Mom said?"

"Tell me."

"She said your heart only has room for so much love, because once it gets damaged it shrinks."

He thought of Misty, of the things he had done.

"Is that what you worry about, that I won't have room to love you?"

She did not answer.

And when she slept he leaned in close and wanted so much to kiss her soft cheek. "I'll always be here for you. I swear it."

170

An hour into the first day of the new semester, he opened the gallery and shuffled through the mail, fretful as Charlotte had left it late to tell him that her sneakers hurt her feet. It was as he went to place the mail in the pile for Sammy that he saw the envelope fallen down the back of the desk.

He was about to drop it into the sack, ignored, when he saw the postmark.

By noon they had joined Route 63, Charlotte pulled from school, the lady in the office eyeing Patch like an abduction was playing out but she was too polite to intervene.

Charlotte watched an eternity of greens, craned her neck when they passed through Jefferson City and over the Missouri River.

They stopped for lunch in Columbia, across from the university, the columns and lawns. Charlotte picked at her fries, watching the students head up the stone steps.

"You ever think about what you want to be?" he said.

"Maybe a writer. I'll tell stories and dazzle people with my words. I want to go to Harvard."

"Like your mother."

"But I won't be a dropout."

"She was smart."

"And then you knocked her up. I know I was an accident. A bastard out of Boston."

"That could be your pen name."

She ate two slices of pie, coveted a third till he caved, and then puked out the window beside the Finger Lakes State Park. "I feel better now it's out," she said, and puked once more outside the Silver Fork Buddhist Temple.

"Pretty sure that's a hate crime," Patch said, as he dabbed her mouth with a napkin.

"You have to purge before nirvana can be obtained," she said, and he questioned the library books he allowed her to choose.

She slept a little, woke when the sprawl of Minneapolis unfolded on a horizon dying out.

They threaded through city streets as office workers spilled from high-rise buildings, crawled in traffic by the Mississippi River, Charlotte watching the lights as he found the tree-lined Saint Paul Street.

The house was gray clapboard; the wire fence kept broadleaf weed from reaching the neighbor. They knocked at the door and waited, though it was clear enough the place had lain empty for a long time.

That night as she slept in their cheap motel room, he took the phone into the small bathroom and closed himself inside, the door jamming the wire as he dialed her.

"Where are you?" Saint said.

"I don't know."

"How's the girl?"

"I don't know that either."

He smelled the mold, the pall of smoke woven into each fabric, and next door heard the light moan of a woman plying her trade.

"I got a letter," he said.

"I thought you were done with the letters."

"This one had fallen out. Like a sign. And it carried a Saint Paul postmark. Grace once mentioned the way city lights bounce from the Mississippi River."

He heard the tired in her voice. "So you drove five hundred miles to an empty house."

"I got the name though. The neighbor came out and said the Carters moved a while after their daughter went missing. Said he'd call me here if he finds out where they headed."

"Charlotte should be at school."

He clutched his knees, hid himself fully in the dark. "The missing girl's name was Rosie. Will you run it if I give the address?"

She sighed, quiet awhile. "You know I will."

"You ever think of the child you used to be, Saint?"

"Take her home."

His voice caught. "These . . . the missing, they're

like a flicker of light on a map of the dark. I see one and I head toward it, but it blinks out before I arrive. And then another. And they're just . . ."

"I'm working a murder. We got a confession but still we work each angle. We compile till that window of doubt is closed up tight. Statements and background, phone records and credit card receipts. We answer each question before they get asked. I still track abduction cases with a loose fit. I still do that."

He cracked the door. Moonlight lay on his daughter.

"I spoke to the professor at State. They'll get Tooms another stay," Patch said. He'd made a dozen such calls over the past decade, each time he presented, one time even wrote a couple of thousand words asking the judge to be lenient. They thought he was doing the noblest thing, that he'd found a god that stole the thirst for revenge, the restoration of some perceived equilibrium.

"People are self-serving, Patch."

"You can't—"

"You have a daughter. You drag her from state to state because you need absolution."

He looked at the lime basin, smelled hard water, the room bereft. "How do you figure that?"

"You ever hear of survivor's guilt?" she said, her voice a note quieter.

"Good night, Saint."

"Hey. We don't do that."

He sat in silence awhile.

"How come . . . how come you never painted me?" Saint said, quiet.

"Because you never needed me to."

He listened to Saint breathe. And after a long time asked if she was sleeping, and she did not reply.

171

In the room he took a blanket from the closet and placed it in front of the door. He checked the windows were locked then lay down. His head beside a valance that smelled of dust as he checked his daughter and knew she should not be there.

The phone rang and he answered before it could disturb her.

The neighbor had found a forwarding address for the Carters. He wrote it down. It took ten minutes to find out they were unlisted.

North Dakota was eight hours at least.

In the stars he saw everything written and did not know how to change the fading script. He had seen things entirely beautiful. Fall on the Kancamagus Highway, the tear blue of Crater Lake. Sunrise over Lake Tahoe, two million years to carve out its place. Sunset over a spring Skagit Valley, the tulips absolute in each shade. He had stood beneath the two-thousand-yard canopy of Angel Oak. And each of those times he had been reminded that it was not

God's work, for alongside each of those sights he had seen missing faces and shelled souls.

Patch knew right then he had reached his last crossroad.

For much of the night he played out the first half of his life.

He'd thought it had led him nowhere good.

But it had led him to Charlotte.

And as the earth rotated enough, and their cheap motel entered the first washes of sunlight, he took the address, tore it in half and tossed it into the trash.

"I have room for you," he said, so quiet she did not stir.

Right then he knew he had found his daughter.

And he had lost Grace.

THE BREAK

1995

172

A quiet year had passed since that day he'd said goodbye to Grace.

A year during which he walked his daughter to school and noted seasons changing by the clothes she wore. In January they'd sat in the Mad House with Saint and her grandmother and watched the 49ers shred the Chargers at the Joe Robbie Stadium. That evening Charlotte had found an old football in the attic, headed into the frozen yard, and practiced till she could throw long passes, picking out Patch in the cherry tree end zone, her fingers so red he took her inside to thaw. "I think maybe I want to be a football player," she said, over a dinner of toasted ravioli.

"Contact sports will turn you barren," Norma said.

"What's barren?" Charlotte said.

"Unable to have children," Norma said.

Charlotte shrugged. "I might not even want children. I might be lesbian, like you."

Norma sighed.

They drove over to the Alamo Theatre and watched a movie on the last Friday of each month, sharing popcorn, Charlotte shaking with fear as Freddy Krueger slashed his way through a New Nightmare.

"Are you sure this is suitable?" he said.

"Yes," she said, her face buried in her hands.

Spring they huddled together and watched a bomb tear the heart from Oklahoma, Charlotte unable to sleep that night, her mind on the families, on the nineteen children. He sat in the chair by her door till sunrise. At nine they joined a cluster at St. Raphael's, dropped their heads and lit candles.

Charlotte read of a mother who had lost her daughter in the rubble. For seven hours the woman feared her dead before the girl was pulled from the debris, her face blackened with dust, their reunion caught by a single camera that would turn into the world's lens as it ran on every newspaper not as a symbol of what was lost, but as a symbol of hope and promise against the harshest of odds.

The next day she asked Patch about the missing girls.

173

Over a month she pinned the photographs to a board and collated names and locations, a little of her father's madness rubbing off, though she was more ordered and better equipped.

During a July heatwave, as the town of Monta Clare sweated, Patch picked up his paintbrush for the first time in more than a decade. This time he kept ordered hours during the day, made sure he spent time with his daughter, that she practiced at the baby grand that took up much of the den. And only when she slept did he sketch, and only before she woke did he paint by morning light.

Sammy noticed the color splashed onto Patch's jeans, the dried shades beneath his nails. He did not ask, did not smile, just breathed a little easier, like he too had found what had seemed lost.

Three girls over six months. Patch spoke with their parents during late-night calls, learning about their lives, their traits and hopes. He could not guess how this background affected the snapshot in time he brought to life, just that knowing them made it easier to find their tone. As another winter drew in the two caught **Toy Story** at the Alamo, Charlotte declaring it a bullshit kids movie before dabbing at her eyes when Buzz discovered his true identity. Patch noted girls had started dressing like his mother, bell-bottom jeans and long, straight hair.

"The seventies are back," Charlotte said.

"So I'm finally in fashion again?"

"No."

Before the lull of the fire Charlotte would lie on her stomach on the thick rug and reply to letters dating back a decade while Patch lined up the missing girls, each on their own easel, before calling Sammy.

"I have something for you," he said.

"Finally," Sammy replied.

174

"This makes a change," Saint said, as Patch ladled Brunswick stew into her bowl.

"Charlotte made it."

"Under duress," Charlotte said.

Saint took a mouthful and smacked her lips. "I can taste the duress."

Charlotte rolled her eyes and headed down to the basement.

"I remember that same move on her mother," Saint said.

Patch smiled. "The way you look at Charlotte . . ."

"What?"

He sipped his wine. "You just . . ."

She tossed a piece of bread at him. "Eat up. You're looking skinny."

Afterward she left Patch to clear up and went down to the basement where Charlotte worked on her bulletin board, her small nose turned up in concentration, bare feet on the floor.

Saint marveled at the detail, the scale of the map

and the sheer number of names and dates placed on it.

"What are the colors?" Saint said.

"The blue girls were definitely abducted. The green ran away. The orange disappeared without a trace."

From Texas up to the Dakotas, from Oregon to Virginia.

"And the red?"

Charlotte kept her eyes on the map. "Those are the dead girls."

Patch joined them, handed Saint a glass of wine, and settled on the low couch.

For a long time Saint just stared, the task at hand too much, growing too fast.

She recognized some of the names.

Saint moved forward and added Crystal Wright in red.

Charlotte watched her quietly, respectfully. "I know them by heart," Charlotte said, and it was not a boast, just a fact that left the three of them mournful.

"Angela Rossi," Saint said, beneath her breath as she stared at the map.

Charlotte pointed.

"Summer Reynolds," Saint said.

Charlotte found her.

"You've written Colorado's Kingdom," Saint said, and squinted at the girl's scrawl.

"Old name for Breckenridge. I like it better."

And it was then, after two glasses of wine, two helpings of Brunswick stew, and a decent slice of chocolate cake, that Saint made a match.

Saint told them good night.

Heart pounding as she raced back to her car.

175

Saint played the interview tapes in her apartment. Tapes she had not listened to in more than a decade.

She sat there the whole night, the blind open to a waning moon and city sounds and the comfort of car engines.

Her own map pinned to the wall.

On the stereo the sound of Patch's voice, fourteen years old, as he recounted verbatim each word Grace had said.

"She told me about the sky at Baldy Point, how Lake Altus-Lugert spills from the dam, crashing its way along the Fork Red River."

Saint marked the Quartz Mountain State Park and the burial site of Sky Jones.

"The gold rush. From California to summer in Colorado's Kingdom. Of course, it's not just precious metal buried in no-man's-land, but you get the idea."

Saint marked Breckenridge. Summer Reynolds.

She paced the room, head light as she breathed deep and tried to calm the adrenaline kick.

"How long have I been here?" he said.

"Ten sleeps."

"It must have been more than—"

"Your head is up in the—"

"Clouds," Patch said.

"Yeah, but the peak of the clouds, with the angel. You see the Misty Moon from up there?"

Saint marked the Tensleep Creek. Fed from Cloud Peak. Angela Rossi.

She paced again. Sat through two more hours.

"Paint me," she said.

"I need to see you."

"I'm standing on a north shore, pink beneath my feet because nor'easters strip rhyolite so pretty I can't even bear it. Maybe it'll preserve me or something. Forty-two miles down with the crystals. Mummified in pink. I hope to hell I keep my looks."

Saint marked mile forty-two of the North Shore scenic drive. By the pink beach. Crystal Wright.

Saint sat back, the room spinning, still dizzy when she picked up the phone and dialed Himes.

"Grace."

"What about her?" he said.

"She was leading us to the other girls."

He took the news with maddening evenness. "How many?"

"Four. So far. But I still have a couple hours of tape."

"Anything else?"

Saint played it again. Loud.

"Maybe one day I'll be the first to see him after the Resurrection."

"Mary Magdalene was the first to see Jesus after the Resurrection," Himes said.

"And if I'm chosen, he'll send me back to the three persons."

"The Trinity," Himes said.

"And they'll hollow me out. Watch my blood flow over black rock like I never even was."

"What does it mean?" Himes said.

"Something," Saint said. "It all means something."

176

Sixty-eight degrees in Central Park.

Patch strolled past the monument on the south side and threaded through suited men and women and nannies pushing strollers filled with wide-eyed kids trying to make sense of the cacophony. For a moment he longed to find the water, the ferry, and ride it till the island was nothing more than a piece of land without such weighty expectations.

Charlotte guided him through the maze like a native, firing out scowls to everyone who jostled close, flipping off a truck driver as he leaned on the horn before Patch could close a fist around the offending finger.

"It's New York, kill or be killed," Charlotte said, locking eyes with the driver and miming a decapitation with the nail of her thumb across her throat.

She nodded to a doorman, moved to head in when Patch stared up, the building so grand it leaned on him.

"Your grandmother brought you to the Plaza?" he said.

"It's her dime. She keeps saying she can't take it with her. You think she doesn't know how inheritance works?"

Sammy met them at the champagne bar at six, wearing a navy tux, white shirt, and gold tie, his watch wafer-thin platinum, his cufflinks shone as he ordered three slugs of Macallan 18 then told Patch he would be claiming each back from him as an expense.

Patch frowned at Charlotte, who attempted to Scottish her Coke as Sammy nodded his approval.

"How about a mint julep? We're reading **Gatsby** next semester," Charlotte said to the bartender.

"When in Rome," Sammy agreed.

"She's twelve," Patch said.

Sammy waved him off. "I took my first finger of Pappy when I was a mere—"

Patch breathed again when Mrs. Meyer crossed the grand room. Chandeliers dropped from ornate moldings before gold curtains that framed a view of Fifth Avenue and the Pulitzer Fountain. Elegant in a green dress and heels, she summoned Charlotte to go change out of her jeans and sneakers.

"Nervous?" she asked Patch.

He shrugged though she read him, reached forward and touched his arm as she left.

Sammy appraised him carefully, from the dark jacket to the cream slacks, the white shirt beneath open three buttons to skin tanned from working the yard.

"You look—"

"Like a cunt?" Patch offered, quiet into Sammy's ear.

He watched the city through the window, thought of the evening ahead, for a moment wanting to head back to his hotel and hide away, to let Sammy do what he did and report back when it was over.

"You're doing it for them," Sammy said. "And for the girl."

Patch did not know which girl he meant, but he guessed both of them. Charlotte's future, the memory of Grace.

Patch attempted to order a Yoo-hoo from the barman, and Sammy sighed.

"Shaming me never gets old," Sammy said.

"I have no idea what you're talking about."

"We should take a Van Winkle Special Reserve in commemoration," Sammy said, signaling the bartender.

Patch checked the menu and saw the price and died a little inside.

177

The gallery took a red brick building on Wooster Street. Patch stepped out from the noise and took a moment for himself, watching cars roll over the cobblestone road, drivers craning to get a glimpse through the double-height windows where two hundred people Patch did not know but who seemed to know him looked over the better part of his life's work and did not flinch at the numbers when they inquired. Charlotte had collated with Sammy, and Patch saw sketches he scarcely remembered, early work so rough he almost felt shame that people were casting their critical eye over his learning curve.

The stars were the missing girls, titled only by their first names, from Lucy to Anna, Ellen to Eloise. People vied to stand before them, to read the small notes beside that told not nearly enough about their lives.

They stood in their coterie, monochrome blazers and stiff shirts and easy smiles. And soon enough there were bids for the conjures of his mind; a lady from Sacramento paid a small fortune for a sketch he had completed in the bones of a night so starved he had gathered the carpet in an old motel room and slept on the bare boards beneath as moonlight served black mold on the aluminum coping. There was no glamour to any of it.

He had asked the lady why she wanted it.

"Can't you see how beautiful you make tragedy?"

"No," he said, and Sammy escorted him out, worried he might sully each sale.

Through the glass he watched his daughter, luminous in a pink dress that recalled her mother, and for a moment he missed Misty, the pain still able to catch him out, like the loss would forever be fresh.

"You're skipping out on your own showing?"

Patch turned and saw her, his smile genuine for the first time that night. "Hey."

"Hey, kid."

He hugged Saint tight, held on for a little too long because when he broke he saw that concern there and wondered if he would always be fourteen to her.

"I like the eye patch."

He reached up and touched it with an absent mind, his daughter insisting that night would be the closest he ever came to a wedding as she tossed the skull and crossbones at him before she left.

"I'm surprised you made it," he said.

"I'm working something nearby."

"Of course."

"And I wanted to see you. To see your success. Lot of people in there."

"Sammy."

"Right." She moved close to the window, cupped her hands around to block the glare. "For a moment I thought that was Misty Meyer. Goddamn she's . . ."

"I worry it's for nothing. All of it."

"We've been here so many times, Patch."

"I feel like I'm acting. When I'm being a father, when I'm being a friend. When I make something to eat or take a shower. I'm playing a part in a story deep down you know cannot end well."

"So how does it end?" she said.

He looked up toward Washington Square, his boots on the flagstone. "How about on a beach someplace far from here."

"Or a ship."

"Or some faraway town—"

"Making honey."

"Is that what you kids are calling it now?"

She laughed, a teenager once again.

"Sometimes I convince myself she wasn't real. We know Tooms is crazy, he'll say anything, but she . . . you never found a thing. Nothing. So if she wasn't real, I'd take that now. Even if I had to look back at so much loss it can't even be counted."

"You ever think maybe it wasn't loss."

"How do you mean?" he said.

"She opened your world with her eyes. You've lived. And how many of us can say that, really?"

She saw the painting hanging in the center.

Grace Number One.

He would not sell it.

"Look at us, Saint. Look where we are."

"Did you find out?" she said.

He looked puzzled.

"If rose trees grow in New York City. Don't tell me you forgot, kid."

He smiled. "Tell me you still play piano now."

"I do. I worried I'd forget, but turns out some things just stay with you, you know."

Though the street filled only with the sounds of cars and the quiet rush of steam from vents, he took her in his arms and slowly began to move with her.

"Are you buzzed?" she said.

"A little. I blame Van Winkle."

"Fucking Sammy."

Patch pressed his head to hers. "I thank the Lord there's people out there like you."

178

An hour later he crossed the street and did not look back as he headed up Sixth Avenue, lost among strangers as he breathed sugared almonds that reminded him he had not eaten all day. He moved with ease, his muscles loosened with each step as he passed the sleeping carousel in Bryant Park, the pulsing heart of Midtown West and bright theaters.

At ten he found his way to a reservation in Barbetta and took a seat alone and ate garganelli in tomato and basil sauce. He drank red wine and tipped heavily.

"How was it?" the waiter asked.

"Almost perfect," Patch said.

He walked all night, alone and adrift, though certain he trod in her footsteps.

The sun rose over Manhattan, and Patch strolled in the shadow of the Brooklyn Bridge as trucks lined up before the fish market. He thought of Skip and his crew, that fateful night when he journeyed into Boston and the universe conspired.

He joined the hustle at the Union Square Greenmarket, and beneath peaked tents he watched people shop fresh fruit and farmstead cheeses, artisan bread and heritage meats. He fell in with a thousand commuters flooding from subways before vanishing into silver buildings clad with green glass. He saw tourists, families, heard talk of Battery Park and boats. The Twin Towers, so prominent he stopped for a long time and committed the skyline to memory.

When the hour was decent enough, he stepped into the Plaza and found a quiet corner.

Sammy was the first down, fresh enough because he had not yet been to bed.

Together they sat at a white-clothed table and Sammy told him they sold everything in the first hour. By the second, new buyers sought the old and offered them twice what they had paid. Sammy had not seen anything like it in two decades of dour sales.

"You'll send the money to—"

"I know, kid. I know."

It was not a sum that would raise eyebrows in the art world, but it was a sum that would give the families of the missing girls a little freedom to search, to mourn, or maybe just to take some time for themselves.

At eleven Charlotte carried a newspaper into the fabled champagne bar, where Sammy nursed a Bloody Mary beside Mrs. Meyer, who nursed one of her own.

Charlotte spread the paper across the table, then turned to the Arts section, where they saw the full-page spread, the photograph, the headline.

A PIRATE TAKES MANHATTAN

Charlotte turned away because she could not check her smile.

Her father had made it into **The New York Times.**

179

The Long Island Expressway.

The heater blew drowsy air, and Saint cracked the window of the rental car and watched the buildup of traffic from the Queens–Midtown Tunnel and out. Through Nassau County and Suffolk the grays greened, and she felt a low knot in her stomach tighten as she met woodland toward Riverhead.

Patch's voice spoke through the stereo.

Like it did on every journey she had taken since.

She needed to hear Grace's voice one last time to make the journey worth it.

"Maybe one day I'll be the first to see him after the Resurrection. And if I'm chosen, he'll send me back to the three persons. And they'll hollow me out. Watch my blood flow over black rock like I never even was."

Saint threaded her way through small towns and beach communities long since bared for the winter approach, the summer gloss scraped off by bracing winds. She parked a good way from the church and turned her collar up as she strolled a wide lane of skeletal trees and dormant grass that ran to family homes, most already shuttered.

The town was Black Rock.

She stepped back and looked at the sign.

ST. MARY MAGDALENE

TRINITY ROAD

180

Saint took in the steeple rising from a turret dark like iron, and beneath that loggia through arches capped with fine mosaics.

Through the main door and into a vaulted nave so stunning for a moment Saint could do little but wish her grandmother could see it.

She thought of Grace.

Of why exactly she had led her to this church, in this town.

Saint wondered if there had been another girl buried here. She had searched the archives four decades back but could not find anything close enough.

Through a maze of rooms and across a rear courtyard, she moved into a smaller building where books rose from hardwood cases stained black. A woman sat behind a cash register that Saint guessed did not see much action.

Her name badge read Sister Isabelle.

Outside Saint circled to the building behind, the children's home, the concrete beside colored with chalk lines and numbers and smiling faces. She saw a perfect feather and held it up to the light. The gray of a mourning dove. Norma had once told her it represented protection and love and guardian angels. She placed it into her pocket.

For two hours Saint tried to decipher a code that was not there. She stopped locals and asked about the history, strolled the graveyard and checked each of the stones.

She showed file photos of Eli Aaron to the nun at the register, and then to the old men gathered at the church door.

At the pulpit she traced Latin, ran her fingers over the carvings on each of the benches.

"What are you trying to tell me, Grace?" she whispered before the chancel.

Saint stepped to one side as the sisters passed.

Though she kept her head bowed slightly, she noticed the way they walked, the reverent way they carried themselves.

She looked at their sandals.

Noted their veils and tunics, their medals and coifs.

And then.

The rosary beads they carried.

181

"Show me," Sister Cecile said.

Saint removed the bag from her case and carefully set the rosary beads down on the desk.

"Yes," Sister Cecile said.

"You can purchase them?" Saint said.

"Not on display . . . not enough shelf space. People go for the cheaper options now. But these are cedar wood. Black glass. Sister Agnes made them, and she had an eye for the beautiful. The medal. It's Mary Magdalene."

"The patron of penitent sinners," Saint said.

"In my experience there isn't another kind of sinner. Not come the end."

Saint's mind ran to Marty Tooms as she took out the file photographs of Eli Aaron and placed them down on the desk.

Sister Cecile replaced her glasses and stared. "Robert. He was an altar boy. I remember them all."

"Robert?" Saint said.

"Robert Peter Frederick. I haven't seen him in . . ."

"He went missing. Likely died."

She took the news without shock. "And you found the rosary beads on him, of course."

"Why would you say that?"

"Robert was . . . challenging. He took the word as gospel."

"That's what you're taught, right?"

Sister Cecile smiled thinly, like she was dealing with a child. "We teach forgiveness. Ours is not a vengeful God. Robert would have been in the care of Sister Agnes before she passed."

"She gave them to those she believed needed saving? So why did Robert need saving?" Saint said.

Sister Cecile cleared her throat. "A local woman fell pregnant. Unmarried. And she came to confession, and Robert overheard and followed her home."

Saint stared at her.

The first hint of color in the older woman's cheeks. "Nothing happened."

"You told that to the police?" Saint said.

"The woman was unharmed. She didn't wish to file a complaint."

"And Robert?"

"Left shortly afterward."

"We know him as Eli Aaron," Saint said.

Sister Cecile sighed. "And he stands in judgment."

"How did you—"

"Eli, son of Aaron. He officiated in the judgment seat. The Old Testament."

"And what happened to him?"

"He was let down by his children. He did not punish them firmly enough when they sinned, and so God cursed him."

"He was not harsh enough," Saint repeated.

Eli Aaron had been raised in a children's home. He traveled. There were likely more graves out there someplace. More missing that would never be found.

She followed her back into the bookstore, where the cash register stood unattended. Sister Cecile moved to a drawer where she retrieved the last set of rosary beads.

Saint took them and was heading out when she ran into Sister Isabelle. The two almost out into the cold air when she heard it.

"Second set of those we've sold this year."

Saint stopped.

Cold.

And turned.

"Who bought them?" Saint said.

Sister Isabelle was maybe her age, her face weighty, her skin smooth and unblemished. "A man."

Saint paled.

"It can't be," Sister Cecile said. "He . . . how did he die?"

"I set him on fire," Saint said, reaching for the photograph.

There was a moment when she knew. Despite the time that had passed.

She read the look in Sister's Isabelle's eyes.

The look of a woman who had just seen a ghost.

182

"There's a chance she's mistaken," Himes said.

"I saw it in her eyes."

They sat together in a café outside the federal building, a place they went when they needed solace, to forget, or maybe to remember why they gave so much of themselves.

Saint had spent the week digging into the life of Eli Aaron. With a little more to go on he'd found a ledger that gave the date he arrived at the home. Only six years old. His mother had a record, a woman who sold her body for money. Addiction. Overdose. A tale so played out she had not flinched as she read.

She got the name of the woman he had followed home from confession a lifetime before. Got no more from her than Sister Cecile had given.

"I really thought I killed him, Himes. He's already dead," Saint said.

"So he purchased more rosary beads this year?" Himes asked.

"Yes."

Himes picked up his burger. "You know what that means."

She closed her eyes.

"It means you have to kill him again."

183

"Can I see the place where your eye should be?" Charlotte asked.

"I can think of better gifts to give you. It's not every day a girl turns thirteen."

The buildup had begun a little under a year before, with Charlotte claiming that hitting her teens would likely change her beyond all recognition. She told him she would need a new bra, the kind that gave her cleavage. He had called her grandmother immediately, and she had appeared at the door that afternoon and whisked the girl into town to see Miss Delaine. Fittings ensued, purchases were made. Patch hid himself in the yard until he was certain the matter had been handled.

Charlotte also claimed she would need a key to the Mad House, which he duly had cut at Monta Clare Hardware. She would need a dress for the day and another for the evening. Another trip to Miss Delaine, this time Patch stayed out on the sidewalk as the girl and her grandmother attacked the racks with ferocity.

"And I'll need to throw a party," she said over a breakfast of muffins and bacon.

Patch looked up. "What kind of party?"

"Elegant, extravagant, wild in a way, and opulent."

"They need to change the reading list at your school."

"There should be a tray of prophylactics should things get rowdy."

"What, like antibiotics?"

"No. But picking up some penicillin isn't a bad idea."

He kept her back from school on the day, spoke with her teacher Miss Lyle, who frowned and pointed out school policy, and also that she had seen his work hanging in Sammy's window. Patch agreed to come teach an art class and a trade was agreed.

At six he led her down to the kitchen where a jewelry box sat on the counter.

She removed the necklace and held it up, a single stone hanging from a chain, the same blue as her eyes.

"Like Mom's," she said, for a moment quiet before she rallied. "I mean, it's not what I'd choose, but perhaps I could pawn it one day. Keep me from doing actual porn."

"It's all I ask."

And then he handed her the piece of paper.

The sketch he had completed near fourteen years before, as her mother slept. The sketch Misty had bequeathed so that he might remember that in their world, in their life, something special had happened.

Charlotte stared at it for a long time.

"I drew that the day you were conceived."

"Fucking gross."

Saint showed up like she could smell the muffins, and outside on the driveway beneath the flutter of fall leaves she left a trailer, and on top of it was a 7 comb and a cedarwood hive with observation window.

Charlotte circled it. "Beautiful. What is it? Some kind of mobile meth lab?"

Saint talked high-temperature waxing, auto flow combs, and honey keys. "Way simpler than the one I had."

"You doing okay, Special Agent Brown?" Patch asked.

"I'm okay," she said, and wondered if that had ever been true for either of them.

"Anything?"

"No." She had told him about Eli Aaron. How cops in every state had a photo and description that were far out of date. She had spent a week trawling security camera footage in a fifty-mile radius of the church where Eli Aaron had picked up the rosary beads. The sisters could not be sure of a date, only the season. The work was painstaking. She had gotten nowhere at all.

"Is there a chance . . . all these years?" Patch said.

"There's a chance."

"And if you find him."

"Then he might lead us to Grace."

184

A half hour later Sammy stopped by, and the three gathered as he set a large brass and leather case down on the counter, flipped the lock, and lifted the solid pine lid.

Charlotte peered inside, blonde hair falling over eyes smoked with shadow.

"You bought her a shotgun?" Saint said.

"Boss and Co., London. 1912. Story goes it was used to dispatch an Irishman over gambling debts."

Charlotte let loose a long whistle as she held it up and cocked it. "It's just . . . it's just perfection. Thank you, kindly, Samuel."

"It'll keep the boys away," Sammy said, and winked at Saint.

"Or draw the right kind in," Charlotte said, and winked at Saint.

"And then you can arrest them," Patch said, and winked at Saint.

"Technically it's just a blink when you do it," Saint said.

Patch frowned.

Saint had to head back to Kansas, so they made the eighty-mile drive just father and daughter, Charlotte talking of the party, about some kid called Dallas who Patch took an immediate dislike to.

"I mean, he's got three girlfriends already, but they won't put out, so I figure I've got a real shot, and if that fails, now I can take an actual shot," Charlotte said, as they rode the four-lane highway, a whisper of trees all that cut the gray.

He watched her speak animatedly. His touchstone, his anchor to every good thing. After the piece ran in **The New York Times** the letters had reached the point where Sammy threatened the mailman with legal action, so they were redirected to the Mad House, where Charlotte continued to collate them, vowing to reply to each, even just to tell them her father would not be painting for the foreseeable. The story had been picked up by several news outlets and crawled its way from New York along the coast and across much of the country.

Before they left, they had stopped by Misty's grave, and Patch had left Charlotte there with her mother while he walked the perimeter of St. Raphael's. On his return he saw her eyes red, offered her his hand, which she shied from. "A bird shat in my eye," she said.

They parked in the lot and walked through the gates of the Culpepper Zoo.

In crisp sunshine he watched as she unfurled a

map and took a pen from her pocket and marked them a route that took in every enclosure, for a moment allowing herself to be a kid.

He bought her feed for the farm animals, and she held her small hand flat as the goats came to the fence. In the soft hue of the aquarium she pressed her face to the glass at the passing of a clown loach. As she pushed open the heavy door and led her father into the reptile house he began to feel it. The heat crept up, his skin cool and damp.

He tried to shake it off, to reason away the flight of his pulse as too much coffee. He managed to smile for her, but reached out and clutched the slick stone wall to keep himself upright. He pressed a hand to his chest, then his neck.

He heard her call him to come see the snakes, but his muscles tightened. He cursed under his breath, zeroed in on her and the way she watched the reptiles as he tried to find his center. It grew worse, his hands beginning to shake as his body fought against him. He saw her as he closed his eyes. Grace's face so present and real.

The last thing he heard was the cry of his daughter on her birthday.

185

Patch woke in an operating room, for a moment so lost he was fourteen again, seeking out the nurse, the doctor to tell him just where the past year had gone. Maybe he had dreamed it all, and he'd walk down Main Street and see Misty Meyer on Chuck's arm, his mother sleeping off a night shift. Another shot at making new mistakes, these ones lesser in every way.

Across from him windows opened to sparse tree-tops, the sky a clear lake, the vista peaked with the umbrella ribs of a thousand white flowers.

He saw a silver trolley, a computer, and above him a cluster of alien lights that blossomed from a steel stem. On the wall was a monitor and beside that a white desk with a man sitting behind it.

It took Patch another moment to remember, and then he sat up and sent the trolley clattering.

The man turned and raised a calming hand, looked into his eye like he knew him. "Your daughter is with Keeper Jen. I believe they're feeding the meerkats at the moment. You fainted. Not the first person to faint at the zoo, so don't even worry about it. It usually happens in the summer when the heat gets up. People don't wear hats, don't hydrate."

"It was . . . the snakes. The smell of them or something."

He had a kind face, though did not smile.

"Are you sick?"

Patch shook his head.

"Are you taking any medication?"

"No."

"Maybe go see your doctor. Always best when these things happen."

Patch stood, a slight pain in his head. "You're not a doctor?"

"No. Not for humans anyway." He smiled and handed Patch a bottle of water.

"I'll have to clear you out in a moment, got a wolf with tuberculosis."

Patch thanked him again, then turned, and that was when he saw the man's name etched on the door.

Jimmy Walters.

186

There was a moment before it came to him, before he questioned the cold trail of fate, and in that moment he saw his daughter, wearing her new necklace and tending her bees, just as Saint had once done with her grandmother.

He stared at the man, at his hands and arms, his mouth and lips and eyes. Patch knew well about the rot that set in just beneath, how you couldn't tell shit about someone from the way they looked or the job they did. To see it you had to gut them; you had to look deep inside for the poison in their veins.

Jimmy said something else, added a laugh, but Patch heard none of it, just saw Saint, his friend, in all her pure and good. He saw her crawling through tangled woodland, the bite of winter deep in her bones as she pushed on looking, seeking him out while the world around had long since buried him. He saw the way she cared for her grandmother, the way she was with Charlotte, how this man had taken so much from someone who only gave.

Patch knew there were moments when you made your bad decision even when you were fully aware of what would come.

He also knew that he would not allow his daughter to grow up in a world where the good stand by idle. In a world where her father did not stand up for the few he cared for. He once told Nix he had left the old version of himself back in the dark. But he knew then that wasn't entirely true. He had once told Saint they were a team. Come at one, come at both.

"Jimmy," Patch said.

Jimmy nodded.

"You remember me?"

"I remember you, Joseph," Jimmy said.

"And you remember Saint. You remember beating her. You remember telling everyone in town—"

"That she murdered my child."

Patch knew about the notion of purpose, of free will and a divine goal. He knew about determinism and the need to shape a future.

He knew it might have been the one bad thing Jimmy Walters had done. That maybe he could rewrite that turned chapter and save his own story.

There was much that Patch knew.

But nothing that could change what would happen next.

THE PRISONER

1998

187

The window was tall and narrow like a letterbox flipped on its side.

Around the width of a human head, it mirrored a striplight to the ceiling so that from his bunk Patch would sometimes imagine the roof was open to the heavens.

His view of the world rose across a thousand acres of prison land, and beyond that a water tower standing on six spindles, the same white as winter cloud, its belly darkened, bulging with rainfall. Telephone cables crossed, and sometimes he heard them crackle with a thousand voices racing to be heard. He imagined mothers and daughters dissecting Monica Lewinsky, the plight of Hillary and her **Today Show** conspiracy, following Bill standing strong and noble, adding layers to his card house, the foundations unimpeachable. Maybe a couple of guys talking Dale Earnhardt and the nature of a hard win. A line to big cities where traders talked their books, the Dow scorching new highs as unemployment plumbed new lows. A Thurston school shooting, another in Arkansas. A tornado in Minnesota, another in Birmingham.

The prison was the third oldest in the country, and its years could be counted in the fractures of bare stone walls and intermittent electrics, in dust that coughed through vents and the run of slave trade blood spilled a hundred and fifty years before.

From that window he watched the new prison take shape; cement foundations lay in blocks as yellow backhoes drove rutted roads and scooped soil loosened by jackhammers so loud the walls of his cell shook. At the end of hard days, the men sat on their machinery and smoked and looked back at the housing. Patch would raise his hand, knowing they could not see him at all. And when they were done, they passed onerous checks before hitting the eight-mile road that led back to civilization, where they could stand in scalding showers and wash the drag from their skin and memory.

Though the prison was different, the sentence and route in, Patch mostly picked up where he had left off, his time outside a temporary reprieve from a judgment that began so long ago.

He left his cell at seven, ate a little, then headed to the prison library in the sternum of the central block, down whitewashed corridors that might have fit into a tired hospital had bars and heavy locks not accompanied each door. A year of sedulous care and he was granted a single key that he would collect from a utility station manned by an unsmiling lifer.

Inside the prison library he switched on the godly lights, so bright he gave his eye a moment to adjust as he went through the shift pattern, emptied the drop box and began to shelve the returns. Four thousand books. He worked with eleven others on rotation, overseen by two librarians who bused in from neighboring towns and fielded questions mostly on law and enterprise. Patch worked the reference section, building the art collection as an aside to pointing the new in the direction of self-help, meditation, and cognitive behavioral therapy.

At nine the librarian Cooper showed, newspaper tucked beneath his arm, bitching about the construction work, eight miles breathing dust as he followed a concrete truck in.

He wore glasses, his hair a little long for current fashions. Six feet tall, broad and lean, he kept order with the tone of his voice, followed protocol because it was ingrained. He'd started work a month after Patch arrived, the two feeling their way together. Patch offered just enough, towed the straightest line, added smiles when he had to. And then, after five hundred and thirteen days, he wrote his letter to Warden Riley.

Two months after that Patch was hauled out of his cell an hour after lunch, cuffed, and led from the main floor through two sets of doors and out into the yard. The guard's name was Blackjack, and he did not speak a word till they were clear of the reception center.

"Warden's office, what the hell did you do, Patch?" Blackjack said.

Patch threw a glance at the man. Six feet five, maybe two hundred twenty pounds. Most of the inmates called him The Wall and said the state of Missouri could've saved a couple of million dollars on security simply by placing Blackjack in front of the main gate.

"I know you weren't fighting. I would've seen the sheet."

"How's your girl?" Patch said, and the big man smiled.

"Aced it."

The girl was Blackjack's daughter. Eleven years old, she had been tasked with a school project on precious metals. Patch had pointed Blackjack in the direction of Gustav Klimt.

They walked slow because Blackjack knew that feel of sun on skin was something.

"I always thought I knew you, always thought your heart was in the right place, but why the hell did you go kill that zookeeper?" Blackjack said, same each time.

188

Inside they waited while a secretary busied herself with a call from the Twenty-fifth Judicial Circuit. Patch heard talk of recusal and a change of judge as the woman made notes.

They waited in silence for twenty minutes, Patch content to leave his confines, to stare at the wood paneling, the patterned carpet and gold flag stands.

Blackjack handed him off as Warden Riley told him to lose the cuffs.

"We're gentlemen," Riley said, like they were to take iced tea overlooking his plantation of lost souls. He shook Patch's hand a little too hard, his face a bluster of burst capillaries, hangdog eyes, and shaving nicks. He wore pinstripes, his shirt a little tight at the neck so surplus flesh spilled over like potted meat from a tube as he ushered Patch to sit before the mahogany desk.

Riley slumped into a brown leather chair, and as he moved to pull it in Patch saw the large wall behind him, and the single painting that hung in the center beneath a satin nickel wall light, like it had been placed there by God's hand as a reminder.

There was a moment when Patch looked around, like a prank had been pulled on him.

And then he stared for a long time at the scene.

Main Street bursting with color he knew well. A diner took one side, a vista of rolling hills fed blue slate rooftops beneath a sunset that dazzled with two dozen hues.

"Beautiful, isn't it?" Warden Riley said, turning to look. "There isn't a person that comes in here that doesn't spend a little time lost in that painting."

Patch had not seen it in near twenty years. His first sale, his touch crude, he saw only imperfections. Flecks where he had overloaded his brush, his hand heavy at the bleed of the sidewalk.

"Where did you find it?" Patch said, transfixed.

"Aileen. My wife. She decorated this office a half dozen times, picking swathes and swatches. That painting is the only constant. Hell, even my chair was chosen not to detract from it."

Patch remembered to smile when the man laughed.

Riley rolled his shirtsleeves back over plump arms and reached for the letter on his desk. "You want a library service for the gentlemen on C Level."

"Yes, sir."

Warden Riley leaned back, the chair creaking as he steepled his fingers and furrowed his brow, like what had already been decided still left room for further thought. Patch tried not to notice the lure of the painting, that low pain in his gut, in his bones. He tried not to see Sammy's face as he worked, Saint's as she stopped by with a plate because his mother could not care for him. He tried not to see Nix, Misty, the Mad House, and the town of Monta Clare. But mostly, when he lay down in thunderous silence each night, he tried not to see Charlotte.

"The Federal Bureau of Prisons makes certain recommendations."

"Yes, sir," Patch said, and tuned him out awhile, his mind on grinding out the past year, fixing so hard on keeping his head down low enough. Not reacting when a yard fight got out of hand, when a Kansas City biker got in his face and threw a hard right. Patch had dropped to a knee, spit his own blood in the dirt, and took a couple of kicks to the ribs. That night he'd coughed hard and knew his ribs were broken, didn't say shit about it the next day, just went about his library work.

A week later the biker's people wanted him involved in a hustle, Patch guessed at drugs. His resistance cost him a couple of teeth, knocked loose before Blackjack stopped it. That night Patch lay in his bunk, swallowed down his blood and watched the keening breeze chase shadow across his cell till morning. A table and bench bolted to the wall. A steel basin and toilet without a lid. Sometimes the smell of shit flowed the walkway like a river, creeping beneath doorways like a reminder of the sewage among them.

"You've got a daughter, but she doesn't visit?" Warden Riley said, flipping through a thin file, tutting at the crime like it was the first he'd heard of it. Like it had not been in the newspapers, the story of the known painter who had thrown a single punch at the beloved veterinarian who struck his head as he fell back.

"And you go to chapel?"

"Yes, sir."

Warden Riley nodded like it lent legitimacy to the ask. "In your letter you said you were willing to deliver books yourself, because we can't spare the men. I daresay it's not a place people want to spend more time than they need to."

"I want . . . I turn to reading when times get hard. Lose yourself for a while, we all need that sometimes. People say they don't deserve it, that none of us do. But we're serving our time. A lot of us won't breathe free air again. Reading isn't a privilege, sir. I believe we all have the right to leave our problems and escape into another world, if only through the written word." Patch heard the words leaving Cooper's mouth as he spoke them verbatim. Six months practicing. A single shot would miss or hit.

"And the people on C Level—"

"Be kind and compassionate to one another,

forgiving each other, just as in Christ God forgave you," Patch said.

"Okay," Warden Riley said.

That night Patch did not sleep.

The next day he would visit C Level.

Death row.

189

Saint was sitting behind her desk at the Monta Clare Police Department when the phone rang.

Deputy Michaels flinched a little when he patched the call through.

"It's the school, Chief," he said. Michaels was a decade younger and too eager, his uniform as sharp as his haircut, buzzed at the sides like a marine who'd taken a misstep and landed far from the action.

Saint sighed and stared out at Main Street as she spoke with Mildred, the principal's secretary, the two so close now that Saint knew to sometimes bring the woman a slice of pecan pie from the Monta Clare Bakery on the way in.

She took the walk slow, heard the early spring call of a junco as she looked up and watched Mitch Evans painting the sign for the opticians. The forest green had been approved at a town council meeting so heated Saint had threatened to draw her gun to defuse it. She stopped to collect a Monterey pine cone, checked the scales and carefully slipped it into her pocket.

Mitch raised a hand. Saint would've rather he kept it fixed to the ladder.

She passed Sammy, who crossed the street with a brown paper bag, guessed where she was headed, and chuckled because he read the thunder in her face.

Old stores with new fronts; cars that did not dare double-park so circled round looking for an opening; the faded white skeleton of graffiti so primitive Saint had narrowed the culprits down to a group of junior high kids, then made them spend a weekend collectively scrubbing as acetone filled the air and locals tutted at the chain gang as they passed by. People whispered she was tougher than Nix, worked harder and smarter, cared more and took each infraction so personally crime levels had dropped to nonexistent. In truth it was perception, the FBI veteran who returned to her hometown to become the youngest police chief in the history of the state of Missouri. The respect and fear fell short of acceptance, for she would always carry the trace of Jimmy Walters.

"Fuck them. And fuck the church," Nix had said, as he stopped by on his way to the pharmacy on her first day, his name in gold lettering still on the glass door in a show of respect that would endure.

At Monta Clare High she sat in the familiar hallway, shot the shit with Mildred.

The principal was new, the routine was not. Saint did not need to plead Charlotte's case because they all knew, everyone knew. Saint guessed that was part of the problem as she agreed on a week's suspension.

Outside they walked beneath a high sun, and the girl bled attitude. Saint was tired enough that she no longer smiled at transgressions that carried the haunt of one, Patch Macauley.

"You want to get this done?" Charlotte said, hair streaks of blonde, skin so pale and delicate despite the fire that simmered just beneath.

"Who was it?" Saint said.

"Noah Arnold-Smith."

Saint knew the kid, knew the kind, did not know how to be a mother or guardian no matter what Patch's wishes had dictated. "You popped his shoulder out."

"You showed me how," Charlotte fired back.

They stopped on the edge of Walnut Avenue where the big houses had slowly been remodeled, and foreign cars sat on cobblestone driveways beside postcard lawns bordered by blue sage and crested iris.

"You shouldn't have done that," Saint said.

"He grabbed my ass."

Saint thought of Noah Arnold-Smith, and how the popular still carried that smirk. Her mind ran all the way back to Chuck Bradley and how he had treated her, and Patch. "You still . . . you shouldn't have done that, Charlotte."

"You know his family. Sammy told Grandma that Mrs. Arnold-Smith is a double-barreled cunt."

Saint looked away for a moment, bit her lower lip till it hurt, same each time the girl cursed like that.

Saint sat on the bench and waited an age for Charlotte to join her.

"You don't come here," Saint said.

She looked across at Misty's grave, the flowers changed each week by Mrs. Meyer.

"Will you tell Grandma what I did?"

Saint shook her head.

Charlotte tucked her hair behind her ear. "She's close to cutting me off. And I desperately need the five bucks a week she gives me if I'm going to save enough for that new life in Vegas."

"Right."

The girl swallowed. "I don't need to come here, like it's a reminder of who I'm letting down."

"That's not—"

"Less than four years till you can stop pretending to give a shit, Saint."

190

Saint had read parenting books in the small library in Pecaut, fielded advice from Norma when the girl stopped eating, from Dr. Caldwell when the girl stopped sleeping. She had consulted with Mrs. Meyer when the girl's grades fell, the two taking tea together each Monday afternoon, watching rolling Missouri clouds the same gray as their frets. Each Saturday they spent a couple of hours with Sammy, while Charlotte locked herself in her father's old studio and played Nirvana so loud Sammy took to dragging a leather armchair out onto the sidewalk and sitting in the afternoon sun. She did not paint a single stroke.

Tuesdays after school Saint dropped her at a small house on the edge of Thurley State Park, where Charlotte sat in total silence in the office of Rita Kohl, M.D. The bills were sent to her grandmother, the shrink quietly marveling at the girl's prevailing vow of silence.

Saint spoke quietly, "There's another piece about

your . . . about Patch in **The Washington Sun.** My grandmother clipped it for you. People collect his work now . . . the paintings you have are—"

"She can just toss it in the trash."

Sunlight broke past the tower. Saint had tried to visit with Patch a dozen times. She could make the drive blindfolded. She could pick out distant mountain ranges from the lot, knew each pothole in the eight-mile track. She knew the building was too old, the cells like ice in the winter, a furnace come summer. Saint quietly campaigned for change, added her name to petitions for humane facilities, to expedite the construction schedule. Sometimes she made it to the tall gate and remained on the outside, talking to Blackjack, the giant of a man so sweet on her he shied when they spoke.

"What you did to Noah . . ."

She felt the girl glance at her.

"Maybe he'll think twice before he does it to another girl," Saint said.

"Yeah?"

"I'm not good at this. I didn't have a . . . I have my grandmother, and I love her, but she's not . . ."

Charlotte watched the grave. "I want to be left alone. I don't want to talk when people ask me to talk. Or paint. Or share goddamn feelings I don't even have. I don't want my ass grabbed. If I want to rage, I'll rage."

Saint stood. "This weekend I'll show you how to disengage a testicle."

191

Norma once told Saint that it took a village to raise a child. Though she did not have a village, on the last Friday of each month Saint threw open the doors of the tall house on Pinehill Cemetery Road and cooked a meal for her grandmother, Charlotte, Mrs. Meyer, and, with blazing reluctance, Sammy.

At six Charlotte emerged from the yard with a jar, then stood beside Saint as she mixed the cornmeal and flour. Charlotte sprinkled in a little sugar, beat the eggs and buttermilk. They had agreed on an allowance of two dollars each week, for which Charlotte acted as sous chef, quickly honing her skills till Norma declared her cornbread superior to Saint's. In return Saint declared her grandmother Judas and threatened to withdraw from the kitchen entirely.

Mrs. Meyer arrived with a bottle of red, Sammy, with two bottles of Buffalo Trace Bourbon.

Saint fixed glazed skillet chicken while Charlotte took her blueberry buckle to the corner to fold.

Mrs. Meyer dressed the table, the three women working together in orchestra while Sammy and Norma quietly got drunk.

They ate on the porch, Charlotte watching the fired sky, her grandmother beside her. "Sweetest chicken I ever tasted," Norma said.

"Charlotte's honey," Saint said.

"Fuckers only stung me thirty times during production. That aftertaste is likely my blood," Charlotte said.

Mrs. Meyer sighed. She wore a white virgin wool jacket, Dior lipstick, and crystal-embellished mules. Each time she showed at the door Saint would silently note the combinations then seek to copy the outfit at the Three-Rivers Outlet Mall. She used to wonder if the lady was going on someplace grander afterward till Charlotte told her that her grandmother only left the house to visit with them now.

Charlotte brought out the dessert, which Sammy tried to decline till Saint threatened to subpoena his second bottle.

"It's the finest honey I ever tasted," Norma said, smacking her lips till Saint threatened her, too. "I mean . . . Saint's produce was fine enough, but Charlotte here has a true farmer's touch."

"Is that why all the boys want me to milk them?" Charlotte said.

"Jesus," Saint said.

"Don't blaspheme," Norma said.

Mrs. Meyer sighed once more.

"Charlotte is the closest thing I have to a great-granddaughter," Norma declared. "I was waiting on Saint, but I reckon she's running my clock down now, and hers. No time to fall in love—"

"And produce a clutch of eggs?" Saint said.

"Don't need a man for that," Charlotte said.

"You're not talking about . . . what's it called?" Norma slurred.

"Spunk donor?" Sammy offered.

"Jesus," Saint said.

"Don't blaspheme," Norma said.

"It's all delicious," Mrs. Meyer said, aiming to bring it back.

Saint smiled. "I registered Charlotte with the American Beekeeping Federation."

"Sometimes I worry she knows me too well," Charlotte said.

"Sass all you want, but I reckon you'd be a shoo-in for this year's Honey Princess," Saint said, raising an eyebrow at Charlotte.

"And that could also be my stripper name," Charlotte said, to a deep roar of laughter from Sammy.

When it was done, when the last wine had been drunk, when a drunk Sammy aimed a goodbye kiss at Mrs. Meyer, who swerved with such finesse that he toppled from the front step and disappeared into a ninebark, Saint sat at the old piano and played.

She watched the painting of the white house as she did.

"Why do you always play this song? Norma said

it was your wedding song," Charlotte said, standing behind her.

"It belonged to two people way before I got married."

"Will Patch die in there?" Charlotte said.

"No."

"Shame."

"Don't say that."

"You can't think there's a heaven for people like him?"

"It's the only thing that I pray for."

192

Twenty cells, eighteen of them in use.

Silver bars red rusted at the centers, where arms sometimes leaned, hands flexing, orange sleeves rolled back over thinning forearms. Natural light came from a line of windows opposite, too high to see more than a sky dappled gunmetal.

Blackjack opened the final gate, and Patch hauled in a canvas bag spilling with books. There had been a library service once before, in the late eighties, before Warden Riley wielded budget cuts, the business of correction not entirely immune to the world outside. Inside, the cells were much like his own, maybe with a little more color, the posters numerous, a couple of cacti, a radio played quiet. The first man was Ricky Nelson, and Patch guessed him to be sixty. He asked for cigarettes and declined reading matter. The second man was Howie Goucher, and he did not acknowledge Patch at all. A couple of guys took a random selection. Patch picked out **Blood Meridian, Lonesome Dove,** and **Huck**

Finn. His fingers traced over **Gatsby,** the memory of his daughter catching him dead, tightening his jaw and neck.

Patch knew the average wait was fifteen years in a cell eight by ten, also knew a quarter would die before the state could kill them. He knew they were more prone to disease, malnutrition, psychosis. Sleep was broken every thirty minutes for counts that rattled locks. Patch knew four percent would be innocent. No religious rights, despite what the Supreme Court ruled. Patch knew these things because he had spent his first year in the prison library reading and listening and working his angle.

So when he made it to the final cell, he slowed a moment to recall the past, to hear the voice in the dark, to feel the touch on his skin.

The radio sang of pale blue eyes.

The man was thinner, kept his hair parted neatly, his hands by his sides. He looked down at his own boots.

For a long time Patch could not find the words he had practiced.

He could not even remember to breathe.

He could not imagine how a man could exist for nineteen years without even the company of hope.

And then, finally, their eyes met.

"Hello, Joseph," Marty Tooms said.

193

"You did so much to live, only to come die in here," Tooms said.

"I practiced what to say," Patch said.

"Okay."

"But now I'm here . . . I want to reach through the bars and grab your throat and make you tell me where she is."

"I'm sorry," Tooms said, and Patch looked at him, at the lines that crept from his eyes, the way his hands shook lightly, and saw that he was.

"You said she was dead."

Tooms glanced at the window, at a sky that lay over a world he had lost. In seven months he would be taken to a room with a single window. Straps would be placed across his legs and stomach and head, and a couple of IVs inserted in case his veins failed. Sodium thiopental would knock him out cold. Vecuronium bromide would paralyze his muscles. Potassium chloride would stop his heart from beating. After twenty years of waiting, his life would be ended in ten minutes. Activists would make it to the big gate, light their candles and sing and bear witness to their own beliefs. They would fall silent for those ten minutes when their government carried out one murder in vengeance for another. Local news would cover it, and they would speak of a crime long since forgotten, maybe note the irony that the only survivor was incarcerated in that very same prison, though that in itself was not so unusual. There would be no one there for Patch. There would be no one there for Grace.

Patch saw Blackjack at the door.

"Did you really kill her?" Patch said, a tremor in his voice.

Marty Tooms kept his eyes on the skyline.

And then began to cry.

194

She checked in with Himes once each month.

He had taken her resignation with an even hand, told her she would be back, that he understood, but that she was destined for greater things.

"Anything?" she said, as she looked through the glass wall of her office and out into the twilight street.

"If there was anything, don't you think I would have called?"

"What are you eating?"

"An egg."

"Whole. Like a snake."

"Eli Aaron. Each month ahead of speaking with you I get the team to reach out. Nothing."

"It's possible he changed his MO," Saint said. It was a fear she would not ever shake. Each night when she sat on the porch with her grandmother and a car slowed up the street she would feel a slight flutter in her chest, that she had the acute responsibility of keeping Charlotte safe from whoever was out there.

"It is. Carl Eugene Watts. He—"

"Stabbed. Strangled. One time raped. Weapons. Hands," she spoke with dispassion.

"I forget who I'm talking to."

On her desk was a coffee cup and inside it warm milk. In her drawer was a romance novel.

"Sister Isabelle wears trifocals," Himes said.

"I like that you know that, Himes."

"Poor sight. Good chance she was mistaken."

"You'll send me the case file."

"It won't do you any good."

He said that each time they spoke.

195

Patch waited each week for his time with Marty Tooms in a state of suspended agony, not sleeping more than an hour the night before, the questions bouncing around those hard stone walls till he caught the most pertinent and filed them away.

He grew quieter in the day, Cooper pulling him aside during his library work and asking after his mental health. In the yard he watched big men shoot hoops as he strolled the perimeter fence. The workmen in their dustbowl kicked out so much of it Patch could feel the sting in his eye. On his second lap he was joined by an old man known as Tug on account of his crimes. In 1964 he had been gambling on a St. Louis riverboat when the dealer hit such a streak that Tug lost a year's rent money. Tug followed him up to the lido deck and tipped him over the side, claiming to the jury he just wanted to wipe the smirk off his face. Unfortunately for Tug, and the dealer, a tugboat was passing at that same moment. Six hours later they fished the man's body from the Mississippi River.

"So you can order in books?" Tug asked.

"What do you want?" Patch said.

"Just making talk, Pirate. A man can't inquire?" Tug's fuse was short, like his stature, a little under five feet. Patch mostly spoke to the top of his head.

They walked another revolution. "Ursula Andress."

"Excuse me?" Patch said.

"Honey Ryder."

Patch sighed heavily.

"Dr. fucking No. The Bond girl. Ursula Andress. Born March nineteenth. Pisces. I've been in love with her since 1955. Used to picture her face when I—"

"Jesus. I can't get movies."

"I see the shit you've got in that library. Fucking books on soap production. Who the fuck wants to produce soap in a prison? You know how dangerous that shit is in the shower block? And you can't get me nothing with my love in it?"

He ranted awhile longer, the disappointment palpable.

"I'd like to ride me one of those," Tug said, and pointed in the direction of a tracked excavator. He wore his white hair long like the moustache that traced the downward swing of his mouth. He carried a kind of optimism Patch had not seen in men who would die in prison.

"Make you feel bigger?" Patch said.

"What the fuck does that mean, One-eye? I'd drive it at these fences and tear them down right during yard time. Watch them scramble." His grin turned into a laugh so high and manic Patch guessed that optimism was born of the loose screws in his head.

"Only way out," Patch said.

"Quickest way out."

A watchtower stood a thousand yards out.

"Anyone ever make it?" Patch said.

Tug's moustache twitched a little as they looked out toward the wilds, the land bowing to the ravine. "Not for forty years. Sonny Parker. Tunnel."

"Pickax?"

Tug rolled his eyes. "No one tunnels out of here. You see that machine over there? It's a pile borer. Missouri bedrock. You can't get deep enough without mechanical intervention."

Patch watched the steel core of the drill, wider than his shoulders at the flutes. "So how then?"

"Sonny had a crew. You don't break out of any-place without assistance. So his crew drilled a shallow hole and tunneled in over where the new five-wing is. Only twenty feet and they were under each fence. This hole was about ten inches round."

Patch frowned. "Small enough for a rabbit."

Tug grinned. "Big enough for a gun."

"They smuggled a gun into prison?"

"Sonny used it to get himself out, Dillinger-style."

They turned when a fight broke out. Nothing

meaningful landed before Blackjack scooped up one of the men and dumped him against the fence.

"You're not thinking of trying something, Pirate?" Tug said.

Patch saw a couple of drops of blood on the ground, soon trodden into dust. "I've got no place to go."

196

That afternoon he stood outside Tooms's cell and stared at the heavy sheet hung from the inside across the bars, blocking everything within. Near a hundred degrees, Tooms had built himself an inferno rather than stare into the face of his crimes. Patch glanced back and saw Blackjack had retreated into the cool of the captain's office.

When he started talking, he watched the other men appear, arms through the bars as the radio died. "She was brilliant in ways you can't imagine. In ways that don't sound real when I tell them. She took me from the dark and showed me her world. She could recite poems and stories and knew facts I thought she had made up. She knew that prairie dogs kiss, that ghost crabs growl using teeth in their stomach. She knew that koala fingerprints are so close to ours they could contaminate a crime scene."

"I fucking told those cops it was the koala that did it," Ricky Nelson called out, to laughter.

"She was kind. Not enough people are. The cops

said I remembered too much, that some of it must have been imagined. I know her. I still know her. I miss her. I carried her with me each day of my life. You can give her back to me, Tooms. You're in this place, where you can't do shit. Where you've got nothing. But you can do this brilliant thing. It's inside you to do it. Just tell me who she was. Tell me where she's buried."

Blackjack tapped his stick on the metal as Patch snapped from it.

On his way back he handed a copy of **The Color Purple** to Howie Goucher in cell two. He would keep it for a month, telling Patch of the glorious Celie.

A little after that the row would fall silent as Howie was led from them.

197

"Who is this boy she's out with?" Norma said.

They sat together on the porch as a fine spring evening unfolded.

"Matt Leavesham," Saint said, watching the street though she knew Charlotte would not return from the movie theater for another few hours.

"I know the Leaveshams. His mother is diabetic. Self-inflicted," Norma said.

As the air cooled a little Norma fetched a box and dropped it beside Saint.

"It's from Himes," Saint said, checking the label. "The Eli Aaron case file."

"Oh, I know that."

"When did it come?"

"You have your hands full enough."

Saint glared. Norma glared back.

"It's important, Grandma."

"Important is looking after that girl."

"I'm doing the best I can."

In Norma's hands was a novel, the pages dog-eared. She wore a cardigan Saint had once knitted for her.

"Is there something you want to say to me?" Saint stood, paced to the edge, and leaned to touch a baluster, the rot setting in at the bottom rail.

Norma shook her head, but Saint saw it in her eyes.

"Don't spare my feelings now. Not after you've spent years being cold."

"Nonsense," Norma said.

Saint glared.

"It's just, you might have been better equipped for this had you . . . with Jimmy."

Saint turned her back for a moment.

"Did he not deserve more time?" Norma said, quiet.

"I—"

"You aborted his baby, Saint. And then you divorced him. For what?"

Saint turned. "He wasn't a good husband. He wasn't—"

"He wasn't Joseph."

Saint stemmed her tears and took a breath. "That's not—"

"Men don't start out as good husbands. You didn't give him time. Jimmy is a good man. I know it. I was the one that pushed the two of you together. I made you give him a chance because I saw him at church, and I knew . . . I knew he was what you needed. And you tried for the baby, and when it happened you—"

"Please," Saint said, her voice barely holding.

Norma swallowed. "You made a pact with God. You promised that if he brought Joseph back then you would live a good life. You would—"

"You don't understand. Jimmy, he—" Saint cut in, and then stopped. And for a moment she saw her grandmother, the woman who had raised her. And Norma stood, and walked toward her and opened her arms.

Saint stepped into the embrace. Right then it was all she had. It was all that kept her standing.

"What about Jimmy?" Norma said.

Saint closed her eyes and leaned her head on her grandmother's shoulder. "He's not Patch."

198

Saint fretted her way through dinner, fielded a call from Mrs. Meyer, who'd seen the Leavesham boy in the Monta Clare Drugstore and surmised he was purchasing either condoms or some kind of sedative to make her granddaughter more pliable. Saint had hung up the phone, gone back to fretting and fighting the urge to call round to the Leavesham house and draw her gun on the diabetic mother.

At nine she paced.

At ten she made calls, and at eleven she found the Leaveshams' address, where at the window she saw Charlotte and Matt making out in the den. She hammered the door and pinned Matt to the florid wallpaper in their neat hallway with her forearm.

Saint caught up with Charlotte at the end of Cotterham Avenue and reached for her arm.

"Don't you fucking touch me," Charlotte said, her cheeks burning.

Saint took a step back, her face just as flushed. "You broke curfew."

Charlotte glared. "You're not my mother."

"And I thank God for that every day." Saint spoke the words before she realized, before she knew they would later strangle her with shame.

There was a moment when Charlotte took the full force of that blow, winded till she reared.

"I suppose if you were my mother I wouldn't even be here," Charlotte said.

Saint took a step back. "I don't know—"

"That's what you do when you get pregnant, right?"

Saint shook her head.

Charlotte went on, told Saint truths she already knew, how the girl was ashamed to live with her, to be seen with her. "You keep that trunk in your closet. You collect leaves and pine cones. You sit home with your grandmother. You have no life, so you fuck around with mine. You couldn't even keep your husband. You—"

Saint felt it build, felt the conversation with her grandmother from earlier that evening. Saint felt the way the girl looked at her, the way everyone in Monta Clare looked at her. And she could not stop the words before they spilled from her. "He beat me."

Charlotte stopped.

And the two faced each other in the street.

Saint closed her eyes to the moon and the stars. "I was pregnant and Jimmy . . . he beat me. He fractured my eye socket. And my jaw . . . it still clicks when I eat."

This time Charlotte shook her head, the words too much.

"I saw a dentist because one of my teeth stayed loose."

The street died around them. The town and the woodland and sky. And what had once seemed so beautiful and safe was lost.

"My grandmother said hatred is misplaced fear. And maybe she's right, because when I lie down to sleep each night, I still feel scared that he'll come do it again. No matter that I'm a cop. That I carry a gun. I'm scared—"

She stopped then because she saw the look on Charlotte's face.

And then Charlotte turned and ran.

199

Saint tore through the town. She woke Michaels and two auxiliaries, pulled Sammy from the gallery, and met Mrs. Meyer on Main Street.

For an hour she near lost her mind, roused half the town and had them moving through every street, the dull pain in her stomach moving up to her head as she recalled two decades before.

From St. Raphael's to Monta Clare High, she checked her watch as minutes ebbed to the torture of nightfall. She doubled back to the house, saw Norma standing on the porch.

"Jesus," she screamed it, hating herself fully.

"She'll turn up."

"When and in what state?"

She stayed on foot because she knew each and every shortcut.

Saint stopped at the Brayer house and woke Melissa and her parents, did the same at Madeline Collins's. The only names she could remember the girl speaking. Right then she realized she did not know nearly enough about Charlotte's life.

Back on Main Street she saw Sammy comforting a crying Mrs. Meyer, the night sobering him cold, the fear they all carried, all of those that remembered Patch and Misty, and the doctor, Marty Tooms.

In the old spot in the woodland she pushed through ropes of vine and looked for tracks with the bright of her flashlight, but the ground was loose dust. She felt the heat of her gun burning her hip like a reminder she was no longer a rookie, that she would shoot first if anyone went close to the girl that was Patch's and in bourgeoning ways her own.

As she cleared the woodland and jogged down Rosewood Avenue she saw the light burning in the Mad House. Her breath rushed out in a burst of relief when she saw Charlotte sitting in her father's old chair, staring at the television light.

"Goddamn, Charlotte. Goddamn. I've got half the town up and you're sitting here watching television."

Charlotte did not turn her head from the screen. "Saturday nights we watched movies together."

She might have berated her, might have kicked down what little was left between them had she not seen what the girl was watching.

The channel dramatized the moment, two years before, when the girl had been returned to her father, the two of them embracing in such a way that even the reporters fell silent for a moment so rare it had almost been forgotten.

Outside a Texan hospital, on artificial grass, the two held each other while the cameras cut to a single shot of the girl when she had gone missing two decades before.

Eloise Strike.

Saint gasped not because she recognized the name, but the face. The face she had stared at in the window of Monta Clare Fine Art for three summers.

"It was his painting," Charlotte said.

Saint watched as the story unfolded. The reporter told how an Arlington woman had been visiting her sister in New York City when she happened across a painting hanging in the window of a small gallery in Tribeca. She'd stopped dead because she recognized the girl. The same girl she saw at the window of a single-family home by a Fish Creek Linear Park access point back home in Texas. Each morning as she took her walk she saw the girl sitting by the rear window, looking out over the woodland. She had not known the girl was being held, that she hadn't left that room in near two thousand days. The woman went into the gallery, heard a little of the story, and immediately dialed 911.

"Jesus," Saint said.

Only now did the girl and her father, Walter Strike, feel strong enough to share their story.

Saint knelt beside Charlotte, breathed the perfume she wore, noticed her red sandals, her denim skirt and the gold clips she wore in her hair. She had hoped that her first date would have been just that. It didn't have to be love; it didn't have to lead anywhere at all. It just had to be a night when she could slip from that long shadow.

She looked up and saw the first tears on the girl's cheeks. She knew better than to try and comfort her.

"What you said," Charlotte began.

Right then she knew Charlotte needed her truth more than Saint needed her silence.

"Your father, he did it for me—"

She would play that moment back and wonder at a universal network of fate, each decision rippling out from the wings of a butterfly, searching a grid of pattern that had been laid in another life.

She would wonder if it would have made a difference to any of them.

But as she turned and saw Sammy at the door, his cheeks ashen, she knew there was no one at all in control.

"Your grandmother," he said.

200

That night in the ICU Charlotte would not leave, distraught that her actions had brought about the heart attack, no matter that Saint told her of Norma's age, a family history, an addiction to honey and bourbon and cigar smoke. Still, she shrugged off her hand, curled up on the bench and stared at the television, at the roll of news that did not sleep. A California serial killer; Embassy bombings; updates on an Indiana train collision.

Mrs. Meyer sat beside Sammy, who lay his large coat on her chair because he worried about the cream of her dress.

Saint knew the room well. It was a place she had waited for a life to be saved, for a story to begin and end.

A little after three in the morning a nurse came to collect her, and she was glad the others slept. The nurse was old and knowing and did not need tell her it was time, for Saint read it in the mourn of her smile.

"She's ready," she said, and Saint did not tell her that she, herself, was not.

Saint took the chair beside Norma and was left with only the steady organ of the machine that inflated Norma's chest, the fading flutters of a heart that had beat long enough.

She looked around at switches and canisters and machines and plugs. She looked to the window where she had once pressed her face and begged the stars to spare a boy who would become a brilliant man.

"Goddamn," she said, as she took Norma's hand and told her sorry for cursing. Her hand. Norma had held hers when she was seven years old as they crossed the street. When they first heard the hum of bees. She had taken it as they strolled to Monta Clare High for graduation. And now it was Saint's turn to take hers.

She whispered, "I promised God I wouldn't sin. I promised him that if he saved Joseph then I would live a decent life, and I wouldn't hurt anyone. And every day I'd be kind to people."

She pressed her cheek to Norma's hand.

"It might sound like a big ask, like too much to promise, but I knew I could do it, Grandma. I knew I could do it because I had you to show me how."

She finally looked up and saw her grandmother, her wrists now so thin.

"You told me I was named Saint because I brought you all so much joy. But I worry . . . I worry I only made your life harder. You are the absolute best of us."

They would ring the bells at the church.

"Why do we hold on to the bad things and forget the good?" She posed the question to the small medal clipped to Norma's sleeve, to the empty halls, the green glass and leather benches, the lead roof and the clock that counted them down.

"I want you to take me for ice cream at Lacey's. I want to ask God to make that happen. But I know I've already asked for so much."

She leaned over and kissed her grandmother's cheek. "I'm so sorry I let you down, Grandma."

She wet Norma's face with her tears.

201

"They confiscated a round of Beaufort d'Été," Sammy said, shooting a hard glare at the guard. "I told them the first thing that dies in a place like this is the palate. Fucking barbarians."

They talked awhile, a little about the market, the demand for his work so scaling Sammy said **Grace Number One** would likely fetch seven figures. Patch stared impassive, tuned him out when he spoke of securing Charlotte's future, because Patch knew between Misty and her grandmother Charlotte would want for nothing.

"How is she?" Patch said.

Sammy sobered a little, glanced around at the other men, most sitting with families trying to cling to the last strands, the loss written in the smiles of children old enough to realize. "She's . . . she started painting again."

"Yeah?"

"Nothing much, maybe just getting a feel. Wasted a couple canvases."

"Thank you, Sam."

Sammy waved a hand. "The tab."

"I need a favor."

"Anything," Sammy said.

"There's a box in the attic of the Mad House. The only belongings I have from when I was a kid. Inside there's a copy of **Playboy.** June 1965."

"You know porn has come a long way—"

This time Patch held up a hand.

Sammy lowered his voice. "I've got a collection that would—"

"Stop."

They sat awhile.

And then Sammy loosened the collar of his Oxford shirt. And he told Patch that Norma had died that morning.

"Saint—"

Sammy smiled, shook his head.

"Will you tell her . . ."

"Of course," Sammy said.

Patch watched a little girl sat opposite her father, drawing something, gripping a crayon with a tight fist and streaking her colors. "Just tell her I . . ."

"I will."

Sammy stood and moved to leave him.

"You never asked," Patch said.

Sammy had made the trip a dozen times, claimed he had business that way, but Patch knew his network did not extend to those lost acres. He had come to the arraignment, sat at the back and sipped from the sterling silver flask, his hands shaking a little as the sentence was read. He wrote sometimes, never more than a quote, often Oscar Wilde and his creeping common sense. Other times he sent postcards of a single color, always a shade Patch had used in his work. Patch kept them in a large tobacco tin Tug had given him. Sammy was not mawkish enough to say that he missed him, that he missed sitting in contented silence on the small balcony, sipping their whisky together and watching the workings of Monta Clare.

"You never asked why I did it," Patch said.

Sammy buried his hands deep in the pockets of his velvet blazer and straightened his rabbit felt hat. "I never needed to."

202

That next visit he told Tooms of Grace's dancing, from sauter to tourner, glisser to élancer. He spoke to the heavy sheet, had the ear of the other men, who took to peppering him with questions about her, his words bringing color to their day. Tooms did not appear, so Patch slipped a copy of "The Raven" through his bars, the letter inside almost as thick as the book itself. He no longer begged or asked, instead wrote a little of his hopes for the rest of his own life, stating he would not get to watch his daughter grow up, to become much like the woman her mother was.

Patch sat on the concrete, his back to the bars.

The other men lost interest.

"I was sorry about your mother. I never told you that. But I was sorry."

Patch did not turn toward the voice, just felt Tooms, his back against the same bars as they faced away from each other.

"She tried her best," Patch said.

"I don't doubt that, Joseph."

"Why do some people fall so short?"

"It depends what you measure against."

At the distant end Patch watched a rat scurry. "Are you afraid?"

"Yes."

Patch turned a little and saw the shape of him, the profile of a man he once knew to be kind.

"How did you end up here?" Patch said.

"How long have you got?"

"Longer than you."

Tooms laughed then.

Patch laughed, too.

203

The following week they sat for an hour because Blackjack was called to a fight in the block.

Back to back, like it lessened the pressure somehow.

"I never wanted to be a doctor," Tooms said. His voice was soft, emanating compassion and care.

"I never wanted to rob a bank," Patch said. "Actually, that might be a lie."

Tooms laughed, a sound Patch heard often, a sound he matched often, too.

"My sister died when I was fourteen," Tooms said.

"How?"

"She was nineteen and fell pregnant."

Patch ran his hand over the cool cement.

"I found her. I don't know how she got the rope up over the high branch. Hell, I don't even know how she learned to tie a running knot. She never was an outdoors type," he said, chuckling, but Patch heard that note of shock some memories still carried.

In return he asked Patch not of his search, or his struggles, but of himself. Of the things he enjoyed.

Of Misty, and, though it hurt like a physical pain, Charlotte.

"I remember, after your father. Your mother came to see me, and I could see it, that she would struggle more," Tooms said.

Patch listened to his voice, to the soft tone.

"You looked out for me," Patch said.

"I didn't do nearly enough."

"Still."

"As a parent, what do you want for your children?" Tooms said.

"More than you want for yourself."

"So the bar is low in your case."

Patch smiled.

"I'm sorry you're here, Joseph. But, damn, it's good to hear your voice."

204

As they turned onto Main Street, Saint saw each of the storeowners standing in their doorways wearing their finest, heads dipped, then they fell into step behind her. That morning the town of Monta Clare mourned one of its own, and the great St. Raphael's burst its old seams and spilled onto its lawns. Those inside were blessed by Saint, who took to the organ and played Chopin.

The Reverend Franks led them, and when it was her turn Saint's knees shook as she walked the chancel and stood engulfed at the altar and bridged her grief with focus on Norma's life, from a distance so simple and honest, but up closer a marvel of endurance and love. She looked out at the swell of faces, some from the bus route, some distant cousins who had made long drives. Nix sat alone in the far corner, smiled when she met his eye, though in his she saw a hollow that dampened the stained glass, the triforium, the clerestory of color.

Sammy took the other corner. He wore bold pin-stripes and a white-and-pink cravat, and beside him a hardwood crook cane leaned against the stone.

Her mind sought Joseph Macauley, who should have been there with them. She had received a card, a simple sketch of the old porch on a winter's evening, the three shapes sitting together nothing more than a blur. He had used only two shades.

In the morning sun they placed Norma into the ground. Saint had once wondered if her grandmother would want to be buried back in the city, with her husband and daughter. Norma told her no, she wanted to stay close to the tall house, the memories they had made there.

They ate sandwiches on the small green. Mrs. Meyer took care of the details, had Lacey cater and Charlotte bake a selection of cakes.

Saint fended hugs, smiling her way through stories she had heard countless times before. She looked around for Nix, but he had gone, looked for Sammy and found him alone on the bench. He drank from a flask, offered her a slug, which she took and regretted.

It was at the close of the day, as Charlotte read quietly on the porch, that the telephone rang.

Saint stood alone in the kitchen.

Numb as she listened to the voice of Sister Cecile.

"Eli Aaron just visited here."

205

"In my time studying, in my years practicing, I never came close to finding such a medical marvel, such a wonderful affliction," Tooms said.

Through the window Patch watched a dry storm seize the distance, each shaft of rainfall sublimating, like it was for show, for them.

"It's an emotion," Patch said.

"Oh it is, that's not in doubt. But it's more, right? It turns you off your food. It stops you sleeping, stops you thinking."

Patch heard the smile in Marty's voice as he spoke.

"So you've felt it then," Patch said.

"Once. A long time back. But turns out once is more than enough."

"Who was the dame?"

Marty laughed. "I guess maybe someone all wrong for me in the ways that counted least. We fell in love and it was like . . . you know when all of a sudden there's meaning. Actual true meaning and purpose."

"Like color in the dark," Patch said.

"Yes. Exactly yes. Nothing is so dark with them in the world."

"How did you meet?"

"I was just seventeen. Each year my parents would farm out work to local kids when the harvest was due. I mean, it was tough work, backbreaking."

"Fun."

Tooms laughed. "So fun only one kid from school showed. We spent that whole summer just the two of us on my family land. Got to know plenty about each other. We had our differences, but the fundamentals . . . to be kind, it was ingrained, you know. A good heart. Not much in the world more important than that."

Both settled in silence awhile. "What happened?" Patch said.

"Hearts were broken, and then healed, and then broken all over again. But we lived, Joseph. Just like you. We lived and laughed, and we loved each other without condition. And so when it happens, when they lead me into that room, I know I can seek out a single picture in my mind to carry me away."

"Paint it for me," Patch said, the steel hard against his back.

"A smile. Doesn't sound much, but when it was aimed at me, I knew for sure it was the only one I ever needed."

The storm moved from sight. Only calm remained.

"There's so much I don't understand," Patch said.

"I can't tell you where she is, Joseph."

At that they both turned.

And Patch saw it clear enough in his eyes.

"Because you don't know."

Tooms glanced toward the gate, where Blackjack stood and reached for his key.

"But you do know something," Patch said, following his eye. "You have to tell me. You can't leave me like this, Marty. Not after everything."

Blackjack crossed the stone floor slow.

Patch gripped Marty's hand through the bars. "Please. I'll beg . . . I'll fucking beg you. I can't go on the rest of my life."

Marty looked at him, tears in his eyes. "I'll see you next week."

"And?" Patch held his breath, felt the sweat on his back as the air left them, what remained little more than a morgue.

Tooms nodded.

He would tell him.

206

Patch wrote letters to the supreme court asking for a stay for the man who had abducted him, the date looming like a swell on calmer water.

He wrote ministers at a dozen churches, asked them to lobby the district attorney to slow the runaway train. He read books on the history of capital punishment, legal tomes fatter than his arm. He learned of loopholes that would not benefit Tooms, precedents that had been set and rescinded.

In his first month he had learned of Teddy Fawn Durston, a Democratic candidate who would run for governor of Missouri. Patch found an old newspaper interview where the man talked moratoriums. That evening he'd called Sammy and told him to donate twenty thousand dollars to the campaign.

And then, on September 14, Cooper carried in a copy of the **St. Louis Post-Dispatch** and gently set it down on the desk beside Patch.

Patch picked it up and read.

"I'm sorry," Cooper said.

Patch read it again, knowing it would come, not believing it would come.

In a little over two weeks Marty Tooms would be put to death, and with him, Patch knew, Grace would die.

207

Saint landed in the bustle of Miami International Airport, moved through vacationers and climbing humidity.

Her shirt clung as she collected her Ford Crown Victoria and headed seventeen miles along 95 Express, the ocean holding the horizon but not her attention. She'd coordinated with Himes, come close to thanking God himself that the FBI had signed off on fitting surveillance cameras outside the church where Eli Aaron had shown and picked up another set of rosary beads. Sister Cecile told how he had gone into the chapel afterward and lit a dozen candles, told Sister Isabelle he was doing God's work, that he was heading south, where it was hotter in many ways.

They had license plates.

They had the make and model of the van.

They tracked him back through the city and then lost him, figuring he'd switched either vehicles or plates.

Roadblocks and checkpoints and a dozen agents scrolling a thousand hours of surveillance footage. They'd mapped the likely route through Philadelphia, south through the Carolinas. They had him hugging the coast, Wilmington, Myrtle Beach. They moved him inland to Interstate 81, Virginia, picking up Interstate 77 through Charlotte.

Either way they joined in Jacksonville. Interstate 95 toward Miami.

It was thirteen hundred miles and more than double that in variations.

It took five hours to get a hit at a toll booth fifty miles from Boca Raton. The guy working the booth noted the plates were different, but the picture of the van that had been circulated was a clear enough match.

Saint opened the window to the sounds of Miami-Dade County, the skyline fractured by gray high-rises that edged off the colors.

"I'm coming for you," she said.

208

Agent Gil, on the second floor of the Miami Division building, took her through what they had.

"Ashlee Miller. She's twenty-two. Taken two hours ago from the corner of Crystal Avenue. Van mounted the sidewalk."

"Goddamn," Saint said, wiping sweat from her lip.

"How's he choosing them?" Agent Gil said.

"Sinners."

"That narrows it down then."

Saint sighed at the frustration, and the ticking clock, the time and the lives slipping by so maddeningly.

For an hour they sat in the airless office. Agent Gil working the phone, Saint pulling together the file, and the memories.

"Tell me everything you know about Summer Reynolds," she said to Patch one Sunday afternoon.

Patch reeled off information like he kept it right there at the forefront. "She was sixteen when she

went missing. Had a boyfriend her father didn't approve of."

"I have the background. Give me something else."

"She played piano. She wasn't popular, wasn't alone. Good at math and maybe thought of becoming a teacher."

Saint sighed.

"And she was a Girl Scout."

Saint frowned. "Like with the cookies."

"A Gold Award Scout. From Daisies through Cadettes. She could map a route through Big Bend alone. Pitch a tent and snare dinner. The girl could survive."

Saint looked at the other files. "Ashlee Miller. Did she ever go camping?"

Agent Gil worked the phone, got the field agent at the house. "Her girlfriend said they spent last weekend at the Ocala National Forest."

Saint felt the air cool. "Eli Aaron once told me he liked to camp. Maybe he saw her. Maybe he came back for her."

Agent Gil moved quick, put out calls, knew the plates had likely been changed again, but had every patrol car in the area move along the campsites of the Keys.

It took less than an hour for the call to come.

209

In a messy sedan they tore from the town to the Tamiami Trail toward the Big Cypress National Preserve. From stands of hardwood hammocks through pinelands to sawgrass marsh, she looked out over a million acres of everglades. The road sliced it without mercy, a blight on natural wonder.

The call had come from a local cop who saw a van that matched their description outside of the Black Coal campground.

Ahead they saw cruisers, four of them. Distant sirens told more would come.

Saint stepped out into brutal heat so heavy she moved to fan it from her face so she could draw breath.

Sweat dripped as officers spread out.

Along the bank she saw a hundred waterbirds she did not know the names of, the arcs of them beautiful as she drew her gun and felt her skin sink between the grip. In her mind she might've tracked him alone. In reality it had taken fifty agents across eleven states pooling their investment and knowledge until a break came.

They moved together along land that fell into bogs they skirted with care as mosquitoes swooped. Saint did not move to bat them away as they crossed a timber footbridge and met a hiking trail.

A trooper raised his hand, pointed to a line of blood that led into plumes of muhly grass, four feet high, a sea of purple come fall.

They spread apart, a hundred yards between them as they waded, their guns ready for a man likely lying low. Saint knew the protocol, also knew he would kill again if they did not stop him.

She took measured steps into undergrowth forged from the runoff, the Gulf of Mexico flowing down a peninsula now rivers and streams. Lake Okeechobee and the waters that ringed Kissimmee, emptying into Florida Bay. Her grandmother had once told her that in the winter the grasslands were fields, unflooded for precious months like a rising submarine.

She was about to turn and check progress when she stumbled.

Saint cried out when she saw her.

Ashlee Miller lay face down.

Saint turned her over quickly.

Pumped her chest.

And screamed.

210

They ate on brown trays atop polished metal tables with rigid plastic spoons.

Tug picked at his taco, the meat stained brown, beside that a bread roll, the edges beginning to green. Each week a cluster of inmates took the center tables in the library and worked on a class action suit led by Larry Medeau, a former Kansas City lawyer who had shot dead his gardener in a dispute over bull thistle. Larry argued the food was so subpar it amounted to cruel and unusual punishment. Cooper ran a book on how quick a judge would dismiss it.

"So they're putting Tooms to death," Tug said, picking corn from his teeth with a fingernail. "You see him when you head in there?"

Patch did not answer.

"Damn noble what you do. Quickest way to shed ignorance is to read a book. Strips it each page you turn, letting knowledge in, you know. You want your shell?"

Patch tossed it to him, glanced up and saw a couple of guys with Brand affiliation. They stood apart, sleeves pushed back over tattooed forearms, the inking crude, the shamrocks bright.

"You see them?" Tug said, still eating. He had not looked up or around once.

"I do," Patch said, biting into his bread.

The men beside them stood and left, food mostly untouched.

"You disrespect them?" Tug said.

"A while back."

"They don't forget."

"They'll do it here?" Patch said.

Tug nodded. "Fish. Got to prove themselves. Same shit for thirty years now. Can't blame them. Probably got the same sentence as you. Might as well serve it with some backing, right?"

"Right."

Patch tried to keep eating, but his mouth dried out, the dough like gum as he swallowed it down with water, his hands shaking a little.

"Too late to do what they ask of you?" Tug said.

"Too late."

Tug stood, nodded once and then moved on as they moved in.

There was a moment before it began when Patch felt the hall fall quiet. The high windows leaked the last of the day. A dozen pillars propped the roof, painted white and buried into a floor coated with specked rubber, the ingress of meals trodden in.

One of the two looked young, maybe a teenager, fear in his eyes as they crossed toward him.

Patch knew he had options, none of them good. He could stand and run, but they would not forgive his slight, not forget that he once dared tell them no. Maybe he would see out another week, a week where he would lose the last of himself entirely. Lose the kid with the eye patch who came out swinging because it was in his blood. Likely in his daughter's blood. He thought of the Barbarossa brothers, sailing flaming North African seas five hundred years before. The red beard Aruj fighting on when the Spanish sliced his arm clean off. Patch knew he could fight most, but knew he could never fight his own fate.

So when the kid pulled the sap from behind his back, when the big guy clenched his fist, Patch took a breath, picked up his tray and swung.

211

The cell was seven by twelve.

No window, the bed so close to the toilet the mattress pressed on the rim. Tug once told him the solitary cells had been out of use since the seventies, but with workmen tearing down the old seven block, Patch found himself staring at a slice of history best forgotten. The stone walls breathed damp, cold and slick to touch. The bars faced a bank of brick shedding lime paint. The only light came in from yellow bulbs.

Patch lay on the bunk, both fists swollen. He'd gone easy on the kid, sent the big guy to the infirmary. He knew things would be different after, that he was as much a dead man walking as Marty Tooms.

He closed his eye and in the confines of that cell found a memory of her came easier.

"You get out of here and you don't look back. Never. You promise me you make it out and leave all this behind you," Grace said.

"You know I can't do that."

"You can. You get out and get on. You live. You fucking owe it to me."

Right then, in that room so stark, he wondered just how much he had failed, not only at finding her, but in every way a person could fail.

"Pirate."

He heard the voice of the kid in the cell beside his, a little nasal, his nose clean broken.

"You okay?"

"Yeah, kid," Patch said.

He heard the boy breathing, a line of stone all that separated them. Patch did not hate him. There wasn't the room.

"I didn't . . . I don't want to be here."

Patch studied his own hands. "Don't cry, kid. It'll be worse."

The boy cried.

"Tell me something," Patch said. "How old are you?"

"Nineteen."

Patch heard a slight drawl, reasoned it was the nose, maybe even a few teeth loose. "Dentistry is the oldest profession in the world. They had long enough to practice. You'll be smiling right again soon."

"We were supposed to kill you."

"You will."

For a moment he wondered what the boy had done, what exactly got a teenager locked away for the rest of his life.

"What's your name?"

"They . . . all of them call me White. I don't got my birth certificate or nothing. Lou, he's my foster father. He called me Tommy, but I never felt it, you know. Maybe Tom. Just Tom."

Patch listened to him talk awhile, mostly about nothing much at all, the kid trying to stave off his own thoughts, the weight of silence more than he could deal with. He talked like a kid, like he didn't realize that everything would harden and die. Friends he once knew, stores and girls and places.

Patch knew well that the replacement would be gradual and total, until he was born in the system, everything before the turned pages in a book no one would ever pick up again.

212

"He was tougher than I thought . . . the way he looked at me."

"Who's that?" Patch said.

"Warden Riley. I mean, the big fellow hauled me right to the warden's office, didn't even fix up my nose or nothing. I dripped a little blood outside."

Patch thought of Warden Riley, knew the man would have a couple of inmates come scrub that pathway clean before the kid's blood could print a reminder of how he plied his trade.

"He yelled like I was at school or something . . . Tell you, on the outside I might have—"

"He's tough because he has to be. Don't worry about it."

"I ain't . . . I mean, I was looking right by him, that painting he's got hanging like this ain't prison but something fancier."

Patch drummed his fingers on the bed frame as he thought of his painting.

"You seen it? I reckon it . . . you know how some

people can just paint or sing or play guitar. Like Lou used to say it can be taught, but that ain't true."

"You can learn in this place, Tom."

Another sniff. "Not like that. It's like being right there, you know. Leaving this place and heading back. You reckon I can ask them to get me a copy or something, place it in my cell."

Patch thought of the kid's future, then his own, so tired he knew the fighting was done. All of it. He would hand back his library key, dip his head when the time came, acknowledge another loss in a life spent losing each fight he took on. He would say a silent prayer that Marty Tooms went quick. And then he would wait on the Brand to move again, and this time he wouldn't swing. He was not a pirate. He was not a father or friend. He did nothing noble. He lived a little life.

"You reckon he's been there?" the kid said.

Patch yawned. "Who?"

"The painter. You reckon he's been to the town or just saw a photo or something. I mean, it ain't all correct but close enough."

Patch opened his eye, the cell a blur of golds, the smell so thick it caught in his throat. He didn't speak for a long time, just played the kid's words back over before it fully dawned. "What are you talking about, kid?"

"Alabama."

Patch moved to the bars, his arms through them as he pressed close to the stone divide.

"I ought to know it. I grew up two towns over. Might as well have been a world away though. They got the fancy school and all."

Patch gripped the bars tight, the sound falling away till all he heard was the gentle rush of his own blood.

"The town . . . you're saying it's real?" Patch said.

"Of course, it's real, Pirate. I've been there a dozen times. Used to case the big houses when I was fifteen, but they got the dogs and all."

"Are you sure about this, Tom?"

"I am."

"Tell me the name."

Patch held his breath and felt the old walls beginning to crumble. His body trembled, his forehead on the rusted steel as the moment ran.

"Grace Falls. The town in the painting is Grace Falls, Alabama."

213

Not a thousand yards away Saint sat in her cruiser in the parking lot, watching the building that housed her only friend.

She wanted to tell him how close she came.

How because of him she'd led them to Eli Aaron in time to save the life of a young woman named Ashlee Miller. A woman who would go on to live her life.

She wanted to tell him how she trawled through swampland, her gun out and ready to shoot, but could not find the man that would lead them to Grace. But she was close. So very close.

At the turn of day to night she found the nearest bar and took a stool and ordered bourbon, her hands resting on the gnarled counter as a couple of guys played pool beneath a sign that flickered red over the green felt.

A television took the top corner above photographs and banners tacked to hardwood paneling yellowed by the touch of cigarette smoke. Saint placed the glass to her chin and breathed in the smell.

She closed her eyes to murmurs of conversation, took the spices deep until she might have been beside her grandmother on their porch.

She opened them only when she heard the news reporter at the Culpepper Zoo, standing before a decent crowd as they marked the opening of the new enclosure. And then the dedication, in memoriam one Jimmy Walters. Saint stared up at his face, at the smile she remembered, the decency she did not.

She launched her glass and it shattered the television screen.

There were shouts.

Saint felt a big hand on her shoulder, and she was gently led out.

"You knew the man on the screen," Blackjack said.

"He was my . . . he wasn't a man. Not a good man."

He did not ask if she was okay, he did not stay, just went back in to settle her bill and cover the damages.

She gulped air beneath a sky she did not blame or judge or understand.

214

Warden Riley knew well enough the factions that made a prison, each kings of their domain, from the captains to the guards to the inmates. Each had a hierarchy, and though it was his name alone at the highest peak, he didn't labor under the illusion that he ever had full control.

So when Blackjack filed his report, Warden Riley knew it would not have been Joseph Macauley that started the trouble, but the report also stated clear enough that it was Joseph that ended it. Riley saw to it that the bigger man, Mick Hannigan, would be transferred once he left the infirmary. The boy, White, it was a first offense, so he'd do a month in solitary, then move back into general population, where the Brand would punish him worse than Riley ever could. And as for Joseph, Riley took a little pleasure in taking back his access to death row, and in turn their access to the library, as if he had foreseen this long before.

"I take no pleasure in this," he said.

Patch stood.

"You watch yourself," Riley said. "And you know why I say that."

"Yes, sir."

Blackjack walked him back and handed over the sack of books removed from the lifers' cells.

It was only as Patch returned to the library and began shelving the returns that he felt it.

In a beaten copy of Janie Crawford's story that had lain in Marty Tooms's hands.

Patch removed a single envelope hidden well enough.

He stared at it, Tooms's handwriting a beautiful sweep of cursive so archaic that for a moment Patch did not register the name on the front of the letter.

And how he knew it.

215

Patch ate his breakfast with Tug, the noise too much, the heavy chewing and teeth meeting, the hollering and laughing as food sprayed from mouths. There were a few stares because he had handled the Brand a little too well, but most were used to it; two against one wasn't always decided by math alone.

At three Sammy came and the two sat in near silence. Sammy made no jokes, didn't grouse about Blackjack or the guards, the journey in or the heat in the visitation room. He didn't ask about Patch's hands, still cut, the blood dried dark between the lines of his knuckles.

And when it was time, he moved forward and gripped Patch tight.

"I never had a son. I think it was God's way of protecting the world. But, if I did, then—"

"Then you'd hope to hell he turned out nothing like me, Sam."

Sammy smiled.

"I owe you . . . my tab. A real man settles his debts," Patch said.

"Consider it settled. I'd have paid it a hundred times over, just for the honor of knowing you."

Sammy hugged him, the only time in his life.

Patch slipped the envelope into Sammy's inside pocket.

"You're the boy that saved the Meyer girl," Sammy said.

"The only good thing I ever did."

"There's still time."

216

They cleared much of the land themselves.

Over a long weekend Saint and Charlotte worked beneath a high sun, grunting as they tore at fronds, bent low and hacked roots of mountain laurel, witch hazel, and wild blueberry. They broke to eat a lunch of beans and ham hocks on cornbread the girl had perfected. In the shadow of the tall house and the memory of Norma, they worked to the background hum of Charlotte's bees.

On Sunday morning an arborist came and felled half a dozen oaks, didn't charge because he wanted the timber for his father's mill. Saint gave him a couple of pieces of butter cake. Charlotte groused because she'd made plans for every crumb.

They took their shovels and wheelbarrows and went back to work, clearing out a section thirty by thirty. In a week Sammy's contractor would come lay the foundations for the studio. Charlotte had balked at first, told Saint she was crazy if she wanted to waste her money like that, then eventually conceded she might like a little space of her own.

"Don't think I'll turn out like the pirate, making you all wealthy," Charlotte had said as they looked at blueprints in the gallery.

"No chance of that at all," Sammy said, a little too sadly.

Charlotte came up against a Douglas fir, found a short-handled axe in the woodshed, and hacked at it till her shoulder burned. When it fell she climbed on the carcass, stared down and spit on it and called it her bitch. Saint rolled her eyes.

By early evening the land was clear enough for the machine to come in.

"I miss Norma," Charlotte said.

"People say it gets easier, but that's only because each day we get a little closer to seeing them again."

Charlotte looked over at her.

"You're going to say you didn't think I believed because I don't go to church," Saint said.

"I see you pray."

"Maybe when we pray we're not asking for intervention. We're just reminding ourselves of the things that matter. You screw up and ask forgiveness of yourself. Someone loses their way, and you search your own mind for the guidance to help them."

Charlotte walked the perimeter of the clearing, arms out like she balanced on tightrope.

"I think your grandmother likes Sammy," Saint said.

"I think I've got a better chance of making Honey Princess than he has of slotting my grandmother."

"Slotting?"

Charlotte laughed so hard she lost her footing and sprawled. She cursed as Saint knelt to help her up.

Blood dripped from her elbow. "Something sharp down there," Charlotte said.

Above the sun set at a low angle, the light spread violet through heavy moisture over the St. Francois Mountains as Saint held something up to the purple sky.

"What is it?" Charlotte said.

Saint set it down, then dug out another, moving quickly, tilling the concretion till the shape was born. Charlotte knelt in the dirt beside her.

"Is that—"

"Bones," Saint said. "A whole lot of bones."

Charlotte stood as breeze shifted thickening trees, giving glimpses of the land behind.

Where the old Tooms house stood.

She looked back when Officer Michaels emerged from the side gate.

"What is it?" she said.

"There's been a murder."

217

Saint made the drive sixty miles out to the small town of Darby Falls.

She saw the distant spires of a church and rolled her window down because right then she longed to hear the bells.

The street carried a wholeness like the memory of the girl had been varnished over with bake sales and white paling, fall parades and striped lawns.

A lone cop waited out front.

"Still waiting on the forensic team," the cop said. He was young and skinny and anxious. "The neighbor said Richie didn't collect his newspaper this morning. Peered through the window and saw him."

"Okay," Saint said.

"You know Richie was a cop—"

"Yeah."

The cop stayed out front. She felt his anger.

Inside was the heavy movement of a grandfather clock, the green carpet bleached pale beneath each window. There was no smell at all in the lounge. Just

Richie Montrose, with a single bullet hole in his chest. It was neat and ordered, and Saint knew the real mess would be found behind his body, seeping into the cream throw.

She knew how to read a scene that was not all that complex.

Richie had known his killer.

Maybe they sat and talked first.

There was no struggle, nothing knocked down or broken. It was an execution, someone intent on removing Richie from the world with as little fuss as possible. A price to be paid.

On the mantelpiece Saint saw a single photo in a gold frame.

Callie Montrose, frozen in time.

Saint recalled going to the girl's vigil in a time so distant, yet she could still feel it entirely.

And on the table beside Richie Montrose was a letter.

Saint picked it up in a gloved hand, saw the envelope beside.

Richie Montrose.

I'll see you in hell.

It took Saint less than twenty minutes to locate a neighbor's security camera footage.

When she watched it back she saw him clear as day.

He had made no attempt to conceal himself or evade being seen.

She closed her eyes.

Her heart ached.

218

Saint drove twenty miles out of Monta Clare, away from the mountains, both windows rolled down to the vineyards and fruit stands, and, as she climbed, a network of old trade routes mostly swallowed by the flourish of woodland.

The house was bordered on each side by the sweep of fields. She pulled into the driveway and climbed out into heavy summer air, and for a while stood and looked at the Shaw house across the street where she had once taken piano lessons.

The Nix house was small for the lot, neat and simple. The white paint fresh, the porch sanded and varnished. As she strolled the path she looked out at the okame cherry, unsullied and perfect.

Saint took the deepest breath, drew her gun, and knocked and waited.

She saw his Ford so wandered around back, her shoes crunching the gravel. The land unfolded till the views stalled her; the distant fields glowed warm with canola. A couple of stables looked empty. A riding mower lay in the shade.

She tried the kitchen door, and her stomach flipped a little when she found it opened.

"Chief," she called, for a moment forgetting who carried the title, who carried the gun.

The kitchen was dated and clean. She moved down the hallway, instinct pushing her onward. The den was bright, the carpet deep synthetic shag. A line of vases at the window burst with wildflowers plucked from the land.

Three bedrooms, made up for guests she could not imagine him receiving. Saint heard the rush of water in the bathroom. She kept her gun trained and gently pushed the door.

The tank seal was broken, the flow constant.

Outside in sunlight she walked one of the tandem paths that led to the stables.

And then she saw him.

Nix carried a shovel and a smile.

Hay was bagged by the door, and a long way out she saw a couple of horses grazing.

She kept the gun aimed at him.

"Just like I taught you," he said.

He made no move to walk toward her, and for that, and a million other reasons, she loved him totally.

219

"I went to see Richie Montrose," she said.

Nix stood tall, still handsome though the years had almost caught him. He carefully placed the shovel down, slow and steady. Nix stared off toward the horses. "Smart animals. Only have one less bone than us, you know that?"

She shook her head.

"They can see three hundred and fifty degrees around themselves. Mostly monocular. The depth perception is poor. They only see the surface."

"Sometimes that's all you need."

"That's right, kid. You see a body, you find out who and how. The why don't mean shit when all is said and done. Not in the eyes of the law."

Saint wiped sweat from her head quick, her gun still locked on him. "But I still need to know."

"Aim a gun at someone and the truth will come out."

"And here I am, aiming a gun at you," she said.

He smiled once, quick, like she had grown up

CHRIS WHITAKER

under his gaze. "I'm afraid it's not my story to tell, Saint."

"I fucking hate this day," she said, and though her eyes blurred with tears she was tough and did not let them fall.

"Can I at least grab my hat? Then you can walk out with a little of the old me."

She managed a smile. "Sure, Chief."

Later, that night when she closed her eyes, she would wonder about each move she had made. And, if she knew, whether she would have done a single thing different.

She watched him walk into the stable, and she did not react until the door slammed closed and the bolt slid across.

Only then did she move.

Saint sprinted to the door.

And she screamed and she begged, and she hammered the sawn timbers till her hands tore.

Till her throat burned.

Till she heard the single gunshot.

And she turned and pressed her back to the wood and slid down to the dirt.

220

At seven-fifteen that evening, as Patch was sweeping the floors in the metal shop, the power went out.

It wasn't an unusual occurrence. Blackjack was bitching out the workmen at weekly intervals. Warden Riley reasoned the whole system would be overhauled, with a commercial-grade generator taking the place of the old Kohler.

Until then the lights flickered as the workhorse powered up and the ventilation system went down. Patch heard distant hollers from men who knew the night would be insufferable, each cell an oven. He did not stop sweeping, even when the bright lights faded and emergency yellows took their place, the long corridors dim, the whole place carrying an air of jaundice, a store soon to be out of business.

When he was done he set his broom, bucket, cloths, and cleanser back in the supply cupboard, and then he walked deep into the building and stopped by the library, where Cooper was finishing up. The last Thursday of each month Cooper took stock, complained that the state didn't pay overtime but also enjoyed the quiet.

"I have to hand you my key," Patch said. "Warden said to see out the month till we train someone up."

"You help with these boxes before you go?"

Patch heaved a couple into the storeroom. Cooper followed him in, the books numerous.

When they were done, he headed back, walked the same route burned into his mind, two lefts and then he turned right back into the main block, where the dayroom sat empty. He fussed with his eye patch, and then he walked up the metal steps and into his cell, lay down on his bunk and fished a book from beneath the mattress. The new guard locked him down for the night.

In the library Cooper took his hat from the rack and slipped it on, carried a raincoat over his arm, and reached for his worn leather satchel. Inside was a single book, an apple, and a copy of **The Examiner.** He locked up, strolled down toward B Block, and passed through two doors, the lock catching for a moment.

At the desk he dropped his keys into the drawer and waited to be buzzed out.

Blackjack thumbed the Sports section, whistled low to himself when he saw the Yankees heading toward the record books, whistled again at the Tiger chasing down all those white men.

"They reckon he's the new Jack Nicklaus," Blackjack

said as he stared at the picture of the boy, a smile on his face.

"About time, though not really my sport," Cooper said, as he signed out, flipped the page and signed in again for the morning.

"Not mine neither, though it might be now."

Cooper laughed and raised a hand to Blackjack, who hit the buzzer.

Had he looked up from his newspaper he might have noticed.

That night Cooper walked with the slightest limp.

221

The call came a little after nine and dragged Saint from broken sleep.

She'd spent the afternoon and much of the evening at the Nix house, dealing with the coroner, writing up her report, and fending off the couple of neighbors who stood at the foot of the driveway distraught. There were pieces she could not begin to figure out, questions that remained in a free float, reached for and let go.

She sat upright when she heard Himes's voice.

"Joseph Macauley escaped from prison this morning."

For a moment she sat there disheveled, took in the bright walls of her room, the slick dread that slowly dawned.

"He locked a library worker in a storeroom this morning, stole his hat and keys and then vanished."

"What the fuck do you mean he vanished?"

Himes's voice held steady, though he was clearly

eating. "Guards have it that no one left through the doors."

She found her shirt. "Guards have it? Where's the fucking cameras?"

"Main power was out. Generator gives what's strictly necessary. Still got no ventilation, and they've got quite a scene there. Big fight broke out this morning. Geriatric named Tug riled them up and then it was mayhem."

She buttoned her shirt with one hand. "He can't have gotten far. I mean, they count them, right?"

"They do. But as I said, the fight broke out and he just . . . they got the place locked down, blocked the roads. I'm sending Peterson and Lina—"

"I'll do what I can."

"I know that."

"He'll be okay."

"I'm not sure that's the concern."

"He's not a threat," Saint said.

Silence awhile. "He killed a man."

"He's not a threat."

"Do I need to send someone to you?" he said, posing the question like he was asking himself. "His daughter is in your care."

"He's not stupid enough to come back home."

"But still, do I?"

"You're questioning me. I was the one who shot him, who brought him in for something—"

"I'm not questioning you, Saint. I'm just wondering

how much pull you have with surrounding areas. I've got the map here, reckon you can reach out to four departments and get them mobile."

She caught herself in the mirror. She knew who she was, throughout. "I haven't been out that long, Himes. I know how to run a hunt."

"You'll come back in for this last one?"

222

Patch sat in woodland opposite Monta Clare High School.

Timber beds held morning glory. He had not smelled sweeter air.

When the sun rose he caught himself mirrored in a water table, and for a moment the panic took hold as he frantically smoothed at his hair and wished he might've shaved.

Someone once told him that the bad things no longer matter if you choose not to repeat them. But as he saw the first clusters of children ease into their day, he knew second chances were the hardest earn, sometimes beyond reach no matter how much you willed and pushed.

He sat there on the old fallen oak an hour till she showed.

He was not prepared for just how beautiful his daughter had become.

The moment stretched far over the St. Francois Mountains that held them in that wondrous frame.

When he took steps toward her he felt himself grow smaller, all the way back to fourteen years old, sitting beside her mother.

He was about to call out, to let her know. But then he saw the cruiser pull through the gates, and he slipped back into the trees.

He did not deserve her.

She did nothing to deserve him.

223

Saint met her at the main gate and leaned on the hood of the cruiser.

"Your father escaped from prison this morning," Saint said.

Charlotte did not react at first.

She wore a summer dress, her thick blonde hair in a single Dutch braid that curled over one shoulder. Even then as the stragglers passed they shot looks at her like she was some kind of exotic pet, as likely to bare her teeth as she was to ignore you.

"There's a chance he'll come here, and if he does you need to tell me. For him, you need to tell me. Cops around here . . . cops everywhere, they'll shoot before they ask a single question."

They drove through the town, left the car by the old railroad and walked into the woods together. Saint slowed by the spot, the memory stubborn.

"You ever know something, but sometimes you're able to convince yourself it isn't real?" Saint asked.

"Santa. I caught my grandmother eating the cookies

when I was six. Didn't stop me believing entirely. I never told anyone that."

"Because once you say it, it makes it real." Saint fixed her eyes on the water as she spoke, not wanting to see the world around. "What I said before . . . Jimmy Walters . . . the man died when . . ."

"I know enough."

"You rarely see all of someone. Not for a long time. And often, when you do, it's too late. Jimmy was kind and decent. Until he wasn't. The good parts, they still leave so much room for the bad. . . ." She watched a heron so still, slowed her heart to the cicadas' song. And then she felt Charlotte's hand slip into her own and hold it tightly.

Saint kept her tears back. "I didn't want to be your mother, when you said that. I know I don't deserve to be, to anyone. I just wanted to be your friend. Because I never . . . since I was thirteen, I didn't ever have another friend of my own."

"You said before that he might come here."

Saint nodded.

"He won't. Not for me. I never come first," Charlotte said.

"That's not—"

"I remember the first time I met him I told him Grace was his rainbow connection. Dumb kid shit. But . . . but maybe you only get one, Saint."

224

The Montrose murder was put to one side as Saint gave her entire focus to Joseph Macauley.

She spent the afternoon fielding calls from Himes, the Alwyn County Sheriff's Department, and every other police department in a couple of hundred miles around. She did not say it, but Patch had spent the better part of his life seeking, so she had little doubt he'd learned a thing or two about hiding. She saw his face on local news reports, then the national news at six. Evening news followed a dozen sightings. They gave it a lick of flavor when they ran the piece in **The New York Times,** talked of his paintings, his history, the fact that he'd been a pirate since birth.

"He's too famous," Michaels said, sitting on the corner of his desk, biceps thick beneath his shirt, anxious like he was waiting for a starter pistol to fire. "No way folk aren't noticing the eye patch."

Warden Riley stood before the prison and fielded questions like an ailing politician. Saint did not like the look in his eyes. Humiliation brought the meanest streak. He told the people of Alwyn County to lock their doors but also not to worry; they'd find him and they'd put him back where he belonged. They cut to cops moving door-to-door, to dogs straining leashes through the woodland surround.

Early evening she crossed the street and found him upstairs on the balcony, toasting the sky as the church bells rang seven.

She noted the bottle of Laphroaig, the number forty emblazoned. "You celebrating something, Sammy?"

He poured her a measure and she finally sat.

They watched the slowing of Main Street as a bruised sky reigned over mountaintops.

"I heard about Nix. I only saw him yesterday. He took some mail from me, knew the address when I asked. Always looking out for everyone, you know," Sammy said.

She ignored the buzz of her radio, the sight of Michaels fielding calls instead of locking up. She traced back her years and found Nix in each.

"I know what the press doesn't," she said.

Sammy, his skin tanned, tie loose, and gold cuf-flinks on the table. "What do you know, Saint?"

"I know that at seven last night a construction worker cut through a main cable that fed the prison."

Sammy drank.

"I mean, this cable is armored and thick, and the guy went at it with a track saw."

"Mistakes are made."

"Maybe. Then you've got Cooper, the guy that works in the library. He's tall like Patch, lean, strong enough. But he's locked in there and can't bust his way out or nothing. And you got the guard who did the last count, swears blind Patch was in his cell. I mean, he would say that; otherwise he's in for it, too. You got Blackjack on the gate that night, saw Cooper leave, but left his post in the morning because a veteran starts a brawl at morning count."

Sammy leaned back a little and lit a cigar.

"You got all these people. Some of them are clean, right. We do the backgrounds, hell, you have to be clean enough to land the job in the first place. But we've also got the feds on it. And they've got whole departments that'll roll over these guys till every secret they ever kept comes spilling. You understand me?"

Sammy ran a hand through his curls. "Not even a little bit."

"If there's money, if it leads anywhere close to you . . ."

"You want him to die in there?"

"Goddamn you, Sammy."

He held both hands up. "I didn't have anything to do with this."

"I want to believe you."

He watched the town. "But?"

"I know you love him as much as I do."

225

After twenty-four hours of fruitless searching, they'd covered a hundred miles around the prison.

Work on the new wing was halted, most of the prisoners existed in a state of frisson, and the guards kept their heads down. Local cops crawled over nearby towns, checking barns and silos and bunkers. Farmers woke in the night to flashlights on their land. A man was arrested in Arrow Port simply because he had lost an eye in Vietnam. Diners filled with out-of-town cops sipping coffee, already weary from the chase.

In Monta Clare reporters stood at the basin of Main Street and spoke of the pirate. They found the Mad House and photographed it, still standing so beautiful because Charlotte now tended it each week. She called it an investment in her future. Saint knew it was a little more than that.

By late morning Warden Riley was so mad he put his hand through the glass cabinet beside the painting. His secretary fetched a handkerchief for the cut, then beat a retreat because his mood bounced from every surface. He summoned guards and screamed at them, his cheeks crimson as spittle flew and landed on their faces. He fired the new guard, and the entire construction crew even though the delays would be costly.

"Who the hell was he close with? Someone knows something," Riley spit.

A half hour later Tug was pulled from the yard and sat in front of the warden.

"You're the one who started the trouble," Riley said.

"No ventilation . . . this place ain't fit for cattle."

"The morning count was missed because of you." Riley slammed a hand on the desk between them and issued all kinds of threats. Tug smoothed his moustache, crossed one leg over the other, and glanced at the painting, and then at the fine paneling and Persian rug.

"I once heard that there ain't much more dangerous than a man with nothing to lose."

"What the hell does that mean?" Riley said, looking to Blackjack, who shrugged.

"It means . . . there also ain't much more frustrating to you than a man with nothing to gain."

Riley paced, weighing up how many ways he could make the old man's life worse, and just how likely that was to work. "What do you want?"

An hour later a barber was fetched from the city of Hartville. He worked right there in the warden's office, Tug's white hair falling to the plush carpet.

The pompadour rose high, the sides and back cut short. The barber held out a mirror, and Tug smiled at himself. "This still how they wear it?"

Blackjack dropped his head to shade his smile, bit his lower lip when Tug requested a wet shave and a little shea butter to cool the skin.

"I also like a dot of apricot kernel for moustache maintenance. Y'all still carry that?"

The barber looked to Blackjack, who looked to Riley, who walked from the room. Tug raised a hand; he'd ridden it further than he'd hoped.

When the barber was dispatched, the room vacuumed, and the warden returned, Tug leaned back in his chair.

"I want assurance you'll bring him back safe. He's as decent a man as I ever met."

Riley nodded.

"He's got a girl up there in North Dakota. Bismarck. Ain't nothing stronger than the want of the human heart."

Riley ordered Blackjack to take Tug straight to solitary.

They walked out into the sun together in silence.

At the door Blackjack handed Tug a large book on soap production. "Cooper said this came in for you."

In that small and dank cell Tug breathed the richness of sandalwood oil, lay back on the mattress, and flipped open the book.

Inside was the June 1965 issue of **Playboy**.

He flipped to the twelve-page pictorial and smiled at Ursula Andress.

And then he closed his eyes and smiled again, this time at the thought of Riley and his cops heading a thousand miles in the wrong direction.

226

A hundred miles to the south, Patch sat by the bluff and followed the snake of the Mississippi River up to the oxbow. His hair cropped close, face clean-shaven. Beside him sat a blue leather satchel with clothes and money and most everything he would need. He had found it in the trunk of Cooper's car before he dumped it a couple of miles from anywhere.

He wore a ball cap that shaded his face, and though it bothered him something awful he left the eye patch in his pocket and wore dark glasses.

Patch strolled along till a sunset chased iron water from bold to abstract, and land and sky met for a moment he wished he could paint.

He found a copse and beside it lay down low before the sedges, his bag a pillow as he waited on nightfall. The next day the checkpoints would move and he would cross into Tennessee.

The next day he would be closer to her.

227

Saint drove forty-five minutes to an apartment complex so soulless it called her back to her first days as an agent.

As with the Eli Aaron hunt, Himes had her on temporary reinstatement, gave her access to everything they had and told her to use what she needed. She did not need much.

Cooper lived alone, the place devoid of life. His clothes hung on an open rack. A single sofa in front of a single window that overlooked a parking lot, the blinds drawn, but light glowed through and lit the man who regarded her without interest.

"You've had a rough time," Saint said.

He was tall and slim, and his face carried the kind of symmetry that should have given him confidence as he went through his statement once more. She checked it against the original, found he hadn't strayed.

"I don't have anything on you, no background. Nothing," she said. The prison office was overrun,

Warden Riley's line so busy his secretary pulled the plug.

He spoke of a staid life, had a decade working in public libraries before he took the job at Hannington. No wife or kids, no mention of the preceding years.

"There'll be more questions. You should get a lawyer," she said, as she stood to leave. He stood with her, polite as she headed toward to the door.

It was as she turned that she saw it.

A single photograph beside the bed.

She crossed to it, struck by the likeness of the dark-haired girl. Saint picked up the small gold frame, the only show of life in the place.

Like a forgotten memory.

Or a reminder.

She studied it intently, so faded it was hard to place detail, the full lips and green eyes so familiar.

Saint looked at him again, then stepped toward the door. "I'll be seeing you, Mr. Cooper."

"Actually, Cooper is my first name."

Saint turned.

This time he met her eye and smiled. "My surname is Strike. My name is Cooper Strike."

228

The news vans departed. Lacey's emptied till only the locals remained, and over sweet cream pancakes, sausage links, and coffee Saint listened as talk finally turned to Nix.

The pace would slow enough for them to mourn the man who had kept order for near thirty years. A couple of old guys raised cups of coffee.

Charlotte picked at her French toast, then the two walked to Monta Clare High.

"It's tonight," Charlotte said. "They execute the man that took Patch."

"Yes. You want to talk about it?"

"Will it hurt?"

"No."

Charlotte stared at her, mouth tight. "It should. Why does he get to go out easy?"

"I'll bet there hasn't been much that's been easy for Marty Tooms these last years."

At the station she took a call from Himes, who told her Patch was likely headed to North Dakota, where Warden Riley said he had a girl. Saint rolled her eyes, then filled him in on Cooper Strike.

"Joseph Macauley brought his missing sister home," Himes said.

"Gave her life back."

Saint hung up in time to watch Jasper stroll out of his law office and cross the street. He took the seat opposite her and dusted lint from his lapel.

"Nix left you his house."

"Excuse me?"

Jasper took a monogrammed handkerchief from his pocket and wicked the sweat from his forehead. "He dropped off his last will the morning before . . . before it happened."

"Why?" she said, a question he could not answer.

He placed a stack of papers and a set of keys down on her desk. "It'll take a while to go through, but in case you want to keep the place tidy. I know he's got horses."

"What the hell I am supposed to do with a horse?" she said.

He checked his reflection in the glass cabinet behind her, his salt-and-pepper hair lending him an air of distinguished, despite the ambulance chasing. "I don't believe he had anyone else."

Saint walked home alone, where she met a forensic examiner named Stevie Harris in the yard, her tech van across the driveway. Saint had almost forgotten about the bones they had found in the yard.

The two walked down to the clearing, work delayed a few days.

"You building?" Stevie said.

"A studio."

Stevie had been there an hour, dug out a little but stopped when the picture cleared enough. She had not brought a team; the job was of low importance.

"The bones . . . canine," Stevie said. Her hair was long but tied, her eyes dark and tired. "Been there a long time."

Saint thanked her, walked back to the van to see her off when Stevie fished something from a clear bag and handed it to her. "Found this beside them. You can toss it out."

Saint looked down at the simple gold tag, caked in grime, a couple of strands of leather entwined it. Inside the phone rang and she made it just in time to catch the call.

229

Himes spoke with a mouth full of something. "We brought in the construction worker who cut the power, but got nowhere. Guy's a veteran and tells it like it's a genuine mistake, easily made."

"Name?"

"Owen Williams."

Saint pinched the bridge of her nose. "Let me guess, daughter named Lucy?"

She heard the rustle of paper but did not need wait for the reply.

Saint fielded another call, this time from the James Connor Correctional Facility, and she thanked Warden Thompson for getting back to her.

They made a little small talk, with Thompson unable to hide the cheer from his voice when he asked after Warden Riley.

"I just wanted to know if Joseph Macauley was close with anyone during his time incarcerated with you. I know it was a long time back but—"

Thompson's voice was rich and smooth. "Just a

guard. Looked out for the boy. Other than that I don't recall. You think he made a connection that led to this?"

"No. I'm checking the detail, is all. This guard, what was his name?"

"Darnell Richardson."

Saint searched her memory, came up blank, so she thanked him and filed it, then climbed into the attic, the space so hot sweat gathered, her forearms slick as she found the box. She blew dust from it, dragged it down the steep ladder on her shoulder, and for the first time in a dozen years, opened the Macauley abduction file.

She thought something might reach out and let her know where he was headed, where he had been. She played the tape over the big speaker, almost smiling when she heard his voice.

Backdropped by Grace and everything he remembered, she turned the pages of her first case, stuck notes to the board in her office, and recounted each photograph and interview transcript. Soil reports from the Tooms farm. Fingerprints and material analysis. She worked long into the afternoon, Charlotte with her grandmother, Saint breaking only to sit on the porch when her mind clogged. She found her old map: locations where he'd hit banks, met with families, painted scenes Grace had once painted for him.

It was early evening when she came to Tooms. She sat back in the old leather chair, breathed the smell of cigar smoke, and for a stunning moment could not believe she would never get to speak with her grandmother again.

"We've been through this. I was looking for the dog," Marty Tooms's voice filled the room. Saint closed her eyes and saw him clear. Right up until they arrested him he hadn't wavered, hadn't drifted from his version of the truth.

"I don't know the breed, maybe a cross because his legs were too long, and his ears hung almost to his eyes. I bought him a collar in case . . . I know they sometimes pick them up. Called him Scout. Bought him a medal, too. I used to worry he'd end up in some pound. The way they put them to death like that . . . no rights at all."

"So you believe in the right to life?" Nix said.

Saint frowned at the question.

Tooms paused for a long time.

"You don't believe in playing God?" Nix said, calm in his voice.

"I'm a doctor. It's my job to play God. I spend my waking hours trying to get better at it."

"To save lives but not take them."

"They say it's humane, but I can't help thinking it's murder under any other guise."

His story had seemed tall, his reason for being in those woods that morning.

Nix again, his tone unforgiving, like listening to a ghost. **"So it just showed up now and then. And you fed it? And then it stopped showing, so** you searched for the thing, even though it wasn't yours to search for. A stray mongrel."

"You're not a dog person."

"I was. Once."

A cough. "I don't know what to say. It just appeared on my land, sometimes coming from the woodland behind. It was too skinny. I wanted . . . I guess helping is in my blood."

She played it so loud the silence crackled. And then she wound it back, played it again, and reached for the map of Monta Clare. She noted the land boundaries as he told that the dog appeared from the woodland.

She traced the line and came to her grandmother's land, the shrubs knotted too tight to pass.

Too tight for a human to pass.

Saint stood and fished out the gold tag from the trash. She ran the faucet hot and washed the dirt, then set at it with a wire brush, gently bringing it back.

She stared at the faint letters as they stood proud, then traced a finger over the indented curves.

SCOUT

230

A day in Union City beneath a fierce sun.

He'd walked since first light, stopped only to notice the lake, more bayou. The sodden willow limbs that teased the water, their roots sunk beneath combs of algae. He saw logjams, shifting sandbars, and distant cypress. He made sure to breathe in all of it. He rode three buses, head down, but no one noticed him or cared much. When they passed cop cars he breathed even, too tired to worry, too close to turn back.

On city streets he kept his cap pulled low but moved with a casualness as he shopped windows, then settled into a corner booth at a coffee shop and nursed a coffee. He stood in the shadow of the first monument to the unknown confederate dead, for a moment thought of his father. He'd take an awkward route, board whichever bus left soonest. The first would leave Union City at eight-thirty the next morning. It would head back up to Evansville where he'd spend a little over five hours waiting for the 1167, which would carry him through the night and across the state.

At four in the morning, as the first cardinals sang, he would step out into Alabama.

231

That evening Saint sat at her desk with the Macauley file.

Patch had derailed her thinking, her process. The fallout from Richie Montrose and Nix would amount to more work than she had handled since she took over.

Deputy Michaels took a call out back, his girl-friend riding him about the hours. Though Saint told him to head home, he'd sat there like he knew he'd be needed.

She ran through what she knew and what she needed to know.

Nix had taken his gun and driven fifty minutes to Darby Falls, where he'd walked into the home of Richie Montrose and fired a single shot into his chest. She knew that Tooms might've been telling the truth about the dog, but also how that didn't mean shit. That he could've been searching for it, and an opportunity presented itself in the shape of Misty. So many variables, nothing made sense but the coldest fact. Callie Montrose's blood was found in Marty Tooms's farmhouse.

She was about to head out when the phone rang. Saint expected to hear Himes's voice but instead it was Lucy Alston from the lab.

"Got some prints for you," Lucy said.

"The letter," Saint said, her mind running to Richie Montrose and the envelope she found beside him. **I'll see you in hell.**

"Got a match to Nix."

"Right."

Saint closed her eyes and rubbed her temples at the beginning of a headache. "Nothing else."

"Actually a couple. Lifted clear enough from the paper."

Saint gripped the receiver tight.

"Match to Martin Tooms. And Joseph Macauley."

232

Saint used the key to let herself into the Nix house.

Barely a day had passed, and she felt the void like a pain lodged deep in her chest. A glow from the landing light, the shade orange, throwing everything a little sullen, a little softer. She moved quickly from room to room but found nothing much at all. No signs of life outside of his job, no hint at the depth of the man she had looked up to her whole life.

Utility bills and vehicle insurance. Details of a checking account that carried a little over twenty thousand dollars. In the bathroom cabinet she found Advil and cologne and shaving foam and toothpaste. There was nothing hidden at the back of his closet behind his dress shirts and navy pants and old uniform.

She stood at the window in his bedroom and stared out at the land and the buckle between hills like the clouds weighed too heavy out there. And then she recalled his last moments. How she had drawn on him and seen no fear, just acceptance of an ending he had expected. She thought of his face, how he had emerged in slacks and a shirt even though he had come from the stable.

Her eyes fell to it.

There were too many stars out as she walked the path, her flashlight a guide as she drew up beside the stable. The horses had already been collected by a neighbor with enough land.

She took a breath as she opened the heavy door, and inside the scene had mercifully been tended because the red hay had been swept up neatly.

Saint pulled a cord to drear light from a naked bulb, saw nothing and sighed, until she looked up.

The ladder was strong, and she placed her feet carefully as she opened the hatch and emerged into a preserve of loft space neatly boarded and insulated. She heaved herself through. Boxes were stacked high, and in the center was a single rocking chair.

She carefully took a box down, sat back on the chair, and began to open the albums.

Hundreds of photos.

Nix through the years.

She traced them back, from recent to rookie, his moustache thinner back then.

And then before.

She sat back stunned.

For it told the very beginning of a story that ran a lifetime. She picked another one out, taken up by the Meramec River, their smiles unalloyed and beautiful. She saw Thanksgivings and white winters, easy summers and mountain hikes. Though most, she noticed, were taken on the same acres of land. A sanctuary she had struggled to understand the importance of.

Chief Nix once told her that to love and be loved was more than could ever be expected, more than enough for a thousand ordinary lifetimes.

And then, on the shelf, placed haphazardly, as if it would be discovered by chance on some distant date, she saw a single letter.

And on the envelope, her name.

233

She woke Deputy Michaels, told him to shut the fuck up and listen. And then she told him to get the office of U.S. District Judge Mark Cully. To call Attorney General John Lester's office. The Missouri Supreme Court. To wake the whole fucking state.

Marty Tooms was innocent.

"I can do all this," he said. "But in a little over an hour Marty Tooms will be executed."

Saint sprinted to the cruiser and flashed the lights as she found the highway. She called the prison as she drove, the lines jammed. Only Judge Cully had the direct line. Tires wailed as she passed a line of trucks, one hand on the wheel and the other calling the Life Project. The phone rang so long she cut when Michaels called through.

"Tooms doesn't have a lawyer. No one to make the calls."

"You get Cully?"

"Jammed. Protestors."

"Fuck, Michaels. You drive to Cully's and grab him by his fat face and make him listen."

"Yes, Chief."

She knew he'd go, a direct order was what Michaels lived for.

She pared miles of darkness, the blue lights meeting a herd of deer, their black eyes catching moonlight as Saint saw the dash blink once. The fuel gauge red. She screamed every curse word she knew as she slammed her hand against the dash. Saint kept her foot down until the car died and she almost cried out.

On a cold stretch of highway she planted her feet in the middle of the road and flagged down an old Jeep, hauled the driver from his seat, and aimed her gun at his face when he moved to resist. She spun the truck around and left him in the dust. She opened the windows to the night heat, cursed herself for leaving her cell phone in the squad car. No radio, no time to stop at a phone booth, no way of knowing if any of their messages had landed.

She tuned in the radio and found a news station debating capital punishment, same each time. The heavy truck shuddered as she cleared a hundred, then flashed her hazard lights and tore down the wrong side of the road past an old man who raised a fist from the window of his Dodge.

When she saw the sign, the turn, and lights she felt her adrenaline kick harder. Guards had been brought from the category B over in Fordham, and they built out a blockade at the mouth of the track. She careered through ROAD CLOSED signs and took the dirt road at seventy, each bump sending her hurtling high from her seat as she gripped the wheel tight. Half a mile from the prison lights she met a rolling roadblock, its feet embedded in the dirt, the yellow low-bed truck hitched to it empty.

She jumped from the Jeep and ran, her sneakers in the dust as she finally hit the mayhem. News reporters cast their lenses over heavy placards planted in the soil that declared Human Life over Human Vengeance, Premeditated Murder Promotes Violent Society. She hustled past clusters sitting in peace on the ground, hands joined in prayer led by a pastor and beside him a man with a thin white wooden cross. Candles burned, and cops kept peace on the most violent night.

Saint pushed her way to the line, screamed her way to guards who shoved her back, not heeding her badge, more than ready for trouble. She called out her name and rank, asked for Blackjack and Warden Riley. She was ignored.

Saint felt the panic rise as cries intensified. She shoved her way deeper into the crowd. Only when she heard those first notes, and those gathered sang of his presence every passing hour, did she wipe her tears and check her watch and see that second hand make its final approach that day.

I fear no foe.

She thought of Nix and Tooms, and Patch and

Misty, and the random convergence of innocence and guilt. She thought of two decades laid out like a twisting path. Her grandmother above them waiting to shepherd another into the lost kingdom.

"Goddamn," she cried. "Where are you? Why is it all on us?"

Saint said her silent prayer.

Drew her gun.

Aimed it toward the sky and shattered the heavens with her fire.

234

They sat together.

Tooms was not cuffed. There was no trace of the hours before, of how close he had come to losing his life. She marveled at what a person could endure.

"How was that last meal?" she said.

He laughed, the tension spilling from him. "Grilled cheese. Ain't a better meal on this earth."

She caught the inflection and smiled.

The night sky made it through the smallest window as he finally sat back and talked.

"I still remember the smell that morning. Summer . . . it's got its own feel in Monta Clare, right. Before the heat wakes for the day. Nix had a dog growing up. I guess if you're a dog person you get it, how they're family. His face when that mutt showed up . . ."

She let him speak; the drain of the day before blazed in her eyes, her skin and bones.

"I was just out looking for Scout."

Saint smiled. "I found him. He disturbed the hive

in our yard. Bees will kill to protect their queen, even if it means giving their own lives."

Blackjack knocked, set two coffees down, but not before Saint noticed his name badge.

Darnell Richardson.

For a moment she stared at him, his smile and the kindness in the big man's eyes. She sighed as he left them, no longer knowing which side of the coin was up.

Tooms breathed the steam.

"I know what you did for those girls," Saint said.

He did not speak, still, maintaining an oath he would die to protect.

She smiled again, but it was entirely broken. "You gave them a chance when no one else would. Maybe you saved lives."

"But not all of them."

She thought of him visiting high schools, hanging around outside in case they sought him. Just being there so they knew they were not alone. She thought of the girls, some not even older than she had been back then, turning up at the farmhouse and being led to the room where he took one life to save another. No questions were asked. No blame apportioned. Girls from church towns, from unforgiving families. Wealthy. Poor. He gave them their lives back. And then someone found out.

"Tell me about Eli Aaron," she said.

"Eli Aaron was a bad man. I knew that the day he

came into the school to photograph the children. I heard him, with Misty Meyer, with the other girls. So I went to his house, to tell him, to let him know someone was watching him."

"And he—"

"He let me know someone was watching me."

"That's why we found your hair fibers at the Aaron house."

He nodded.

She felt the chill. "That's how he chose them. He was doing God's work. He chose penitent sinners. The pregnant girls who came to you for an abortion."

Tooms said nothing.

"You could have warned them," Saint said.

"I thought he was just taking their money, promising to make them models. When he told me he knew what I was doing I worried for them. That he might tell their parents or something. And I did try to tell them, but I didn't even take their names. It was safer for them."

Saint closed her eyes. "So you took to waiting outside the schools. To try and warn them to be cautious."

"I should have done more to protect them."

She placed a hand over his. "You did enough. You did everything."

There was no pride, no sense of doing right. He stated a fact because it was just that.

"You told me you killed Grace," she said.

He straightened a little. "I treated Joseph's mother for over a decade. I watched her getting worse. It was my duty to inform Social Services."

"But you didn't."

He shook his head. "I failed that boy fully."

"You lied about murdering her."

He nodded. "He lost so much of his life. And I knew he would spend the rest of his days searching. Nix told me she wasn't real. That Joseph conjured her."

"You wrote me . . . you wanted to tell me because you knew Nix wouldn't agree to it."

"I gave Joseph an out. I was being put to death anyway. Grief is a part of life. It's the unknown that truly ruins us."

She thought of Patch.

"When I saw Joseph here I cried that night because I knew I had failed. I knew I had made the wrong choice. To hear him speak, to offer compassion and hope when he himself had none. I didn't deserve to look him in the eye. And then he escaped. And in those hours when I sat with the chaplain and waited for them to put me to death, I used my last prayer to ask that he never returns."

235

Saint took a deep breath because she knew what would come. But she was in no way ready for it. "Tell me about Callie Montrose."

Marty Tooms cried then. He did not stop to breathe, to explain. He just cried in a way that was difficult to witness, an unraveling of a story he had held inside so tightly and for so long.

When he calmed he drank a little. "The hemorrhage. It's always a risk, but there was just . . . I just couldn't stop the bleeding."

Saint had not realized she was crying, too.

"I didn't know he'd come back with you, and he'd see it on my face, because I could never lie to him—" he cried again. A wrenching sound.

"Who?" Saint said, but knew. She thought of the photographs. Saint knew love, she knew it was sewn into the smallest gestures, the kindnesses barely perceived. And she knew it was responsible for the largest and darkest acts, the sacrifices and the rawest pain.

And when Tooms spoke his name, she heard it in his voice. "Nix."

"That first night I showed at your house—" she began.

"Was the night Callie died. You led Nix to my house, and he saw what I had done. I told him to call it in, but he wouldn't."

"So he made it go away," Saint said.

Tooms nodded, like he could no longer find the energy to speak.

"You met him at school," she said, and for a moment found a smile.

"I loved him the first time we spoke. Of course, it was different back then, with the church and all. The judgment."

"Maybe not so different still," she said.

"We never hid it. Just didn't advertise it. We had our place at the farm, and we shut out the world and just—"

"Lived," she said.

He smiled. "Loved."

Saint took a moment. "He didn't know what you were doing? Helping these pregnant girls?"

"I would never have told him. It would have put him in an impossible position. I just, I saw what was happening. Hell, what is still happening out there."

She took his hand, and it was a moment that stunned him. Maybe it was because he had not felt the warmth for so long, or because he didn't feel he deserved it. But when Saint looked at him she saw nothing but heart.

"Nix didn't want you to tell the truth?"

"Oh, he did. He came to visit me each week. Over a thousand times he threatened and blustered and damn near broke. He told me to tell the judge I was helping the girls. That's why the blood was there."

"But you wouldn't save yourself."

Tooms wiped his eyes. "I wouldn't betray Callie. She deserved my protection in death as she had done in life. I wouldn't betray Nix. And I know how that sounds."

"Noble, Dr. Tooms. It sounds nothing but noble."

"Callie was pregnant. You know that. But when she lay there, when she started bleeding, when she started to fade, she told me who the father was."

Saint took a breath, and she thought of Nix and Richie Montrose. And she thought of Patch and Eli Aaron. She thought of the best people and the worst, and how the two so often collided.

"I couldn't tell anyone without betraying Callie," Tooms said.

"So how did Nix—"

"He always suspected something was wrong. Callie went to see him a little while before she disappeared. Got four buses just to find a cop who wasn't linked to her father."

"Nix sent her back," Saint said.

"The girl went a little off the rails, and so he thought it was best handled by her father."

"The father that raped her," Saint said, empty.

"I wrote to Richie. I needed him to know that someone knew. That he wouldn't live out his days in peace. I wrote to Richie, and I gave the letter to Patch. I thought maybe he'd give it to Sammy to post."

"What did it say?" Saint asked, though knew.

"Something that needed to be said. Something I couldn't post out of here because it would have been seen as a threat when they checked my mail."

He took a breath, calmed a little.

"Callie Montrose. Where is she now?" Saint said.

"I didn't ever ask. I just told Nix she deserved to rest somewhere beautiful. Somewhere she wouldn't ever be troubled or disturbed again."

Saint exhaled till her shoulders dropped.

She hugged him for a long time, and when she turned to leave she wondered at the price of trust, and the toll it took to offer it, and to betray it.

236

Past Greek revival plantations and hardscrabble farms far from anywhere, he kept his face close to the glass window and watched the moonlit confluence as the sleeping town rose like a prosperous afterthought. The Cumberland Plateau lost in the distance to forested ridges over a land that carried such fractured history.

At a phone booth he made the call.

"I'm sorry," he said, when he heard her voice.

"You shouldn't call," Charlotte said, almost in a whisper though he knew that Saint would be at the station. "Why did you run?"

"I think I found her."

"She's real," she whispered.

"A town called Grace Falls. It's just like the painting, Charlotte."

"There's cops looking for you. It's on the news. Saint said they'll—"

"I came to see you. I came to tell you that—"

On the other end he heard the street door.
He heard Saint call out to the girl.
He heard the dial tone.

237

The telephone rang as Saint was about to climb into bed, the long day almost over.

In the bathroom she'd splashed water on her face. Blackjack would watch Tooms as he was led back to his cell. In time questions would be answered, until then Saint placed a call to Jasper and told him to head to the prison, where Tooms would retain him. Jasper had groused about the hour, sobered at the revelation, salivated at the attention it would generate. Saint did not know what the future would bring, but she did know that Marty Tooms would walk free in the coming days; whatever his wrongdoing, he had served his time. He had paid enough.

Saint listened as Himes talked.

Too tired to even summon anger because deep down she knew he was right to have put a trace on her telephone line.

She checked on Charlotte and saw her sleeping.

The girl would not forgive the betrayal.

Even if Saint brought her father back safely.

238

Patch could not sleep after, felt each moment on that bus like a lifetime of waiting, his stomach empty.

At Rowan Bridge a woman moved to use the restroom and stared at him for so long he contemplated leaving at Birmingham, instead held his nerve and waited the hour alone, the night still warm enough that the driver kept his window down.

An hour from dawn Patch took his small bag from the seat and stepped out into Alabama air. A few cars cruised by slow till they crested the hill and dropped into half dark. A full moon held as the sun rose east of the horizon.

In the river city of Montgomery, the white dome of the state capitol stood.

The streets filled with sounds of morning workers as Patch rode his last bus from the city, his head lying back on the seat rest until he climbed out, checked his map, and breathed deep as he walked the last miles.

At the sign he reached up and touched the lettering.

GRACE FALLS

239

He passed family homes and winding avenues, reached Main Street and stopped dead because he already knew the place. He almost rubbed his eye at the sight, almost reached out to check it was real. Each building lifted from his painting. He still heard her voice like it was moments before.

I'll tell you what I miss. I miss when the moon slips under water and turns everything blue. I miss the four faces of time. I miss yellow brick roads and tin men. I miss silver woods.

Green awnings hung over bleached white arches, red brick laid like royal carpet in the center of the sidewalk. He walked up to the gold-faced clock, stared at the time like it had been frozen for twenty-five years. Silver maples held the horizon.

In the Moon Under Water Diner he sat dazed in a red booth and ordered coffee from a girl too young to look so tired. He watched the waking of a town he felt he knew well, trying to ignore the frantic turns of his stomach as people walked to the bakery and the grocery store.

"You lost or something?"

He looked up at her. She wore an apron, and her hair fell in chestnut waves. Serious eyes but the corners of her mouth stood in amusement. "You want a refill?"

"No. Thank you. I'm not lost. I don't think I'm lost."

Patch sat there an hour, till sunlight warmed the street and the fountain at the far end spilled water over the stone pool around it. It was a beautiful town, not all that different from Monta Clare. He looked down at the scars that crossed his knuckles. He saw a woman with a stroller bend to fuss with a kid. Normal lives flickered like fireflies, so luminous he wanted to reach out and hold on to them awhile.

"Now you say you're not lost, but you've got that look about you, like maybe you are but you're too stubborn to ask for help. My daddy was like that. He once drove a hundred miles in the wrong direction because he was too proud to flag someone down."

Patch smiled.

"You reckon it's a man thing?"

He nodded. "Could be."

Her name tag read Katie and she took the seat opposite, bent forward and rubbed her calves. "Nine hours on my feet."

"Must be tough."

She waved a hand. "Tough is not paying the bills. And round here, lot of rich folk now so the tips are decent. Unless the cops come in, treat the place like home. One time even grabbed at my ass like the badge gave him warrant."

"Truth is I'm looking for something, but I don't really know where I am."

She smiled. "So tell me, just how long you been lost?"

"I don't recall a time when I wasn't."

Behind her a small television was fixed to the corner wall. He knew that a few days before she might have seen his face on it.

"You want to tell me what you're looking for?" She raised one eyebrow.

"A house."

She raised the other to match.

"It's . . . it was white."

"You're looking for a white house in the South." She smiled.

"There's a long driveway reaching to it, with tall trees on either side. Trees that reach over like they're linking arms to protect the people that walk under them."

She stopped smiling and listened.

"And grass so green it might have been painted. And in flower beds beneath sash windows butterfly weeds glow like campfire."

She stopped rubbing her calves and motioned for him to go on.

"There's shutters at the windows, and a balcony that runs around the entire building. There's a staircase that winds its way from the yard to the bedroom, and in winter you can see it because the praying trees shed leaves till the house emerges like a snowflake on a summer day."

She stared at him.

He swallowed, afraid to ask about what he now saw in her eyes. "You know the house?"

Katie slowly smiled. "Yeah. I know the house."

240

Saint touched down at Birmingham-Shuttlesworth International Airport not twenty-four hours after she saved the life of Marty Tooms.

She jogged through the airport, passed weary travelers hauling cases, found the rental desk, and collected her Taurus.

Saint opened the window to Alabama air, found the highway, and hit the gas.

241

The Bleached House lay a mile out of town.

Shadblow leaned over a half mile of winding fence beside woodland trails and cross vine. A river cut its way, and Patch stepped near and saw the silvers and golds of crappie.

He walked slow, like he knew it was the last stop on a railroad long since forgotten.

And as he drew nearer to the ornate gates, with each step he shed a year from his life, till he was nothing but thirteen again.

He found the rusted metal parted enough to let him through.

And just like she said, the trees curved above him, their arms linked in prayer as he noted the grass too green. So when the house came to view just like she had painted it, he knew he had found her.

A mirror of the Mad House, only hers had long since caved to the elements. There were signs of a restoration that might take a lifetime, the timber framed windows rotted, the stucco broke, and the pathway cracked and uneven.

He walked the last steps in something like a dream, too tired to smile, to do anything but press his head lightly to the heavy wood. Grand pillars of peeling white rose on either side. The arch above carried glass stained in midnight gray.

He raised his hand and knocked and took a step back.

242

Seven hundred miles from there, the kid Tom White reached his third day in solitary, closing in on ninety hours, his body not used to such strain. The mattress thin like paper on a bed of steel. The smell burned his throat; the steady drip of brown water from the rusted pipe that speared the wall above loudened with each fall till he placed his fingers into his ears. His stomach ached with hunger. Till then he had thought he was tough. Tough like he'd been at school, where he could swing till the other boys couldn't. Tough like when his foster father started in on him. Right then he knew he'd take a beating over Warden Riley's open call to leave him there till he learned his mind was not his anymore.

He cried with the shame.

Then he stood and pressed his face to the bars and hollered till the guard did his check.

"I need to see the warden," he said.

The guard just stared, waiting.

"I know where the pirate is."

243

Patch waited five minutes, knocked a dozen times, and then peered through a window hazed by seasons, where algae clung to the copings.

Inside he saw bare floors, a large reception room where wildflowers stood in empty milk bottles, the only sign of warmth in a room where wood shutters were propped against tall windows so thin Patch could only imagine the bite of winter.

Another window and he saw wallpaper heaped by baseboard and left there to yellow by the sun. He moved along sunken beds where no flowers or weed grew, and he cupped his hands to the glass and saw more empty rooms in shades of disrepair, one with a couple of paint cans beside the feet of a wooden ladder.

Down the side of the house he came to stone jardinieres and purple wildflower and a small water feature that had long since dried out.

The grass had been cut, but the size of the grounds was overwhelming, and in the distance Patch saw two barns, and beyond that hills that followed a wide arc around the land.

He tried the back door but found it locked, and through a cracked glass pane saw a kitchen counter lined with jars and pots of homemade jams and preserves. He saw a stove. He saw signs of life.

He was about to circle the house when he heard the faint crackle of thunder.

Patch looked up as the storm moved in.

244

Saint slowed as she breached the town of Grace Falls and watched kids freewheeling down a wide street where trees towered every fifty yards. She pulled over and checked her map. Big houses occupied wide lots, the camellia bold against white clapboard. She traced a finger over the route as she took the call and listened to Himes.

"You there?" he said.

"I am."

"I pulled satellite images of the town. I know where the house is."

Saint gripped the phone tight as he gave her the road name. She watched a mother stroll with her children, the youngest on reins. A distant storm cloud gathered.

"I hear Alabama State Troopers are moving with local PD," Himes said.

"They'll shoot him dead."

"So you find him first."

245

On the first strike of lightning Patch ran over to the nearer barn that stood in the crest of wheatfield beside the house.

He opened the large door to six bents, the bays between empty. A ladder at the far side led to a mow he could not see.

Rain lashed down so hard he closed the heavy door behind him.

The darkness total.

The days caught him then, the fear and the hope, the sheer exhaustion of it all.

He sat on hard wood slats and smelled hay and closed his eye.

The sky chorused and rained down harder on the old roof as he wondered what he had found, certain it was her home but not knowing if she'd lived there since, if the place had been sold or just left to ruin.

There was nowhere left to look, no avenues he had

not walked down, no corner of his mind that had not been sifted.

Patch lay back and swallowed drily, and for a wretched moment felt tears brim in his eye as he tried not to feel the devastation he had wreaked, the lives he had dictated in his search for a girl that had spanned the better years of his life. From boy to man. From Monta Clare to robbing banks, art exhibitions to prison. He had lost a daughter, a friend, a love, and a parent. He had lost more than could ever be counted.

And when he felt a hand slip into his, he knew that it was in his mind, that it could not be real. That maybe it had never been real at all.

His breath caught as she let go and traced her way up his chest and across the hollow of his throat.

Her fingers moved through his tears as she gently stroked his cheek.

He tried to shake her from his head, to find himself once more, but then she spoke in a whisper he could recall, from a memory he would never forget.

"Someone once told me you could hear a smile."

And when he spoke he was thirteen, and he had his chance to do it all again. "Bullshit."

Her voice began to break. "Say something and I'll tell you if you are."

"Though it's dark, I'll always find you. Though you're stronger than me, I'll always make sure that you're safe. To me, you'll always come first."

"You're smiling."

"Because it's true."

She pressed her head to his.

"Grace," he said.

"Yes."

246

Alabama State Troopers swept through the town of Grace Falls, moving from door to door, flashing photographs and checking garages. They blocked the two roads in and out of town as they waited for Dallas County cops. Agents from the FBI office in Birmingham were deployed. The rain fell in waves so heavy flak jackets were zipped and caps pulled on as boots trudged mud.

When they came to Main Street they split into four teams and tried to maintain calm as riled-up locals headed home to fetch shotguns and hunker down till both storms passed.

Inside the Moon Under Water Diner they found a waitress named Katie Mitcham sitting out back, seeing off the last of a night shift with a coffee, a cigarette, and a level of amusement that pissed State Trooper Sadler off something rotten as he crowded her beneath a sun canopy sagging with the fall.

"We're looking for this man," Sadler said, and Katie took the photograph from him and squinted.

"Nice looking."

"He's a murderer."

She looked some more as he waited, and then she shook her head. "I ain't seen nobody like that."

247

Patch could not breathe.

For a long time he gripped her tightly, and she held onto him like he was the life preserver she had been without. He pressed his lips to the parting of her hair and breathed her.

He ran his hands over her arms and up her back to the nape of her neck. He traced her face lightly and knew for certain, for it was a face he had painted a hundred times and dreamed of a thousand more.

The relief did not come. His bones ached for her, his heart and his head, and he gripped the cloth of her dress tightly in his fingers, his hands shaking, his body shaking.

And as lightning flashed and made its way through gaps at the height of the gable, she illuminated.

The delicate purse of her lips, the full green of her eyes. He looked at her skin and legs and feet and hands. Her hair was richly red, her dress pinched at a narrow waist. A mirror of **Grace Number One,** so close it was like she could not have been real.

"I found you," he said.

"I waited for you," she said.

248

Saint drove out of town in the shadow of the storm and the local cops, the cruisers numbering in double digits as word spread far. Rain battered the windshield, falling so hard for a moment she stopped dead in the middle of the quiet road and waited it out, looking for a break, looking for calm however distant.

She found it when the house came to view.

The very same house that had hung on the wall above her piano for a lifetime.

Saint watched it like a mirage, like at any moment it would vanish and she would return to chasing shadows.

She eased the car up to the gates, climbed out, and set off up the driveway on foot, not moving to shield herself from the rain, not noticing that her hair matted down and her clothes soaked through.

Saint knocked on the door, followed in Patch's footsteps as she rounded the house and peered through the windows, looked for life but found none at all.

She looked out over land that drowned beneath midnight cloud, the thunder so deep she felt each roar.

Her eyes found the barns.

One stained a shade of red that had not dulled, the timber newer.

She crossed the grass, did not flinch when lightning struck the horizon, the air charged as she made it to the red barn and gently pushed the door.

249

They lay side by side in the darkness in a mirror of before.

"You can't be here," she said, and there was something frantic in her words. "But I'm glad that you are."

The rain eased enough so that he could hear her breathe in his ear.

"I've been searching for a long time."

"I stayed here. Right here. I was born in this house, and it looks grand, but it's falling apart, and there's no money to fix it up like it once was. But I knew if I moved I'd never see you again. So I begged him to let us stay."

He clutched her hand like they weren't strangers, like they knew where each other had been.

"You're real," he said.

"You were my dreams and my nightmares. I've lived this moment a thousand times, but it was selfish, and you have to go."

He shook his head, felt that fire still burn inside. "Why?"

She squeezed his hand so tight. "In case my father finds you."

250

It was dark inside.

Saint smelled it first.

The chemical so barbarous she pressed a hand to her mouth for a moment till her eyes adjusted.

She made out shapes, a chair and metal lockers, a couple of steel tables and a basin, and on the walls were papers she could not make out.

"Patch," she called, quiet because the storm was dying, despite the last flashes, the death twitches.

She saw plastic trays, tongs, papers. On a shelf were bottles.

Rapid Fixer.

Indicator Stop Bath.

Vario Fix Powder.

Saint reached the far end of the barn, stopped before a false wall, and squinted through the darkness to make out the papers.

The thunder stopped as sudden as it began.

And when the sun emerged through heavy rain,

and light fell through the open door, only then did she see what she was looking at.

The girl in the photograph was terrified.

Tears streamed down her cheeks.

Squinting at the camera, her glasses missing.

Saint stared at her teenage self as she drew her gun.

A hand found her mouth.

And stifled her scream.

251

She dragged him by his hand, her body thin but strong as she heaved the heavy door open and the light fell on her fully.

Grace.

He stumbled after her, pulled back a little just to stare at her.

To see that she was real, standing right there as the rain soaked her dress through, her hair and her porcelain skin.

He tried to pull her back into the barn, but she pulled back just as firm, her eyes wild as her nails dug into his skin.

Grace slipped to her knees, fought back to her feet as the rain lashed down.

Patch wrenched his hand free.

She squared to him, her eyes darting behind as she shoved him so hard he fell back. "Go now. You've seen that I'm here. That I'm okay."

He stood firm, wiped the rain from his face and

pushed his hair back and shook his head. "I'm not leaving you again."

Anger flared in her as she shoved him once more. "You have to go. I don't need saving."

Another shove.

"Get the fuck away from me. From here. You don't understand." She was crying, desperate, panicked, but he held his ground and caught her hands as she tried to push him again, and he pulled her close as she sobbed into his chest. "He'll kill you, Patch. He promised me that. He swore it. And he doesn't break a promise."

"Tell me what happened."

She closed her eyes tight, like it was a dream, like his being there was just a dream as she spoke. Grace told him how she had grown up in the beautiful house, till her mother fell sick and passed away. She had no other family, so her father had been sought, and he took her with him across the country, from state to state on a quest she could not comprehend.

"Eli Aaron is your father." He said, stunned.

He took a moment as, slowly, pieces more than two decades old begin to fit together to make a picture that near broke him apart.

"I was too young to know," she said.

"It's not your fault."

"And then when I did, I was too scared to—"

"He didn't kill me," Patch said.

She cried, "I begged him. You hadn't sinned. You

wore a cross. In his mind he was doing God's work. But he figured you saw him, that you knew where the house was. So he kept you there. And I sneaked down when I could."

"He wanted to take Misty."

"He saw her on the front of the newspaper. The day Jane Roe won her case. And he didn't forget her face."

Patch thought of Misty holding that placard, smiling because for once human decency won out. He thought of those times when Grace was gone, the horrors he had conjured now different, but no less.

She smoothed the hair from her eyes. "For three hundred and seven days you were mine, Patch. You were my connection to something real, something pure and real. I could be someone different. That's the thing about the dark. You could look at me and not see the things I'd seen. I could teach you everything I learned from books, everything I saw when we traveled. I could lead you where I needed you to go, to make right what I could not."

He gripped her hand so tight, afraid she might slip from him again.

"And then the girl came. And I watched her on the cameras."

He thought of Saint. Of the bravest person he had ever known.

"And I willed her to pull the trigger. To end it all. But then I saw the smoke. And I felt the heat. And you were so sick, but I dragged you out and left you.

And my father took me. There's a hundred ways off that land that the cops didn't find."

She was crying harder.

He moved to tell her it was okay, but he knew that it wasn't. None of it was.

"I saw the flashlights and the cops, and I knew you'd be okay, because you had a mother, and you had friends and a school and a life. And you could move past it. You could move past me."

I didn't, he thought. **I couldn't.**

"We drove back to Alabama."

"You didn't go to the cops?"

He saw the terror in her eyes, fear he had once known well. Fear that claimed parts of you till you no longer knew your own mind.

"He'd kill me. There's cameras here. There's a room just like the one you were kept in. And when he leaves me there . . . I'm so grateful when he comes back. I'm so grateful to see the light again."

Patch died for her, for her nightmare that had run far longer than his.

"And then I saw you in the newspaper. You were just a kid, but your paintings. The house. This house."

He cast his mind back to that first exhibition in Monta Clare.

"My father saw it, too.

"If I tried to escape, he promised he'd go find you after he killed me. He doesn't lie, Patch. He doesn't ever lie."

He pressed his forehead to hers.

surmise her wins and failures, her gains and losses. To think of Charlotte and her grandmother, and Jimmy, and Patch.

Instead there was gunshot, and there was Eli Aaron losing part of his skull.

253

Patch helped her up and out into the light.

The storm clouds dismantled till blues sketched the horizon. Saint fell to her knees and retched and coughed as Patch knelt beside and placed a hand on her back.

"You're safe," he said.

"You killed him," Saint said.

She panted, coughed again, and felt the pain sear her throat, her chest weak. She sat back and he knelt beside her, stroked the hair from her eyes and pressed his hand lightly to her cheek. She saw him then. She thought of Tooms and Nix, thought of Monta Clare and how far they had drifted from home.

The gun lay on the ground, and with a heavy heart she picked it up and climbed to her feet.

His smile met her tears.

She held her gun out, level with his chest.

He stared at the barrel, at the steady of her hands.

Patch turned and did not run, instead raised his hands in a surrender that near broke her.

Saint looked past him, at the big house that stirred a memory of their town, of finding Charlotte watching the screen, her father's work bringing a family back from that total loss of hope.

"The house," she said. She looked at him, at the toll of each year, a boy and now a man, a shadow in the light. "Tell me it was her, Patch."

"It was her." He looked in the direction of the barn, where Grace stayed and hid and waited for the end.

Saint cried then. The search was over.

"You'll look after her," Patch said.

"You know that I will."

"You look after everyone, Saint."

"Just not the one person that matters most."

"You do the right thing. Always. And I love you for it."

She kept the gun out, wiped her tears. "They're coming for you, kid."

He smiled. "I think they're already here, Saint."

She slipped the handcuffs from her belt.

"How is Charlotte?" he said, as he watched her.

"She's doing good."

"She's tough, like her mother. Like her friend."

"And like her father."

In the distance she heard the call of sirens, the troopers closing the net. In hours he would return to prison, where he would pay for a crime he had committed. Saint knew that for some it was written in the stars that no matter how hard they fought their road did not lead somewhere good.

"At first I thought it must've taken someone pretty smart to get you out of there. Maybe some money. Some bribes. But then I realized it just took a lot of heart. A desire to right something wrong," Saint said.

"You got me now. You don't need to—"

"I won't. I'm not interested in who exactly helped you escape. Though I could guess who was at the center. And he'd never survive on common food," she said.

He took a breath and looked back toward the barn, where Grace stood like a ghost, like a vision he could finally let go.

Patch smiled at her as he spoke to Saint. "So this is how it ends."

She took a step closer. "Regrets?"

"Too few to mention."

Saint hugged him tightly.

Behind them the clouds eased apart for a rainbow of light they did not notice.

The sirens grew louder.

They held together.

Saint would not let him go.

To love and be loved was more than could ever be expected, more than enough for a thousand ordinary lifetimes.

She did not understand that until then.

MYTHS AND LEGENDS

2001

254

It was a fine spring morning as Sammy stepped from the gallery and out onto Main Street.

He took coffee with Mary Meyer, the two comfortable enough in each other's company to sit with their newspapers, him scowling at a smiling Carter and Castro as she read of the sweeping investigation that now covered seventeen states. Led by the FBI, and police chief Saint Brown, they had used the interview transcripts with Joseph Macauley to map a detailed trail of the life of Eli Aaron. They had recovered the final body from Pearl River County, by the Hemmsford Swampland. Comfort was small, but to the families starved of so much, it was a chance to lay their pain to rest and begin the process of grieving. There had been no mention of Grace in any newspaper or report.

"Justice is served," she said.

"And it only took three decades," Sammy said.

"Karma, Samuel. Do you believe?"

"More so each day."

"Getting romantic on me," she said.

"I can still picture your father's face."

"If you had your time over . . ." she asked him that often, and he would smile, as if he were not going to satisfy her with a response.

"I would tell your father, and Franklin's father, to go fuck themselves. I'd leave the Rothko where it was, because I already had something far more beautiful to make a life with."

She rolled her eyes but could not fight the smile, and then she turned the page and noted the listing. That night he would take her to the newly reopened Palace 7, where they would see a return of **Cleopatra.**

He would take her hand.

She would let him.

255

At nine Sammy checked his pocket watch, stood and kissed her cheek, and in hues of sunshine climbed into the waiting car.

He sank into the plush leather and closed his eyes to the quiet of the engine. As they took a wide arc around the town of Monta Clare, he opened his window to sweetened air as front yards bloomed and he breathed content.

The driver almost missed the turn, the track appearing like a notch in the wild. At the old farmhouse Sammy climbed out and took in the view, from the flats of the grassland toward the St. Francois Mountains. It was a place he had not visited before, but now he understood the enthrall.

He found Marty Tooms behind the house, digging out a patch of bindweed. When Tooms saw him he rose, offered a smile though they were now perfect strangers.

"You must be from the bank," Tooms said, wiped his hand on dark jeans and extended it. "I spoke with Mr. Fulbright, and he said it was alright if I came tidied the land ahead of the auction this weekend. To be honest there wasn't all that much to do."

Sammy smiled. "That's because I heard the old police chief used to come by each month and tend it. He was all heart, you know."

Marty smiled, for the smallest moment unable to find his words. "There are some places where the good memories are easier to locate. You'll find a buyer now people know, I'm certain. I hope they love it like . . . like me and the chief did."

"I'm not from the bank, Marty."

Tooms kept the smile but frowned a little. He stood tall, no outward mark of the past years. Sammy knew he rented a small apartment two towns over. Days he worked at a timber yard in Preston, weekends he volunteered at the Thurley State Park, tagged trees and checked footpaths, gates, and stiles. He'd been freed without fanfare, did not make a claim to be compensated because by his own admission he had done so much wrong.

They found the body of Callie Montrose buried beneath the cotton candy wings of the okame cherry on Nix's land. Saint had sat on the small bench beside it, same as Nix had for twenty years, and took a moment to remind herself of the simple complexities of life as colors spread from the crown.

Sammy knew that right and wrong were subjective terms, also knew some men set their own price on redemption.

They walked toward the house.

Tooms kept his eyes down until Sammy drew the thick envelope from the car.

He noticed the tall man's hands shook a little as he opened it and thumbed the pages.

"I don't understand," Tooms said.

"The land is yours, Marty. The house, the acres. The memories. Everything you can see. It's all yours again."

Tooms looked around.

"Someone left you a painting. It's worth a fair amount of money. I took the liberty of giving you a loan against it, buying up this land because I know Ernie Fulbright is tired of keeping it on the books."

Tooms cleared his throat. "A painting?"

"A painting I spent the better years of my life staring at. A painting that I'd like to leave hanging where it is. Alongside the others. Because they remind me of . . . of a friend. That's your interest payment. We can sort the finer details, and of course you can come view it whenever you like. Or you can tell me to go to hell."

Tooms looked at him.

"I know this doesn't make an awful lot of sense to you, but maybe it will when you see it."

256

At the gallery Sammy held the door and then led Tooms through, where Callie Montrose took space on the vast white wall that ran the depth of the building.

There was a moment when Tooms didn't speak, just stared, the painting so blinding and brilliant.

Sammy left him there for a long while, sharing a moment with a girl he had tried to save, a girl he had given his life for, certain he would do it again in a breath.

And then Tooms stared at the painting to the left, the one that many said was the true dime in a collection that would fetch many millions.

"Grace Number One," Marty said, reading the plaque.

"Newly acquired. I made the same offer I made to you, only this time it was to a young lady in Alabama. She'll use the money to turn her house into a home," Sammy said with a smile.

Afterward they sat on the balcony in shallow spring warmth, Monta Clare going on beneath them.

For a long time Marty Tooms did not know what to say, even when Sammy handed him a check to go along with the house. The only work he need tend to was his land, back in his name, his memories secure.

"And the painting in the window?" Tooms said.

"The white house. I just acquired it from . . . from a dear friend."

"You don't sell them on?"

Sammy smiled. "I'm a collector, Marty. And this collection is sewn into the fabric of Monta Clare like folklore. Like a reminder that sometimes, against the longest of odds, hope wins out."

"Thank you," he said, finally.

"It's not really me you need to thank," Sammy said, and sipped cured oak bourbon.

"Joseph Macauley," Tooms said, and finally broke a smile. "I don't know where to find him."

Sammy raised his glass toward the sky. "That's the thing, nobody does."

257

Saint made the journey alone.

She drove highway miles with only the rolling northwest plains and the low claw of nerves for company.

In the trunk was everything she had: gifts dated with each of his years; letters and cards. Seashells she had found, conches intact, ormer with oil slick greens and purples, and a triton that whispered crashing waves when pressed to her ear. A magnolia leaf, a conker, and a mourning dove feather. A Monterey pine cone that survived intact because she lightly varnished it. Alongside each she attached a small card that told of where she had been when she found it.

There were photographs she had taken herself: the sun setting over the St. Francois Mountains; morning mist over the rooftops of Monta Clare. The old church where her grandmother lay beside a police chief who had shaped her life; Main Street and

Charlotte's hive; and the tall house where she had lived the best parts of her life. She packed in clippings she'd found in a trunk beneath Norma's bed, each case she had worked, from Joseph Macauley through bank robberies to homicides. The day she found them she'd lain on Norma's bed, wrapped herself in a blanket, and felt her grandmother's love and pride envelop her. A single book, **Where the Wild Things Are.**

In her final letter she wrote of Charlotte, how the girl had come to stay when she was a near stranger, of how she had bucked and kicked until only recently, when Saint had discovered that trust was a two-way street. Of how Charlotte was quite brilliant, each day dazzling her with a poise and ease Saint hoped would open the world to her. She included a single sketch Charlotte had made, the two of them sitting on the porch, from a memory replenished each evening no matter the weather.

It was over those long days and months, over dinners with her grandmother and Sammy, that Charlotte slowly came to realizations about her father, and then took to her small studio where art gave her an outlet she had been seeking. And though Sammy declared her work shit, she grew in talent, and with talent came confidence. At school her grades settled and rose, and despite a line of boys readying, she spent her weekends hiking the Thurley State Park, where she would note Saint stopped to smile at the tall man who kept the routes clear, his eyes kind, his smile always present.

Saint told him how Charlotte was heading to college, to Boston, where her mother had studied. Only Charlotte would eventually study law. Infected with her father's need to help others, she had already pledged her future to defending the poor, whom Sammy defined as pretty much everyone in comparison to the young princess of Monta Clare.

When Saint reached the green of Madison County she passed covered bridges and found the hamlet of Robins Elk, stopped at a gas station, and fussed with the dress Charlotte had picked out for her.

It took ten minutes to find the land, the track forged in tire widths of loose gravel that led to a red-roofed farmhouse grand and perfect.

She pulled up at the foot of their land and opened the trunk. Inside was a leather cabin box the rich color of horse chestnut seed, the brass buckles polished, the base lined with soft cotton. She had spent too long choosing it, making sure the gifts were parceled neatly, the letters bound, the chronology correct.

She lifted it out with care, set it down beside their mailbox, and did not dare think of him inside there, growing up in that house, free on that land so beautiful she felt a swell of longing grow heavier still.

She might have been okay, might have driven back safe in the knowledge that she had not interrupted his life until he was old enough to know, had she not been seen from the large kitchen window of the farmhouse.

Saint stood there with her head bowed low as the woman crossed the long driveway. It was not until she neared that Saint recognized her from the hospital room so many years before. Candice Addis, so much a woman and mother that Saint smoothed her own dress down and cursed herself for pairing it with sneakers.

There was a moment that passed between them, and then Candice crossed and hugged her tight, and Saint did all she could not to break right there in her arms.

Candice stepped back and appraised her and smiled. "I always hoped you would come."

Candice led her to a small bench in the shade of a silver maple, and together they talked. The yield of the farm, the prices of acres, Saint's work, and how Candice had once seen her on the news when the young man escaped from prison.

"You were there?" Candice said, brown eyes a little wide at the thought.

"I was."

"But you didn't find him?"

Saint thought back to that afternoon, how the state cops arrived at the large white house. How she had taken Grace from the scene and worked with Himes to keep her from the media's glare. How together they had listened to a story that left even Himes unable to eat. Grace had told them that she wanted to stay at the house, where her mother had once lived. Saint checked in with her often, made sure she had the support. The road back would be long and difficult, but with freedom came hope.

"Joseph Macauley escaped," Saint said, just like she'd told Himes, who'd watched her awhile, the wheels turning fast and then grinding to a halt because she'd laid foundations so strong she could not be questioned. She knew in her heart what was good and right. She no longer needed her badge for validation.

They spoke of Theodore, of how he excelled at sports, math, English, pretty much everything he came across. For a long time Saint listened, her cheeks aching as Candice spoke of such a fine boy.

"Of course, he knows about you. Would you like to meet him?"

Saint looked toward the house and beyond it before she caught herself.

"God . . . no, that shouldn't be my choice. I just . . ." she swallowed, resolute, each boundary crumbling as she sucked in breath and fought the tremble in her hands, bit her lower lip to stop the shaking. "I just wanted him to know . . ."

Maybe it was the memory of Jimmy not letting her finish, not letting her tell him she had visited the clinic but could not go through with the abortion because she had once made a promise to God, a promise that saw her friend return safe from his own hell, a promise that saw her cast out, whispered of, a pariah in the small town that she so loved.

Maybe it was the memory of the way she folded herself away from his punches and kicks and cradled the life that grew inside of her.

Or perhaps it was simply the touch that broke her, the way the older woman pulled her in and told her it was okay. It took everything she had left not to let her small body wrack with sobs, to focus on how beautiful the land was behind the house, the cross of spring-fed streams, a thousand acres of tillable land that would be his.

"The farm," Saint said.

Candice looked at their land.

"You'll . . . it'll be okay." For more than a dozen years Saint had been into the law offices of Jasper and Coates and had them track the accounts for the Robins Elk Farm, resting easy in bountiful years, fretful when the returns fell.

"I'm waiting on the new farm bill, but Nicholas . . . he said he'd rather lose the place than overproduce," Candice said, and in her eyes Saint saw the only trace of concern. She remembered Nicholas a little, from all those years ago when she had handed them her son and the best pieces of her heart.

"There's something in the box, something to . . . to say thank you. It's not even money I earned. I had a painting and it . . . and I made the check out to Theodore, but I know he'll help you and—"

Candice tried to shake her head, to tell her no, but when she saw the imploration, the need, she simply hugged her once more.

They stood, and Candice followed her to the car, but not before Saint heard it as the wind finally died.

"You keep bees?" Saint said.

Candice smiled. "Theodore does. He found an old hive buried in the woodland. Sweetest honey I ever tasted."

Saint waited till she was free of their land, till Candice and the farm faded in the mirror, and only then did she pull to the side of the road and cry.

For the girl she once was.

For the man he would become.

258

It was a small showing.

Mostly family and friends, though Daisy Creason brought a camera and promised a quarter page in **The Tribune.** Though her hair had long since grayed, and her hand shook a little as she wrote shorthand in her notebook, she did recall a similar showing near three decades before.

Charlotte wore a simple yellow dress, her hair tied back and only the lightest touch of makeup. And she worked the room with an effortless ease, smiling for her friends, hustling potential customers just like Sammy had taught her.

"You'll miss her when she heads to college," Saint said.

"Best assistant I ever had," Sammy said. "She once sold a Rosenquist print to a tourist who came in to use the restroom. You could tell he couldn't afford it. Most beautiful thing I ever saw."

"How lovely."

Sammy wore a satin jacquard twill tuxedo jacket,

left three buttons of his tailored shirt open to tanned chest, and stood in the far corner of Monta Clare Fine Art, for once content not to hold court.

Saint strolled slowly, taking in each of the landscapes, wishing her grandmother were beside her, so that she might point out scenes from their town, from the woodland and the water before it.

Most, she noticed, carried a small red sticker on the comment beneath.

"She's popular," Saint said.

"Telephone bidder," Sammy said, swirling his whisky. "Always looking for the next big thing."

Mary Meyer followed her granddaughter with unabashed pride. She wore a floral embroidered silk evening dress, and Saint could not help but admire the refinement of the Meyer women, her mind on Misty, on just how wide her smile might have been.

"I saw you in the newspaper," Sammy said.

Saint shrugged, like it was nothing.

The FBI Medal for Meritorious Achievement. Himes had shaken her hand, posed for a photo with a hotdog cupped behind his back as he commended her lifelong work on the pursuit of Eli Aaron. She'd suffered nightmares awhile after, still saw his face in that Alabama barn, and would wake sweating, only to find Charlotte had slipped into the bed beside her, the girl feigning sleep until Saint's heart calmed enough. By morning she would be gone. They did not speak of it.

When the last wine had been drunk, the last

painting sold, and the visitors had spilled into the arms of a summer evening, Daisy asked for one last photo of the girl and her family.

Charlotte placed herself between Saint and her grandmother, then called for Sammy to join them.

Sammy shook his head. He knew that he was not the missing piece of that particular puzzle.

"Please, Grandpa," Charlotte said.

"You don't fucking call me that," Sammy said, jabbing a finger and sending Dalmore splashing over his arm.

Outside, Charlotte locked the door.

Ahead, Mary Meyer took Sammy's arm, and the two strolled toward the hill.

"Sometimes I imagine them having sex," Charlotte began.

"Jesus," Saint said.

"But then I think there's no way he can summon an erection with all that booze."

Saint nodded somberly and did not tell the girl of the blue tide of pills sweeping the country.

"Do you think he's a good man?" Charlotte said, and looked to Saint with those eyes.

"No."

Charlotte glanced at the church.

"But he tries," Saint said, and smiled.

"Can I stop by Mom? Sometimes Grandma throws me a couple extra bones when I tell her I visited."

"Sure."

And while Charlotte visited with her mother,

Saint took a little time to sit before Norma and Chief Nix. She did not pray much anymore. Though she still believed. Entirely and absolutely.

Had she turned her head she might have noticed the oak tree, and in the right hour of sunlight the faint initials still carved into its face.

Sometimes she imagined him out there somewhere, painting, working, living the kind of small life that did not impinge. Charlotte spoke of him more, that first year raced to the telephone when it rang, the mailbox when the post arrived. She watched the news each evening, badgered Saint to check in with Himes each week. For a while her father lit up the national news, but Saint knew in time the heat would cool until such day that his name would slip from memory, sometimes whispered in prison yards as the man who bested Warden Riley and half the Missouri police force. Himes filled her in on the rumors, that he had robbed another bank in Texas before crossing into Mexico, that he was likely dead, that his paintings now quietly changed hands for millions of dollars that were somehow funneled to him. She believed none of them. They were merely the myths and the legends.

It was as they climbed the creaking steps to the porch of the tall house that Charlotte saw it.

The small package bore her name.

"Secret admirer," Saint said.

"It better not be Noah again. His testicle has only just reengaged."

Charlotte settled herself on the porch swing as Saint let herself into the house and fixed them cocoa, a routine passed down. A routine that still made her smile each evening as they sat together and watched fireflies spark from the St. Francois Mountains.

Saint carried two mugs out and settled beside the girl, who had kicked off her shoes and sat curled on the seat.

Saint sat beside her, only then noticing what Charlotte gripped in her hands.

The jar glowed.

Charlotte held it to the moonlight, the colors shifting from cardinal to mulberry.

Otherworldly.

Impossibly beautiful.

"What is it?" Charlotte said.

Saint took a breath. "It's honey. It's purple honey."

259

In the embers of summer they loaded Saint's truck and set off an hour from dawn.

Two weeks before Charlotte would make the journey to Boston, where Saint had already planned to visit often, if only to bring the girl some decent home cooking.

A little over a thousand miles, they planned the route lazily, just highlighting a couple of stops they would make along the way.

A road trip, not mother and daughter, but friends. Friends that had been through so much together.

They detoured at Mount Vernon and followed a long sweeping curve toward Nashville. Charlotte wore denim cut-offs and placed her bare feet on the dashboard as she sang along to Dolly Parton and Hank Williams, Loretta Lynn, and, of course, Johnny Cash.

By the time they made it to their motel, Saint's ears were ringing from the din, and her mouth aching from laughing.

"You sing like your mother cooked," Saint said.

They ate hot chicken and strolled the glittered walkways, Charlotte drawling Elvis as she posed for a photograph before the lights of Music Row, her top lip quivering till Saint doubled over with laughter.

They stopped at the Cherokee National Forest, the girl turning quiet as the sky crimsoned over Appalachian mountains so lush they mirrored the sheen of deep river gorges. They hiked a couple of hours and Saint fired off pictures of eastern box turtles and five-lined skinks, juncos and peregrine falcons. In time she would fill another book, her mind on Theodore as she carefully pasted in photographs he might one day look at.

At a waterfall that cascaded over ridges and brows of russet rock, Charlotte stopped and turned to her.

"What I said . . . about not wanting you as a mother—"

"I know," Saint said.

"I mean. You're everything. And you—"

"I know that, too."

Charlotte hugged her quickly and tightly.

A day later the horizon spread from the Blue Ridge Parkway beyond. They played games, spotted bumper stickers, and assigned points for noting WWJD, SHIT HAPPENS, and, as they neared their destination, OBX.

They stopped for lunch, Charlotte tapping her foot to bluegrass though Saint could see the way her shoulders tightened, her smile a little less as she quietened. It was not a trip with a clear destination or aim. It was unsaid, though hope gently warmed in the pit of their stomachs.

The jar of purple honey carried a label.

And after a day carving through the Piedmont they came to Hillcrest Farm.

It was not a place that would appear in any guide-book, and as Charlotte found matching jars on the shelves, Saint took the calculated risk of showing a photograph of him to the young girl that worked the counter.

A shake of the head.

The crushing of a dream that perhaps had always been out of reach.

Charlotte did not speak much afterward, as they drove aimlessly through a plateau of low hills, the land beginning to flatten toward distant coastal plains.

"He's keeping you safe," Saint said.

"He could be dead," Charlotte said.

They spent another day moving through North Carolina in heightened silence. They met traffic as they coasted out of Raleigh.

Nose to tail.

"The bumper sticker again," Saint said, and Charlotte noticed it and smiled.

The letters OBX, and beside it a skull and crossbones.

They saw it a half dozen times as they drove toward the flats.

At a truck stop far from anywhere Charlotte

stopped by the car next to them and stared at yet another bumper sticker.

This one carried the same letters, only instead of a skull and crossbones it bore the face of a pirate.

"What does it mean?" she said, to the big guy climbing from the car.

He was tall, and beneath broad shoulders was a bulging stomach.

"Outer Banks, North Carolina," he said, and shot Saint a smile.

"Why do so many people have it?" Charlotte said.

Another smile, this time a little wider. "You ever been to the Caribbean?"

Charlotte shook her head.

"You head to the Outer Banks and you won't ever need to."

Charlotte squinted at the setting sun. "And the pirate?"

The man leaned on the hood of his car. "That's Blackbeard of course."

"Blackbeard," Charlotte said, in a whisper.

"The pirate, Edward Teach. Of all the places in the world, and he chose to hide out in the Banks."

260

Outer Banks. A hundred miles of open shoreline.

Of ivory sand and water so clear rocks jeweled from beneath.

They moved slow, through small towns and tourist traps. Charlotte wore a wide-brimmed hat and stood in the sand watching the white fins of distant sailboats beyond the crescent of barrier islands.

Through bustling marinas.

Pirate Cove.

Safe Harbor.

Names that conjured the kind of ending Saint prayed for. For Charlotte. For herself.

They lost days looking out, their hope rising and falling with the waves. And it was as the islands thinned along with the tourists that they came to the final harbor.

When the heat eased and the sun began to drop, they watched the first fishing boats begin their return.

Charlotte stood, her feet in the water as she kept her eyes fixed on each vessel, hands by her side. Saint stayed back, counting off the boats, her breath shallow as another appeared filled only with locals.

She felt the soar of the girl's heart, and then the break as the boats began to thin.

A sunset fired colors that splintered over the water.

Charlotte turned once, and Saint closed her eyes to the girl's tears.

She was about to stand, to tell her sorry, that she had felt so certain, when she saw it.

The sailboat was white, maybe fifty feet long, and it sliced the water so gracefully. The deck a teak bleached by the sun. Light met the hull, rubbed down and painted fresh. Saint looked to Charlotte, who watched it, for a moment still, like she expected another vacationer.

And then they followed the mast.

Saint smiled when she saw it.

The flag was small. Black.

The skull and crossbones lit beneath the burnt sky.

She sat back on a rock, felt the stir in her muscles, in her heart as Charlotte stood still as the boat eased to stop at the small berth at the end of a long jetty.

He stood on the hull, the moment frozen as he saw her.

Patch jumped from the boat. His walk turned to a run as Charlotte began to move toward him.

They met at the water's edge, Patch's smile taking
Saint back to a time she had worried lost forever.
Two steps from each other, the girl held back.
And then he opened his arms.
And Charlotte stepped into them.

261

It was warm enough for Charlotte to lie out on the deck.

And beneath the stars she fell into a contented sleep.

Saint sat beside Patch, the sailboat gently swaying. He watched his daughter, and Saint watched him.

His hair light, his skin gold.

Saint did not ask how he had survived, how he had purchased the boat and stayed so hidden. She did not need to, as through the hatch she saw a fine bottle of cognac, and beside it, two heavy-bottomed crystal glasses.

"I think of you," he said.

She smiled. "I thought you might have left the country."

"I once made a promise to Charlotte that I would always be here for her."

"It's a risk."

"And we both know I don't take many of those."

Saint laughed.

"I stay for you as well," he said, meeting her eye.

She turned her head for a moment, took a breath. "We were lucky to catch you," she said.

"I sail each day, return at sunset. I dream . . . each time I come in I dream of seeing you both waiting for me."

"What do you do out there all day?"

"I paint."

"You paint?"

He told her of Grace, of the letters she'd sent that sometimes ran to a hundred pages. She wrote of her childhood, her memories of her mother, the grand home they had shared, and the beautiful town she was named after. And of the missing girls, whose graves she planned to visit, whose memories she would share with their forgotten families. Grace told of how he had kept her alive with his paintings, his story, his strength to right their past, to find his passion. To love. Grace sent photographs of the white house, the barns demolished, and in each he saw not the size of the task at hand, but only the slow emergence of hope against the harshest of odds.

In her latest letter she told of how she had once lost her faith, had once prayed for nothing more than survival. But how, though theirs was a story now told, it was a story whose end had yet to be written.

For her part Saint told him of Charlotte. And of Theodore. And for an hour he sat and listened, and smiled and laughed, and wiped her tears.

And only when she was done did he take her hand

and carefully lead her through the hatch, the ladder steep, the cabin it opened into simple.

Mostly bare and functional, except for the wall, where a single memory lay on canvas.

"I saved the best till last," he said.

She stopped before the painting, the only one he had kept for himself. Though later, when it was time for them to leave, he would insist that she take it.

Saint knew the scene well.

Impossibly valuable, but to no one more than her.

Saint smiled as she looked at the two figures, lying beneath the stars, their heads side by side, their feet the north and south of a compass.

The thirteen-year-old pirate.

And the beekeeper that saved his life.

ACKNOWLEDGMENTS

My readers. I'm a slow writer, but I want you to know it's not because I don't work hard. Thank you for waiting for me. Thank you for sending me messages, photos, gifts, kindness, and love. I hope I never let you down.

Charlie. George. Isabella. I'm finally okay with all the times I messed up, but only because they were part of a very specific path that led me to you. All the words are written for you. And Victoria, for being a wonderful mother. Life hasn't been easy for us, but I know that we've finally come out clean on the other side.

Amy Einhorn. It's hard to know what to say here. We've come a long way since Duchess, and you've kept betting on me ever since. There are very few people in my life that have shown such faith, and I'll forever be grateful to you and your amazing ability to guide me toward the story I felt certain was beyond me. I'm not particularly clever or talented, but you make me feel both.

Emad Akhtar. I'd long heard rumors of your talent, and then I got to experience it for myself. Some people are put on this earth to do amazing things, you are one of those people. Thank you for helping to make the last four years the most creative of my life. I absolutely could not have written this book without you. I am lucky to know you.

Jennifer Joel. For taking a chance. For being fearless. For making me a better storyteller and knowing exactly how to handle every situation. I breathe easier just for having you in my life. And am much fatter after our NYC meals. **But we didn't even order corn crème brûlée?**

Jason Richman. I fell deeply in love with you from that first lunch. Thanks for being so kind, talented, clever, and patient. For laughing with me. For seeing this story in ways I never could. And for being a phenomenal drinking partner. So much wine. So many chasers.

Cathryn Summerhayes and team CB.

Sindhu Vegesena and team CAA.

Annabelle Janssens and team UTA.

Felicitas von Lovenberg, Anne Scharf, and all at team Piper.

Richard Herold and all at team Natur & Kultur.

My wonderful foreign publishers. For showing the world what we can do.

Jordy Moblo. No one has waited longer and more (im)patiently for this book than you. Thank you for listening to my very meandering Ivy pitch all those years ago. For sticking by me and guiding me with such vision and heart. And mostly, for being my friend. I love you, buddy.

Lori Kusatzky. For always having an answer to every question I think of. For tireless work on this story. You're the best.

Julie Cepler, Dyana Messina, Bree Martinez, Rachel Rodriguez. Thank you for helping readers find this story, for being so passionate and creative, and for not laughing (much) at the very British pedestal I put Penguin on. I'm very lucky to be on your team.

Chris Brand and Anna Kochman for the stunning jacket.

Production superstars Heather Williamson, Natalie Blachere, and Christine Tanigawa.

Ashley Alberico and Natalie Muglia for getting this book out there. I'm so grateful for your hard work.

David Drake, Annsley Rosner, and everyone at Crown, for making that penguin tattoo less of a drunken regret. I'm proud to be with you.

Helen Carr. For, attempting, to, teach, me, grammar, Americanisms, geography, and basic spelling. I know I am your worst student. Thank you for never giving up.

Robin Slutzky, for pointing out that I can't have four characters called Mitch.

Conor Mintzer. I miss you. Vegas.

For all the booksellers, book clubs, bloggers, and reviewers who gave their precious time to me. You've changed my life. I will always be grateful.

My author friends. For letting me sit at your table.

Patricia Cornwell. For advice, kindness, laughter, and for making your secret service dudes pretend to care about my wellbeing, too.

Jenna Bush Hager. For being so cool, kind, and into this story from the very beginning.

Sue Naegle. The safest, most skillful guide for putting words on screen. Also for relationship counseling, life coaching, and making me laugh.

Gubbins. There's no one in the world I trust more with this. I am lucky to know you.

Nick Matthew. Nickelback. Nicaragua. For producer meetings/Soho House merriment/offering me your spare room. You are Manny levels of cool.

Tommy Kail. The Angelica/Eliza to my Peggy. For teaching me how TV is made and never laughing at my questions. "Yeah, but how do you get the little actors into the screen?"

Sinead Daly, for caring as much as I do.

Jennifer Todd and all at Twentieth TV.

Disney, although that mouse is a real shit to negotiate with.

Nicci Cloke. My Pixar hangover cure. My ham. For blue chair movies. Monday night roasts. Quicksand. Butter that pretends to be cheese. For never letting me play Wordle. For turbulence, trying to put me to bed early, triple letter yum, and general sensationalness. For always seeing in me the things I worried weren't there. For being the most spectacular person I have ever met (and for not realizing it).

I know you'll be rolling your eyes at this, and telling me "you want to get a life, Stace," but it's important you know just how lucky I am to have found you. I love you.

Let's do it all again in another four years. (Sooner, Amy and Jenn, I promise.)

ABOUT THE AUTHOR

Chris Whitaker is the award-winning author of **Tall Oaks, All the Wicked Girls,** and the **New York Times** bestseller **We Begin at the End.** Chris lives in the UK.

Follow him on X @WhittyAuthor
And on Instagram @chriswhitakerauthor